NEMESIS

NOMAD SERIES — BOOK 2

K.A.FINN

Also by K.A. Finn

ARES

PERSES

CHAOS

MANIA

Coming soon

CRONUS

K.A. Finn grew up in Co. Wicklow, Ireland and now lives in Co. Meath, Ireland with her long-suffering husband, bossy children, crazy dog, slightly bad-tempered cat, and stick insects.

After working as a veterinary nurse for many years, she was forced to change career as she ran out of room for any more strays. She spent the next few years in banking before moving to Herefordshire, then back to Ireland.

When not looking after the demanding two, four, and six-legged residents, she writes and works as a freelance proofreader.

Visit me online:
www.kafinn.com
(trailers, excerpts, artwork, playlists etc)
Twitter @K_A_Finn
www.facebook.com/kafinnauthor/

Coming soon

MANIA

CRONUS

Book 5 & 6 in the Nomad series

Cover design by Deranged Doctor Design

www.derangeddoctordesign.com

Published by Cooper Publishing

ISBN: 978-0-9932073-4-1

First Edition: January 2016

Second Edition November 2020

NEMESIS

NOMAD SERIES – BOOK 2

K.A.FINN

To my best friend Cooper
Thank you for 16 years of friendship.
It won't be the same without you lying at my feet

Terra ducks to avoid Bray's attack. 'I thought you said you've been practising?'

Bray snorts and twirls the sticks in his hands. 'Not as much as you, clearly.'

She smiles and slowly circles her adversary. The lone fan bolted to the stone wall does little to ease the stifling heat of the underground training room. Readjusting the bandanna controlling her unruly dark locks, she launches a counterattack. The Hunter curses loudly as the wood makes contact with his upper arm. Not stopping her attack, she spins on her toes to land another blow on the back of his shoulder before finishing with a strike to his chest. 'Too much time in the company of Ultaran ale is slowing you down, Commander.'

Massaging his shoulder, Bray closes the distance between them. He pulls her body close against his as he leans down to kiss her. Laughing, she pushes him back playfully.

'Hey, I was enjoying that,' Bray complains.

'You can't get around me that easily. Training was your idea.'

Bray smirks and the skin around the small metal crescent beside his eye crinkles. 'I can think of other ways to train.'

Turning away from him she prepares to fight again. 'Not going to work, Bray.'

'You're no fun.' He takes up a defensive stance, then nods indicating he's ready.

They duel, ignoring the other crew milling around the area. The small alcove they're dancing around sits just off the main corridor leading to the underground hangar. In the ten months since the Port was destroyed, the training room has become like a second home to Terra. When not at work, she can be found here or jogging around the large lake to the west of the base. The lake is one of the few places she can be alone. With the destruction of the Port, colonists are obviously wary of retaliation by the Foundation, and had flocked to Ultar for protection. The underground tunnels have become home to hundreds of refugees and empty space was quickly becoming a rarity. With the imminent threat of the Foundation hanging over everyone, Ultar provides the security that many off-world colonists need.

So far, Sayber and his Hunters have kept other rogue groups from taking control, but they are struggling. And they're not the only ones. Morale is at an all time low. Terra hasn't found the transition to Outer Sector life a chore, but many of the Foundation crew are struggling with their new luxury-free living. She's lost count of the amount of times Roman and Aleena have been called away to settle disputes between the locals and ex-Foundation. While on *Infinity*, Roman would always find time for her. Even if it was only ten minutes a day to see how she is, quiz her on ship information or novels he forced her to read. Between dealing with the unhappy colonists and gathering intel on the Foundation, he barely has time to eat, let alone have a deep and meaningful conversation with her.

As they train, she feels the tension roll off her shoulders. Sparring is the only way she has found to unwind and switch off from her new day-to-day life. With a base full of Nomad and some Hunters, she isn't short of training partners.

The intercom crackles, calling an end to their session. 'Commander Rush and Commander Bray to the conference room.'

'Saved by the bell, Commander. Guess I'll have to postpone winning until later.'

He laughs and shakes his head. 'You've got a very different view of this competition than I do. What do you think it's about?'

Terra shrugs. 'Only one way to find out.' She throws her towel at him and walks out the door ignoring his verbal protests.

∞

A guttural scream from the adjoining cell drags Gryffin back to consciousness. Forcing his eye open he takes in the same view he's had for the last few months — rusted metal bars and bare concrete floor. Very different to the lakeside he visits in his dreams. Using the chains attaching him to the wall as leverage, he manages to pull himself upright with his flesh arm. He leans back against the solid metal wall of the cell and looks over at the man in the cell next to him. His lifeless eyes stare at Gryffin as blood pours out of his mouth. Judging by the state of him, he only has minutes left. The man came back from surgery a few days ago with a large metal plate screwed to the side of his head, covering the internal implant in his brain. He's not the first to have the procedure and he won't be the last. Even after months of being examined, the Scientist is no closer to figuring out how to replicate what he did with Gryffin. He managed to get working models, but the men die horribly soon after surgery.

Gryffin's neighbour makes a strange gurgling sound before taking his last breath. If Gryffin knew what the hell made him different to every other man here, he'd tell the Scientist, just to stop the experiments. He turns away from the man's lifeless eyes and watches the water slowly drip from the ceiling to gather in a puddle opposite him. Anything, even watching water drip, is better than looking at the death he'd indirectly caused.

He presses his hand to his face as a surge of pain spears through his left eye socket. Having the crowbar shoved into his eye on the freighter didn't hurt as much as his new, state of the art eyepiece does. A few months ago, losing another piece of himself would have bothered him. Now he couldn't care less. He'd already lost an arm, a leg, some of his chest, and a portion of his face — what's an eye on top of all that? Absently, he scratches the raw skin under his collar. The metal ring hangs loosely around his neck — the one advantage of not being fed regularly.

A door bangs at the end of the corridor and Gryffin's stomach clenches. Hopefully they're not coming for him again. It must have been at least a few days since the Scientist last worked on him. Time doesn't exist down here so it's making it difficult to keep track. Time is judged by the condition of his wounds. The most recent incision on his chest has only just started to seal. It can't be time yet.

Pulling himself to his feet, he leans heavily on the wall and waits. One of the newer cyborgs marches past his cell and opens the one next to him. The cyborg pulls the dead man out, drags him past Gryffin and disappears down the dark corridor. Gryffin slumps to the ground and lays his head back against the rough metal.

He massages the tender flesh on his upper right arm. The large chain welded to his metal stump is irritating the hell out of him. He never thought he'd miss his metal arm, but he does. Anything would be better than having a chain permanently welded to him, securing his arm to the wall. He can barely stand, but his captors aren't taking any chances with him. Even if he managed to tear the chain from his arm, he'd never break the one securing his collar to the wall.

He closes his eye and waits while his other eye shuts down. Alone in the safety of his head, his thoughts wander to the battle at the Port. He's tried to figure out how he ended up here, but he can't remember. He knows that Sayber knocked Terra out and took her from the ship. He knows that he tethered the freighter to Balfe's ship. But that's it.

The injury from landing on the corner of the console should have killed him. The trail of blood he left across the floor of the freighter confirmed his fate, but instead of dying, he lost consciousness and woke up here.

He can handle the examinations and the pain — he's well used to it. The thing slowly driving him crazy is not knowing. He doesn't know if Sayber and Terra got away in time. He doesn't know if Chayse and Aleena managed to launch *Nemesis*. He doesn't know if *Ares* was destroyed. He doesn't know a damn thing. The Scientist and his pet cyborgs don't talk about anything of that nature while he's on the operating table.

If he knew for a fact that everyone was still alive and fighting the Foundation, it would somehow make all of this worth it. It would make leaving Terra worth it.

Screams erupt to his left. Gryffin lies on the floor and puts his arm over his head. He squeezes his eye shut and forces an image of Terra to the forefront of his mind. In the false safety of his head, he puts himself beside her at the edge of the Ultaran lake. It's the only place he goes. He spent so many hours there when he was on the surface. It was one of the few places he could shut off and just be himself. He concentrates hard, trying to remember every single detail on Terra's face. Her sharp green eyes look at him as she brushes some hair from his face. He'll wait here in his head. Stay with Terra until he's dragged back to reality again.

∞

Terra takes a long drink of water and places the glass back on the wooden table in front of her. Bray winks at her from the seat opposite and she can't help but smile back. She dreads to think how her life would be if she hadn't let him close to her. In the months following Gryffin's death, she had withdrawn into herself. She had even pulled away from Roman and Milla. Everyone wanted her to talk, but it hurt too much. Just saying his name tore at her heart. Strangely, the only person she could spend time with was Bray. He may be Gryffin's brother, but he wasn't in the slightest bit interested in reminiscing about him.

Their friendship grew over time, but it wasn't until nearly six months after the fight at the Port that she finally took the next step with him. Initially, kissing him felt wrong. It felt like she betrayed Gryffin. But he'd died and she needed to move on.

She glances up at the Hunter Commander. There's no escaping the fact he looks a lot like his older brother. Bray may have more of his mother's facial characteristics, while Gryffin inherited his from Roman, but the more she sees Bray, the more the similarities stand out to her. If that isn't enough, some of his mannerisms also remind her of Gryffin. He's strong willed, stubborn, and a little hot-headed, but it's something he can control. Bray certainly wouldn't do something stupid or reckless like sacrificing himself without a second thought.

Her stomach tightens as her anger builds. For months, she's replayed the final events over and over in her head and is convinced Gryffin could have done it differently. She has no doubt he could have found another way of destroying the Port. If she had only known about the collar being rigged to blow if he left the ship, she could have found a way to take it off him. But he didn't give his own life a second thought. He charged into a dangerous situation without thinking about how his actions would affect the people that cared about him. Like the Nomad. Like her. Compared to Gryffin's 'act first-think later' attitude, Bray is a breath of fresh air. He's safe, unlike his emotionally and physically dangerous brother.

His hazel eyes narrow and he tilts his head to the side. 'You okay?' he mouths across the table.

She is. She never thought she'd be able to recover from what happened, but she has. Bray may never fully repair the hole left by Gryffin. She will probably never feel the same intense emotions that Gryffin gave her, but she does feel something. It's too early for love, but not for hope. She can hope for a future with him. With Bray, she can have what was impossible with Gryffin — the possibility of a future together. He's still staring at her with a worried expression on his face. Terra smiles widely and nods. His face lights up as a large grin takes over.

The smile is quickly extinguished as Roman and Aleena enter the small conference room. They close the door to the meeting room, blocking *Ares* from their view. The line of cargo containers take up the right wall of the cavern and provide a private area in the main hub of the base. The hangar serves as the brain of the facility. Most of the main computers are set up in an area to the back of the space while the transport and any ships undergoing repairs take up the rest of the area. At the moment, the hangar is home to *Ares*. It took nearly a year, but the Nomad flagship is back in one piece again.

'Thank you all for coming at such short notice.' Roman sits down and turns on the screen at the front of the room. 'I'll let Chayse explain what he found.' Chayse's handsome face fills the large screen. Milla instantly brightens when she sees the young Nomad captain. Terra envies her friend and the innocent and happy look on her face. In the space of a few seconds, just seeing Chayse has transformed her. Terra had forgotten the way another person could make you forget there was anyone else in the room.

She glances at the Hunter commander. He's staring intently at the screen, one elbow on the table. His head is resting on his raised hand and disappears behind the lock of thick brown hair that hides the side of his face. Even without seeing his hand, she knows he's running his finger over the small implant beside his eye.

'Terra?'

She blinks and the colour races to her cheeks as everyone in the room looks at her. 'Sir?'

'You with us?'

'Of course,' she replies. Bray hides a smile behind his hand and shakes his head. It seems he can make her forget there are other people in the room — much to her embarrassment.

'What did you find?' Roman asks.

Chayse leans forward to bring himself closer to the screen. His blue eyes search the room and he winks when he sees Milla. 'We've been getting some strange energy readings from an area two days travel from the site of the old Port. *Nemesis* has patrolled the area with some Hunter ships, but we haven't been able to figure out what's causing the readings. Until today.' He pulls information from another screen onto the main display causing the atmosphere in the room to grow instantly serious.

Bray frowns at the screen. 'That looks like a Port.'

Chayse nods solemnly.

'So, the Foundation set up a new Port right under your nose and you knew nothing about it?'

'Hunter ships are patrolling the area with *Nemesis*, Commander. You got a problem, maybe you should talk to them.'

Roman slams his hand on the table. 'Give it a rest! Chayse, please continue.'

Chayse clenches his jaw and glares at Bray. This isn't the first time the Nomad and Hunter have gone head-to-head. Relations are strained between all the groups and unless something changes, the situation will only get worse. For some reason, Bray and Chayse seem intent on beating their chests at every opportunity. She's tried to talk to Bray about it, but he won't back down. The Nomad and Hunters have been enemies since Sayber split from Gryffin. It will take a lot to change what has been part of normal life until very recently.

'The new Port is roughly half the size of the original one Gryffin destroyed. However, it is big enough to transport the fighters we battled a few months ago.'

Roman manoeuvres in his chair. 'I knew they'd send ships here, but I never thought they'd go so far as to build another Port. The expense alone must be incredible.'

Milla tucks her blonde hair behind her ear. 'We stole a shiny new ship, Captain, and then blew up the Port. I'm guessing they are annoyed.'

Roman scoffs. 'We should be flattered they're investing so much to find us. Chayse, how strong are the Port defenses?'

'Five patrol ships so far and more artillery on the Port itself.'

'Send over all data you have on the new site. Knowing the Foundation, there'll be more ships watching than you can see. There's no way they will take any risks. Loosing the main Port will have been a massive financial hit. I guarantee they won't make the same mistake twice.'

'So, we just sit back and do nothing?' Bray asks.

'We go in now, we'll lose any advantage we may have.'

Desyl steps out from the corner to join in the conversation. 'Can't believe I'm saying this, but I agree with the Hunter. It's time we stop hiding in the shadows and take some Foundation out of the picture.'

Bray nods. 'We've been stagnating here for months. Every day we sit and do nothing, the Foundation gains more ground. We have to fight back.'

Roman pushes to his feet. 'Enough!' He puts his hands on his hips as he faces the mismatched group. 'Hasn't there been enough deaths already without wanting to race headlong into another battle? I understand the need for revenge, the need for retribution, but without all the facts, they will destroy us!'

'You know you'll have to fight them at some point, right?'

Roman visibly tenses at Bray's remark. The Hunter hit the nail on the head, and everyone in the room knows it. None of the Foundation personnel are eager to go up against their former comrades. The people they'll be fighting — killing — could be friends. They've had no contact with Earth since the Port was destroyed and have no current intel about the Foundation. Terra can't imagine doing harm to any of her old classmates. Roman feels the same. It's natural and understandable, but detrimental to the group. If Roman doesn't give the go ahead soon, the uneasy reconciliation among the groups will suffer.

Roman clears his throat and nods slowly. 'I know that, Bray. Trust me — I know.' He clasps his hands on the old wooden door that serves at the desk. 'I can't force you to work with me on this. I can't force any of you to work with me at all. The only thing I can do is ask all of you to wait until we get more information from Chayse to make an informed decision. If... when we make the move against the Foundation, I want as many of us to come back as possible. Too many lives have already been lost to them. I refuse to hand any more over to them on a platter. When we fight them — I want us to win.'

A few minutes of grumbling follows, but one by one, they agree to his terms.

'Good. I'll make sure everyone gets a copy of the data within the next thirty minutes. Thank you.'

The room empties, leaving Roman alone with Terra. Roman turns off the telecommunication screen when Chayse signs off. Terra leans back against the table beside Roman. 'What's going through your mind?'

Roman sits down beside her and runs a hand through his cropped hair. 'We brought this on everyone.'

Terra brushes her braid off her shoulder. 'Sir, *Infinity* was sent here in the first place to colonise. That was the decision of the Foundation Council. We were just following orders. It wasn't our decision.'

'Yes, and we dutifully obeyed those orders without hesitation.'

'We didn't have a choice.'

He looks at the ground and sighs. 'I know. I'm just thankful we realised the truth before it was too late. So, Commander, if you were me, what would you do?'

Terra shuffles back to sit on the table top. She swings her legs as she looks at the map of the Sector on the far wall. 'We have two options. We can do nothing as the Foundation sends ships here to destroy us all, or we fight back.'

He smirks and shakes his head. 'It sounds like you've taken a leaf from the Nomad or Hunter book. I never thought I'd say that about you.'

She shrugs. 'Times change. People have to adapt. The Foundation brought this on themselves.'

He focuses on the screen in front of him and nods. 'I know.' They sit in silence until he eventually speaks. 'So, we haven't had a chance to speak recently. How are you?'

She looks at the screen and shrugs again. 'Busy. *Ares* is taking most of my time.'

'I mean you, not your workload.'

'I'm good.'

He turns to face her and frowns. 'Try that again.'

'I'm good, really.'

He smiles. 'A certain Hunter have anything to do with that?'

Terra winces. She really doesn't want to discuss Bray with Roman. 'Yes, sir.'

'Ah, so we're back to sir. Not comfortable talking to me about it?'

She gapes at him. 'What? How...'

He laughs and wraps his arm around her shoulder. 'I know you, Terra. I'm happy that you've found someone. Really, I am.'

'So you're not angry with me?'

He turns to looks at her. 'What made you think that?'

'Gryffin.'

He nods in understanding. 'Firstly, who you socialise with has nothing to do with me. Secondly, my son is gone, Terra. Not for one minute did I expect or want you to stop living your life. I'm not going to pretend to know Gryffin, but I doubt he'd want you miserable either.'

'Yeah, but his brother?'

Roman grimaces and shrugs. 'They're brothers by blood — apart from that, they're strangers.' He squeezes her shoulder. 'Just be happy, Terra.'

'What about you? How are you doing?'

11

He wipes a hand over his face. 'This is a big bloody mess and I can't find a way out of any of it. Until this is dealt with, it has to be my main priority.' He sighs as he examines the map of the Sector. 'There's just so much to do.'

She squeezes his hand. 'One thing at a time.'

He laughs and looks back at the map of the Sector opposite him. Red dots are scattered over the map, detailing Foundation sightings. 'Those dots are growing in number. Each day more are appearing. At this rate, I don't have time to deal with each problem individually. We've got to come up with something before they take over and we all end up on a one way trip back to Earth.'

Gryffin jumps from his unsettled, nightmare filled sleep as someone pulls sharply on the chain attached to his arm. The unfamiliar cyborg guard unlocks his limb then roughly drags him to his feet by his collar and out of the small cell. Gryffin's legs struggle to keep him upright and moving forward, but the guard clearly couldn't give a damn. Every time he stumbles, the guard seems to increase his pace, which in turn, forces Gryffin's weakened legs to move faster.

They wind through the dark facility, past row after row of small cells — some are empty, but compared to the last time he was dragged this way, there seems to be more occupied. He doesn't know where the hell the Scientist is finding all these people, but there seems to be a never-ending supply. At least this time they're all adults. Not that it makes what the Foundation is doing here any easier to stomach.

Gryffin leans heavily against the railing for support as they climb the metal stairs and turn the corner into the room the Scientist uses as his makeshift lab. The guard slams Gryffin against the edge of the table and he grunts in pain as his tender ribs clash with the metal. The guard grabs the base of Gryffin's top and tugs the stained material over his head. Gryffin hisses in pain as it drags along the fresh wounds on his chest. He is pushed back against the surface by his neck and held in place as the portly technician gingerly approaches the two men.

Gryffin concentrates on the small circular lights embedded in the ceiling as the man secures him to the table. As usual, he works in nervous silence as he bolts the chains to the table. Gryffin watches them work in the polished metal ceiling above him. He doesn't recognise the reflection staring back at him. The blood stained, painfully thin man looks like something you'd find in a morgue. The thick black sutures holding his chest together stand out in stark contrast to his dirty and pale skin. He closes his eye and swallows back the scream that desperately wants to be released. It would be a futile act that would just waste the little energy he has left.

Once he's satisfied Gryffin isn't going anywhere, he reaches over to attach the monitors to his ocular implant. Gryffin ignores him and focuses on slowing his breathing down. The man fixes a mask over Gryffin's face and turns on the anaesthetic. The drug won't knock him out, but it will help keep him drowsy and less likely to put up a fight. As soon as the mask is fitted, the guard turns and leaves the room.

Gryffin wills the technician to work faster, but the stupid man continues to fumble with cables and adjust the monitors. He can feel some of the anaesthetic work into his system. It won't be long before he succumbs to its effects. If the technician doesn't leave soon, he's going to be worse than useless and another day will be lost in this hell. Gryffin forces the panic away. If he's going to get out of here, he needs to keep calm.

The technician eventually stops adjusting the monitors and wires and leaves him alone while he gets the Scientist. If the man sticks to the same route as every other time, Gryffin will be alone for about ten minutes. Hopefully it will be long enough.

Using the connector going into his ocular implant, he connects with the computer controlling the anaesthetic. He gains access and after shutting off the alarms, turns off the machine. He then works his way around the system to link with the internal sensors. After dodging the firewall he finally breaks through. According to the system, the Scientist is still in the lab at the far end of the facility. It's now or never.

The last few months have been leading up to this moment. Initially, he would force himself to drift off while the Scientist was operating on him, but after a few weeks he realised he could access the main system through the monitoring connectors. He had never connected with something so large and initially the effort was too much for him. He'd had a few close calls, but luckily the Scientist thought it was his procedures that almost killed him — not hooking into the system.

Once he figured out how to control the link, the next problem was moving through the system while keeping his readings the same. If the Scientist got wind of what he was doing, he'd be screwed.

But he didn't find out. Instead of dreading the procedures, Gryffin would plan what to explore the next time they hooked him up. Having something to work on, to fight for, had kept him sane through the months of being repeatedly cut open. He knew everything he needed to know to escape — security numbers and locations, defences, transport types and their key codes, and the layout of the facility.

Gryffin shuts down the power going to the locks on the table and clenches his fist. He pulls back hard and is rewarded by the sound of chain snapping. He firmly grips the chain locking his collar to the table, takes a deep breath and pulls. The chain breaks, but the collar won't budge. Without the Scientist's code, he won't be able to get it off. He releases his torso and then leans over to deal with the remains of his right arm. Once free, he rolls off the table and lands in a heap on the ground. Pain shoots through his chest and blood seeps from the barely closed wound. At this rate he'll bleed to death before he even leaves the room.

He pushes up onto his knees and reaches up to use the table to pull him upright. As soon as he puts pressure on his right leg, the pain drives him to his knees again. He pulls up his trouser leg and grimaces when he sees his metal thigh. The damn thing has been nothing but trouble since he was given it on the freighter. It was supposed to make him faster, but he can barely walk, let alone run. The Scientist replaced a perfectly good thigh with a piece of scrap metal.

He bites back a curse as he forces his metal leg to support some of his weight. He fumbles in the drawers beside the table and finally finds a roll of bandage, which he hastily wraps around his torso. It'll have to do for now. He pulls on his filthy scrub top taking care not to disturb his patch-up job on his chest. He needs to leave, but he's not going anywhere without his arm.

Moving as fast as he can, he pulls open cupboards and drawers but there's no sign it. 'Damn it! Where did you put it?' It's then he spots a metal case on the floor under a storage unit. He throws the lid open and smiles when he sees his arm. His elation is short lived though. His arm is damn all use to him. Even if he could get the chain off his upper arm, the welding has damaged the connectors. He's going to have to carry it. His metal leg protests as he rises to his feet again. He swallows deeply as the room spins. Forcing one foot in front of the other, he limps over to the instrument table.

He rests his metal arm on the table and examines the collection of knives. Two large knives slide into the waistband of his scrubs before he stumbles towards the door with a third in his hand and his metal arm stuffed under his upper arm. He leans heavily against the doorframe and squeezes his eye shut. The drug is still affecting his vision. It will take another few minutes before his implants neutralise it completely, but he doesn't have time to wait. The Scientist will be on his way.

Gryffin carefully peers around the open door before he moves out into the corridor. He'd be a hell of a lot happier if he had his gun or his arm attached. He misses the feeling of additional power in his arm, but a prisoner that can electrocute his torturers is a bit too risky.

He reaches the end of the corridor and pauses. Footsteps approach his location so he presses his body tight against the wall. A man passes by, but doesn't see Gryffin until it's too late. The knife is lodged deep into his heart before he realises what's happening. Gryffin lowers him to the ground and relieves him of his gun and belt. He would have liked to take his boots too, but the man's feet are ridiculously small. He uses the belt to strap his metal arm to his leg before leaving the safety of the corridor. There's nowhere to hide the body and time is definitely against him.

Using the map he downloaded from the system, he stumbles along the corridors, each painful step taking him closer to the transport bay. As he nears the location, alarms scream to life. Seems he's been missed. He quickly locates the control panel in the wall outside the bay. Gryffin hooks up to the panel and loads the program he designed. It has remained dormant and hidden on the system but now it's time to let it do its job. He shuts down all lighting to the bay. The cyborgs will probably be able to see in the dark like he can, but the humans will struggle.

He rolls his shoulders and takes a deep breath. There's no time to hide in the shadows. If he's going to get out alive he has to move now. He steps out of the corridor and into the transport bay. Quickly he scans the chaotic bay. Humans stumble in the dark, but it's the cyborgs that get his attention. They stand motionless at their posts. Gryffin watches as one of them roughly pushes a human aside when he wanders too close. So, they can see in the dark. Not ideal, but there's nothing he can do about it. They're in his way — that's all he needs to focus on.

He zooms in on a small transport in the far corner. He recognises the model, but more importantly, he also knows how to deactivate the tracker on it. That's his target.

He's come this far. There's no way he's going to turn around and go back to his cell. Whatever happens in the next minute or so, he knows one thing for sure. The Scientist will not be cutting him open again. He'll die before that happens. He's beyond caring if this is the battle that finishes him off for good. There will be no more cages for him.

He raises the gun and hopes the adrenaline coursing through his body will keep him upright. His vision keeps swimming, everything hurts and his damn feet won't move in the same direction as each other.

His use of the main control implant in his brain has been carefully monitored and controlled while he's been here. He doesn't even know if he can access it on his own anymore, but there's no way in hell he's getting out of here without help. The added strength might just keep him and his feet heading in the right direction. He closes his eye briefly and tries to link, but nothing happens. He clenches his jaw and tries again. Finally, the familiar buzzing feeling builds at the base of his skull. It slowly spreads up his head and along his new eyepiece. He bites back a groan of pain when the new eyepiece throbs as power surges through it. Gryffin opens his eye and breathes a sigh of relief as his vision sharpens.

Before he loses the connection, he steps out of the corridor and walks purposefully towards the transport. That ship is more than just his escape. It's his lifeline. It's the thing that can bring him back to the Nomad and back to Terra. The thought of possibly seeing her again gives him a new strength. One of the cyborgs notices him and shouts the alert. Before his cyborg friends have turned to face him, Gryffin shoots him in the head. One down. He doesn't feel guilty for the death. At least the man isn't suffering anymore. Gryffin targets the next cyborg as they near him. A small smile pulls at the corner of his mouth. For the first time in months, he actually feels in control of his future. With an image of Terra firmly in his mind, he roars and charges into the group of cyborgs blocking his way.

Aleena stands at the edge of the hangar and watches Jensen Roman as he speaks to a group of Foundation personnel. Not for the first time, she is grateful she allowed *Infinity* to land on Ultar all those months ago. If not for her decision, she may never have met Jensen. He is unlike any man she has encountered previously. Perhaps it is his strict Foundation upbringing, but his dedication and devotion to their cause is unending. She's had to physically pull him away from the base many times just to get some rest.

The last few months have been particularly difficult on him. The grey has crept further into his dark hair and his piercing blue eyes have earned a few more lines. Instead of weakening him, the betrayal by the Foundation has only made him stronger and more determined than ever to stop them from taking over the Sector. She can't help but smile. Jensen and Gryffin are similar in that regard. Neither father nor son has allowed the Foundation to control them. Aleena bites the inside of her cheek to stop the tears. Gryffin's absence is like a gaping hole in her chest. She tries to remain strong for Jensen and Terra. They lost a son and a lover, but she lost a dear friend. Aleena straightens her shoulders and takes a deep breath. Gryffin would want them to fight, not cry.

She weaves through the crates of supplies surrounding the large Foundation ship. *Infinity* will be leaving in an hour to collect some refugees from a neighbouring world. A Rogue group has just attacked and destroyed the small town. The population of the once small farming community had increased tenfold in the last few months. The defences Gryffin put around the planet keep it safe from any attackers and means it is one of the best protected places in the Sector... for the moment. She is under no illusions that the Foundation will find a way to break through — it is only a matter of time.

Jensen smiles as she approaches. 'Come to see me off?'

'I always do.'

He brushes her long blonde hair back and drapes his arm across her shoulder. 'Don't think I'll ever get used to deciding where *Infinity* goes without checking with a superior.'

'As I said when we first met — Nomad don't have to answer to anyone.'

He laughs and looks down at her, his eye brows raised. 'You're saying that I'm a Nomad?'

'Perhaps. Would you call yourself Foundation?'

Roman sighs and looks out the cargo doors at *Infinity*. The large vessel sits in the field beside the base with transports and personnel milling around her. 'Can't say that appeals to me. I may sound a little naive when I say this, but I'd like to think that the Council are the exception, rather than the rule. I refuse to believe everyone on Earth thinks the same way they do.'

'So, perhaps you and your crew are New Foundation. You have certainly brought about a new era for the sector.'

21

He smiles and nods. 'You know, I like that.' He straightens his shoulders. 'Anything is better than being associated with the current Council.'

'Are you worried about this new Port?'

'I'd be crazy not to take it as a serious threat. *Nemesis* and *Epsilon* are on their way to meet with us. Once Chayse and Lucan get here, we'll decide what to do.'

Aleena can't help but smile. She misses her old security detail leader. After the trouble at the Port, Admiral Avoca had withdrawn into himself for many weeks. The truth of what he'd been involved in affected him deeply. Initially, he spent every hour next to Bray's bedside. It took a week for the young Hunter to wake up after what the Scientist did to him. He may have recovered from the procedure, but Sayber commented that Bray had lost some of his previous light-heartedness.

Even though Gryffin probably would not have approved, Lucan agreed to captain *Epsilon* when Avoca stepped down. Her Nomad security detail leader was the best candidate for the role and surprisingly, the crew of *Epsilon* agreed and have eagerly followed his command. She cannot help but smile at the thought of what Gryffin would say if he knew one of his men was the captain of a Foundation ship.

'How is Terra?'

Roman blows out a breath, which speaks volumes to her. 'I'm worried about her, Aleena, and I haven't got a clue how to help her.'

'She appears to be happy.'

'She is. Bray has a lot to do with that. Don't get me wrong, I'm delighted she has someone. For a while, not even Milla could get through to her.' He purses his lips and looks at the ground.

Aleena gently squeezes his arm. 'You are more concerned about who is helping her.'

He nods. 'Got it in one. Bray's his brother. You have to admit the two even look alike. I guess I'm worried she's...' He looks up at the stone roof and sighs. 'I don't know.'

Aleena understands what is troubling Jensen. She has had the same concerns. 'Perhaps we should trust Terra to know her own mind. Bray is a good man. I truly believe he would do nothing to hurt her. You have said it yourself — she is happy.'

'It's the anger I'm worried about. Bray hates his brother. I don't know why, but that much is clear as day. I just hope they have more to talk about than their hatred or disappointment or whatever they're feeling towards Gryffin.'

'Has she spoken about her father yet?'

He shakes his head. 'That's a banned subject. She flat out refuses to discuss him. It's not healthy to bottle everything up like she is.'

'And you?'

'What about me?'

'Your childhood friend faked his own death so he could work with the Foundation on this secret project. The same project that tortured your son and changed him forever. Your friend and your son are connected in a way you could never have imagined. Surely, you are affected also?'

'I can't afford to give it much thought. It could easily consume me if I let it. Until I'm face to face with him, until I can ask him what possessed him to do what he did, I'm at a dead end.' He straightens his shoulders and shakes his head. 'At the moment, my personal feelings will have to be ignored.'

∞

Gryffin growls and raises his gun as Forty-Three steps out from behind the transport to his left. The man's red eye locks on to him and Forty-Three smiles as he raises his weapon to point it at Gryffin. He hates Forty-Three almost as much as he hates the Scientist. In a way, having the cyborg work on him was worse. Forty-Three went through similar procedures in the past thanks to the Scientist. Having him now help the man who changed them both against their will is messed up. The only thing Gryffin wants to do when he's around the Scientist is rip the man's spine out through his chest. Being his dutiful assistant would never cross his mind.

'You're not leaving here, brother.'

Gryffin's jaw pops as he clenches it tightly. Every time the man calls him 'brother', he feels like he's going to throw up. The word sounds unnatural coming from his mouth.

'It's clear you're malfunctioning.'

'He tortured you and you're helping him. Ever think you're malfunctioning?' Gryffin tries to keep his outstretched arm steady, but the damn thing trembles with the exertion.

'He made me stronger. That is all that matters.' He walks around Gryffin, slowly turning him so his back nears the wall. 'There's nowhere for you to go. I've been watching. You have no bullets left. This is where you belong.'

'Damn that.' Gryffin drops the gun and throws a knife at Forty-Three. The blade embeds itself in the centre of the optic implant. Sparks dance across his head as he roars in pain. Gryffin stumbles away from the downed man and hones in on the transport again. His legs don't feel like they belong to him anymore and his chest is on fire so he allows the implant a little more control. The added power helps his torso and legs connect again.

The distance between him and salvation shortens. Forty-Three's screams still echo behind him. He risks a quick glance over his shoulder. The other cyborgs are standing in a circle around Forty-Three.

The first punch glances off Gryffin's chin. The second punch doubles him over and expels the air from his struggling lungs. He drops to his knees and screams as the impact jars his metal leg. He looks up at the large cyborg in front of him. Definitely an ex-prison inmate. This one is huge, all pumped up muscles and snaking veins. He clenches his massive fists and smiles down at Gryffin.

He has every reason to smile. It was one hell of a shot. Outside of having the wind knocked from him, which he always hated, Gryffin notices a fair amount of pain. The cyborg is strong. Not exactly something that's going to do him any favours in his current state. Usually, he'd be a match for the man, but months of torture has weakened him. However, he has something on the large cyborg — experience. He's been operating with his mods a hell of a lot longer than his opponent has.

He pushes the pain to the back of his mind. Living in this shithole has conditioned him against it. Even being out of air is something Gryffin knows how to deal with.

He ignores the protests from his body and stands up straight. His purple eyes glow with rage as he stares at his opponent. In those brief few seconds, Gryffin sees everything he needs to. Fear. His opponent didn't expect him to get up again. The cyborg tries to stand tall, but it's too late to redeem himself. Gryffin has him where he wants him.

'You're... in... my—' Gryffin takes a lurching step forward with each word, striking the cyborg wherever he can hit. On the forth step, he swings his fist at the man's face. 'Way!'

The blow is going to miss. Gryffin knows it the second he launches his fist. The large, smirking cyborg ducks under it. Before Gryffin can even register the dodge, however, another body shot, this one to his ribs, sends fresh ripples of pain through his already damaged torso. He plants his feet to make sure he doesn't fall, but it's not easy and uses too much energy. Usually his reputation ensures hand to hand combat is avoided by anyone that crosses him. If they saw him now, his reputation will have already taken a beating.

The cyborg goes in for another shot. Gryffin shoves him off. Seeing the man crash back against the wall gives him a much needed second wind. He quickly covers the distance between them and throws three more punches that do land. The man falls to the ground in a heap. He pulls the gun from the man's belt and turns towards the transport again. The few seconds it takes to run to the ship feels like hours to him. He drags himself up the small cargo hatch and slams his palm against the door control. Using the walls as support, he pushes himself up to the cockpit and drops heavily into the pilot's seat.

He looks out the window and notices the cyborgs are getting themselves together. The ship shudders to life as he starts the ignition sequence. Gryffin keys in the code for the transport bay door and holds his breath. He spent weeks memorising the code. Each of the numbers and letters will be permanently burned into this brain. He can't read, so he doesn't know what the numbers and letters are. Growing up in the lab taught him about pain and how to survive — reading was a luxury well above his entitlement as a test subject. The large red light over the door flashes and he releases his breath.

He lifts the transport off the ground and turns to face the door. The craft shudders as it is hit again and again by whatever weapons the remaining guards can find. Gryffin ignores everything except the ever-increasing gap in the door that will lead to his freedom. Men race towards the transports. He can't tell if they're human or cyborg. It doesn't matter. They all work for the Scientist so he has no regrets about what's about to happen.

As soon as he can, he forces the ship out the door, scraping the sides as he squeezes through. Just as the craft clears the doors, he sends a four-digit code to the station, pushing the trigger on the final piece of his plan. The inside of the transport bay lights up as the remaining transports explode one by one. Gryffin smiles to himself and accelerates away from the destruction. He can't believe it actually worked. Overloading the power cells on the ships was a lot easier than he thought it would be. But even though his plan worked, he can't relax. He's bought himself a couple of days at the most.

He enters the coordinates for Ultar into the system and closes his eyes. There's a bench seat and a med kit in the main compartment, but he doubts he can even make it that far. Without the strength to hook to the system, he can't figure out where he is or how long it will take to get to Ultar. Aleena's patching-up skills are just what he needs right now — he never thought he'd feel like that.

Whether through sleep or unconsciousness, he allows the calm blackness to carry him back to Ultar — he hopes.

4

Terra packs her tool kit away and wipes her hands on an old rag sticking out of her pocket. She stretches her arms above her head to loosen her weary muscles. The morning was spent under a console on *Ares*… again. It's how every day seems to go for her at the moment. She slaps the Nomad working with her on the back and grins. 'I'm off for lunch.'

He wipes the sweat from his forehead with his sleeve. 'No problem. Give the Hunter a kick from me.'

She doesn't bother replying to his remark. The feud between the Nomad and Hunters is a part of life in the Sector. It's a given, just like day and night. Luckily, Desyl and Lucan ensure her relationship with Bray doesn't cause any problems for her. She pauses as she gets to the top of the loading ramp. A group of Nomad and colonists are gathered at the bottom, engrossed in conversation.

As she approaches, they stop talking. They always seem to do that when she's around. She smiles and greets them as she walks past.

Once they think she's out of earshot, the murmur of conversation continues. She knows they're talking about Gryffin — wondering where he is, whether he's coming back, what happened to him? They don't fall silent to disrespect her, quite the opposite. They're respecting her need to distance herself from the memories.

Gryffin is the topic of many conversations around the base. Bar a select few, most of the inhabitants have never actually seen him. To them, he was this entity that arrived in his ship, did what had to be done, and then left again. They all knew the stories. They all knew what he was like and what he was capable of. He was like a mystery figure — a myth. The silent threat of him was always there. You stepped out of line, attacked a colony, did something someone didn't like, you knew there was a possibility he would be sent after you. It helped to forge his reputation and the myth surrounding him, which in turn helped to ensure the safety of the colonies he protected.

She's heard the stories about him. Apart from a few embellishments, she fully believes most of them. It's not difficult to think of Gryffin being able to fight his way out of any situation he was in.

As a result, a lot of people don't believe he's actually dead. Someone like that, with that myth, that reputation — they don't just die. They don't think of him as a flesh and blood man, but as an indestructible cyborg. They hadn't seen what Terra had on the freighter though.

She squeezes her eyes shut as the image of his torn, bloody body hits her. They didn't see the large hole in his chest. They didn't see the blood pouring out of his body, to gather in a puddle on the floor. They didn't see the grey hue of his skin as he lost more and more blood. They didn't see his eye dull as death called to him.

If they knew all that, they'd lose the hope his reputation kept alive. For the moment, they're happy to bury their heads in the sand. Even though the freighter exploded, they still couldn't believe he was dead. Terra knew there's no way he could have survived his injuries, let alone the explosion. His human side couldn't come through that.

She steps out of the cool base into the Ultaran sun. The warmth is a pleasant relief to the chill deep in her bones. Thinking about what happened on the freighter always left her cold. The sun helps to warm her a little, but the chill still remains deep within her.

For a while, the truth of his demise threatened to overwhelm her. She fought against the attraction to Bray, against the connection between them, the comfort he offered. But she could only fight for so long. Over time, she realised she needed him and she wanted to be with him. He was the one ray of light that managed to break through the crippling grief constantly surrounding her. He never pushed her — he was just there for her. He would stop by her room regularly with a tray of food, with a drink, or just to have a chat. Apart from Milla and Roman, she couldn't talk to anyone like she could talk to him

He was easy, uncomplicated. Unlike his brother. But they were very similar in other ways. Both are... were strong, imposing, unyielding men that could more than take care of themselves. But unlike Gryffin, Bray is not afraid or unable to express his emotions. Terra knows he cares about her. He's told her he does enough times. And she's told him the same. They talk like normal people do. He'd ask her a question, she'd answer, ask him one in return and he'd answer. There was no dodging questions, no abrupt and aggressive attempt to stop the conversation. She knows about his childhood. She knows where he grew up. About the death of his parents. About living with his grandparents on one of the border colonies. She knows how he felt when they died. How he took the wrong path in life and ended up in the prison where Avoca eventually found him. She knows about his life on *Perses* and how much he loves being a Hunter. She knows every detail.

She could never have that with Gryffin. Apart from her father, no one knows what happened to him when he was a child. How did he vanish from Earth and reappear out here? People have asked, but he never answered. She laughs and shakes her head. She doesn't actually know anything about Gryffin — not really. It sounds silly when she admits it to herself. Bray shared more with her in one day than Gryffin ever did with her. It doesn't make sense for him to have this affect on her.

She nods to herself and walks through the trees towards the village. When put like that, it's hard to justify her extreme reaction. Clinging to the weak reasoning, she picks up the pace — her boyfriend is waiting for her.

∞

'What's the problem?'

Desyl points to an unknown signal on the screen. 'We picked it up about ten minutes ago. It's a small craft, heavily damaged and only operating on ten-percent power. There may not be anyone still alive in there. Could explain why there's no response.'

Roman examines the small craft on the screen. 'Don't suppose you recognise the design?'

Desyl shakes his head. 'There's no such thing as 'designs' out here.'

Roman grunts. It was a stupid question. He looks at the large clock on the wall. '*Nemesis* is due within the hour. Get Chayse to pick it up on the way here. He's not to take any chances though. This could be a trap.'

Desyl contacts Chayse and relays the order while Roman organises security teams to meet the ships when they arrive.

'Contact Aleena and tell her to get everyone inside, just in case.' Desyl nods and activates his radio. Roman hopes there will be no need for all the security, but with things the way there are in the Sector, caution is certainly advised. Over the last few months, many transports and larger ships have come to Ultar. Some were seeking refuge, but more than a few seemed intent on destroying the colony. It didn't help that there are ridiculous rumours that Gryffin is being hidden on the surface. Many colonies put a bounty on his head after what he did. Unfortunately, with the situation so unstable, there are many groups eager to either destroy Gryffin once and for all or to cash in on the bounty.

Everything is ready when they get word the battleship and the mysterious craft have arrived. Roman and a security detail consisting of Nomad, Hunters, Foundation and Ultarans, arm themselves and make their way to the surface. The large steel doors slide open and he squints as the sunlight hits his eyes. The team makes their way to the large field to the South of the base. A year ago, the field was used to graze cattle, now it serves as a landing zone for the ever growing fleet of ships gathering on Ultar.

He glances up as the sound of engines disturbs the otherwise peaceful surroundings. *Nemesis* breaks the cloud cover and hovers over the field. The sun glints off her hull, highlighting the large purple griffin marking her as a Nomad vessel. Roman activates his radio. 'Chayse, welcome back. We're in position.'

The thick steel tethers extend from under *Nemesis* and slowly lower the smaller craft onto the ground. The large locks release the transport and withdraw back into the ship. Roman gestures to the team and they surround the ship. He shields his eyes from the dust and debris thrown up by *Nemesis'* powerful engines as she comes in to land at the far side of the field. Her engines shut down and the sudden silence is strange after the roar of her engines.

The ramp lowers and Chayse steps on to the surface. He jogs up to Roman with a team from *Nemesis*. Roman shakes his hand and nods towards the battered transport. 'No need to bring a gift, Chayse.'

The young Nomad smiles. 'Yeah, well we don't know if it's a gift yet. Probably best to hold off thanking me.' He pulls out a gun from his belt. 'Ready?'

Once everyone is in place, Desyl opens the back of the transport. The hatch shudders and slowly lowers to the ground. The ship's internal alarms sound as the back opens. Lucan and Chayse slowly move into the ship, constantly scanning the interior for any signs of trouble, while Desyl and Roman remain outside. Lucan covers Chayse as he approaches the cockpit. He spins around the corner, his gun raised in front of him. 'What the hell?'

Roman, Desyl and Lucan cautiously approach to join Chayse at the front of the vessel. Roman's breath catches in his throat when he sees the pilot slumped in the seat. 'Gryffin?'

Chayse holds him back as he tries to get closer. 'Don't go near him.'

Roman pulls his arm from Chayse's grip. 'What are you talking about? He's hurt.'

Chayse pushes Roman back into the main body of the ship. His pale blue eyes lock with Roman's. 'Think for one minute. Nearly a year with no sightings, no intel. Not a damn thing. Then out of the blue he arrives here by himself, all wrapped up in a neat ship — a little convenient, don't you think?'

Lucan joins them in the back of the ship. He drapes an arm over a seat and gestures towards the cockpit. 'Chayse is right,' Lucan says. 'He's in a bad way. Can't see how he'd pilot this ship like that. No harm in checking his programming just to be sure — for everyone's sake. The Foundation have already programmed him to kill us once. Not a stretch to think they'd do the same again.'

Roman looks over Lucan's shoulder at the cockpit. The unnerving and unfamiliar emotional pull towards his son is powerful, but common sense is breaking through. It is a little too convenient. 'Very well. Take whatever resources you need. If his programming is clear, I want him off this ship and with Milla as soon as possible.'

Even though every fibre of his being is telling him that he needs to stay on the ship, he forces himself to turn and walk down the ramp, leaving Gryffin with Chayse and Lucan. These Nomad are two of Gryffin's most trusted men. He's in safe hands.

∞

Milla pushes through the gathering crowd. News of Gryffin's apparent rising from the dead has flown through the village faster than she thought possible. Not gaining much ground, Milla stops. 'Would you all get out of my way!' Her outburst has the desired effect. The crowd divides to allow her a clear path to the ship. 'Thank you.'

She locates Roman at the bottom of the ramp. His usual confident presence is gone leaving him looking lost. She rushes over to him and places a hand on his arm to get his attention. 'Sir, I just got word. Is it him?'

Roman nods solemnly. 'Chayse and Lucan want to be sure he's not... I don't know... booby trapped I guess.'

'Is he awake? Is he in one piece? How did he get here?'

Roman holds up his hands to stop her rapid-fire questions. 'All I know is that he's badly injured and unconscious — at least I hope he's unconscious and not...I don't even know if he's alive. The life support in the ship failed. I know his implants can keep him alive, but we have no way of knowing how long he's been in there. There's so much blood, Milla. Can the implants help with blood loss?'

'I honestly don't know, sir. Without examining him, I really can't say.' She looks over his shoulder and sees Aleena hurrying towards them. 'Stay with Aleena. I'll see what's going on.' She steps into the ship, but Chayse jumps up from the floor of the cockpit and stops her from getting near. 'Stop right there, Milla'

'Let me help.'

'You're not going anywhere near him until I know he's safe to be around.'

She squeezes his hand. 'I'm a big girl, Chayse. Please let me be here for you, for him.'

His cool blue eyes bore into her, but she stands her ground. He finally looks away and shakes his head. 'Fine. I know I'm wasting my breath.' He kisses her briefly. 'Hi, by the way.'

She smiles at him. 'Hi back.' He takes her hand and leads her into the cockpit. If not for the recognisable implants, she wouldn't have known the pilot is Gryffin. He is slumped in the pilot seat, leaning against the side wall of the ship. Blood soaked, dirty, once white scrubs hang off his painfully thin body. Wires snake out from the centre of a new eyepiece and disappear into his matted hair. Every bit of exposed skin is discoloured with heavy bruising and large cuts, and his metal arm is missing. 'My God. Where is the blood coming from?'

Instead of answering, Chayse leans over and slowly peels Gryffin's top up. Milla swallows deeply at the sight of sodden bandages struggling to keep his chest together. 'He piloted the ship like that? I need him in theatre. Now, Chayse.'

He holds on to the back of the chair to block her path. 'No, Milla. Lucan is nearly finished.'

'Look at him, Chayse. He'll die before that. Gryffin is unconscious. What exactly is he going to do in that state?'

'Look around you! You've seen what he can do first hand. The Ultarans have suffered enough. Until we know for sure that he hasn't been programmed to finish what he started here, he doesn't move from this ship. Understood?'

'"Understood?" Seriously? You're even starting to sound like Gryffin. Well, at least let me bandage his chest and try to stem the blood flow. Or would you prefer to kneel in it while you test him.'

Chayse lets go of the chair and allows Milla to squeeze by him. She removes all the bandages from her kit and opens the packages. Ideally, she'd remove his top and clean the wound first but it would be a futile act. He needs surgery, not a flimsy bandage. Instead, she instructs Chayse to support his weight while she places all the padding she has with her over his chest and wraps the bandage around his upper torso. Within seconds of laying him back in the chair, the blood seeps through the fresh bandages. 'This is ridiculous. He's going to bleed dry at this rate.'

'Almost there,' Lucan replies. He rises to his feet and hands the tablet to Chayse. 'From what I can see, his programming has been altered a lot, but nothing that's going to stab us in the back. I hope.'

'Not filling me with confidence,' Chayse grumbles.

Lucan wipes his bloody hands on his trousers. 'It's the best I can do in here and right now. Milla's right, it's time to get him patched up.'

Chayse stares down at his former captain for a minute, saying nothing.

Milla stands in front of him and attempts her best stern face. She understands his hesitation but that's not going to do Gryffin any good. He's alive, but that can all change in the space of a few minutes unless they act now. 'Chayse, he's going to die. He's back after what... ten months! Are you really going to let him bleed out?'

She can see his internal battle written clearly on his face, but he nods once. 'Bring him in. Take his implants offline as soon as you get him in the med bay. Use an isolated system to support him until we can do a full systems check.'

Milla calls for a gurney as Chayse and Lucan carry Gryffin into the back of the shuttle. Milla drapes a sheet over Gryffin to hide him from the onlookers before her team hurries towards the underground tunnels with their precious cargo.

She can't quite get her head around Gryffin's sudden appearance. They spent months wishing he would come back. And suddenly here he is — like the miracle they all need. It's all a little too convenient.

5

The Scientist slowly walks around the examination table. He picks up the anaesthetic mask and squeezes it in his hand. 'How did he get out of the state of the art restraints?'

The technician fidgets with the cuff of his lab coat and swallows deeply. 'I secured him well. The catches seem to have been broken.'

'But how did he break them if they were strengthened by the power to the table? He either wasn't secured sufficiently or he somehow managed to break the restraints when he was suddenly overcome by a surge of strength. Now, considering the procedures he's been through over the last few months, I find that incredibly difficult to believe. Was the table powered?'

'Of course!'

'So, he wasn't sufficiently restrained.'

'I... I don't know how—'

The Scientist places a hand on the man's trembling shoulder. 'Well, how about I give you thirty minutes to find out how my most prized possession escaped on your watch.' He leaves the technician and slowly strolls through the prison. Years ago, the facility was the main prison used by the Foundation, but concerns about prisoner wellbeing had forced them to shut it down and build a newer one in Foundation space. Prisoner wellbeing. The Scientist nearly laughs out loud at that. The notion is ridiculous.

He enters what's left of the transport bay and steps over the body of one of the security guards.

'How many test subjects were destroyed?'

Forty-Three climbs off a mound of rubble and approaches his creator. 'Twenty-one.'

The Scientist can feel the anger build in his body, but pushes it aside. Losing his temper will do nothing to help the situation. 'How long will it take to repair what the prototype did?'

'Unknown at the moment. There is extensive damage. I estimate a month.'

'Pack up. We'll move to the new facility. We'll just have to make do while the building work is being finished. Any remaining subjects are to be there within the day. We cannot afford to lose any time because of this. I doubt the Foundation will appreciate a delay of any kind — no matter how valid. Once you've organised everything, I want you down in the lab. You're no good to me with a damaged eye.'

Forty-Three nods once and then turns to carry out his orders. The Scientist leaves the transport bay and the carnage behind. This whole situation is laughable. The prototype was weakened considerably by the examinations, yet he still succeeded in breaking his bonds, killing twelve security personnel, twenty-one cyborgs and stealing a craft. It is a setback, but it's also a great achievement. The modifications he made to Thirty-Five clearly helped him in his escape. While a regular man would have died or accepted their fate at some stage during the examinations, Thirty-Five fought back and won. This round anyway.

There is too much at stake for him just to walk away and let his main project have a happy life. He enters his personal quarters and sits down on his bed. He picks a picture of Maggie off his bedside table and runs his finger tenderly down her cheek. She is going to be so disappointed in him. He let her son escape. He places the picture back on the table and removes his glasses.

He's so close to saving her. So close to having her with him again, but time is running out. A person can only survive in a stasis pod for so long. Eventually, they will succumb to death. If he can't figure out how to incorporate an implant with an organic brain, he won't be able to help her. He rises to his feet and walks across the concrete floor to his personal computer on the desk. The situation is infuriating him.

He closely studied Maggie's son for months. Every single implant was scanned and tested — whether outside his body or inside. He knows every intimate detail of the prototype's body. The position of all his implants, the colour and length of every piece of wiring, the locations of each of his scars. He knows it all except for one valuable detail. How he has survived all the procedures. Physically, there's nothing special about the young man. He was a late addition to the project and he was just used to test the implants before they were fitted to the main subjects. There was no anaesthetic used, no fancy stitching or aftercare of any kind. He should have died after the first operation.

He calls up the project files and scans through the lists of test subjects. Dozens of healthy young prisoners were tested and all of them failed. What is it about the prototype that makes him different? The other men are the same age group, they're all strong and fit, but it doesn't make the slightest difference. They all die after having the control implant fitted. It's the one critical piece of the technology and he can't get it to work without killing the subject. There's no way he can risk fitting it to Maggie if he keeps getting results like this.

He examines Thirty-Five's file and comes to an uneasy conclusion. He is going to have to disappoint Maggie. He can't save her without sacrificing her son. If he is to succeed, he needs to remove the control implant from the prototype. It's the only sure way of replicating and improving on his original design. The procedure will kill the prototype, but it will also bring him closer to saving her.

His mood lightens slightly. He checks his watch. Thirty minutes have passed since he left the lab. Time to speak to his technician again.

∞

Terra slides out from under the console and wipes her hands on the hem of her shirt. 'Try it again.'

The Nomad working on the comms system with her nods and activates the computer. 'Still no power, Commander.'

'Seriously?' She pulls herself to her feet and examines the readings on the monitor. Terra rubs her tired eyes and leans closer to the screen. *Ares* is the bane of her life. Even though she spends every spare minute on the ship, there always seems to be something else that needs attention. If they were in a Foundation space dock, the ship would have been finished months ago, but with little resources and antiquated diagnostic equipment, the process is painfully slow. It also doesn't help that *Ares* is a mix of so many different systems and modified parts from countless ships. It's a hard enough job just figuring out what everything does let alone try to fix it.

She ignores her Nomad companion and stares at the screen. She hates being here. Hates the feelings that stir to the surface whenever she's on board. When the decision was made to rebuild *Ares*, she thought she'd be safe. The Nomad don't let women on their ships, so naturally she assumed that also included having woman on the repair team. Unfortunately, Aleena convinced Desyl otherwise. *Ares* has to be in the air as soon as possible. In order to do that, they had to drop the 'no woman' rule. That decision placed her in command of the repair crew. Just her luck.

Terra traces her finger along the path of the connection and taps the screen. 'There. I must have missed something on this path. I can't think of anywhere else the issue can be.' She lowers to the floor and slides back under the unit. 'Next time Desyl feels like crashing *Ares* into the ground, tell him to do it with a little less force.'

The Nomad officer laughs. 'Will do. Never thought we'd get her flying again. When I saw her buried in the field, I was sure that was the end for her.'

'So did I. If she was in Foundation space, we wouldn't even have bothered stripping her for scrap.'

He shakes his head. 'Never an option. The Nomad would never scrap *Ares*. She's Gryffin's ship.'

Terra flinches at the mention of his name, but recovers quickly. 'Yeah, well you're lucky she was salvageable. Might not have had a choice.' Terra holds out her hand. 'Pass me the hammer.' He places it in her hand and she beats it against the underside of the console a few times.

'Gentle female touch, huh?'

'Whatever works. Try it again.'

There is silence for a moment then the ship's intercom system crackles to life. 'At long last. Good work, Commander.'

She slides out and takes his offered hand. 'Right, mark that one off the list. If anyone breaks the system again I don't want to know about it. How long is the repair list now?'

He flicks through page after page on the screen. 'Just one or two... pages. Next on the list is the comms panel in the captain's quarters. Your team mentioned a time delay on incoming messages.'

Great, Gryffin's quarters. Just where she wants to be right now. Terra pushes her shoulders back, but her reaction hasn't been missed. His eyes soften. 'You know what, I can handle that myself.'

'No. Let's go.'

They pack up their gear and step out of the room and straight into Desyl. 'There you are, Commander.'

'Everything all right?'

'He's here. Gryffin's here.'

∞

'How is he?'

Milla closes the door behind her and turns to face Roman. Chayse leans against the closed door and drapes an arm over Milla's shoulder. Milla takes a deep breath. 'Well, the good news is that he's alive. That in itself is a pretty big miracle. I honestly can't begin to imagine how he did it, but he piloted the shuttle with a full neck to waist incision. They cut him right through his muscle, and only put one quick line of sutures in. We had to go in and put him back together.'

Roman swallows deeply and clears his throat. 'Do you know what else they did to him?'

She consults her unit and sighs. 'He's malnourished, dehydrated, has numerous surgical incisions and newly healed fractures to three ribs, his left arm and left eye socket. He has deep lesions on his wrist and ankles from presumably being restrained. The collar Terra described is still around his neck, but the explosive side has been deactivated. We're still figuring out a way to remove it. There's also severe tissue damage to the flesh above and below the new metal thigh. From what I can tell, his body is rejecting the modification, but I really need to examine it in more detail once he's cleaned up. Add all that to the trauma of numerous operations, including what we had to do to him today and he's in serious condition.'

Roman licks his dry lips and crosses his arms to stop them from shaking. He has never felt more ashamed and disgusted to be associated with the group responsible for those injuries. 'And his implants?'

Chayse examines his boots. 'It's still early in our testing.' When he looks back up at Roman, he can clearly see the anger in the Nomad's eyes. Some of that is directed at him. Chayse has never fully moved on from the fact that Roman was the one to physically hand Gryffin over. Not that he can blame Chayse. It's not something he will ever forgive himself for. In his own eyes, he's as responsible for what's happened as the Foundation is. 'His arm was removed a while ago. Probably after he disappeared. Luckily Lucan found it under the seat in the shuttle.'

'Can you reattach it?'

Chayse shakes his head. 'Not yet. There's a chain welded to the connectors. Until that's removed and the arm is tested and repaired, we can't do anything. Your people clearly examined him regularly and aggressively.'

'They're not my people anymore.'

Anger flashes in Chayse's eyes. 'That doesn't wipe your slate clean.'

Milla stands in front of Chayse and places a hand at either side of his face. She forces him to look at her instead of Roman. 'Hey, blame won't help Gryffin. We have enough to do already without wasting energy on things we can do nothing to change.' He slowly nods before Milla releases him.

'As I was saying, he's had some alterations. His eye is the noticeable one. They replaced the eye that was destroyed on the freighter with a plate that fits inside the original implant. It looks like the optic on the centre works like an eye. Until he wakes up there's not much more I can tell you about it. Like Milla said, there's a lot going wrong with his metal leg. Don't know what they were thinking, but it's really messed up. We should be able to make some adjustments, but it may be a lost cause. As for the internal components, the Foundation did him a few favours.'

Roman frowns. 'Excuse me?'

'When I joined *Ares* as Gryffin's aide, I was given access to some of his medical records. According to these reports, Gryffin has always suffered episodes of severe pain in the tissue surrounding his implants. He'd get a searing burst that would last for a minute or so. It was random and usually affected his head, but he got them in all the implants occasionally. Klay couldn't figure out a way to help.' Chayse snorts and shakes his head. 'Can't say if he was actually trying or not though. Anyway, after checking the scan data over the last few months, we were able to figure out that the pain was caused by overloads in the old implants. They weren't designed with the... host body taken into account. From what I can tell, everything except the main control implant in his head has been upgraded. Hopefully, that will reduce the pain. Lucan is still checking his programming, but it's a mess. Our initial examination doesn't show any changes that will cause problems, but there have been upgrades.'

Roman runs a hand over his hair. 'I don't understand? I thought they wanted to — what did Avoca say? — finish him. Apart from minor alterations, what exactly did they take him for?'

Chayse shakes his head. 'Looks like he was just examined.'

'Examined?'

Milla nods. 'There's severe damage to his chest around his implant. He was definitely opened quite a few times. I agree with Chayse. There was a lot of poking around inside him, but not a lot actually done.' She shakes her head. 'A whole lot of pain and suffering, and for what? I know I'm a doctor and I shouldn't say this, but they deserve a taste of their own medicine.'

Roman grunts. 'Couldn't agree more. Will he wake up?'

Milla sighs. 'I really can't say, sir. His body has had to depend on the implants over the last few months just to keep him going. They weren't designed for that, so I have no idea what it's done to his body.'

'Can I see him?'

'Of course.'

She leads Roman into the room and waits at the door as he steps closer to his son. He pauses beside the bed and his shoulders slump. 'Why do you need all these monitors?'

'Just a precaution,' Chayse explains. 'We've hooked Gryffin up to the system temporarily. The computer at the head of the bed is supporting and running his internal implants. I'm bypassing the main programming in his brain until I can properly examine the implants. After what happened last year, it's for our safety as much as Gryffin's.'

'How long will it take him to check his programing?'

'I'm working through it with Lucan. The system won't be able to support Gryffin for too long. We've probably got about twenty-four hours until we have to unhook him.'

'What about the implant mod?' Roman asks Chayse. 'Will you be able to fit it?'

He shrugs. 'Technically yes. We don't quite have a working model yet, but with him actually here, it should speed things along.' Chayse nods towards Gryffin. 'I have to get back to his programming. He needs to come off those computers ASAP so we don't damage him.'

Roman nods, dismissing him. Before he leaves, Chayse kisses Milla. 'See you in a bit.'

Once he's gone, Milla steps up to Roman. 'With the greatest respect, sir, no one is cutting my patient's head open. Do you hear me?'

'Doctor—'

Milla holds up her hand. 'Don't you doctor me, Captain. It's far too early to even consider that. We have no way of sedating him. Do you really want to put him through that while he's conscious?'

'He's not conscious, Doctor, that's my point. Surely it's best to fit it now while he's still out. It's not something we can ignore, Milla. As long as that control implant is open to new programming, he's a threat. Anyone can take control of him and use him as a weapon. Chayse's mod needs to be fitted — for Gryffin's safety as much as ours.'

'I understand that, sir, but there's no way he'd survive brain surgery in his current state. He's been tortured for months. Is he not entitled to a break? I'm not going to put him through that, not yet.'

Roman makes a non-committal grunt. 'I understand what you're saying, Doctor, but this has to happen. He doesn't leave here until that procedure is carried out. It's going to be difficult enough to integrate him back into the fold after what's happened. At least if the mod is fitted, people may be more inclined to trust him.'

'So, he has to have brain surgery in order for ex-Foundation members to trust him.' She mutters a curse under her breath. 'Excuse me, sir, but that's pretty shite if you ask me.'

Roman wants to respond to her harsh comment, but he doesn't disagree with her. She's hit the nail on the head in her own unique way. It's not fair, but neither is the alternative. At the moment, Gryffin's future isn't secure. As impersonal as it sounds, without that mod, he is a weapon. Plain and simple. 'After seeing first-hand what he's capable of, what someone in control of him is capable of, we can't risk not fitting it.' He steps closer to Gryffin's bed. 'I don't want this any more than you do, but it's happening. That's an order, Doctor.'

Milla glares at him but slowly nods. 'Yes, sir.'

'Thank you. Chayse is leaving in a couple of days. You'll need to fit the mod while he's still here. Keep me posted.' He looks at his son one last time then leaves before he changes his mind.

Terra lifts her head into the spray, hoping the hot water will wash away some of the unwelcome feelings threatening to consume her. After she ran from *Ares*, she had picked the first person she saw in the training room and worked out until she could barely stand any longer.

He can't be alive — not really. Not after all this time. She increases the water temperature. The freighter had exploded. She watched the footage often enough to know it was true. Even Gryffin couldn't have removed the explosive collar and made it to a transport in time to escape. He had a gaping hole in his chest from the fight. Without medical attention he wouldn't have had a hope. Gryffin still being alive doesn't make sense. It must be a mistake. It has to be.

Strong arms circle her waist. 'You okay?'

She turns to face Bray and smiles. She wraps her arms around him then reaches up to kiss him while dragging him into the cubicle with her.

'Hold on, Terra, we need to talk.'

She runs her hand along the side of his face to trace the line of the small piece of metal from the corner of his eye to his ear. 'No.' She pulls at his shirt, but he takes her wrists in his hands.

'I'm serious, Terra.'

She wrestles her hands free and grabs a towel off the rail beside the stall. 'We don't need to talk.'

Bray leans against the sink and crosses his arms. 'You just found out Gryffin's still alive. Of course we damn well need to talk.'

Terra slips into her robe and roughly ties the belt. She pushes past Bray and stands in front of the mirror to brush her hair. After a few minutes of silence, he sits on the edge of the bed and clasps his hands on his knees. 'He's alive, Terra.'

'Yeah, I heard. The news is all over the base. You'd swear the Foundation had disappeared overnight.'

'You can't blame people for talking. He was dead.'

She angrily pulls the brush through her hair. 'I know that!'

'I'm worried about you, okay? You've had to deal with a lot over the last few months. What with your father, being trapped in the Sector, the Foundation, Gryffin dying and now this. I'd be surprised if you aren't a little, I don't know... off. I mean you were in love with him. This has to—'

'We don't talk about my father. Ever,' she addresses his reflection in the mirror. 'As for Gryffin, it was a one-way thing. I've told you enough times that there was never anything tangible with him. I'm with you Bray. You. The fact that he's now alive doesn't change a thing.'

He looks down at the worn wooden floor and sighs. 'Listen, I know you and my brother have a history. I get that. Whatever there was between you... it ended abruptly. It's only normal for some feelings to resurface now that he's back.'

She throws her brush on the bed and searches for a pair of trousers. 'Normal? What's normal about any of this? He died, Bray.

We all mourned him and moved on with our lives.' She stuffs her feet into the legs and pulls on a pair of black combat boots. 'What about you?'

Bray frowns. 'Me?'

'Gryffin is your long-lost big brother. You got him back for what, a few hours, before he died... again. Surely you must have some feelings about his return?'

Bray scowls and crosses his arms. 'We're not talking about me. As far as I'm concerned he's a stranger. Nothing has changed for me either way.'

Terra randomly picks a shirt from the drawer and ties her hair back in a messy bun. 'Yeah, well it's the same answer for me. He made his decision when he stayed on the freighter. As far as I'm concerned, he can stay dead.'

She slams the door behind her, ending the conversation.

∞

'Roman just told me you're leaving. When were you going to tell me?'

Chayse excuses the three Nomad with him at the bottom of the loading ramp leading to *Nemesis* and turns to face Milla. 'Can you try to be professional when my crew are around? It's hard enough trying to keep everything together without you speaking to me like that.'

Milla crosses her arms and glares up at him. 'Professional? Forget that! We're supposed to be in a relationship. Do you know what that means?'

He turns from her and climbs the ramp. 'I don't have time for this, Milla.'

She races up the ramp and stops in his path. 'With the greatest respect, Captain, make the time. What in the blazes is going on with you?'

His icy blue eyes refuse to meet hers. '*Nemesis* is needed along the border.'

She jabs her finger in his chest. 'You're running away! Why?'

Chayse glances around the cargo bay at his men. She couldn't care less about his reputation at the moment. 'Forget them and talk to me. Gryffin's back. That's a pretty big deal. I don't understand why you want to leave as soon as you can. I don't get it.'

He finally locks on to her eyes. 'Just because he's back doesn't mean I get to relax. It'll be weeks, months before he'll be any use to us. Until then, *Nemesis* has a job to do.'

Milla frowns and shakes her head. 'Any use to us? He's your friend not a computer. What's changed in the last few days?'

'Nothing. I have work to do.'

She grabs his arm and leads him to the corner away from prying eyes. 'I don't buy that for one minute. You don't go from practically idolising someone to turning your back on them at the first opportunity. Do you not think you should fill him in on what's been going on? Tell him about Klay and how he was behind the mysterious attacks and malfunctions. He deserves to hear that from you.'

Chayse looks towards *Nemesis* and shakes his head. 'Everything is recorded on the system for him.'

'Heaven forbid you actually talk to him. That would just be too much,' she replies sarcastically. She turns away from him and looks up at the ceiling. 'You and Terra are as bad as each other.' She faces him again and steps closer. 'If it didn't go against my oath as a doctor, I'd quite happily beat some sense into the two of you. The way you're behaving is bloody ridiculous. Yes, he's indirectly responsible for a lot of deaths, but you've been defending him all along. You've been the constant voice of reason, pushing the fact that he had no control over what the Foundation programmed him to do. You're the unofficial leader. You should be the one to talk to him.'

'Leader? I've done a great job, haven't I! The Nomad don't exist anymore! We're hiding in the shadows like vermin. That happened on my watch, Milla.' She rests her hand on his arm but he pulls away from her comforting touch. 'Don't, Milla. He trusted me with this and now there's nothing left.'

'Chayse, what happened to the Nomad is not your fault. It was a mix of, well, what Gryffin unintentionally did, the colonists' reaction to that and the Foundation. I doubt Gryffin himself could have done anything about it. You can't think he's going to blame you for everything.'

He runs a hand over his blond spikes. 'You don't understand, Milla. The Nomad are the most important thing to him. *Nemesis* was a life line — something to save the Nomad. I've done the exact opposite.'

'You're looking at this from the wrong angle. *Nemesis* did exactly what she was meant to do. Ultar is safe and the Foundation haven't been able to get a hold on the Sector.'

He laughs and shakes his head. 'That's down to blind luck. Milla, I haven't got a clue what I'm doing. What was he thinking putting me in charge? I was his aide.'

'He believed in you. Believed in your commitment to the Nomad.'

'Yeah, well, I've only got Aleena's word that Gryffin chose me because he really believed in me. Why didn't he try to find some way to block any modifications to his programming? I could have helped with that. None of this had to happen.'

'Maybe he thought nothing could be done about his programming. In his eyes, *Nemesis* was the only solution he could find.'

'He knew full well that I'm an engineer. Of all the people on *Ares*, I was the best one to find another solution.'

'I don't have the answers for you. But, luckily, the man who does is in bed along the corridor from here. When he wakes up you can ask him.'

'Are you crazy? I can't face him.'

'For the love of-' Milla mutters under her breath. 'Why not?'

'I let him down. When he died, the fleet looked to me for

leadership. I went from being an aide to a captain and I blew it.'

She shakes her head quickly, loosening some locks of hair from their tie. 'No you didn't! I really think you should stay until he wakes up. Everything could be cleared up in one conversation.'

'You've met Gryffin, right?'

She raises her eyebrows and nods. 'Fair point. I just don't want you to race away from here thinking the wrong thing. I seriously doubt he'll blame you for any of this. Please stay. I'm sure he'll be grateful to see a friendly face when he wakes up.'

'Yeah, well that's not me, not when he finds out what I did to the Nomad. I'll help you fit the mod, then *Nemesis* is leaving.'

Before she can muster a reply he turns and walks away from her without another word. She stares at his retreating back, barely resisting the urge to throw something at him.

∞

The head of the Foundation Council clasps his hands behind his back as he surveys the city through the reinforced glass. It had taken him ten years to work up to the illustrious title of One. The rest of the Council would turn to him for the final word on all main decisions. From an early age, he knew his future lay with the Foundation Council. Academically, he suited the role perfectly. His parents were delighted when, at the age of seven, the school made it official and entered the role against his name in the database. Dozens of names were entered but only twelve were selected.

Although he wants nothing more than to celebrate the promotion with his family and friends, they can never know. The identities of council members must remain a secret to protect their relatives. All meetings and public addresses take place behind a mask. Remaining incognito makes him feel powerful. While wearing the mask, he can make decisions that will directly impact millions of people. Then, at the end of the day, he can go home to spend a pleasant evening with his wife — the perfect balance.

He turns away from the view and settles behind his large wooden desk. One runs his hand along the solid gold edging and leans back in his leather chair. A small light flashes on his screen and pulls him back to his job. He opens the message. It's a report from a Foundation ship stationed in the Outer Sector. He scans through the message and his good mood melts away. *Infinity* has been causing trouble for them again.

Stationing *Infinity* in the Outer Sector had been his idea. If he brought the lawless region under Foundation control it would assure him a place with the great leaders of the past. At the time, he trusted *Infinity* would meet little resistance. What resistance could the Sector offer with inferior, old ships, barely any weapons, and no recognisable structure to speak of? But, they proved him wrong.

Then things deteriorated when *Infinity* was stolen from the group. Losing the ship is a greater inconvenience than losing the personnel. People can be replaced easily. The ship, however, is a different story. When Roman was given her command, she had just left the space dock. One clenches his fist tightly on the top of his desk. By commandeering *Infinity*, Roman had earned his place under the Nomad leader on the Foundation wanted list.

He thought time would help ease the feeling of betrayal and anger at Roman's actions, but it had the opposite effect. Roman continues to parade around the Sector in a Foundation ship. How dare he! *Infinity* is fitted with state of the art trackers and sensors. Or at least it was. Roman must have had outside help to disable them. A state of the art vessel disappeared and there's nothing he can do about it.

Time is running out for him. At the moment his great plans don't seem as great. Instead of turning the colonies, they are joining to fight against the Foundation. He needs those colonies under Foundation control. The populace expects him to deliver.

He takes a deep breath. The smell of his expensive leather chair fills his nostrils. He deserves this role and he will not let a rogue captain and a defective cyborg destroy everything.

∞

Terra sighs loudly and drops the tablet on the bed — Gryffin's bed. Well, technically it's Desyl's bed now. He's the captain so presumably this will be his room now.

'You okay, Commander?'

She turns to find Bray leaning against the doorframe. 'Yeah. Just can't get this antiquated system operating again. What are you doing here?'

He shoves his hands in the pockets of his navy combats and shrugs. 'Just thought I'd see how you are.'

Terra forces what she hopes is a convincing smile on her face. 'I'm good. I'll be glad when we sign *Ares* off as being fit for duty.'

Bray steps across the threshold and brushes a lock of hair behind her ear. 'You know that's not what I mean. I don't want to argue with you. I care about you, Terra. That gives me the right to be worried.'

She squeezes his hand. 'I'm sorry I acted the way I did. I guess I'm just tired. Seriously, Bray, there's nothing to worry about. Well, apart from the comms system on *Ares*.'

Even though he doesn't look convinced he nods and bends down to kiss her. She can't explain why she turns her face slightly so he kisses her cheek instead. The hurt is visible in his eyes as he pulls his hand back and steps away. Without a word, he turns and disappears down the corridor, his footsteps fading as he moves away from her.

Terra slumps on to the edge of the bed, suddenly not caring who it belonged or belongs to. What is wrong with her? She has an amazing man like Bray in her life and she's still not happy. She should leave the past in the past and focus on planning a future with him.

She glances around the empty room and her heart aches. Over the months, she thought Bray had managed to fill the void left by Gryffin. Until the Nomad leader crash landed back into her life, she had convinced herself she was over him. Those last few minutes with

Gryffin on the freighter play in her mind like a horror movie. "Terra, I can't go with you." She didn't realise at the time how much those six little words would change her life.

"I'm sorry, Terra." She nearly laughs out loud. Did Gryffin really think that everything would be made whole again with his final words to her? It was Bray who slowly managed to put her back together after Gryffin pulled her apart with his words. She can never forgive Gryffin for that or for giving up on them so easily.

Terra wipes tears from her face before she chastises herself for weeping over him yet again and storms into the bathroom. She splashes cold water on her face and looks at her reflection in the mirror. Yeah, she looks as horrible as she feels. She knows she should go after Bray and apologise, but she can't face him just yet. She needs to get her own head sorted out before she even attempts to speak to him. The last thing she wants to do is make things worse.

Terra faces her reflection again and grimaces. She's emotionally attached to two brothers. How can it possibly get worse?

Milla wraps her arms around Chayse's shoulders and buries her head against his neck. 'Please don't go like this.'

He sighs and holds her close to him. 'I have to, Milla. The most important thing is to get Gryffin up and strong. When he finds out the truth about the Nomad, I'm going to be the last person he'll want to see.'

She pushes back from him and looks into his ice blue eyes. 'I really think you have it all wrong. From what you told me, you were the closest thing he had to a friend on board. He'll stick by you, Chayse.'

He shakes his head. 'He'll have enough on his plate without dealing with me. If I can somehow figure out what's going on around the Port, maybe even keep more of the Foundation from coming through, I might be able to make it up to him.'

'But—'

'But nothing, Milla. I have to go.' He pulls her tight against his chest. 'I wish you could come too.'

'You really mean that?'

'Of course I do.' He takes her face in his hands. 'I-I love you, Milla. Have for a while now.'

Her mouth drops open. 'Why the blazes didn't you tell me?'

He shrugs. 'I'm not exactly a good prospect. I wanted to wait until I fixed this.'

Milla doesn't know what to say. She never planned for anything more than a casual relationship with Chayse. Serious commitment wasn't something she sought out — ever. After living with a mother who was discarded by man after man, Milla swore never to place herself in a situation like that. She would control where the relationship went and usually ended it before it went too far.

Somehow, Chayse managed to throw her off her game. She didn't realise until he said he loved her, how much she had let him in more than she initially planned. It's all Terra's fault. If Milla hadn't been preoccupied worrying about her friend's feelings for Gryffin, she would have noticed she was falling in love with Chayse.

Milla frowns and Chayse crosses his arms. 'What?'

'I'm in love with you?'

He laughs at the confusion in her voice. 'Asking or telling?'

Milla takes a deep breath and meets his pale blue eyes. 'Telling, I think?'

Chayse places his hands on her shoulders and leans down so he's level with her. 'Weren't expecting it either, huh?' He uses a finger to tilt her head up slightly. 'Hey, took me by surprise too. But that doesn't change the facts. I love you Milla Collins.' He shrugs and smiles his lopsided grin. 'Have to admit, I'm kinda glad you're acting like this. Makes me feel a little better.'

'What do we do now?'

He shrugs and looks over at *Nemesis*. 'Not a lot we can do. I still have to get on that ship and leave you.' He tucks her hair behind her ear. 'I meant what I said. If I could, I'd take you with me — no question.'

57

Milla forces herself to stay cheery. 'You and me trapped on a ship? We'd probably kill each other.'

Chayse gathers her in his arms. 'Yeah, but think about all the making up we'd have to do after.'

Milla laughs in spite of the large hole steadily growing in her chest. 'When do you think you'll be back?'

Chayse's chest rises and falls as he takes a deep breath. 'In a few weeks. Roman and Aleena want us to take some supplies to a few of the outer colonies.'

'Can't someone else go?' Milla hates the desperation in her voice. She's never needed a man the way she needs Chayse.

'The other battleships are allocated. Anyway, you'll have your hands full getting Gryffin back on his feet again. Just remember not to take any shite from him.'

Milla laughs. 'That your best attempt at an Irish accent?'

He shrugs. 'Made you laugh and that's what I was going for.' He kisses her then pushes away. 'I gotta go. I'll contact you as often as I can, okay?

She nods and attempts a smile, but doesn't quite manage to pull it off. Chayse pauses at the top of the ramp and smiles at her before he disappears into his ship.

∞

One looks up from his screen as Leeson enters the room. The look on the Admiral's face immediately makes him uneasy. 'Why do I get the impression you're going to ruin my day?'

Leeson sits in front of him and nods solemnly. 'The latest batch of cyborgs the Scientist shipped to us have all expired.'

One clenches his teeth and shoves his chair away from his desk. 'Are you certain there are no survivors?'

Leeson shakes his head. 'None.'

One paces the ornate rug behind his desk as he tries to rein in his temper. The Scientist is costing him a fortune and he is getting nothing but useless bodies in return. He examines the large map of the Sector covering the far wall of his office. The Outer Sector had been painfully mapped and each of the new development sites chosen. The future of their civilisation depends on these new sites.

He rubs his temple and lowers back into his seat. How he wishes he could face his predecessors and show them his disdain. Their bad decisions have left him in a difficult position. The system that allocated professions to the populace has a major flaw. Over time, in order to improve the social status of the inhabitants, careers involving manual labour of any kind were slowly eradicated. Everything that involved physical exertion was left to the drones. The robots could cope with most jobs but they also had a flaw — they needed to be programmed. Without knowledge of the task, how could they possibly complete it effectively?

There were those that fought against their allocated roles, but the first Council had an answer for that too. Anyone who would not conform was sent through the Port. The social cleansing had created an Earth of elite and peaceful people. It was not to last.

Since he took control of the Council, he found the flaws in their great plan. Thanks to their extreme actions, Earth is running out of food — fast. The dwindling food supply has pushed pricing to an all-time high. The Council agreed not to inform the population of the real issue behind the shortage. If they lose faith in the leadership of Earth, the Council could find themselves overthrown. What they desperately need is a steady supply of food.

He opens the file on the prototype cyborg and leans closer to the screen to examine the sketch Balfe was sent by Roman over a year ago. Balfe had no knowledge of the true problem facing Earth. His focus on growing a controllable army will do little to help their current crisis — it can be adapted however.

The Outer Sector provides the best solution. The resident colonists can farm the land to provide the elite with as much food as they need, once again securing the future of the elite. Unfortunately, in order for all that to happen, he needs the cyborg program.

Earth needs an army. An unstoppable one. The Foundation fleet performs well, but they don't have enough personnel to capture and control the Outer Sector colonists. In order for this to work, the general population must remain in the dark. The Council cannot afford for word to get back. If they can modify the prisoners and use them to keep the colonists in line, he will only have to send a select few to oversee the efforts.

When he was elected, he promised the population two things: that he would provide them with an army without taking people from the main population and that he would relocate the prison moons. The cyborg program solves both problems while also addressing the more vital, food issue. Due to a change in the law just after he took office, many citizens found themselves in prison for crimes that some would see as petty. He couldn't care less. Earth deserves strict order. It is an extreme pleasure to be allowed to stay on the planet. If people choose to do something that angers him, they will be punished. It's for the greater good of society as a whole.

He turns away from the screen to address Leeson. 'Where is the prototype?'

'Still with the Scientist on the other side of the new Port.'

'Has our dear Scientist uploaded all of his data?'

'Yes, sir. Everything is with our team of experts. I will request the Scientist sends the prototype with the next batch.'

One shakes his head. 'Not necessary. The data is sufficient for now. Leave it in the Outer Sector.'

'Yes, sir, but do you not need the prototype on Earth to serve as a demonstration model? The populace will need to see proof the project works.'

One slowly sits back in his chair and clasps his hands on his rounded stomach. 'Yes, but not yet. Does the Scientist know why the units are failing?'

Leeson nods. 'In spite of the longevity issues, the control implant works. Being able to study the prototype was useful. The Scientist was able to assess that it is not just the one implant that he must focus on. All of them working in conjunction with the control implant is key. Initially, the units work as Thirty-Five does, but their usefulness runs out after a month, two at the most.'

'What happens at that stage?'

'They die of a brain aneurysm.'

One rubs his jaw. 'Interesting. How does the prototype avoid this particular side effect?'

Leeson frowns. 'That's the unsettling news. He doesn't. Well, what I mean is that he may have avoided it so far but, according what the Scientist can determine, it will happen to him too. The reason it hasn't happened yet is still unclear.'

'So, it's on borrowed time also. Did the Scientist give any indication as to when we should expect it to shut down?'

Leeson shakes his head. 'He's yet to determine why Thirty-Five is reacting differently to the others so it is impossible to say when he will die. All we know for sure is that the more he uses his control implant, the more likely it is to kill him. Eventually he will lose the ability to control it and then he will die.'

One cannot form a sentence. What he thought couldn't get worse, just did. If the prototype fails before he can demonstrate the benefits of the program to the populace, he'll be forever known as a fool. His reputation will be in tatters. He will not let a faulty machine ruin everything he'd worked so hard to achieve. 'I want our team to work on a solution to this problem. Are we clear, Leeson?'

'I will speak—'

'You will not speak to the Scientist. Leave that man out of this. He's been picking the prototype apart for months and is no closer to figuring out his own work. It's ridiculous! The prototype is far too important to continue dissecting it. The Foundation will rectify his fault.'

Leeson nods. 'Yes, sir.'

'When will the next batch be ready?'

'The first ship of cyborgs will be ready to go through the Port within a month. We also have another batch of prisoners from the moons ready to undergo the procedure. Our engineers and doctors are familiar with the Scientist's work and are ready to attempt the surgery themselves once the shipment arrives tomorrow.'

One grunts and nods. That is good news at least. He is uncomfortable placing so much in the hands of the less than sane Scientist. If Foundation doctors can do the basic procedure, it will make him less dependent on outside more uncontrollable options.

'Superb. Dismissed.'

One watches as Leeson scurries from the room. While news that they can carry out some of his plan has improved his mood, he is still uneasy. There is not a limitless supply of prisoners. The priority is fixing whatever is killing them so they can be used to their full potential in the Outer Sector. Ideally, they need the prototype in the lab on Earth. He has no doubts the Foundation could find a solution to the problem if they could actually examine Thirty-Five in the flesh. They will have to do without for the moment. He needs to leave the prototype in the Outer Sector for now. One looks back at the screen again and smiles. No, for now the prototype is exactly where it needs to be.

∞

Milla knocks on the door to Terra's room. 'There you are. How did things go over on *Ares*?'

Terra puts her book down and sits up on her bed, tucking her legs under her. 'Good. Another few days and she should be up and about again. That's not why you're here though, is it?'

Milla smiles and shakes her head. She joins Terra on the bed and mirrors her posture. 'You got me. So, how are you?'

Terra shrugs and attempts her best I'm not bothered face. 'A bit tired. It's been a busy few days.'

'Stop being awkward. I mean how are you about Gryffin being back?'

'I'm glad he's okay.'

Milla looks up at the ceiling and mutters a few choice words under her breath. She looks back at Terra and sighs. 'I swear you've picked up some of my more annoying traits. Are you going to visit him?'

'I'm sure Chayse can fill him in on what's been going on here. My time will be better spent finishing *Ares*.'

Milla bites back her less than friendly reply. Her friend is so caught up in pretending to be unaffected by Gryffin's arrival, she's completely missed the fact that *Nemesis* and Chayse are gone. 'Chayse left.'

Terra's brows shoot up. 'What? When? Why?'

'About an hour ago.' Milla picks at a small hole in the bed covers and shrugs. 'The short story is; he blames himself for what happened to Gryffin.'

'But that's ridiculous.'

Milla nods and swallows back the lump in her throat. She refuses to cry over Chayse anymore. 'It is the way it is.' She looks up at Terra and forces a smile on her face. 'Not a lot I can do about it. Unlike you.'

Terra frowns. 'What can I do about Chayse?'

Milla rolls her eyes. 'For heaven's sake, Terra. I meant you can do something about Gryffin. Go and see him.'

'And say what exactly?'

Milla frowns. 'Terra, Gryffin isn't talking to anyone. He's unconscious. But, maybe if you sit with him, it'll help put some of your demons to bed.'

'I don't understand, he flew the shuttle here. Did something go wrong with the landing?'

'*Nemesis* brought the shuttle to the surface. Gryffin was already unconscious in the cockpit. Terra, he's in a bad way.'

A range of emotions travel across her friend's face before she composes herself. 'Will he be okay?'

Milla shrugs. 'Hard to say at the moment. His programming has been altered, his implants aren't doing what they should and his body...' She purses her lips and shakes her head. 'He's going to need a lot of recovery time.'

'Listen, I appreciate you coming to see me, and I'm so sorry about Chayse, but it sounds like Gryffin needs you more than I do.'

'Oh come on, Terra. You're seriously telling me that having Gryffin less than a five-minute walk from here means absolutely nothing to you. You were in love with him.'

'Exactly, Milla. Past tense. I'm with Bray now.'

'Yeah, don't get me started on how weird that is. It's normal if you're feeling... I don't know, confused or have doubts.'

Terra stands up and pulls on her boots. 'Change the subject. I'm going to get something to eat. You hungry?'

Milla slaps her hands on her knees and gets to her feet. 'Right, so we're ignoring the issue. Fantastic.' She opens the door. 'Well, you enjoy your make-believe world. I have a patient to look after.'

Terra hides in the shadows of the access tunnel and watches the door to the med bay. She feels like an idiot but there's no way she's going to give Milla the satisfaction of being able to say I told you so. The fact that Milla may have a small point just makes the whole thing more irritating. She has to see him. It has nothing to do with any residual feelings she's harbouring for him. This is about closure — plain and simple. She needs to see him one last time so she can finally say goodbye on her terms. This time she is going to have the final say.

She absently rubs her hand along the small scar buried in her hair. It serves as a constant reminder of the horrific time on the freighter when she found out Gryffin's big plan was to sacrifice himself for no reason. Sayber's hit to the head was Gryffin's idea to get her off the ship without any arguments. It was a lot easier than having the discussion with her.

Her attention is drawn back to the door as Milla leaves the med bay. Terra watches her friend disappear around the corner and waits a few minutes before she enters the room. Terra nods at the personnel on duty and walks right past them like she belongs here. She weaves through the space and stops at the glass door in front of her. Before she can talk herself out of it, she opens the door and approaches the bed. Any anger she feels instantly disappears when she sees him. He looks so small, thin, and pale against the stark white sheets.

Terra slides into the chair beside him and her eyes follow the path of the thick cable running from the side of his ocular implant and from the centre of his chest plate. They snake into a screen on the wall displaying data from his implants alongside his vitals. She has basic knowledge of his cybernetics, but not enough to figure out what the problem is, or if it can be fixed.

Without thinking, she traces her finger along the edge of his ocular implant. The new eyepiece sits very neatly inside his implant, but makes him look harsher than he deserves. Numerous new scars are scattered over his chest and arms, some old, but others are still fresh. Her eyes are repeatedly drawn to his right arm. The metal lower arm is missing. His metal covered stump has a thick chain link welded to it where his arm should be fitted. The limb in question is sitting on a table at the side of the room with wires running from it to the main computer.

She reaches out to take his hand and gasps when she sees the thick, angry cut circling his wrist. Terra lifts the sheet from the bottom of the bed to see a matching wound on each ankle. She slumps back into the chair and the world seems to slow for her. What did she think would be accomplished by coming here? All it's done is confuse her even more. It's probably just sympathy at what he's been through clouding her feelings. No one should suffer like he has. That doesn't mean it changes a thing for her.

Bray is a better fit for her. He's safe and reliable. Even with his Hunter background, he's better for her than Gryffin ever could be. It's just not possible to have a meaningful relationship of any kind with someone who can't figure out their own emotions. A puppy would show her more emotion in a minute, than Gryffin ever has.

Her hand moves up to hold the griffin pendant around her neck. It hasn't left her neck since the freighter. She promised she'd look after it for him until they met again. At the time, she thought their reunion would be a few hours later when he joined them on Sayber's ship. It was a reunion he didn't attend. Instead, he locked the freighter into a collision course with the Port then shot the controls. He was so intent on destroying the Port, he had wasted valuable time hooking the freighter to Balfe's ship, *Omega*, just so he could get revenge for what Balfe did to him. Revenge was more important to him than letting her figure out a way to disarm his collar so he could leave the freighter.

Even though a part of her doesn't want to part with his pendant, she unties the leather cord and looks at the small griffin in her hand. It's the exact same design as the large tattoo that stretches from his back, down his arm and across his chest. She rubs her thumb over the raised metal. Roman gave the pendent to Gryffin's mother a few weeks before his parents signed him up to the Foundation fleet. She must have passed it to her son before he disappeared as a child.

She leans forward and, unable to get it around his neck, wraps the cord loosely around his wrist instead.

She gets to her feet and, after a lingering look at Gryffin, hurries from the room before Milla comes back.

∞

Gryffin takes a shaky breath. Instead of blood, he can smell disinfectant. Not something the lab ever smells of. His mind wanders, not fully connecting with anything. Soft voices murmur in the background. Machines hum and beep quietly. Cool, soft sheets wrap around his legs and chest.

He mentally assesses his body. His wrists and ankles feel strange. It takes him a minute to realise he's not chained. The heavy metal has been a constant since the Scientist took him back. Without them, he feels like his limbs are going to rise off the bed and float by themselves. He takes a deep breath and his chest protests angrily. It's not the sharp agony he remembers. It actually feels better. Wherever he is, he's being looked after a hell of a lot better than the Scientist ever did.

He opens his eye. Blinding lights assault him. He squeezes his eye shut and hisses in pain. A voice to his left says something, but he can't make it out. A soft, gentle hand strokes his face as the owner speaks quietly to him again. He feels like his head is submerged in water. He doesn't want to panic, but he can't help it. The ringing continues in his ears and distorts whatever the person is saying to him. More hands examine his body. Gryffin tries to pull away from their touch, but he's too weak to move. Gentle or not, he doesn't want to be examined. He's had enough of that.

In a desperate attempt to defend himself, he tries to charge his arm, but he can't feel anything. His arm isn't attached. Whoever has him, took his arm off. The panic turns to anger. He lashes out and shoves someone aside. He swipes blindly at anyone who gets close enough to hit. He blinks rapidly, but his vision refuses to cooperate. Both his eyes must be damaged. How the hell is he going to get out if he can't see?

He'll worry about that later. For now, he just has to keep them away from him. The beeping from the monitors turns to a high pitched screech as he sits up. His head spins at the sudden movement, but he manages to stay conscious. He braces for another attack, but instead of trying to restrain him or fight back, he hears someone shout for the room to be cleared.

Not quite the reaction he was expecting. Left alone, he opens his eye again to find the room lights dimmed. He still can't make out any details. At least the searing light is gone. He rolls over onto his side and hisses in pain as the action sends knives of pain through his chest. His head finally stops its spiral motion so he reaches out to move over in the bed. Without his metal arm, there's nothing to stop him from falling off the bed with a thump. Pain tears through his metal leg as it impacts with the ground.

The cool floor tiles help him to drag his bare, useless legs into the corner. He slumps back against the wall and breaths deeply. He may not know where he is, but he's not with the Scientist. The room is semi bright and clean. The complete opposite to where he's been. He presses himself into the corner and straightens his legs in front of him to try and ease some of the pain.

He looks towards where he thinks the door is and waits to see what happens next. At least there's only one angle they can attack him from.

∞

'Okay. Everyone back away from the room. Get Aleena here. Now!' Milla remains in the doorway as someone calls Aleena to the room. Milla hasn't got the first clue what to do for him. Hopefully, Aleena will be able to ground him. Of all the people in the base, she's the one he knows the best. If anyone can reach him, it's her.

Aleena rushes along the corridor and slows down as she reaches the door. 'What happened?'

'He woke up.'

'That is great news.'

'Well, yes, but he freaked out when we tried to examine him. It's my fault. I should have known not to touch him until he was fully conscious. I don't think his eyes are working so it'll take a familiar voice to get through to him.'

Aleena nods. 'Very well.'

'Security will be at the door. You won't be alone in there with him.'

Aleena straightens her shoulders and takes slow steps into the room. As soon as she sees Gryffin, she freezes in her tracks. The once powerful leader is huddled in the corner of the room with his arm wrapped around his chest. He blinks repeatedly trying to clear his vision. She takes another few steps and he tenses. 'Gryffin.'

His head whips around to her direction but he clearly can't see her. He scrunches his brow but doesn't say anything.

'Do you know who I am?'

'I'm... not falling for it.'

She moves a little closer and crouches down in front of him. 'You are on Ultar. You arrived in orbit a week ago and have been unconscious since then.'

'I got out?'

Aleena sits down beside him, but doesn't get too close. Milla can't blame her. She can see him practically vibrating with tension. 'Yes, you did. You were a prisoner?'

He squeezes his eye shut and shakes his head briskly. 'I can't see.'

'Will you allow Milla to examine you?'

'No more examinations!'

'You are among friends, Gryffin. You are home. Please, let us help you.'

He leans his head against the wall and his ocular implant hits off the stone with a dull thud. Gryffin nods slowly so Milla cautiously approaches him. Following Aleena's example, she crouches down in front of him. 'Welcome back, Captain. How about we get you back into the bed. It'll be more comfortable for everyone. Can you manage yourself or are you okay for us to help?'

'I need... help.' Without a word, the two women each gently take a hold of an arm. After a couple of false starts, they finally help him to his unsteady feet and back into bed. 'Where's my arm?'

Milla gently attaches the monitors to his chest. 'On the table in the far corner. It's in one piece. Lucan is running a scan to make sure the repairs he made are working before he reattaches it.' She examines his face carefully. 'So, how are you feeling?'

'I'm fine.'

Milla laughs loudly and shakes her head. 'Well, if that doesn't count as the biggest fib, I don't know what does. You've been through a lot, Captain. I don't even know how you made it here in the state you did.'

'What state?'

She frowns slightly. 'You don't remember?'

He clumsily rubs a hand over his face. 'Just fragments. I stole a shuttle. Sent it here.'

'Well, you made it to Ultar just in time. Another few hours and we very well could have been burying you instead. What happened to your chest? You were barely being held together.'

He runs a hand over his chest and frowns. 'They didn't stitch me properly.'

Milla snorts. 'You don't say. It took us a long time to fix what they did.'

Gryffin sighs and runs a hand through his hair, wincing as his fingers brush against a scar on the side of his head. 'That's new, isn't it?'

Milla sits on the edge of his bed. 'Short story — with some help, Chayse developed a mod that will prevent any new programming being loaded to your control implant without your permission. We fitted it just after you arrived.'

'You operated on my head without asking me?'

Milla feels her face losing all traces of colour. It's not going to matter to Gryffin that she fought Roman until the last minute. She had been overruled by Roman, Chayse and Bray. Not that Bray agreeing surprised her. It scares her how much he seems to hate his big brother. 'I was under orders, Gryffin. We just couldn't risk... '

He closes his eye and turns away from her. Milla stares at him unable to say anything else to defend her actions. Aleena comes up beside her and squeezes her shoulder in an act of silent support. Milla looks up at her and smiles. She gets to her feet and hooks the monitors back to the system. He's clearly still awake but is doing a pretty good job of ignoring her. She can't blame him. He escapes from who knows what level of hell only to be operated on without his permission as soon as he gets back. If he ever trusts any of them again, it'll be a bloody miracle.

Aleena slowly gets to her feet and leaves Gryffin to his sleep. She quietly closes the door and finds Jensen sitting against the desk outside. The worry on his face immediately hits her. He is worried about his son but attempting to hide it. As soon as he sees her he gets to his feet. 'Is he okay?'

Aleena is not sure exactly how to answer that. Luckily, Milla appears from her office and saves her from having to answer. 'Hey, Captain.'

'What's going on, Milla? I heard there was a problem with him.'

Milla shakes her head. 'Nothing Aleena couldn't handle. He woke up and kind of freaked out. He's settled now.'

Aleena takes Jensen's hand. He may be trying to stay strong, but it is clear all the emotional upset is taking its toll on him. 'Has he said anything? Is he going to be okay?'

Milla holds up her hands. 'Whoa, Captain. Yes, he's talking. Not about what happened of course, but he has been able to express his anger at what we did.'

'Milla, please.' Aleena agrees with Milla. They should not have fitted the alteration to his programming without his permission, but now is not the time to discuss it. 'Jensen, he is naturally upset. You will need to explain the decision to him.'

Jensen nods, but clearly looks less than happy about that discussion. 'Did you tell him what happened — to the Nomad and the Sector?'

Aleena shakes her head. 'Perhaps we should wait before we tell him. He just woke up. Let him sleep for the moment. There is time enough to give him the bad news.'

'Will he be okay?'

Milla shrugs. 'It's too early to say for sure. He seems to be having a few problems with his implants.'

'What sort of problems?'

'The new eyepiece the Scientist gave him isn't of the highest quality. Some of the wiring that connects the optic with his brain is a little loose. Myself and Lucan will need to carefully study the device before we even attempt to take it off and fix it. He can see for now, but the wiring may come loose again. The chip in his real eye just needed readjusting. It'll take time for everything to get back into sync again. His mechanics have been pushed to their limits just like his body has.'

Jensen visibly pales in front of Aleena's eyes. She clutches his hand tightly and pulls him towards her. 'He is safe now. Let him sleep. Please, come with me.'

He glances over his shoulder at Milla. 'I want to hear if there's any change.'

'Of course.'

Aleena gently leads Jensen away from the med bay. They walk in silence through the base and out into the village. After a short stroll, they reach the lake and lower onto a bench. She watches as the fish jump from the water to catch flies skimming the surface. This is her favourite time of year. Usually, the villagers would be tending to their hay harvest. Long days spent out in the fields cutting and gathering the feed they need for the coming year. Anyone not physically capable would bring baskets of bread, fruit, and cheese to the fields for the workers. The villagers would stay out until well after dark, singing, telling stories and eating. Life progressed very differently now. They still work in the fields, but the jolly, light-heartedness that had previously accompanied the work has been quashed. Their future is no longer secure. The threat of colonisation is always present. Each day feels like borrowed time.

'Thank you.'

She looks at Jensen. 'For what?'

He sighs and smiles. 'Getting me out of there. I'm a little lost.'

'Lost?'

'People depend on you and I to keep the group together. They look to us for strength.' He laughs. 'I'm not doing a great job.'

'You are human. The situation with Gryffin is bound to be unsettling.'

'That may work for the select few who know the truth about Gryffin and I. For everyone else, there's no excuse. I need to, I don't know, control the feelings a lot better than I am.'

'That sounds a lot like what Gryffin attempts and it does not help him.'

'The colonies have to come first. I can't let this thing with Gryffin interfere. The people here deserve all my attention.'

She stands up and puts a hand on his shoulder. 'Do not underestimate yourself. I believe there is enough strength in you for both your son and the colonies. Trust in yourself.' Aleena leaves him by the lake with his thoughts. He will be of no use to anyone if he allows his doubt to shadow what he is doing. If they are to have a chance at survival, both Jensen and Gryffin are needed. So much depends on the father and son. She hopes they are up to the challenge

∞

Roman lowers into the chair beside Gryffin's bed and allows himself to relax slightly. He didn't realise until today how much Gryffin's disappearance affected him. Over the months, he's thrown himself into work. So much had changed in his life over the last few months. He gained a son, lost a son, lost contact with Earth, betrayed his people, and spends every day worrying about what the Foundation is planning. Having his son back makes everything seem less desperate.

But now he's faced with another problem. He wants nothing more than to tell Gryffin they're father and son. There's been too many lies in Gryffin's life so far, he doesn't want to add to the pile of deceit.

Gryffin murmurs in his sleep and his face contorts in pain. Roman leans forward, unsure of what to do. Gryffin's eye suddenly opens and locks on to him. 'What do you want?'

'We've been taking turns sitting with you.'

Gryffin narrows his eye. 'Why?'

'Didn't think you should be alone. How are you feeling?' Roman is not in the slightest bit surprised when Gryffin ignores the question.

'How long was I gone?'

'Ten months.'

Gryffin stops breathing for a few seconds. 'Didn't think it was that long.'

Roman leans forward and rests his arms on his legs. 'Do you remember what happened?'

'Yes.'

'Would you like to—'

'What happened at the Port?' He tries to sit up, but fails and flops back onto the pillow.

Roman clasps his hands in front of him. 'I could ask you the same thing.'

'I blacked out after I launched the tethers. Don't know anything after that. Did the freighter destroy the Port?'

Roman nods. 'Your plan worked.'

Gryffin bends his right leg and rubs the skin over the metal. 'If it worked, why are Hunters here?'

'I give, then you give. An answer for an answer — deal? Did the Foundation take you off the freighter?' Roman watches the anger flash across Gryffin's pale and clammy face. He's not used to bargaining for information. It's the only way he's going to get anything out of him though. Roman needs to know what happened and where Gryffin was. If there's a Foundation stronghold in the Sector and he knows where it is — Roman needs to get that information out. There's also a large part of him that needs to know for different reasons. Personal reasons. 'Well?'

Gryffin's new robotic eye targets him before he finally breaks contact and looks back at the ceiling above him. 'I didn't see any Foundation uniforms, but someone must have been funding the Scientist.'

Roman barely manages to keep the emotion from his face. He was hoping Callum had been taken out of the equation when the Port and *Omega* blew. 'How did you get off the freighter?'

Gryffin's focus remains on the smooth white ceiling as he shakes his head. 'Why are Hunters here?'

'You're right — my turn to answer. Well, we thought the destruction of the Port would give us a year's grace, but we were wrong. The Foundation were already here.' He sighs and leans back in his chair. 'From the numbers we've been experiencing, it seems the Council inserted some ships in the Sector after *Infinity* was sent here. Their presence affects everyone in the Sector. We've arranged a somewhat uneasy truce for the moment. Your turn, how did you get off the freighter?'

'I don't know. They must have come to get me before it blew up. The Scientist had the code for my collar.' He reaches up and touches his neck. 'How'd you get it off?'

'It gave when Lucan attacked it with one of the tools used to cut metal in the hangar. What happened? What did he do to you?'

Gryffin closes his eye and swallows deeply. His chest rises and falls as his breathing increases. Roman considers calling an end to the conversation. Perhaps it's too soon for Gryffin to relive what happened.

'In-depth examinations.'

Roman can barely hear Gryffin's mumbled reply over the hum of the monitoring equipment. He leans closer, hoping for, but also dreading, any further explanation.

Gryffin frowns at the ceiling. 'We found an old transport floating in space a few years ago. For months my crew slowly picked it apart, trying to figure out how it worked, how to repair it and make it work better than it did before. It would be put back together, tested, then taken apart so we could work on it again.' His throat muscles move as he swallows. 'I feel like that damn transport.'

A sudden coldness penetrates Roman's core. There's no response to what Gryffin just said.

'There are thirty-three Nomad ships,' Gryffin continues. 'We couldn't keep the Sector under control without Hunter help?'

Roman is grateful for the change of topic. 'Your... well, death for want of a better word, hit them hard. Colonies pulled away and made things difficult. I'm afraid only three colonies remain loyal.'

Gryffin swallows a few times and opens his mouth, but nothing comes out. Frustrated, he thumps the bed beside him.

'Ultar serves as our main base. The Hunters have joined with us to try to keep the Sector out of Foundation control. Between the Hunters, Nomad, *Infinity* and *Epsilon*, we can patrol and protect the remaining colonies.' He watches as Gryffin squeezes his eye shut. 'We need all the help we can get. Is there anything you remember, anything you can tell us about what they're planning?'

'I was chained in a cell or locked to a table. They didn't discuss anything important around me. Everything was kept on the Scientist's personal unit in his room. No one had access to that — not even his pet cyborg. They just wanted to figure out how the control implant worked.' He turns slightly in the bed to face Roman. 'What about the Nomad and *Ares*?'

Roman pauses.

'What about the Nomad?' he asks again.

'They've disbanded. *Nemesis* and *Ares* are the only ships left in the fleet.'

Gryffin looks back at the ceiling. After a long silence, he finally speaks again. 'You ordered the thing to be fitted in my head?'

'Yes. I apologise for making the decision without your consent, but for everyone's sake, I had to make the call.'

'It was the right one.'

Roman sits up straight in his chair. 'Really?'

Gryffin nods. 'After hearing all that. Yes. I should never have come back here.'

Roman rises to his feet and leans over his son. 'Now you hold on one minute, Captain. There's a ship full of Nomad here waiting for you to take command of *Ares* again. Desyl has filled in as captain during the repairs, but I know he'd much rather step back and give you the reins. They need you to lead them — now more than ever. I know this is a lot to take in. But we're running out of time. We need you back on *Ares*.'

Gryffin closes his eye and the purple glow from his new eye shuts down. Instead of taking the hint, Roman leans back in the chair and crosses his ankles, settling in for another uncomfortable night.

∞

The smell of fresh bread brings Gryffin out of his unsettled sleep. He doesn't think he's ever smelt anything so good. Compared to the rancid, unrecognisable sludge he's enjoyed for the last few months, the bread smells like paradise. He opens his eye and sees Aleena sitting on the chair beside him. She is wearing a large smile as she waves the plate of bread in front of his nose. His stomach growls loudly and his mouth waters.

'From what I can hear, you are a little hungry.' She cuts a slice of bread into smaller portions. 'It is my speciality — cheese bread.'

He pushes himself up. It's like that plate of food is a lifeline. He wants it. Now!

Aleena places a pillow behind his back and hands him one solitary piece of the toasted bread. He raises his eyebrow. 'Seriously?'

'When did you eat last?'

Good question. 'Probably a few days before I escaped.'

Her face momentarily loses its smile but she recovers quickly. 'As I feared. It will take your stomach time to readjust. Little and often for now.'

He tries not to stuff the piece in his mouth, but he doesn't succeed. He nearly moans out load. The bread is better than he remembers. Aleena's eyes begin to water. She looks away and rearranges the pieces of toast on the plate.

'You okay?' She forces a smile on her face and nods. 'Still a bad liar.'

In spite of the tears, she laughs. 'I have missed you, Gryffin.'

He doesn't reply as he takes another piece off the plate. He missed her too, but it's not something he can voice. He settles back against the pillow and tries to control his stomach. It may have wanted the food but it's having a hard time digesting it. He watches Milla rush around through the glass doors of his room. There are about half a dozen people sitting or lying in the beds that line the walls of the bay. He's the only one getting the four star treatment with his own room.

'Would you care to-'

'You already know the answer.' He's never going to talk about the missing time. All he wants to do is forget it ever happened. His new eyepiece chooses that moment to throb — like it's telling him that'll never happen.

Aleena nods and clasps her hands on her knees. 'Is there anything you would like to ask? Anything you wish to know?'

'Terra.' Her name pops out before he can stop it. Her absence is obvious. One thought refuses to leave him — what if she didn't get off the freighter in time? What if his actions killed her? The toast threatens to make a reappearance. He swallows deeply to keep it where it should be. He wants to ask Aleena but he's terrified of the answer.

'She is alive.'

He breathes a sigh of relief. When he woke, he instantly noticed the addition of his pendant around his wrist. He spent a long time just looking at it, unable and unwilling to touch it. He hoped it had been put there by Terra in person and not by someone acting on her behalf because she wasn't around anymore. He's relieved to hear she's alive, but, for reasons he can't explain, it bothers him that she gave it back while he was asleep.

'Sayber and Terra both escaped the freighter before it hit the Port. He brought her safely back to Ultar. It seems you have your enemy to thank for saving her.'

That thought doesn't sit well with him. He's grateful for everything Sayber did for him on the freighter, but that doesn't mean he'll ever thank him. 'Did we lose anyone?'

'I'm sure you remember Commander Evan Stanner from *Infinity* lost his life. After a lot of digging, we discovered that Rayde ordered the ambush and Klay carried it out.' She looks down at the floor and shakes her head. 'I still struggle with the fact he betrayed you.'

He's just glad his metal arm isn't attached. He'd probably drive it through the wall. 'Klay dead?'

She shakes her head. 'There has been too much death. He is in the security facility. I have told him he will not be killed, but I am unsure what to do with him.'

He's got one or two ideas, but his former first officer can wait. 'Who else?'

'There were casualties on all sides. Numbers are not important.'

'How many did I kill?'

She openly stares at him. 'Gryffin, this is not your fault.'

He shoves the plate of bread off his legs in anger. 'Of course it is.' She'll see the good in anything given half the chance. 'Is Terra avoiding me?' Aleena brushes her hair off her shoulder. He knows her well enough by now to recognise that she's stalling. 'I had Sayber take her from the freighter to save her life. He had to knock her out. There's no way she would have left otherwise.' Knocking her out was the only option at the time. She flat out refused to leave him there and time was running out. The collar around his neck would have blown if he left the ship. He was stuck and the Foundation were about to send a fleet through the Port. Using the freighter to destroy the Port, and taking *Omega* along for the ride, solved all the immediate problems. If he had to do it all again, he wouldn't do anything differently. *Omega*, the freighter and the Port were destroyed and she was still alive. Apart from being captured again, it all went as he planned.

'I know that, Gryffin. Terra... she is overseeing the repairs to *Ares*. We are under extreme pressure to get her back in the air. Unfortunately, she is needed there.'

He nods, but isn't convinced. Before he forced Terra to leave the freighter, she told him she loved him. Love... any feeling like that is foreign to him. He's pretty sure that if someone you love came back after being tortured, you'd want to see them.

Maybe he has it all wrong? Maybe Terra just said that to him because they were up to their necks in trouble. He nearly laughs out loud. When he wasn't on the table he was deep in his head with her. He only survived because of her and now she doesn't want anything to do with him.

Klay glances up from his bunk as a Nomad throws a tray of food into his cell. He waits until the door is locked again before he sits up and looks at his dinner. At least the food stayed on the tray this time. Picking dust and debris off his dinner has become a mealtime ritual for him.

He pushes off the bed and clutches his arm tightly to his bruised ribs. After a few failed attempts at bending down to pick up the tray, he gives up and slumps to the floor to eat. He's not hungry, but if he's going to survive more talks with the *Ares* crew, he'll need to keep his strength up. Aleena is sticking to the promise she made when he was pulled out of *Ares*' remains after the ship crashed — he's still alive. Unfortunately, there's not a lot she can do about the angry group of Nomad. It's only a matter of time before her fragile hold on the Nomad falters.

He fully accepts his fate. He chose Rayde over Gryffin. It's a decision he stands by and will die by.

Klay chews on a piece of meat and lies back against the stone wall.

During his interrogations he's tried asking questions about what happened after *Ares* crashed on the surface, but his questions are ignored. He hasn't got a clue what happened to Gryffin or to Rayde.

He doesn't blame the Nomad. In their small minds he broke a fundamental Nomad law — protect your captain at all costs. Their unquestionable loyalty to Gryffin blinds them to the fact he was following that very law. Rayde was his captain and always had been. Gryffin controlled *Ares*, but Rayde controlled Gryffin. Klay squeezes his eyes shut and beats his fist against the floor. He's a bloody fool for letting Desyl take *Ares* from him. He underestimated the young man and look where it's left him. He's alone, sore and being used as a punching bag by the very men he used to command. He doubts Aleena will ever allow him the honour of a Nomad death. He'll grow old and frail in this cell.

After finishing his food, he crawls back over to the bunk and flops onto it. He stares at the ceiling and tries to listen for any sounds from the room outside. Apart from having his food thrown at him, it's the only glimpse of the outside world he gets. He hears nothing for a few minutes, then the door to the room outside his cell opens. He slowly gets to his feet and leans against the bars. It sounds like there are a few people in the room outside. Their raised voices help him pick up on snippets of the conversation. Nothing really gets his attention until he hears two words that send a chill up his spine. He stumbles back from the bars and crashes onto his cot. His racing heartbeat blocks out the rest of the conversation.

Gryffin's back.

∞

'What exactly is going on in here?' Roman shouts as he bursts through the door.

Milla and Gryffin both turn to face him. Gryffin sits on the edge of the bed with a scowl on his face. Milla crosses her arms and blows out a long breath. 'I'll tell you what's going on. My patient here is refusing to do anything I ask him to.'

'You touch me again, I'll break your damn arm.'

'I'm trying to examine you, you stubborn fool. Touching is involved.'

Roman steps between the two before a full argument breaks out. 'Okay, why don't we just take a minute?'

Gryffin glares at Milla. 'I don't want a minute. I want her to get the hell out of here. Now!'

Milla forces a laugh out. 'Oh, nice, you really think I'm going to respond to that? Your chest is still sutured, you've barely eaten anything since you got here and, as a result, you're struggling to support your own weight. If I don't examine you to see what's going on, how do you expect me to treat you?'

Gryffin clenches his fist on the bed beside him. 'I've told you that I'm fine. You did your job — I'm alive.'

Roman gently moves Milla away from Gryffin before she really loses her temper. 'I understand you may have an aversion to being examined but—'

'What does any of this have to do with you?' Gryffin's purple eye locks on Roman. 'I don't answer to you. I'm done following Foundation orders.'

Roman inwardly grimaces. He should have thought how barging in and throwing his weight around would go down with Gryffin. After everything he's been through with the Foundation, he's probably the last person Gryffin wants to see. 'You're right. I apologise. You have absolutely no reason to believe a word I say, but your health, your wellbeing is important.'

Gryffin snorts and looks at his arm sitting on the table across the room. 'That why you haven't reattached my arm?'

Milla points to his arm. 'I told you it will take a few hours to reattach it. I don't even know if the new connectors we fitted will work properly.'

'We're not going to figure it out if I'm here and it's over there.'

'Milla!' Roman jumps in before she lets her temper loose. He gestures to the door and, after giving Gryffin her best glare, she obediently follows Roman from the room. Once the glass doors hiss shut, she curses and runs a hand through her hair, pulling some locks free of the tie at the base of her neck. 'That bloody man is a right pain in the arse.'

'Yes, and confronting him face on won't do any good, will it?'

She opens her mouth to argue, but has second thoughts. 'No.'

'Can you reattach his arm?'

She takes a deep breath to calm herself. 'Technically, yes. It's cleared through the testing, but I was hoping to give his new connectors time to heal properly.'

'Heal?'

'The chain that was welded to his arm damaged the connectors. Gryffin's elbow and a small portion of his lower arm are still flesh. The Scientist fitted connectors to what was left of the organic tissue below and on his elbow. These connectors lock into the metal portion of his arm and let Gryffin move it. Chayse and Lucan fitted new connectors, but there's still some residual damage to the flesh half of his arm. The weight of his metal arm is going to hurt the sensitive skin.'

'The chain was attached to his skin?'

'No, it was welded to the metal casing housing the connectors. Minor detail if you ask me. It was still his arm.'

Roman couldn't agree more. 'Get things ready to fit it back in place. I really think he'd prefer some discomfort to having no arm. While you're preparing, I'd like to get him out of here for a bit.'

'You're kidding, right?'

'This isn't the Gryffin I've heard about. He shouldn't still be in bed a week later.'

'He has been tortured, sir. Is he not entitled to some rest?'

'Of course he is. But, it sounds like he's hit a wall. Unless we can motivate him to fight, he won't get any better.'

She leans back on the desk behind her and crosses her arms. 'I'm not agreeing yet, but what exactly did you have in mind?'

∞

'What do you mean he's escaped?'

The Scientist steps over the body of the technician at his feet. Forty-Three wipes his knife on the dead man's lab coat and slips it back in his belt. The Scientist looks away from the body to the screen. 'I mean he's escaped, Leeson. It appears he found a way to manipulate the system.'

Admiral Leeson's face takes on a strange pink tinge. 'Have you any idea what you are saying? I can't report that back to the Council.'

The Scientist brushes away Leeson's concerns. 'He is no longer necessary, Leeson. I have all the data I need. I assure you, the prototype is no longer vital to the project.'

'No longer vital to the project! You fail to understand that there is no project without the prototype. The Council needs a fully operational unit to prove what they are promising. How exactly do you expect them to do that without the actual model?'

'I have other working models.'

Leeson scoffs and points at Forty-Three. 'That one beside you isn't even in the same league. I'll explain this in a way you may understand. Without a working prototype, they could very well withdraw their funding.'

'Don't be ridiculous. They want this to succeed as much as I do. They wouldn't dare withdraw their funding.'

Leeson laughs and shakes his head. 'You're foolish if you believe that. Your prototype is the only available proof that your work is successful at all. Without him, you're just wasting your time. I suggest you get him back. Now! Both our lives depend on it.'

The Scientist closes the connection and stares at the blank screen.

He suddenly shouts and swipes his hand across the desk. Leeson is his main contact with the Foundation Council. If he says the Council will pull out, then he has to believe they will. He glances over at Forty-Three who is standing patiently at the side of the room. He briefly considers using him instead but quickly changes his mind. The man is barely a cyborg. He does have minimal programming in his brain but it cannot be altered or adapted. None of his new cyborgs will be up to the correct standard either. He's forced to accept the truth. 'Everything is lost without him.' He looks over at the stasis pod in the corner, keeping Maggie alive. 'This can't end now. Not when I'm so close. What would bring him back to me?'

'The woman.'

The Scientist glances over his shoulder at Forty-Three. 'Woman. What woman?'

'Terra Rush.'

The Scientist's legs suddenly can't support his weight. He falls back into his chair and closes his eyes. The last thing he was expecting was for that name to come out of Forty-Three's mouth. 'What did you just say?

'Thirty-Five is fond of a Foundation crew member called Terra Rush. She was held on *Perses* under Balfe's orders until she escaped.'

He pulls his glasses off and rubs his eyes. Terra. His daughter. It doesn't make sense. How did his daughter end up in the Outer Sector and become involved with his prototype? His project is the most important thing in his life, but that doesn't mean he'd forgotten about her. Not a day goes by when Terra doesn't enter his mind at some point. 'Did Balfe hurt her?'

Forty-Three frowns, clearly confused by the question. 'No. Sayber aided her escape.'

He nods, not in the slightest bit comforted by the answer. How dare Balfe involve Terra in the project. The only reason he faked his own death all those years ago was to ensure Terra would be safe. He stands up and walks over to the pod. So, his daughter and Maggie's son are involved. He clenches his fist tightly. The prototype is barely more than a machine. What right does he have to go anywhere near Terra? She deserves so much better. Why is someone with her intellect even looking twice at him? The Scientist shakes his head and places a hand on the glass over Maggie's face. Perhaps it is meant to be. What a great story it will make. His daughter brings Maggie's son back so he can help Maggie. This may just be the miracle he needs.

He smiles at Forty-Three. 'Find out where she is. I need to speak with her.'

∞

'Why are we here?'

Roman enters the captain's quarters on *Ares* and looks around the room. 'I just thought you'd like to see inside again. She took a fair hit when she collided with the surface. The Nomad and the locals worked tirelessly to bring her back to where she was before. After building *Nemesis*, there was more than enough capable people to work on her.'

Gryffin slowly steps into his old room and quietly walks around. He stops in front of the desk and runs his hand over the surface. 'Desyl managed to salvage your desk top, but had to give it new legs.' Gryffin pulls his hand back and gingerly reaches out to touch the dents on the wall. 'I may be reading this wrong, but you seem a bit surprised?'

'These are the captain's quarters. Why am I here?'

Roman rests a hip on the corner of the desk. 'This is your ship and your room, Captain. Desyl has officially stepped down. Your crew want you back in the captain seat. He'll assume the first officer position under your command. So, as far as everyone is concerned, these are your quarters, Captain.'

Gryffin turns to face Roman and quickly shakes his head. 'No.'

Roman sighs. This isn't exactly going as planned. He thought bringing him here would jolt him and help pull him out of whatever hole he's been dragged in to.

A week has passed since he woke up. In that time, he's barely said a word. He's not surprised. Roman can't begin to guess what he went through. All he knows is that he wants five minutes alone with Callum. Five minutes to show him exactly how he feels. For the moment, his main priority is to somehow help Gryffin get over what happened. He's never going to talk about his ordeal. Counselling would be a complete waste of time. You can't get someone like Gryffin to talk, let alone discuss his feelings. All you can do is give him something else to think about. He's had too much time alone with his thoughts over the last week and it's not doing him any favours.

Gryffin stops by his bed. The doubt rears its ugly head again. The Nomad leader looks lost. Milla has promised to reattach his arm as soon as they get back from *Ares*. Gryffin needed some incentive for getting up and coming with Roman. The lack of his metal arm doesn't help him look any more confident. He absently rubs the implant over his eye in a way that makes him look vulnerable, which is not a word Roman would ever have used to describe him. Maybe he is too late. Maybe the old Gryffin is gone forever.

No. He's still in there. He's convinced of it. He just needs to force him back out again... somehow. Desperate times call for desperate measures. 'Gryffin.'

When Gryffin turns to look at him, Roman swings his fist and punches him hard in the face. Gryffin staggers back a few steps and holds his jaw. He wipes the blood from his lips and looks down at his hand. 'What was that for?'

He's going to have to do a bit more convincing. Roman hits him again. When Gryffin still doesn't react, he hits him again and again. Just as he's about to call it quits, Gryffin's face suddenly changes as if a button has been pressed. The doubt and uncertainty disappears to be replaced by a familiar hard expression.

Before Roman realises that he could very well be in serious trouble,

Gryffin strikes back with his flesh arm. He easily knocks him to the floor at the other side of the room. He puts his boot against Roman's neck. Gryffin glares down at him. 'Damn it, Roman! What the hell was that for?' Gryffin shouts.

'To... prove a ... point,' Roman gasps.

'What?' Gryffin demands.

'That you're still in there. Welcome back High Commander.' Roman smiles in spite of his current painful situation.

Gryffin's purple eye stares at him for a long minute, then he slowly removes his foot to let Roman breathe again.

'Thanks, Captain,' Roman says breathlessly.

'That was your plan? Beat the hell out of me?'

Roman looks up at Gryffin and smirks. 'Well, I was going more for beating some sense into you, but whatever works.'

Gryffin shakes his head and slowly breaks into a small smile. 'Same difference.'

Gryffin reaches down and tries unsuccessfully to pull Roman to his feet. Roman brushes off his help. 'You're the one just out of bed. Save your strength.' Roman gets to his feet and brushes off his clothes. He massages his jaw. 'That was an impressive punch. I'm just glad your metal arm is still on a table.' Gryffin's punch has ripped the skin on his jaw leaving a large gash. Roman gingerly presses his sleeve against the wound to stop the bleeding and winces as the material presses into the raw flesh. In spite of all this he smiles widely at Gryffin and bursts out laughing.

The Nomad captain tilts his head and frowns. 'You sure something's not broken?'

'Just glad you're back. You've been missed.'

'We better get you checked out.'

'We don't have time for that now. I don't want to push you. I know there must be a lot going on in your head at the moment. I'd like to give you time to get used to everything that's happened, but time is a luxury we just don't have. We need to know if you can or want to command *Ares* again.'

Gryffin turns back to the window and stares at his reflection in the glass. Roman is fully expecting to wait while Gryffin thinks about things, but less than ten seconds later he turns back to him and nods. 'Yes.'

11

'Commander Rush, we have a private transmission for you.'

Terra looks up from her work and frowns. She never gets private transmissions. 'Where's it from?'

The Ultaran shakes her head. 'I do not know. There is no location stamp on the message.'

Terra shrugs and rises to her feet. She places the toolkit on the table beside her and walks over to the bank of computers in the corner. She chooses the unit in the very corner and puts the headphones over her ears. She places her palm against the unit and the message opens. Terra can't hold back the gasp when her father appears on the screen.

'Hello, Terra. It is so good to see you. How are you?'

She squeezes her eyes shut and shakes her head. This must be a dream. After taking a deep breath, she looks at the screen again. Her father smiles at her like this is nothing out of the ordinary. 'How are you? You died... you're dead. You can't come back to life and just say 'how are you,'' she hisses at the screen.

'I understand this may come as a bit of a shock, but I can explain.'

Her mouth opens and closes a few times. 'Explain? How can you possibly explain how you're still alive? I didn't want to believe Roman when he said he heard your voice on the transport. I was sure the recording was fabricated. The father I loved would never fake his death. He would never leave his wife and daughter.'

Her father clenches his jaw. 'Jensen is there?'

'That's all you have to say? Yes, he's here and just as angry at you as I am. Do not contact me again.' She stands up and lifts her hand to shut down the link.

'Wait! I contacted you for a reason.'

'I don't care.' Terra quickly looks over her shoulder at the rest of the team working at their stations. It doesn't seem like any of them have noticed who she's talking to.

'I think you will, once you hear what I have to say. It's about the prototype — I believe you know him as Gryffin. I need you to convince him to meet with me.'

Terra stares open mouthed at the screen for a moment. 'He's not your property. He's a human and he can decide what happens to him.'

'Fine.' He waves a hand in the air, clearly dismissing her words. 'I just need you to bring him to me.'

'You really are crazy. The next time he sees you I guarantee he will kill you. After everything you did, I can't blame him.'

Callum leans back and clasps his hands in front of him 'So, you know who I am.'

'Yes, I know who you are and what you've done.'

He nods and looks down at the metal table in front of him. 'I don't expect you to understand. What's important is that the Foundation wants me to bring him back to Earth, but I have other plans.'

Terra pounds her fist against the table top, which earns her a few puzzled looks. 'I don't want to know.'

'Terra, please. I want to undo what I did to him.'

She hates the fact that his comment gets her attention. 'It can't be undone.'

He nods. 'Not easily, but I can separate the metal from the flesh.'

Her eyes narrow as she examines her father. She had once broached that very subject with Milla and Chayse after Gryffin disappeared. Both had confirmed it couldn't be done. Gryffin's organs need the implants in order to work properly. Removing the metal would be like removing an organ — he would die. 'Why? What's in it for you?'

'I just need his implants, not him. This way, everyone wins. He gets to live as a human and the Foundation gets the implants. Just think about it. I've attached coordinates where I can be reached once you've made your decision.'

The message shuts down and Terra stares at her reflection in the powered down screen. It may sound like a win for everyone, but she suspects it's not actually the case. Her father is a monster. She's spent hours reading the details of what he did to Gryffin and Bray. Nothing about his treatment of the brothers tells her differently. He tortured them. He could have done what the Foundation needed him to do without causing so much pain.

He's trying to use their family connection to recover his precious prototype. Terra turns from the screen and looks at *Ares* filling the hangar in front of her. She'd love to be able to somehow undo what her father did to Gryffin and Bray, but she's not the naive little girl he abandoned all those years ago. As soon as he has Gryffin again, he'll just hurt him even more. She may be angry with Gryffin, but that doesn't mean she would ever allow him to be hurt again. As long as her father is out there, Gryffin will never be safe. If it comes down to her father or Gryffin, there's no competition. She gathers her things and pushes past a technician in her way. She needs to find Roman.

∞

Three hours after he punched Roman, Gryffin is sitting on a chair in the med bay. Lucan takes the metal arm from the table and slowly approaches, never taking his eyes off the robotic limb in his firm grip. 'It won't break if you drop it,' Milla says.

Lucan smiles. 'Not taking any chances.' He places it on the bed beside Gryffin and lets out the breath he was holding. 'Now for the not so easy part. This may hurt a little, sir.'

'It'll hurt more if you don't get on with it and attach it.'

Lucan nods, clearly understanding exactly who will be on the receiving end of the hurt. 'Place your arm on the bed.'

Gryffin does as instructed and waits patiently as Lucan and Milla attach monitors to his chest implant. Lucan lines the arm up with the connectors on the remains of Gryffin's upper arm while Milla carefully watches the screen. 'Now, no heroics, Gryffin. You shout if anything feels off,' Milla says.

'Just get on with it.'

Milla glares at him then nods at Lucan. 'Ready when you are, Lucan.'

Gryffin lifts his arm up, Lucan adjusts the angle, then pushes the artificial limb over the metal covered stump that reaches to just beyond Gryffin's elbow. As soon as the new connectors lock into place, Gryffin grinds out a curse.

Milla is instantly by his side. 'Talk.'

He shakes his head and takes a breath. 'It's fine.'

'Of course it is,' she replies, sarcastically. She gestures for him to lift his arm and frowns as he grunts in pain. 'It's too soon, Lucan. Take it off.'

'No!' Gryffin tries to push the pain away. 'Leave it.'

Lucan sits on the chair opposite him. 'You won't be doing yourself any favours leaving it on if it's not right.'

'I said leave it!'

Lucan nods and shrugs. 'Yes, sir.' He looks at the handheld. 'Your chest implant seems to be accepting the connectors. Can you move your fingers?'

Gryffin tries but nothing happens.

'You might have to concentrate, sir. Until you get used to the connectors, it'll be like having a new arm.'

Gryffin tries again and is rewarded by a slight twitch of his thumb. Bloody pathetic response, but it's a start. He bends his arm. It doesn't quite make it the full way, but it's better than the effort by his fingers.

'Okay,' Milla says. 'That's better than I thought for your first attempt. How does it feel?'

'Fine.'

She throws her arms in the air. 'Why do I waste my breath asking such stupid questions? I'm going to tell you to rest and take it easy, but let's not insult each other by pretending that's going to happen. I'll give you an extra strong dose of painkiller. Hopefully, some of it will work into your system before your implants neutralise it. The pain should ease as your body gets used to the new parts.'

'I want to talk to Lucan alone.'

Milla nods. 'You're more than welcome, Captain. It was a pleasure as always.'

Lucan watches as Milla storms from the room. 'I think she likes you, sir.'

'Where's Klay?'

Lucan shoves his hands in his pockets. 'Aleena won't let you anywhere near him. She's promised he won't be killed.'

'Have you seen him?'

Lucan nods. 'Myself, Desyl and Chayse have each had some quality time with him. Apart from asking about Rayde and you, he's not saying anything.'

Gryffin flexes his wrist and pain soars up his arm. 'Sounds like he's outlived his usefulness. Can you occupy the guards?'

Lucan smirks. 'It would be my pleasure.'

12

Gryffin stands at the base of the stairs while Lucan talks to the Ultaran guards. He rests his head against the cold stone wall and flexes his fingers, trying to get used to the new connectors. When he faces Klay, he wants to appear in one piece. Being able to move his fingers is fairly damn important.

Before he can stop it, an image pops into his head of Forty-Three welding the chain to his arm connectors. He takes a few deep breaths and forces himself back into the present. He clenches his jaw. Klay helped put him in the lab. He doesn't know why Aleena kept him alive, but it's something he's going to enjoy rectifying.

He hears Lucan laugh with the guards then everything goes quiet. 'Coast is clear, sir.'

Gryffin steps around the corner to find Lucan standing over the bodies of the guards. 'Are they dead?'

'Aleena is going to be angry enough about this without me killing two of her people. Apart from an impressive headache they'll be okay in a bit. So, do you need me in there with you?'

Gryffin shakes his head. 'Don't let anyone in.'

Lucan nods and silently watches as Gryffin steps through the door.

Klay quickly rises to his feet and stares at him as he approaches the cell. 'So, it's true. I heard you were back.'

Gryffin lowers on to the wooden bench in front of the cell before his legs collapse from under him. He silently watches his former first officer. Klay isn't looking the best. His usually cropped hair reaches his shoulders. His large frame seems smaller and dwarfed by the badly fitting clothes. Gryffin smiles at the colourful selection of bruises on his skin. At least he's not getting an easy ride.

Klay sits on the end of his bed and crosses his arms. 'You don't look so good, High Commander.'

After a painful silence, Gryffin finally speaks. 'You know why I'm here.'

Klay nods. 'Your faithful followers have been trying to get information from me for months. Rayde trained us both to withstand interrogation. You know I won't tell you anything.'

'Every word out of your mouth is a damn lie anyway.'

Klay shrugs. 'I guess it all depends on who I'm talking to at the time. Took you long enough to come and have a chat. Why wait until now?'

'I've been busy.'

Klay's eyes narrow as he examines Gryffin. 'You were with the Foundation, weren't you. That's where you got your new eye.' He laughs and shakes his head. 'So, the plan worked. Rayde was right.'

'Rayde's dead.'

Klay's smile falters slightly. 'How?'

'I broke his neck. It was better than he deserved.'

Klay rises to his feet. 'No, the Nomad are better than you deserve. Rayde was the rightful leader. Your pathetic need to protect worthless farmers destroyed what we once were.'

'You sound just like him. I guess I wasn't his only puppet.'

'He respected me, respected my opinions.'

Gryffin snorts. 'Of course he did. He played you just like he played me.'

'Whatever makes you feel better.' Klay laughs. 'You were a leader who could be programmed to kill his own people. If you weren't destroying the Nomad, it would be hilarious.'

Gryffin gets to his feet and leans against the cell. He squeezes the bars in his hands as he stares down at Klay. 'What the hell did you do to my programming?'

'Rayde needed you to be unpredictable so he could throw doubt on your leadership. He knew that if he could make the colonists doubt you, make the Nomad doubt you, he'd have an easier chance overthrowing you.'

Gryffin grunts. 'So you killed the recon officer and the other Foundation crew from our first meeting?'

'The recon officer was easy,' Klay brags. 'I left the ship after you did and waited until you were done. You'd barely left him alive so I finished him off like you would have. The others were just collateral damage.'

'Sounds like you had it all planned out.' Gryffin narrows his eyes. 'What about when I was with Terra on Ultar. Did you make me lose control and nearly kill her?'

Klay nods and smiles. 'Of course. It was too good an opportunity to pass up. Rayde thought if you hurt her it would push the Foundation to act. You'd be blamed for starting the war and he could take over. I didn't expect you to be able to keep control of yourself like you did.'

'How much was me and how much was your programming?'

Klay shrugs. 'I guess you'll never know.'

Gryffin reaches out and grabs Klay's neck through the bars. 'You did all that in exchange for what? Credits? Your own ship?'

'What does it matter?'

Gryffin slams him against the bars. 'Tell me!'

'*Ares*.'

Gryffin barely holds back the growl wanting to escape. He can't believe Rayde would promise *Ares* to Klay. Since the day Rayde rescued Gryffin and brought him on to *Ares*, he's felt a special connection with the ship. She's the first real home he'd ever had. Rayde knew that. After everything Rayde did to him, he shouldn't be surprised that he offered Klay his ship, but it still hurts like hell.

Gryffin drops him to the ground. He pulls the keypad from his pocket and attaches it to the door. The locks open and Gryffin pushes the door back. He stands facing Klay and watches in silence as the shorter man's breathing increases. Gryffin winces as his new eye zooms in on Klay. The ability has its advantages, but the sickening sensation while it adjusts, makes it feel like the room is spinning.

Klay straightens his shoulders. 'I have to admit I'm impressed. I never thought you'd go against Aleena.'

'This is between you and me.'

'She made a promise. You know what that means to her.'

Gryffin steps closer to Klay and smiles. The out of character smile has the desired effect. The confidence plastered on Klay's face is quickly replaced by concern. 'I don't give a damn about anyone or anything else right now. You betrayed me, betrayed the Nomad, and everything we stood for. You and Rayde did everything you could to force the vicious, unemotional, robotic side of me to the front,' He holds his arms out to the side. 'Well, here he is.'

Klay swallows deeply. 'You going to let me go out like a Nomad?'

Gryffin shakes his head. 'No.' He closes the distance between them and shoves Klay against the back wall of the cell. Klay curses and squeezes his eyes shut in pain. 'Open your eyes,' Gryffin commands. Klay does as ordered. 'The people you worked for took their time torturing me.' He pulls the knife from its sheath on his belt and turns the blade in his hand. The purple glow from Gryffin's eyes reflects off its polished surface. Gryffin places the tip of the blade against Klay's forehead then drags it down over the bridge of his nose, coming to a stop on his cheek. Klay hisses in pain and blinks rapidly as blood drips into his eye. Klay struggles to release himself from Gryffin's grip, but it's a futile act. Gryffin holds the blade against Klay's wrist and the man screams as the knife digs in.

'Stop! Just get it over with!'

Gryffin leans down and looks directly at Klay, their noses nearly touching. 'No. You need to pay for what happened to me. We're going to take this slow.'

13

Lucan turns away from the monitors and takes a deep breath. He's never witnessed Gryffin dealing with a traitor before. He breathes in through his nose and convinces his last meal to stay in his stomach. He paces the dusty floor in an attempt to distract himself from Klay's screams as they echo through the empty tunnels.

Lucan has no sympathy for Klay. The man made his bed and now Gryffin is forcing him to lie in it. Being assigned to Ultar, Lucan hasn't worked one-on-one with the Nomad leader often, but one thing quickly became clear to Lucan — the Nomad and the colonies are everything to the captain. Gryffin would have died for any member of his crew without hesitation. Gryffin put everything he had into leading and protecting. The fact Klay wormed his way into Gryffin's inner circle just to hurt and discredit him doesn't sit well with any of the Nomad.

He understands Gryffin's need for revenge, but there is no way Aleena will forgive Gryffin for whatever is going on in the cell. Before he can stop himself, he glances back at the screen. Gryffin is like a crazed animal. Looks like Klay is getting the full brunt of Gryffin's anger and anguish from months of abuse in captivity

Lucan can't help a small smile. He can't think of anyone more deserving.

∞

'This is bloody ridiculous! How does a million credit asset just disappear? What happened?'

One clasps his hand on the table top and looks at each of the other Council members in turn. He had just received word from Leeson about the situation and called an emergency meeting to update the others. 'From what the Scientist reports, the prototype escaped and stole a shuttle.'

'How could he possibly have escaped? I was under the impression he was taken offline.'

One shakes his head. 'It was never taken offline. The Scientist kept it conscious for all of the examinations.' He glances out the window beside his seat as the Council take in what he just said. Citizens scurry around the large courtyard adjacent to the Council offices like ants, busy on their way to work or whatever meaningless social engagements they may have.

'This Scientist is jeopardising the project,' Five says. 'We cannot allow that. We can't afford any more delays.'

One holds up his hands and the room falls silent. 'It is a setback, but I assure you it is no more than that. Our experts have perfected the procedure and improved on the Scientist's previous work.'

'But what about the longevity of the units?' Three asks from her seat to his right.

'That is still an issue. It will take time to rectify.'

Ten leans forward in his seat. 'The prototype will go back to Ultar. I recommend we launch an attack. Take out the colony and bring the prototype back to Earth.'

One shakes his head. 'As much as I would like that, brother, we have still not been able to get close to the planet. Ships are overcome by their defences. Ultar is well protected. We cannot afford any more Foundation losses. All available ships are guarding the main site.'

'Building is progressing well,' Seven reports. 'We estimate it will be ready to receive workers in the next few weeks.'

One nods. 'That is good news. I'm sure you all agree it is imperative we keep all available ships near the new colony.'

'We should send more ships,' Eleven suggests. 'Try to cut off the prototype before it reaches Ultar.'

One shakes his head. 'No. If we send more ships, the populace will become suspicious. They believe the Outer Sector is under control. They can't know the truth about any of this. We don't have Balfe to take the blame for this anymore. So far, the populace has been satisfied with our explanation for the destruction of the Port. There's only so much we can pin on Balfe. If this project is to succeed and move on to the next phase, everything that happens must appear to be above board. Besides, our contact on Ultar has already confirmed the prototype has made contact with Foundation personnel from *Infinity*.'

'Are you sure?'

One sighs dramatically. 'Of course I'm sure.'

'And what of Ultar?' Seven asks.

'Plans are in place. Trust me, Ultar will be destroyed. It is just a matter of time.'

∞

Roman takes a sip of his coffee as he considers how to reply. Terra sits stiffly in front of him. Her hands are under her legs and she's chewing on her bottom lip. The colour has all but disappeared from her face replaced by a sickly grey hue. 'Are you sure you don't want something to drink?'

She shakes her head. 'I'd probably just throw it up again.' She looks down at her legs and frowns deeply. 'I didn't fully believe he was still alive.'

Roman grunts. 'I have to admit, I was of the same opinion. You're sure it was him?'

She glances up at him and nods. 'I wish it wasn't. I can't tell you how much I wish it wasn't.' She laughs up at the ceiling. 'Most people would be thanking their lucky stars if a loved one came back from the dead.'

Roman walks around his desk and sits on the edge facing her. 'After what you told me, I prefer to believe the man that was your father died years ago. The Callum I knew would never have involved himself in something like this. I don't want to add to the issue, but Gryffin confirmed Callum worked on him again while he was a prisoner.'

'Oh, God.' Terra's tear-rimmed eyes meet his. 'This is a nightmare. What do I do now?'

He shrugs and shakes his head. He hasn't got a clue what the best course of action is. 'I'll get the coordinates checked.'

'I mean about what he claims to be able to do. What if he really can reverse what he did to Gryffin?'

That's the big question. The Foundation's medical facility has pioneered the regeneration of organs. Decades of developments have been undertaken with favourable results. He's seen the technology first-hand. A cadet training with him had lost a hand during a training exercise. Within six months, they had grown him a new hand and he was back training. Is it enough to replace an arm, an eye and half a leg? That he doesn't know. It probably won't help that the metal has been fitted for two decades. It may be too much for even the Foundation to correct. He'll get Milla to check it out. 'I don't know. Milla and Chayse were adamant the damage is too severe. The program on Earth was developed to help newly injured people. Gryffin's lived with the metal for twenty odd years. It may be too late for him. I'll look into it though.'

'Should I tell him — Gryffin I mean?'

Another big question. The little he knows about his son guarantees that he'll be less than happy about the communication with the Scientist. He also seriously doubts he'll believe a word out of Callum's mouth. After the last time, he'd be mad to trust the Foundation. 'Probably best we do a bit more digging first. Leave it with me for now.' He rises to his feet. 'No offense, but you look like death warmed up.' He holds out his hand and helps her to her feet. 'I'll take you back to your room.' He stops at the bookshelf against the back wall and plucks a leather-bound volume from the shelf.

She looks quizzically at the book. 'What's that for?'

He wraps his arm around her shoulder and leads her along the corridor. 'I noticed it's been a few months since you've read any of my books.'

She shakes her head. 'I'm not in the mood to read.'

He squeezes her briefly. 'I'll read it to you.'

She stops in her tracks and stares at him. 'Sir?'

'Tonight I'm Jensen. I used to read to you all the time.'

She laughs. 'Yeah, when I was a child.'

He shrugs and pulls her along the corridor again. 'You're never too old to be read to. Besides, I think we could both do with a bit of escapism.'

'When you put it like that, I couldn't agree more.'

'Jensen.'

They turn around to face Aleena, and Roman instantly knows something is seriously wrong. 'What happened, Aleena?' She holds a hand up to her mouth and shakes her head. He gathers her in his arms. 'You're trembling.'

'He killed Klay.'

Her voice is barely above a whisper, but the words cut through him as if she has screamed them. 'How did he get in?'

'The guards were speaking to Lucan one moment, then woke up an hour later. Gryffin casually handed them back the keypad for the door and then walked away.' She pushes back from his chest and meets his eyes. 'Jensen, he beat Klay to death. There is blood everywhere. I've never known Gryffin to act this way before.' She shakes her head. 'What... how am I supposed to deal with this... with him?'

He wishes he had an answer for her, but he's also at a loss. 'Terra, can you take Aleena and get her something strong to drink. I'll see to this.'

He holds Aleena at arm's length and forces a small smile on his face. 'Go with Terra. I'll see you later, okay?'

She nods weakly and allows Terra to guide her away. He looks up at the ceiling, hoping to find inspiration in the metal girders. He needs to speak to Gryffin, but would rather go up against the Foundation single handed.

∞

Gryffin groans as someone knocks heavily on his door. He picks up his blood stained clothes, throws them in the waste disposal, and pulls on a fresh pair of combats. He opens the door and is surprised to find Roman in front of him. 'Thought Aleena would come herself.'

Roman pushes into the room and turns to face him, his hands on his hips. 'I just watched the footage from the cells.'

Gryffin lowers into the seat by the door and stretches his legs out in front of him. 'What happened is none of your business.'

'Aleena has put me in charge of this base so I think you'll find it is.'

'Klay was Nomad. Last I heard, I still command the Nomad.'

Roman blows out a breath and turns away for a moment. 'You didn't have to do what you did.'

'Yes, I did. He betrayed me, betrayed the group, and put the colonies in danger.' Gryffin pauses as a spear of pain travels through his new connectors. The new parts are complaining about the recent exertion.

He looks up to see Roman staring at him with a strange expression on his face. 'You okay?'

Gryffin gets to his feet. 'You've said your piece. You can go back and tell Aleena there's more food to go around now he's gone.'

'This is all a game to you, isn't it? You can't beat someone to death like a—'

'What? Like a savage? That's what the Foundation call people in this Sector, right?' He steps up to Roman and glares down at the Foundation man. 'I haven't forgotten your part in what happened to me.'

'Is that a threat?'

Gryffin shakes his head. 'Klay knew what he was getting in to. You were just a Foundation pawn. You're not worth wasting energy on.' He pulls on a t-shirt and sits on the bed to fasten his boots. 'Klay's dead. It's done. No one has to worry about me going on a rampage.'

'You can't deal with issues like this. He didn't have a trial.'

'Enough!' Gryffin stands up and rolls his shoulders. 'Stay out of Nomad business — for your own sake.' He walks away, leaving Roman alone with the threat hanging in the air.

∞

'What exactly are you doing?'

Gryffin stops sparring with the Ultaran and turns to face Milla. 'Training.'

'I can see that. You've just undergone major surgery. I only let you out of the med bay if you promised to rest. Get yourself back to bed. Now!'

'Back off. I'm fine.'

Milla releases a colourful string of words as she approaches him. Gryffin isn't afraid of many things, but the irate doctor gives him second thoughts about his actions. 'Fine? You are far from fine, Captain. Now, I know that following orders isn't on the top of your list, but when I tell you to take it easy and not train, I expect you to do what I say. Understood?'

Gryffin can't help the small smile that pulls at the corner of his mouth as Milla uses his own statement against him.

'And you can wipe that smile off your face.' She pulls the stick from his hand and points back toward the corridor. 'Walk in that direction before I call in a team to move you.'

The last place he wants to be is back in bed, but he doesn't have the energy to argue. He's still not back to full strength. Usually, when he's feeling off, a good workout helps, but not today. He still feels lousy and the exercise only made him worse.

'So, I heard what you did to Klay.'

'Going to give me your Foundation opinion too?'

She stops suddenly. 'I was actually going to say I understand why you did it. Not how you... did the deed, but I do get why.'

'You do?'

She nods, but doesn't reply as a group of Nomad approach. The men salute him as they walk past.

'I've picked up a few things from working with the Nomad over the last few months. You take loyalty seriously.'

Gryffin grunts and shakes his head. 'I wasn't expecting that from you.'

She shrugs. 'I guess I'm picking up some Nomad bad habits. Don't get carried away though. How you killed him was completely uncalled for.'

He continues on his way down the corridor. 'In your opinion.'

'I think you'll find I'm not alone.' She looks down at his leg and frowns. 'You're limping. Did you hurt your leg training?'

'Yeah.' He's surprised how easy the lie comes to him. If she knows his leg is sore all the time, she'll have him back in the med bay before he can stop her.

She nods, but her narrowed gaze tells him she isn't fooled. 'Any other problems? How are you feeling?'

'A bit tired.'

Milla fakes fainting and steadies herself against the wall. 'My goodness! I didn't know you could say anything other than "I'm fine."'

He grunts and follows her back into the small room next to the med bay. She may have released him, but he isn't allowed to go far.

'See, that's more like it.'

Gryffin sits on the edge of his bed as she fusses in her bag for her scanner. 'Have you seen Terra?' The question is out before he can register what his mouth is doing.

Milla sighs and glances up at him.

'Forget I asked.'

She sits on the ground and crosses her legs under her. 'Gryffin—'

'I said forget it.'

'If you knew anything about me, you'd know I can't do that. Have you tried talking to her?'

'There's nothing to talk about.'

Milla sighs heavily. 'I give up. You're both as bad as each other.'

'Back off and leave things as they are. It's better for everyone.'

'You're a stubborn fool, you know that.' She glances at the clock on the wall. 'Right, you know the drill by now. Attach the monitors and take it easy. I'll get dinner. What do you fancy?'

He scrunches his brow. 'Dinner?'

She stands up and brushes off her trousers. 'Yes, you know, food.' She mimes eating like he's a child. 'It's what people eat to stay alive.'

'I'm not hungry.'

'Now why am I not surprised. Well, I'm going to get you some food and I fully expect you to eat it.'

Gryffin opens his mouth to argue, but the doctor has sauntered back to the corridor.

14

'What the hell are you doing here?'

Aleena bites back her reply and pushes past Gryffin into the dark room. She did not intend coming to see Gryffin so soon after what he did to Klay. After Terra left her room, Lucan had called by to speak to her. She does not know if Gryffin sent him to placate her or if he made the decision alone. The young man had helped offer justification for a situation she did not believe could be justified. Gryffin had to kill Klay — he had no choice. His position as leader of the Nomad would be undermined if the betrayal had gone unpunished. She will never condone his actions or his methods, but after spending some time with Lucan, she can perhaps accept them.

She places the tray of food on the small table and takes a seat on one of the chairs. Gryffin stands at the door and throws his trademark glare in her direction. Aleena takes the cover from one of the plates and spreads a napkin on her knee.

'You here to tell me how much you disapprove of me again?'

'There is no need. You already know. Talking about it will only result in an argument. Sit, please.' He frowns, but doesn't move. 'I would not waste your much needed energy on dirty looks, Captain.' She gestures to the chair opposite her. 'It would be much better spent on eating.'

'I told Milla I'm not hungry.'

Aleena lifts the lid from the other plate. 'You can barely hold yourself upright. Stop being a stubborn fool and do as your doctor instructed.'

Her harsh tone has the required effect. He releases a deep breath, drops heavily into the seat and examines the food. Aleena chews on a piece of meat as she watches him. Milla is right to be concerned. He is a great deal smaller than she remembers him — both in weight and in presence. Usually, his strong, sure posture fills a room, but now, huddled over a table, he appears so much weaker.

'It will not disappear by staring at it. If you do not eat you will be of no use to the Nomad. Eat.'

She hates being so forceful with him, but she cannot see another way to get through to him. He picks up the fork like it is a foreign object, stabs a piece of potato and forces it into his mouth. Aleena smiles. 'Thank you. Milla will be pleased.'

He grunts and swallows. 'Doubt it.'

'She is merely doing what is best for you. She did save your life when you arrived.'

He targets a piece of meat. 'You saying I should thank her for that?'

Aleena's appetite suddenly vanishes. 'You would have preferred she allowed you to die?'

Gryffin swallows, and for a moment, she fears his food will not stay in his stomach. He pushes the plate away, but Aleena returns it to the empty spot in front of him. 'What do you want from me?'

'I want you to eat so you will regain your strength and I want you to answer my question.'

'Can't see what good I'm doing here.' He holds up his metal hand

and Aleena frowns as the limb trembles noticeably. 'Can't even hold it steady enough to fire. It's a damn liability.'

'You are expecting too much from yourself. You have been through a great deal. Your body needs time to heal, to grow stronger. Healing will not be a fast process.'

'I don't have time to sit around and wait. Nothing Milla's doing is helping.'

Aleena crosses her arms. 'You are being unfair Gryffin. She has spent every waking hour attending to you. Her personal life has suffered so she can help you.' Aleena drops her hands to her lap and closes her eyes. She did not mean for that information to come out.

'What do you mean?'

'I did not—'

'Tell me!'

Aleena sighs and shakes her head. 'Chayse left just after you arrived. They have hardly seen each other in the last few months.'

'Why does that matter?'

Aleena looks up at him and nearly laughs at the confusion on his face. 'Oh, Gryffin. They are in love.'

Gryffin runs a shaky hand through his hair and closes his eye.

Aleena reaches across the table and takes his metal hand in hers. He attempts to pull it away but she holds him tightly. 'I misspoke, Gryffin. I did not mean to imply you are at fault in any way.' She sighs and squeezes his hand. 'It frustrates me that you cannot see how much people here care for you. You may not see how valuable you are to us — as a friend and as a leader, but others do. Milla needs your help now. She cannot continue your care unless you assist her. You must take greater care of yourself. Please.'

'Chayse left?'

Aleena nods. 'He was eager to get back to the site of the new Port.'

'Did I... did he leave because of me?'

She tries not to let the truth show on her face, but is not successful.

He gets up and leans on the window frame. 'How do I fix this?'

She joins him at the window. 'There is nothing to fix, Gryffin. Just get better.'

Aleena jumps as he suddenly slams his hand against the wall. 'How do I fix this?' he repeats.

'Firstly, you can refrain from damaging the wall. Control yourself or this conversation will end.'

He turns his head in her direction and she instantly notices the purple glow from his human eye. The centre of the new eyepiece spins as it focuses on her. 'I'm in control.'

Aleena does not believe that for one minute. 'I am not your keeper, Gryffin. If you believe you have to fix this, then it is up to you to figure it out.'

'Appreciate your help, Aleena.' His reply is loaded with sarcasm as he turns away from her and walks unsteadily out the door.

∞

Gryffin stands in the doorway and silently watches Milla. She is frowning at her screen and muttering to herself under her breath. After walking out on Aleena, he spent the next hour at the lake, thinking. Until Aleena told him about Chayse and Milla, he didn't realise how much he's affected Chayse's life — and not in a good way. While Chayse was his aide, Gryffin treated him like dirt. It wasn't intentional, Chayse was a good Nomad. Gryffin just hated having someone close to him. Chayse knew more about him than anyone else and Gryffin didn't like it. It made him feel uncomfortable.

He never thought Chayse might have a life off *Ares*. When he beat Chayse up and gave him *Nemesis*, he thought Chayse would be happy. Going from an aide to captain of a new ship was unheard of among the Nomad. After hearing what Aleena said, instead of helping, he's probably just screwed Chayse's life up even more.

'Hey. You okay?'

Gryffin blinks and looks at Milla. 'Yeah.'

'Aleena said you ate. That's a good start.' She frowns. 'You sure you're okay. You look a little... off.'

'You're with Chayse.'

She blinks a few times then leans back in her chair. 'We're in a relationship... sort of. If I'm honest, we've probably only spent a few weeks together over the last year.'

Gryffin leans against the doorframe and crosses his arms. 'Would you be with him if you could?'

'Of course,' she replies without hesitation. 'Bit difficult with him being where he is and me being where I am.' She shrugs and smiles. 'Fingers crossed things will settle down in the Sector soon and we can all attempt a private life.'

'Have you asked him to join you on *Infinity*?'

She looks at him as if he's grown horns on his head. 'Wild horses couldn't drag him away from *Nemesis*.'

'What do horses have to do with it?'

Milla shakes her head and smiles. 'Never mind.' She picks up a glass of water from the desk and stares into the clear liquid. 'No. His place is on that ship. Leaving aside the fact that he'd rather die than let the Nomad down by leaving — he really loves being in command of her. I think he feels he's making a difference.'

'He is. His dedication to the Nomad is the reason I chose him.' He locks his legs in place as his head spins. Two mouthfuls of food aren't helping keep him upright. 'Why don't you join him?'

Milla freezes with her glass halfway to her mouth. 'Excuse me?'

'You heard me.'

'You mean leave *Infinity*?'

He nods and grips the door-frame with his hand, hoping that he keeps the movement from Milla. 'I've checked the reports. He doesn't have a dedicated doctor. It'll be a full time role. It's yours if you want it.'

She opens and closes her mouth a few times before finally getting the words out. 'Can you do that?'

'Technically, I'm still the High Commander.'

'But... why me?'

He shrugs. 'It makes sense. There is one catch though. You'll have to become a Nomad. The first female Nomad ever.'

'Wow! That's pretty big. Would that not cause problems in the group?'

He shakes his head and winces as the motion rattles his headache. 'Think after all the other things I've done recently, this won't be a problem. Talk to Chayse and let me know. I'll make sure the transfer approval is logged on the system.'

'I really don't know what to say, Gryffin. You have no idea what this means to me.' She gets to her feet and opens her arms to give him a hug, but he backs away. Milla smiles sheepishly. 'Sorry, got a bit carried away.' She claps her hands and jumps up and down. 'This is so exciting!'

Gryffin smiles as he watches her reaction. Seems his idea has paid off. Maybe with Chayse and Milla together, he can start to make it up to Chayse for throwing him into a life changing situation without talking to him about it.

Milla stops her celebration dance and stands in front of him. 'Right, now I have to ask you for one small favour.'

'What?'

'Will you please sit before you fall and take my doorframe with you?'

∞

'Are you sure this is what you want to do?

Milla nods rapidly and leans sits back in the chair opposite Roman. It's clear she can barely keep herself pinned down to the chair. She's practically vibrating with excitement. 'I'm sure.'

He clasps his hands on the desk in front of him and looks at the young doctor. He knew she was close to Chayse, but he never thought he'd lose her to *Nemesis*. While it makes sense for the battleship to have a full-time doctor on its crew, he's wary about granting her application to transfer ships. After working closely with the Nomad and Hunters over the last few months, he knows they operate their ships in a very black-and-white way. You obeyed orders or you were removed from the crew — usually in a fatal way. Aleena filled him in on how Chayse was removed from *Ares*. It turns his stomach to think of Milla being put in a situation like that. 'Are you sure Chayse can assure your safety? You will be the only female Nomad.'

'He's the captain and from what I hear, he's taken a tiny leaf out of Gryffin's book. Apparently, he's not to be disobeyed. He's told me his crew will behave. I'm sure they'll do as they're told. Besides,' she adds with a large grin, 'I'd like to see them try anything. I'll soon put them in their place.'

Roman can't help but laugh. He's seen the petite doctor stand up for herself and knows she'll quickly sort them out if they step out of line. 'I'm not going to lie. Losing you will be a big hit for *Infinity*, but it does make sense for someone with your skills to be on *Nemesis*. She needs you more than we do.'

'Exactly. The team working here are good. They've all undergone Foundation style training with me over the last few months. I'd have no problem putting my life in any of their hands.' She sits on the edge of her seat and looks expectantly at him. 'So, can I go?'

Roman still wants to say no, but that's the protective side of himself stepping in. There's no reason to stop her from going. 'Fine. But only because I know you won't let me live in peace unless I say yes.'

She jumps to her feet and claps her hands. 'Yay! Thank you so much, sir.'

'I'll arrange the transfer with Chayse. It'll probably be a few weeks until *Nemesis* is back in the area. Do you think you can hold on that long?'

She blows a stray bang from her eyes and grins. 'I might just be able to manage it. I can't promise I won't be a complete pain in the butt while I'm waiting.'

'Wouldn't expect anything less from you.' He rises to his feet and holds out his hand. Milla shakes her head and rushes around the desk. She throws her arms around his neck and squeezes hard. 'I'll go and pack.'

After nearly cutting off his air, she finally releases her hold and, after saluting him, quickly hurries from the room.

Roman slumps back in his chair and sighs. A Foundation member on a Nomad ship. He shakes his head. A few months ago the thought would have been ludicrous. It just shows how much things have changed since the destruction of the Port.

Lucan pops his head around the door. 'Just got word. The Foundation have made an announcement.'

Roman groans to himself. 'Why do I get the feeling my day is going to get really bad.'

15

'You have to stop avoiding him, Terra. Do you have any idea how childish you're being?'

Terra pushes away from the counter and manoeuvres around her friend. 'Change the record, Milla,' she hisses under her breath.

Milla steps in front of her and pushes her friend back. 'No! So help me, Terra. I love you to bits, but you're being a stubborn ass at the moment. Gryffin hasn't got the first clue what he's done to make you so angry.'

Terra restrains her anger enough to keep the tray of food firmly in her hands instead of on the floor. 'We're in public, Milla. Not now.'

They walk in uncomfortable silence back to Milla's room. As soon as the door is shut Milla and Terra face off, neither side with any intention of backing down. Terra knows how stubborn Milla can be. When she gets her mind on something, there's not a lot that can move her. 'We've talked about this until we're both blue in the face. Can we please just let it go? I don't want to have another argument about it.'

'That's exactly what I'm asking,' Milla replies. 'I want you to let it go. Let go of all the anger. All the hurt. It's crippling you.' Milla takes her arms in her hands and turns Terra to face her. 'The man you loved died and it was shite. No one is blaming you for being in a bad place. But he's back. He's a bit grumpier than he was, but he's back. Do you have any idea how many people would give anything to be in this situation?'

'My father came back from the dead. That hasn't turned out too well for anyone, especially Gryffin. How can I possibly face him when I know that!' Terra clamps her mouth shut. She didn't mean to tell Milla that.

Any hopes that Milla didn't hear her are quashed when she crosses her arms and nods. 'I see. So, that's the real reason. Why didn't you tell me?'

Terra waves her arm in the air. 'What can you do? It's my problem. I'll deal with it.'

'But it's not just your problem, is it? Gryffin is getting the brunt of it and he doesn't know why. Think about it from his side. Before you left the freighter, you told him you love him, right?'

'Yes, but—'

'And now he's back, but he hasn't seen hide nor hair of you. You vanished without so much as an explanation.'

'Just like he did!'

'He didn't do that for a laugh, Terra. He saved thousands of people by doing what he did. You know full well there's no way you would have been able to disarm his collar and destroy the freighter before the rest of the fleet arrived. Something had to give and it was him.'

Terra's shoulders slump. 'He didn't even try, Milla.'

'Okay. There are enough issues here to keep any therapist busy for years. You have to tell him though. Listen, I know things have been terrible for you since he died, but think how the time was for him. You know what he went through the last time. From his injuries, it looks like he's been through more of the same this time too. After all that, the least he deserves is an explanation.'

'What about what I deserve? What this Sector deserves? We need someone who'll fight for themselves and the people who care about them. He has absolutely no interest in understanding anyone else's feelings.'

'Hey, now that's not fair, Terra. He doesn't have a clue how to deal with emotions. You told me that. Why is his lack of understanding a shock?'

Terra waves her arms in the air. 'None of this matters anymore. Knowing him, he'll leave as soon as he can. There's no way he's going to hang around while his Nomad are in the mess they're in. I guarantee, he'll leave us all again.'

'So, you'll just sit back and do nothing as he flies away?'

Terra shrugs. 'It doesn't matter. I'm with someone else now. Gryffin means nothing to me.'

Milla blows out a breath and sits down at the table. 'I give up. It's your life.'

Terra sits opposite her and unwraps her sandwich. She hates fighting with Milla. Since Gryffin reappeared, it's becoming a common occurrence. All she wants to do is get on with her life in peace. Whatever she feels or felt for Gryffin doesn't matter anymore. After watching Milla taking out her frustration on her lunch, Terra finally breaks the uncomfortable silence. 'So, you wanted to tell me something.'

Milla frowns, then flaps a hand in the air as she forces the food down her throat. 'Great way to change the subject, but yes, I do have something super exciting! I'm transferring to *Nemesis*!'

Terra drops her sandwich to the ground. 'You're what?'

Milla smirks. 'Transferring to *Nemesis*.'

Terra bends over to collect her downed lunch. She slowly targets each piece of the sandwich as she gathers her thoughts. Milla can't leave. It's ridiculous. And joining a Nomad ship? Well, that's the most ridiculous part of all. Suddenly it hits her. It's a joke. She breathes slowly to calm her racing heart. It's just a joke.

She deposits her ruined lunch on the plate. 'Good one. You had me for a minute.'

Milla shakes her head. 'Thought you'd say that.' She holds out her tablet.

Terra slowly takes it and reads the transfer order on the screen. She skips to the end and freezes. That's Roman's signature. She taps on the fingerprint beside it and the computer confirms. It's legitimate. 'I don't understand...'

Milla takes the computer back from her and tucks it in her bag. 'It's fairly simple really. *Nemesis* needs a medical officer. I need to be with Chayse. Two birds.'

Terra hears the words but it still sounds like utter nonsense. 'But it's a Nomad ship. You're leaving the Foundation for—'

'Leaving the Foundation? We left the Foundation a long time ago.' Milla shuffles to the edge of her seat. 'Terra, I have to do this. I have to give myself and Chayse a chance. I can't do that if I stay here.'

'But why do you have to join a Nomad ship?'

Milla frowns. 'Leaving the Foundation. Joining the Nomad. Why are you focusing on the groups?'

Terra gets to her feet and walks to the window. 'Why are you not? This is so much more than just being on the same ship as Chayse. You are seriously thinking about becoming a Nomad.'

Milla crosses her arms. 'Of course I am. Terra, there's a lot more to my decision than a group. I couldn't care less that I'm going to be a Nomad. I'll be with Chayse. Sometimes, being with the person you love is a lot more important than titles or being part of the right group. After everything the Foundation has done, I'm ashamed to have anything to do with them.'

'Is it safe for you to be there?'

'Of course it is. You've been working with the Nomad for months.

You know they're great guys.' She puts her hand on Terra's shoulder. 'This isn't about me. This is about you and Gryffin.'

The brush off dies before it leaves her mouth. She can't do it any longer. Milla is her best friend. She knows her better than anyone, how can she continue to lie? Her shoulders slump and a sob wracks through her body. Milla gathers her in her arms. The doctor holds her as months of sorrow works out of her body. 'Sorry, I'm being ridiculous. I've got Bray. I'm finally happy again. What is wrong with me?'

Milla strokes her hair. 'I've been trying to figure that out for years.'

Terra laughs and wipes her damp face. 'Thanks.'

Milla shrugs and smiles. 'It's the truth.' She sits down opposite Terra and takes her hands. 'Listen, I have nothing against Bray. He's been good to you and he seems like a decent guy.'

'But...'

'But, if you still have feelings for Gryffin you should talk to him. Terra, he asked Aleena where you were.'

'I can't. It took a long time to get over him. I can't go back to that. Not now. It's too late.'

Milla shakes her head. 'It's not too late to turn things around. He's still here.'

'Please drop it, Milla.' Her friend glowers, but nods in agreement. 'What am I going to do without you?'

'You'll be miserable of course. That's why you need Gryffin to fill the gap. I know he pales in comparison, but beggars can't be choosers.'

'Milla.'

She holds up her hands and attempts her best innocent face. 'What?'

Terra smiles as she walks into the bathroom to wash her face. 'So, when do you reunite with your Nomad?'

'Hopefully in a few days. Gryffin's arranging a transport to bring me halfway. *Nemesis* will meet me.'

Terra freezes and looks at Milla in the reflection in the mirror. 'Gryffin?'

Milla nods. 'Yeah, he's been great.'

Terra turns and leans against the sink. 'What do you mean? What does he have to do with this?'

Milla laughs as she gathers their plates. 'It was his suggestion. Once Chayse agreed, Gryffin made all the arrangements.'

A cold feeling settles in Terra's stomach. Gryffin helped Chayse and Milla be together. Milla continues to talk in the background but Terra zones out. All she ever wanted was a chance to be with him. Every single time she brought it up, he shot her down. Why is it okay for Chayse and Milla but not for them?

Terra ignores Milla's questions as she leaves the room.

∞

"I'm with someone else now. Gryffin means nothing to me."

Terra's comment kept Gryffin company while he stormed back to *Ares*. Playing over and over in his head, mocking him. Serves him right for listening in on a conversation that had damn all to do with him. He went to tell Milla he put the transfer order on the Nomad system, but got a hell of a lot more than he planned. He rubs his chest, expecting to find a large hole or an open wound, but it's in one piece. There's nothing to explain the aching, hollow feeling.

It was obvious Terra's been avoiding him since he got back and now he knows why. He tries to convince himself that he doesn't care, but he does. Not that he can blame her for moving on. He was dead and it's not as if they had any sort of real relationship to start with. She had moved on and forgotten about him. It's just a shame he didn't do the same. For months, she was the one thing that kept him going, kept him fighting against what they were doing to him. He stupidly mixed up his dreams with his harsh reality.

He holds on to the railing and squeezes his eye shut as the ache in his chest increases. He had Sayber knock Terra out. That was his goodbye to her. Of course she hates him. She saw his actions as wanting to get her out of the way, but all he wanted to do was get her to safety. He could have handled it better than he did. But there was no time.

He doesn't agree with Rayde constantly telling him to ignore his emotions, but he has to admit he sees the plus side. Having control over his feelings would definitely help him right now. His stomach is churning and his throat has closed. He's already checked his implants and knows everything is working, so he can only put it down to some sort of emotional reaction, but he's damned if he knows what it is.

He breaks the top railing with his metal hand. *Seriously, Gryffin. Did you really think she'd wait for you?*

He's embarrassed and angry to admit a bit of him did think she would. He kicks the bottom railing, focusing on the pain that shoots up his metal leg. Being on the same planet as her isn't doing him any favours. He's a mess and needs to sort himself out. He can only do that away from Ultar and Terra.

Ares has to leave. Today.

He closes his eye and takes a deep breath. A part of him is scared what will happen if he can't get a handle on these strange feelings. Hopefully, being away from her will help. Escaping from the Scientist was easy compared to dealing with this mess.

He looks at the cargo deck below and his bike sitting in the corner. Chayse left it on Ultar for him. He's thrilled to have the machine back in his possession, even if he can't get himself to go anywhere near it. The last time he was on it, Terra was straddling him. If he got on it now, it just wouldn't feel right without her there.

He curses under his breath. He's irritating himself. If he heard one of his crew speaking like this he'd send them to the training room to get some sense beaten into them. Maybe that's what he needs. He's no good to anyone like this. He needs to get a grip — fast. With no other option, he links to the implant and winces as pain shoots across his eyepiece. Instantly, the empty feeling dulls. He takes a few deep breaths as his vision sharpens.

The door behind him opens and Desyl joins him. His first officer glances down at the torn railing, but has the good sense not to ask about it.

'Is she ready?'

Desyl blows out a breath and pauses. 'Sir, your eye is purple.'

'I asked you a question.'

'But, sir—'

'I'm not malfunctioning. Now, answer the question.'

Desyl doesn't look convinced, but wisely moves on. 'She'll fly, but we really need a few more test runs to iron out any other last minute issues.'

'What kind of last minute issues?'

'Nothing major. The mess is still being finished and all the training equipment is piled up in the corner over there.' He points to the large tarps in the far corner of the cargo hold.

Gryffin resists the urge to rip into Desyl. The training room and mess aren't even on his radar. 'Get the crew back. We leave in thirty minutes.'

Desyl opens and closes his mouth a few times before he finally forms a sentence. 'But, sir! We're not ready to leave. The mess—'

'We'll eat on the damn floor. We've operated the ship in a hell of a worse state.'

'I really think—'

Gryffin gets right in his face. 'Think? I ordered you to get the crew on board. Now, either you do as I say or I replace you and leave you here.'

Desyl closes his mouth and nods.

'Thirty minutes.' Gryffin closes the door behind him and goes to pack his things.

Gryffin opens the door and freezes when he sees Terra in front of him. His breath catches in his throat. She looks better than he remembers. He clenches his fists by his sides to stop his damn arms from wrapping around her. This isn't one of his twisted dreams. This is real life. The life that puts her a hell of a way out of his reach. He opens his mouth to say hi, but she pushes past him. Doesn't seem like this is going to be the cheery reunion he would have liked.

'What are you up to?'

He spins to face her. 'What?' She's furious and it's directed at him for some unknown reason. He quickly runs through the last few hours. He's done nothing to piss her off this much.

'Stealing Milla. Did it not cross your mind for one minute that she may actually be needed here?'

He slumps into the chair by the open door and sighs. 'Roman cleared it.'

'So that's it, you just take what you want?'

'It's what I do, isn't it?' She threw that very line at him when they were on Ultar months ago. 'I don't know what this has to do with you anyway.'

'I'm her friend.'

'You don't think they should be happy?'

She frowns at his comment. 'Of course I do. I just don't think this is the way.'

'Why not? He likes her and she likes him. They're both unhappy being apart.'

She pauses for a moment, clearly thrown off by his comment. 'I know they are and I want Milla to be happy, but making her officially join the Nomad — that's a bit harsh.'

Flashes of purple appear in his eye. 'I didn't make her do anything. I gave her a choice. Clearly she doesn't have a problem with the Nomad.'

She widens her stance and puts her hands on her hips. 'Oh right. And I do. Is that what you're saying?' She takes a step closer to him. 'You were the one with the Foundation and Nomad problem, not me. Every time I came near, you pushed me away. Well after you got what you wanted from me.' She waves her arms in the air. 'I even told you that I loved you. Apart from setting up camp on your bed I don't know what else I could have done to show you how I feel.'

'Feel? You still feel like that?'

Colour spreads to her cheeks as she looks away from him quickly. 'It was a slip of the tongue.'

A large hole seems to open in his chest. It shouldn't bother him, but it does. Until he met her, he never cared what people thought of him. She's messed him up and he can't figure out how to fix the problem. 'Milla and Chayse are different. He's not me.'

'Is this about your implants? That's your excuse for everything, isn't it?'

She meets his eyes and Gryffin doesn't fully recognise the person standing in front of him. 'There's no point going over this again.

Whatever your problem with me, it's got nothing to do with this. Leave Milla out of it. She's made her decision.' He gets to his feet and stands beside the door. He never thought he'd kick Terra out of his room, but this isn't getting them anywhere. She belongs to someone else now. He doesn't need her to go over how badly he's messed things up. 'Go.'

Terra's jaw drops open for a second before she composes herself. Without another word, she storms out of the room. He shuts it behind her and slumps back into the chair. That was a bloody disaster. He stares at the wall opposite and becomes distracted by the sickening, hollow feeling in his chest. The fight with Terra made it worse. He can't think straight.

His radio sounds. He acknowledges the message but doesn't reply. Time to go.

He reaches behind the chair and pulls the small bag out. It contains everything he owns: two spare uniforms and his jacket. Without a backward glance, he leaves the room. He's going to be damn glad to get far away from here.

∞

Gryffin glares at his reflection in the mirror. He never thought he'd be back on *Ares*, let alone in his old room. Even though the ship is his life and soul, he feels like a stranger to her now. Everything is more or less the same, but the differences stand out to him. He runs a hand over the new mirror. It's just one of the many new parts to the ship. Before he was taken, he knew every inch of the ship, every piece of metal, every wall panel, but not anymore. Not only is he a stranger, he also has to get to know her all over again.

He's not sure there's any point getting to know her again. It doesn't matter that his crew accept him back as captain without question. It doesn't matter how many times someone tells him how happy they are to have him back. He knows the truth. He knows that after he fixes the mess he's made, he'll be obsolete again. If he's being honest, he doesn't have a problem with that. Being given a chance to put things right is good enough for him. Taking down the Foundation is the closure he needs.

There's a lot to get through before that happens though. Like facing the crew on the command deck as their captain for the first time in nearly a year. Then there's the small matter of leading them into battle. At the moment he can't see how he can lead them to the mess hall let alone into a fight. He doesn't even know where to start. What if he gets it wrong and his orders lead to some of them being killed?

Milla assures him he's still the same person. The modifications to his implants shouldn't affect him, but he's far from convinced. That's the problem. Before, he would never pause in battle. He was always confident in his decisions. If he's unsure now, how can he expect the crew to be convinced? Doubt can mean life or death for a lot of people. There are already too many innocent deaths on his hands.

His thoughts are interrupted when his communicator sounds, requesting his presence on the command deck. Can't put it off any longer, especially if *Ares* is going to be out of the area before Terra's transport gets back from checking the defences. He can't handle seeing her again.

He splashes some water on his face and takes a deep breath. He stands up straight and faces his reflection again, this time without glaring. Time to get back into captain mode. He's been given this second chance and there's no way he's going to mess it up. Gryffin grabs a black bandanna from beside the sink and ties it over his hair to hide the large scar on the left side of his head. It will take another few months for his hair to grow back properly and hide the reminder. It takes a few attempts to tie the material thanks to his trembling hands.

He connects with the implant and makes a fist, relieved when the trembling vanishes. His purple eyes regard him in the reflection. If he has to use the implant to stop his hand trembling, how the hell is he going to command a ship? As much as he hates using it, he's going to have to take some support from it until he gets himself together.

Before he changes his mind, he leaves the room to face the crew.

∞

Desyl keeps his feet firmly planted on the floor and resists the urge to look at the time again. Although he's trying to hide it, the rest of the crew are aware of, and share, his anxiousness. He can't blame Gryffin for taking his time getting to the command deck. If he were in his captain's place he may very well not even show up. It can't be easy to lead the people you betrayed — willingly or not. There are some on the crew less than enthusiastic about his return, but everyone on the ship swore allegiance to the Nomad and to Gryffin. All personal feelings will be put aside. They all know they have a better chance of succeeding with him leading the group.

Desyl just hopes they're not putting too much weight on Gryffin's still healing shoulders.

As if to prove him wrong, the man in question slowly steps up onto the command platform. All personnel immediately stand to attention. Desyl holds back a smile. He knows one look at Gryffin and any of the lingering doubt will be quashed instantly. Dressed in the Nomad head-to-toe black leather topped with a black bandanna, Gryffin looks like the formidable leader he used to be. It also helps that by wearing the bandanna, his usually hidden facial scars and implant are on full display, adding to his fierce appearance.

Without a word, Gryffin walks to his command chair and sits down.

'What are you standing around for?' Desyl shouts. 'Back to your stations.'

Desyl risks a sideways glance at Gryffin and notices that his eye is purple. He hides the grimace. He's used the implant twice in the space of a few hours. That's going to hit the captain later. Desyl tries not to get too concerned about it. Perhaps he just needs it as a back-up. He'll have to monitor the captain to make sure he doesn't depend on the implant too much. If it helps, who is he to argue? Gryffin's muscles strain as he squeezes the arms of his command chair in a death grip. If he doesn't relax, the chair will shatter.

'Sir, what are your orders?'

Gryffin silently stares straight ahead of him for a few minutes. Desyl can feel the eyes of the crew drilling into the back of his head as they all wait for Gryffin to acknowledge him.

Just as the silence verges on the uncomfortable, Gryffin snaps out of his trance. 'Get us away from here. Pick one of the border colonies — I don't really care which one.'

Desyl nods and moves away from his captain. Gryffin watches in silence as Desyl loads the coordinates into the system and *Ares* finally breaks orbit.

∞

Terra looks out the window of the transport and rubs her eyes. The day had been long, but with help from Bray, they managed to install new defences around Ultar. The population had nearly quadrupled since the trouble started, so it was vital to get the planet locked down tight.

Bray comes up behind her and rubs her shoulders. 'You look tired.'

She smiles and nods. 'Busy day.'

He sits down beside her and pulls her against his chest. Terra closes her eyes and tucks tightly against him as he runs his hand up and down her arm. 'At least the colony will be safe now. One less thing to worry about.'

Their transport lands just outside the tunnels and Terra wheels her case of equipment down the ramp. The warm sun is a welcome relief after the air conditioned interior of the shuttle. Her boots crunch through the gravel as she approaches the main access door. As soon as the door slides open she knows something is different. She slowly walks into the large hangar and freezes. For the last few months, *Ares* has been a constant fixture in the cavern. Except for test flights, the ship was always here. She stops an Ultaran walking past her. 'Is *Ares* being tested?'

He shakes his head. 'She's gone.'

The man walks away as Bray approaches her. 'Where's *Ares*?'

'Gone apparently.'

'But she's not completed yet. Where's she gone?'

Terra can't find the words to reply. Her throat has closed up — she wouldn't have been able to get the words out anyway, even if she could think of what to say. He did it again. Just like the last time, Gryffin made a decision without stopping to consider how it will affect the people around him.

Bray nudges her arm. 'Hey, you okay?'

She forces a smile on her face. 'Of course. Would you be able to put my equipment away for me? I think I need to lie down. I've got a bit of a headache.'

'You still love him, don't you?'

The question stops her in her tracks. Her feelings for Gryffin are the last thing she wants to talk about right now, especially surrounded by spectators. 'Bray, not now, okay?'

'Please, Terra. I just want the truth. I deserve that much from you.'

'I told you the truth — I have a headache.'

He folds his arms and snorts, earning a puzzled gaze from a technician working behind him. 'That's bull. Stop treating me like an idiot.'

She frowns and steps closer to him. His raised voice is only drawing more spectators. 'Not here.'

He backs away from her. 'Not here. Not now. When then? I'm done putting this conversation off.' He looks down at the ground and shakes his head. 'I thought we had something. Thought you trusted me.'

'Of course I trust you—'

'Are you still in love with Gryffin?'

Everyone in the hangar instantly goes silent at his harshly spoken question. She glances over her shoulder at the personnel intently listening to every word between them. 'I don't want him. What else do you want me to say?'

He puts his hands on his hips as he paces the empty floor in front of her. 'I saw your reaction when you noticed *Ares* had left.'

'What reaction?'

He lowers his head. 'Please, Terra, I'm not blind. You were heartbroken.' He stops and waves an arm at their audience. 'Everyone in this room probably saw what you can't admit.'

Terra attempts a laugh, which just makes thing worse. 'Bray, this is ridiculous.'

He turns to face her and leans on the large tool cabinet behind him. 'You know, I couldn't agree more. Everyone on this base can see the truth, except you. I'm partly to blame. I knew the truth, but I guess I was trying to hide from it.' He looks down at his boots and frowns. 'I can't keep lying to myself.' He looks back up at her. 'And you can't either.'

The uncomfortable silence stretches on for a few minutes. Terra's first instinct is to push the lie with him. Tell him that he's seeing something that isn't there. She glances around the room and it hits her. Bray is right. They can all see it. She looks back at Bray and her stomach drops. She can't lose him. Can't be without him. His strength is the only thing that keeps her going from one day to the next. She can't survive losing Gryffin and Bray. But, if she tells him the truth, he'll leave. Their relationship will be dead before it's had a proper chance to develop.

If she lies to him, and he somehow believes her, the damage will be done. She has to tell him and hope he can accept her. 'Yes.'

Even though the word is whispered and barely audible, he flinches as if he's been struck. 'For how long?'

Terra wraps her arms around herself and shakes her head. 'I guess I never really stopped.' She meets his eyes and the pain is clear in his hazel eyes. 'I never meant to hurt you, Bray. I really didn't think I'd ever see him again.'

He pushes away from her and rests his hand on the top of the cabinet. He lowers his head and doesn't say a word for a few uncomfortable seconds. Some of their spectators move away. Watching an argument may provide some entertainment, but a relationship being torn apart is a different matter.

'I can't be with you, Terra.' He slowly turns to face her. 'I should have stopped this months ago.' He laughs harshly. 'Hell, I probably shouldn't even have started it. I'll hitch a ride back to *Perses* in the morning.'

Terra quickly approaches him. 'Wait, Bray. This doesn't have to end.'

He gently pushes her hands off his arm. 'Of course it does. How can we continue like this? It's not fair for either of us.' His hands fall to his sides. 'I can't share you.' He kisses her quickly on the forehead and leaves the hangar.

17

The rain quickly soaks through Bray's clothes and chills his skin. Yet again, his brother has managed to mess things up for him. It doesn't matter where he is, even freshly back from the dead he can still manage to ruin Bray's life. Gryffin doesn't deserve someone like Terra. Nomad barely accept women on their ships. How can the leader of a group like that know anything about how to treat her? The robot reject will tear her apart again and push her aside when he's finished.

Bray really cares about Terra. Cares about her too much for his own good. Since he first delivered food to her when she was a prisoner on *Perses*, he's been interested. But he was just fooling himself. It could never work. How could it when there were three people in the relationship and has been since the start? He didn't mean to have an argument in the hangar. He had even planned a romantic meal for her when they got back. Tonight was meant to be just for the two of them. An attempt to put all the madness from the last few weeks behind them, but it wasn't to be.

Ever since his brother arrived back on the scene, he's noticed the change in Terra. She has been over attentive with him. Not that he is complaining about the attention, he just wishes it had been about him and not his brother.

He stomps through countless muddy puddles as he storms away from the base. There's a supply run heading out to rendezvous with *Perses* in the morning and he'll be on it. Sayber is going to have one hell of an I told you so to dish out when he sees Bray. His captain said from the beginning he was playing with fire by hooking up with Gryffin's woman, but he thought he knew better. Yeah, well that backfired on him, big time.

He fully expects to spend the next few weeks being taunted by the rest of the Hunter crew. Serves him right for being an idiot. He stops at the edge of the lake and stares out over the water. The cold rain seeps into his clothes, but he doesn't care. He'd prefer the cold than the humiliation waiting for him.

He brushes soaked hair out of his eyes. Stupidly, he thought once Gryffin left, the problem would go with him. As soon as he saw Terra's face he knew their relationship was over. There was no point trying to work through it. She was in love with Gryffin. Bray knows she cares about him, but it's not love. Maybe, if Gryffin didn't come back, their relationship could have gone that way. He shouts and kicks at the mud with his boot.

Even though he knows his mother would disapprove of his reaction to his brother, he doesn't care. Gryffin is the reason he had to grow up without her in his life. When she died, so did his old life. He went from being in a stable family to being an orphan overnight. His parents were only on that transport because they heard a rumour someone resembling his brother had been seen. Just like every other time, they dropped everything and chased after a ghost. If not for his brother, they wouldn't have been on the transport when it crashed. There weren't even any bodies for him to bury.

That was on his brother — end of story.

He marches back through the rain to the base, bursts through the door to his room and straight to his unit. After booking a place on the supply transport, he tears off his clothes and steps into the shower. He can't believe he actually used to respect Gryffin. All the time working for Avoca on *Perses* had been spent studying the Nomad leader. The whole thing had been a complete waste of time. As far as he's concerned, his brother should have stayed dead.

∞

'You're kidding, right?'

Roman throws the tablet on the table with more force than he intended. Terra catches it before it bounces off the end and onto the stone floor.

'Proof is right in front of you. The Foundation announced it last week.'

Terra quickly reads through the data and the anger slowly builds in her body. Bray, Lucan, and Aleena look at her, waiting patiently for her to explain. 'If this report is correct, the Foundation have stated they have a new, exciting programme that will solve the prison overcrowding.'

Lucan snorts. 'There wouldn't be a prison problem if it wasn't illegal to walk on the wrong side of the road.'

'It's not quite that bad, Lucan,' Terra argues, with less conviction than she feels. She wouldn't put it past them to pass a ridiculous law like that. 'Anyway, they claim to have the ability to remove or block the violent tendencies that made the prisoners a threat in the first place. The rehabilitated prisoners can then be put to work as... well, reading between the lines, any job that the main law abiding populace can't be bothered doing. Their main purpose, however, will be to act as security for the Outer Sector colonists as they...'

'As they what?' Aleena asks.

Terra blows out a breath. 'As they provide the resources the population of Earth require. The locals will be working for the new colonies the Foundation will set up. Their new cyborg army will keep the 'lawless Outer Sector peasants under control.' Their words, not mine.' She drops the tablet back on the table. 'Nice. I knew they were capable of some questionable acts, but this... this is horrendous.'

Roman slumps back in his chair and sighs loudly. 'Bray, is what they're claiming possible?'

He nods solemnly. 'Theoretically. Gryffin said they didn't actually manage to pull it off though. The main control implant fails and kills the poor sod it's fitted to. If they've announced this, they must have found a way to stop that flaw.'

'Or they haven't, and they're bluffing,' Roman suggests.

'Do you think the Foundation still needs him?' Terra silently chastises herself for asking the question. It's a valid one, but she still wishes someone else had asked it rather than her.

Bray looks her straight in the eyes as he responds. 'Gut feeling, yes. Once they figure out the control implant, they can create their obedient and deadly army.'

'Perfect way of emptying Foundation prisons,' Lucan grumbles.

'It's a win-win for them.' Roman rubs a hand along his jaw. 'If the Foundation populace believe what's written here, they have no reason to complain. They're promising new, state of the art colonies, hardworking staff to provide the resources they need, and an unstoppable army to protect them. On the surface, it will appeal to the populace.'

'Wow,' Lucan mutters as he's reading through the rest of the report. 'I have to get the name of their publicist. The procedure sounds like a second chance at freedom for these prisoners. The fortunate convicts will be offered a pioneering procedure that will rid them of their predisposition for violence. In truth, they'll be forced to have implants just like Gryffin and the Commander.'

Roman leans forward and rests his head on his hands. 'One thing

I don't understand. What's so different about Gryffin? How is he still alive?'

Lucan takes a deep breath before he answers, 'I honestly haven't got the foggiest. We've all checked every test result stored on *Ares*, but we couldn't find anything. It would have been helpful if he'd stayed on Ultar long enough to help us work it out.'

'Balfe couldn't figure it out either,' Bray says. 'He thought the subjects were too young. That's why they're using older prisoners. Once the Scientist found out I was Gryffin's brother, he wanted to fit it to me. Thought if it worked on him it might work on me.' He rubs the skin next to his facial implant and grimaces. 'Glad that didn't happen.'

Out of instinct, Terra reaches to take his hand under the table, but stops herself just in time. After spending so much time with him, she knows he struggles with what her father did to him. The implants may not be to the same extent as Gryffin's, but they deeply affect him, both physically and mentally.

Roman takes the tablet from Lucan and shuts it down. 'Nothing we can do about it.'

'What do you mean?' Aleena exclaims. 'Of course there is. We have all the data from Gryffin and Bray.'

'We're locals, Terra and Roman included.' Lucan smirks and leans back in his chair. 'We're all classified as being from the Outer Sector. In Foundation eyes, that rates us at the same level as an animal. No one is going to believe a damn word any of us say.'

'Lucan's right,' Roman confirms. 'Unless we have some physical proof of their intentions and can somehow transmit that information to Earth, not only will they get away with this, they'll also look like heroes for doing it.'

'We can clear the prisons on this side of the border.'

Roman rubs his jaw and frowns. 'Go on, Bray.'

'Well, there are what, about four prison moons just at the edge of the border. If they're empty, the Foundation will have a hard time hitting their quota.'

'That still leaves three within Earth's reach, but they're for less violent crimes. Their whole campaign centres around assimilating the other prisoners. What are you suggesting?'

Bray glances sideways at Terra. 'I'm leaving tomorrow to meet with *Perses*.' Terra manages to keep her expression stoic as every face in the room turns towards her. 'I'd need to clear it with Sayber first, but I think the Hunters could do it.'

Lucan frowns. 'Bit of a risk with no layout.'

Bray smiles. 'Between the Hunter fleet, I'd say there are at least thirty ex-inmates, myself included. I'll talk to Avoca before I leave. He's familiar with the largest of the moons. It's the one he broke me out of.'

'What would you do with the prisoners?' Terra asks. She's not sure releasing violent criminals into the Sector is such a great idea on top of the Foundation threat.

'Let them join the group.'

She stares in horror at him. 'You can't be serious.'

'Of course I am. I thought this group is all about our common enemy. Can't say they'd have much love for the Foundation.'

Roman looks over at Aleena. Terra has noticed that he regularly seeks her opinion on complicated situations like this. She knows this Sector better than anyone. He'd be foolish to ignore her counsel.

'The Foundation's definition of violent differs greatly to ours. I believe these people would appreciate the second chance offered by the Hunters over the one offered by the Foundation. Can we really afford to turn away any assistance?'

Roman places his hands on the table. 'Very well. Bray, talk to Sayber and do what you have to. I'll let Gryffin know what we're planning.'

'I wouldn't hold your breath for a response,' Lucan says. 'Gryffin isn't a fan of keeping in touch.'

Roman pushes his chair back and stands up. 'He's going to have to get used to working with us. Dismissed.'

Terra quietly watches as Bray leaves the room without a backwards glance.

∞

Bray takes one last look around the room that's been his home for nearly the last year. A part of him will miss it, but he's looking forward to getting back to *Perses*. When he put the call in to Sayber, he was half expecting his captain to refuse his request. Finding out that your second-in-command is also working for the Foundation, is reason enough for Sayber to kill him. Even though Sayber told him regularly over the months that he'd overlook the error in judgement, he was still relieved to hear the verbal confirmation.

He shuts the door behind him and his old life. Any memories of Terra will stay in the room. He can't afford to be off his game when he returns to *Perses*. Bray walks through the tunnels and drops his bag in the transport that will reunite him with *Perses*, then goes to talk to Avoca.

His relationship with Avoca is a little strained after the Gryffin being his brother revelation, but he still owes the man his life. If not for him, he could very well be on the list for rehabilitation by the Foundation. The two implants he has are bad enough. Even the thought of something metal in his head, controlling him, turns his stomach.

He finds Avoca tending to his vegetable patch outside the small cottage he's now calling home. After events at the Port, Avoca immediately stepped down, handed his ship to Lucan and assimilated into Ultaran life. The man is struggling with the ghosts of his actions, and knows redemption is out of reach.

He looks up and smiles as Bray approaches. 'It's so good to see you, Brayden. I was just thinking that it's been a few days since we spoke.'

'Got a minute?'

He nods and leans his shovel against the fence. 'Of course. Come in.'

Avoca leads him into the kitchen and sits on the wooden seat. Bray sits opposite him and looks at the picture of Avoca's wife and family in the centre of the table. Avoca's penance is living the rest of his life without his family. They probably think he's dead. Whether he died a hero or a traitor he doesn't know. It depends what spin the Foundation put on it. 'I'm re-joining *Perses*.'

Avoca looks down at his hands and nods slowly. 'I'm not surprised.' He looks up at him again. 'May I ask, why now?'

'Just time to go. Did you see the latest from the Foundation?'

Avoca blows out a breath. 'I thought I had seen the worst from them. I truly cannot believe they can stoop to an all new low.'

'I've spoken to Sayber. The Hunters are going to go for the prisons before the Foundation does.'

Avoca frowns. 'They'll be prepared for that. No doubt, some of the still functioning tests subjects are there at this moment. I'm not questioning your abilities, Bray, but you shouldn't doubt the Foundation's either. If they haven't fixed the fatal malfunction in the new cyborgs, losing your brother will be a big and very unwelcome hit. They may even target you as a second option.'

Bray inwardly grimaces at that thought. 'We can handle it. I know the layout of the prison you got me out of. Do you know anything about the other ones?'

Avoca frowns as he stares at the wooden table top. 'I believe I can recall some details. I'll compile what I can remember and send it to you later today.'

'Thanks. We'll take anything you have.' He pushes his chair back and gets to his feet. 'I've got a transport to catch. You going to be okay?'

Avoca stands up and pats Bray on the back. 'I'm content.

Concentrate on yourself and your crew. I know I've let you down, Bray.'

Bray shakes his head. 'It's done.'

'Not for me. I was so caught up in trying to put right what the project was doing, I failed to think about how it would affect you. I cannot apologise enough for that.'

'You got me out of prison. All the rest doesn't matter.'

Avoca smiles as he walks with Bray to the door. 'If that's the truth, why are you still blaming your brother for what happened? Have you not been listening to a word I've said to you about the project and his unwilling participation?'

'I'm leaving now. The last thing I want to do is have another fight about this. Every time you mention him, we fall out.'

'Very well.' He stops at the gate and gives Bray an awkward hug. 'Please do not underestimate the Foundation. I think of you as a son and I've lost too much to this project. I don't want to lose you too.'

Bray nods and walks away from his mentor.

'Sir, there has to be someone else?'

Roman lowers onto the seat beside Terra. 'I know it's going to be difficult—'

'Difficult! That's an understatement.' She rises to her feet and paces the stone floor.

He doesn't say anything for a moment as she angrily storms back and forth in front of him. 'You're the most suitable candidate. The satellite orbiting Juda is vital to us. If it's not working, the Foundation can occupy that entire area and we'd never know. It should only take a few hours to repair.'

She stops pacing and crosses her arms. 'That's not what I have a problem with. Sending me to *Ares* after that is what I'm objecting to.'

While he can understand her reluctance to see Gryffin again, the good of the group comes before her personal feelings. If that means an awkward meeting with Gryffin, then so be it. 'All I'm asking you to do is land your transport in *Ares* and let the Nomad unload the supplies. You don't even have to set foot on her if you don't want to.'

She slumps into the chair in front of him. 'It's the time element, sir. We have enough to deal with thanks to the Foundation. I don't have time to go on a wild goose chase to track down someone who doesn't want anything to do with us. He's made his decision. If he wants to turn his back on the colonies, let him.'

'I never mentioned convincing Gryffin to help us.'

She looks up at him. 'Yes, you did.'

'No, I didn't. I asked you to deliver the supplies. Terra, what's really going on here?'

'Nothing, sir. I'm fine.'

He can't help laughing. 'You're less than convincing, Commander. You see, for the last few months, you've been impersonating someone who's not miserable and doing a lousy job at it.'

'I'm not miserable.'

'And you're not a good liar, either. I thought we were close. You used to talk to me.'

'I'd talk to you if there was something to talk about.'

'Oh really. What about Bray?'

Colour touches her cheeks. 'He missed *Perses*.'

'The truth, Terra.'

She examines her hands and shrugs. 'He wanted to leave. That's all there is to it. Really, there's nothing to worry about. I admit, what happened on the freighter affected me for a while, but I'm fine now.'

He grunts, not in the slightest bit convinced by her response. It was clear there was something meaningful between Bray and Terra. For the past few months, he rarely saw one without the other too far behind. She'll never admit it, but he knows Gryffin's sudden reappearance is to blame. He can't fault Bray for wanting nothing to do with the situation. Still being in love with a ghost is one thing, but with his reappearance, the dynamic altered significantly. 'You know, Gryffin's not turning his back on everyone. He's still working with them, trying to put right what the Foundation did.'

'What he did, you mean. If he really cared that much, he'd be working closely with us.'

'Terra, you know he couldn't have stopped what happened. You really need to give him a chance. He fought to come back here and try to fix some of what happened.'

'Not everything can be glued back together.'

Roman gives up fighting this losing battle. She needs a swift kick and she's not alone. Gryffin could do with a reminder of what's really important at the moment. Everyone sticking together is the main priority. He sits up straight in his chair and pushes his shoulders back. 'No more discussion, Commander. Fix the satellite then rendezvous with *Ares*. We intercepted a weapons supply run last week. I'm sure they would welcome some of the cases.'

'But, sir—'

'It's not a request — it's an order, Commander. I want you off the surface within the hour. Dismissed.'

He focuses on the reports in front of him as Terra marches from the room. He hates having to take such a firm line with her, but he doesn't have much of a choice. Her feelings for Gryffin and how he acted on the freighter are threatening to destroy her. If she can't get over it, she won't be much good to him or the group. Everyone needs to be firing on all cylinders if they're to have a chance. There's no room for uncontrolled emotions.

He rubs his forehead and sighs. He certainly has to include himself in that. Even though he's tried to distance himself from Gryffin and the fact they're father and son, he isn't always successful. He barely knows his son, but when he died on the freighter, Roman lost a small piece of himself too. That piece came back along with Gryffin. He doesn't want to get carried away though. Even if he does find the courage to tell Gryffin the truth, he knows without a doubt that the Nomad leader will never accept him.

∞

Terra clings on to the arms of her chair as the transport attempts to lose their tail. The ship shudders violently as it is hit from behind. 'Still no response from *Ares*.'

The pilot, Ryan, grimaces. 'Not what I want to hear, Commander. Our guest doesn't seem to be getting the hint.'

Terra grunts as her head knocks against the side of the shuttle. She checks the radar in every direction. No sign of *Ares*. Trust this mission to go wrong. The satellite repair went without a hitch, but their luck changed when they got to within an hour of the rendezvous point. The Rogue scout came out of nowhere and is refusing to leave. Terra grips the handles of the transports gun and fires. The smaller vessel dodges and returns fire. Where is *Ares* when they actually need her? The battleship could easily take down the Rogues with one shot.

Terra opens the emergency channel again. The frequency is reserved for the group and shouldn't attract any more unwanted attention. 'This is Commander Rush. We're being pursued by a Rogue shuttle. Require immediate assistance.' The message and their coordinates plays over and over on the channel. Hopefully, *Ares* will pick it up as they near the meeting point. As much as she dreads seeing Gryffin again, she's not going to say no to his help.

Ryan throws the ship to the left, but the smaller vessel sticks close to them. 'It's no good, Commander. We're fighting a loosing battle out in the open.'

Terra targets the ship again and manages to hit it, but it keeps coming. 'Take us down. Maybe we can lose them on the surface.'

Ryan doesn't bother to respond. The ship dives quickly. The uninhabited dwarf planet is deeply forested and should give them a little cover. They enter the atmosphere and Ryan curses loudly.

'What now?'

'We're about to enter the mother of all storms. Hope you brought your waterproofs, Commander.'

Just another thing to add to their fun. Even though she knows it's futile, she checks the radar. Still nothing from *Ares*. The ship rocks and jolts as it joins with the storm. Rain beats against the ship as Ryan guides it through the mountains while fighting against the raging wind. Terra targets the Rogue ship through her eyepiece. It helps to distract her from the sickening motion of the shuttle. Her teeth rattle in her jaw and she swallows the rising bile. She searches for the Rogue ship, but can't see it anywhere. 'We've lost them!' she shouts at Ryan through the sound of the storm around them.

'Not for long. This area should have been clear.' He jerks the controls to the right steering the ship around a large outcropping.

'They've ramped up patrols in the last few weeks. Chayse thinks they may have heard about Gryffin's reappearance.'

Ryan snorts. 'Suppose with the Nomad still scattered through the Sector, now would be the perfect time to finish them for good.' He struggles with the controls as he speeds up to try and keep their lead on the other ship. 'Taking Gryffin out of the picture at this stage will keep the Nomad unorganised and separated.'

Terra agrees. Targeting a small transport vessel is a lot easier than going after a ship the size of *Ares*. It's just a pity the Rogues don't know how close they actually are to *Ares*. Not close enough to help them, unfortunately.

Ryan aims for the nearest mountain. The Rogue ship reappears and fires on them. Terra curses as the round hits their auxiliary engine. The black smoke billowing from the engine dies away as Ryan reroutes power to the other engines. Their pursuer ducks and dives through the terrain. The pilot is struggling to keep up with them. The modified Ultaran transport easily out manoeuvres them. If they can just keep them out of the open, they might have a chance.

Terra returns fire as Ryan speeds through the ravine. 'They're right on our back, Commander!'

She opens the secure channel and relays her message with a little more force even though it's a futile act. If *Ares* were within range, they would have been in touch by now.

She projects her building anger at Gryffin towards the Rogue ship. Her next attack hits home. The ship falters as her round hits its port engine. The Rogue ship collides with the steep rock wall at the edge of the valley, but it doesn't stop firing. Her elation is short lived. The final shot from the Rogue transport hits their ship with a deafening thump and they fall.

∞

'Sir, we're receiving a distress call.'

Gryffin continues to work on his bike as he addresses Desyl. 'Nomad?'

'No, sir.'

'Ignore it.'

'But, sir, it's a transport from *Infinity*. Commander Rush sent the transmission.'

If Desyl says anything else, Gryffin doesn't hear it. He leaps to his feet and instead of using the stairs, jumps up to grab onto the walkway above him and pulls himself up onto the next level. Gryffin races to the command deck and storms up to the helm. 'Where are they?'

'Twenty minutes from our location, sir. They're being pursued by an unidentified transport — not Hunter or Nomad.'

'Rogues,' Gryffin growls. 'I want us there now. Any reply from the transport?'

Desyl shakes his head. 'The message has been transmitting for six minutes. I—'

Gryffin suddenly turns to face Desyl, startling him. 'Six minutes! Why the hell was the message ignored for six minutes?'

'We were carrying out a routine test of the long range comms system. It's only just come back on line.'

Gryffin closes his hand around Desyl's neck. 'The ship is in better condition than when Rayde took her. Who ordered the test?'

Desyl pauses so Gryffin gives him a not so gently shake. 'Roman, sir. All systems were tested regularly when on Ultar.' He clenches his jaw. What the hell was Roman thinking? *Ares* is a Nomad ship. She's got damn all to do with him and his Foundation rules.

'Sir! Let the Commander go.'

Gryffin blinks and looks at the Nomad standing at the top of the steps. The young man has his gun in his hand and looks willing to use it. Gryffin turns his attention to Desyl, horrified to see his metal hand around his neck. He lets go of Desyl and steps back as his first officer crumples to the floor, gasping for breath. The officer helps Desyl to his feet and glares at Gryffin before returning to his post. All eyes remain on him as he stands frozen to the spot.

He glances down at Desyl and remembers what started the argument in the first place. He opens a ship-wide channel. 'This is Gryffin. I'm only going to say this once so everyone damn well better be listening. Forget any standing orders, any procedures or testing, anything you did or were told to do while working with Roman. *Ares* is a Nomad ship. If you've got a problem with that, you know where the airlock is.' He slams his hand against the control to close the channel.

Gryffin forces himself to sit down. Routine testing of systems is a luxury they can't afford. It's always been reserved for Ultar or, in worst case scenarios when they've had no other choice due to malfunctions. How *Ares* is run has nothing to do with that man and his Foundation policies. His routine testing has put Terra in danger. The unfamiliar helpless feeling closes his throat, just like his collar did. He squeezes his eye shut as the tight feeling moves down to take a firm grip of his chest. To add to his fun, the headache he's had for a few days ramps up to a full blown dagger of pain behind his eye.

He opens his eye and catches Desyl looking away quickly. Desyl clears his throat a few times, but doesn't say anything.

'Have we still got a problem, Commander?'

Desyl turns around. 'Is everything all right, sir?'

'Of course it's not all right. You let the Foundation tell you how to run the ship. What were you thinking?'

Desyl's shoulders slump as he rubs the back of his neck. 'Roman has years of experience on me. I was captain for a few days and managed to embed her hull in a field. I'm not stupid enough to ignore advice from someone who knows what they're talking about.'

'Even if it's Foundation advice?'

Desyl pushes his hand through his short blond hair. 'Yes, sir. And Roman took advice from the Hunters, Nomad, and the Ultarans. We were all working together, sir.'

'Sounds cosy.' He links in with the cargo bay. 'I want a transport ready to leave in ten minutes.' He shuts down the link before he gets a reply.

'What are you planning, sir? Do you want me to get some teams together?'

'*Ares* can handle any in orbit. I'll go to the surface and deal with survivors.'

'Sir, with all due respect, you should stay on board.'

Gryffin's jaw cracks. 'You going to try and confine me to the ship?'

Desyl quickly shakes his head. 'No, sir.'

'Right answer. Conversation is finished.'

He ignores Desyl as the commander hovers on the command deck. Gryffin doesn't care about antiquated Nomad laws anymore. It's not like they've done the Nomad any favours so far. He's the captain and if he wants to leave the ship to shoot some Rogues, then that's damn well what he's going to do — especially if they're attacking Terra. 'What the hell is she doing here?'

'She's part of the supply transport from Ultar.'

'I said what is *she* doing here?'

Desyl shakes his head. 'I don't know, sir. According to the distress call it's just Terra and a pilot. Without checking with Ultar, I can't say why she specifically was sent.'

He vaguely remembers Desyl mentioning a transport will be meeting with them to drop off supplies. His pride wanted to cancel the delivery, but they didn't have a choice. With the reputation of the Nomad in tatters, there's nowhere else for them to go. They'd starve without the shipment. If he'd known Terra was on the ship he would have allowed pride to take over. Of all the people to need rescuing again, why did it have to be her?

Terra opens her eyes, wincing as the pain sears through her head. Her last memory is of Ryan losing control and the ship crashing after it was hit. At least she took out the Rogue ship before they went down. She tests her limbs, relieved when everything moves as it should — although with twinges of pain. Her harness pulls painfully against her body, but it did its job by keeping her firmly in her seat.

'Ryan.' She clears her throat and tries again. 'Can you hear me?' Finally, she's rewarded by a cough and a groan from his seat. 'Hang on.' She tries to unclasp her harness, but the damaged catch won't release. She grunts as she fights with the metal catch, burying her rising panic. Whoever shot them down will no doubt investigate the scene. They have to get out of the ship before that happens.

She freezes when footsteps echo through the ship. Someone has entered the back of the transport. Her breath quickens as a second set of footsteps follows soon after. Crates and boxes are moved as the intruders search for survivors. Licking her dry lips, she ignores the commotion as her hand creeps towards her weapon on her thigh.

A scuffle erupts behind her chair and she shrieks as a man's body strikes the console in front of her, followed closely by a second. Paralysed in fear, a dozen scenarios run through her mind, but none involve the person who enters next. Gryffin stops in front of the men and shoots each in the head. Once satisfied they're not getting up again, he crouches down in front of her. His purple eyes glow brightly in the gloomy transport.

Her shoulders slump as she blows out a breath. 'I've never been so glad to see you.'

He clears his throat as he scrutinises her. 'You hurt?'

'No, but I can't get my harness off. How did you find us?'

He ignores her question as he tears the buckle open to release the blood back into her limbs. 'Stay put.' He steps over the wreckage to the injured pilot. 'What's his name?' he asks, his voice thick and deep.

'Ryan, his name is Ryan.'

Gryffin crouches down beside him and examines his wounds. A large piece of the console has gone through his chest and out the back of the chair. 'Ryan, I'm Gryffin. I need you to close your eyes.'

Doing as instructed, Ryan squeezes his eyes shut. Bloody foam bubbles out of his mouth as he desperately tries to breathe. Gryffin places his metal hand on Ryan's chest and leans over. 'This will help with the pain.' He leans closer and speaks into Ryan's ear. Terra has no idea what he says but a small smile spreads across Ryan's face. As he's talking, a stream of electricity runs down Gryffin's arm and into Ryan's body. Before Terra can react, Gryffin pulls his hand away and stands up. 'Time to go.'

'You killed him.'

He pulls her upright and drags her towards the back hatch. 'It was either that or let him drown in his own blood. He was beyond saving.'

'Yeah, but—'

'But nothing, Terra,' he snaps. 'More Rogue ships just entered orbit. We have to leave now!' He grabs her arm and literally hauls her out into the forest. The rain instantly soaks through her clothes and plasters her hair to her face. She brushes the wet locks aside and stumbles after him for a few minutes until he suddenly stops and throws her over his shoulder in a fireman's lift. Once she's on his shoulder, he continues to race through the trees as if she wasn't even there.

Bouncing along over his shoulder isn't the best feeling in the world. Terra swallows repeatedly and puts all her effort into not being sick down the back of his jacket. She can't tell how long they've been on the move, but at least there doesn't seem to be anyone following them. Gryffin slows and places her back on her feet. She wobbles slightly, leaning against a tree to steady herself. The world spins along with her stomach. Gryffin quietly scans their surroundings. His hair hangs in wet locks over his glowing purple eyes and the red from his implant shines.

'We being followed?' she asks.

He shakes his head. '*Ares* will get rid of the rest of them. They'll come back when it's clear. We just have to lay low until then.'

'You mean we're staying on the surface? Without any back up!'

He glances at her as he reloads his gun. He gestures towards a large outcropping about two miles ahead of them. 'She'll collect us from there. There's a cave half way up the north face. We should be safe.'

'How can you be sure no one is up there waiting for us? Surely it's the obvious place for us to hide?'

'There's no way of getting up.' He walks away without explaining further. She doesn't even want to know what he has in mind. With nothing else to do, she trudges after him through the cold, dark and very wet forest.

∞

Gryffin wasn't lying when he said there's no way of getting up.

Staring up at the sheer cliff in front of them, she can't see any way of scaling the vertical face of rock disappearing into the darkness above them. 'Right, so where exactly is this cave?'

'About sixty feet up the side.'

'How do you intend on getting up there?'

He doesn't even bother looking at her as he answers. 'Stay there. I'll be back for you in a minute.' Before she can say anything, he grabs onto the rock face with his metal hand and climbs. She can only stare open mouthed as he uses his arm to haul himself up the smooth cliff face. He disappears from view and a minute later a rope is thrown down to her.

She ties it around her waist, wincing as the rope presses against her bruised side, and in next to no time is standing in front of him in the cave. Her head brushes the cave roof as she slowly straightens. The cave curves slightly to the right, which should offer them some shelter from the cold wind that drives the freezing rain deeper into her bones. 'Don't suppose you squirrelled anything else away up here?'

He bends down and pulls some energy bars and a bottle of water from a bag on the rock floor. 'We should only be here for a few hours. This'll do until *Ares* comes back.'

Terra takes a bar from him and swallows a mouthful of water. 'How did you know about this place? You come to this world often?'

He crouches down in the mouth of the cave and surveys the forest below. 'We scouted it a few days ago. It's handy to have somewhere to lay low if needed.'

'So is this common practice for the Nomad? Have you got hiding places all over the Sector?'

He nods. 'Saved our necks more than once.'

Terra can't help but be impressed. While it seems like a tedious and possibly futile effort, in her current situation she certainly can't argue. She wraps her arms around herself as a shiver works through her body. If the cold isn't bad enough, every inch of her body feels battered and bruised. No doubt she'll have impressive bruising from her harness. An image of Ryan slumped in his seat enters her mind. She can't complain about a few bruises — at least she's alive. In an attempt to take her mind off her cold and sore body, she turns to face Gryffin. 'You didn't answer my question before, how did you find us?'

'We intercepted your distress call. Got here the same time as another Rogue ship. *Ares* took her down.'

'So, where are the rest of the team from your transport?'

'I came alone.'

Terra stares suspiciously at him. 'Why?'

'What the hell does it matter? You sent out the call and now I'm here. I'll put you back in the damn transport if it'll shut you up.'

She holds up her hands. 'Okay. I was just asking. Why do you always have to be on the defensive?'

'Why can't you ever just say 'thank you'?'

Terra pauses and wraps her arms around herself again. 'You're right. Thank you,' she mutters.

He doesn't respond as he moves back to the entrance of the cave and sits down in the rain. Clearly, he wants to be as far from her as possible. She moves around the corner and out of his field of vision. Terra slowly lowers herself to the ground and huddles against the smooth rock wall. She takes off her sodden jacket to stop the chill running through her body, but her shirt is soaked too. At this rate, she'll be dead from hypothermia before *Ares* comes back to get them.

'You okay?'

She jumps slightly and looks up at Gryffin. She must be not quite herself if he somehow crept up on her without her noticing. She nods quickly. 'I'm just a little cold.'

He frowns as a well-timed shiver proves her point. Gryffin pulls off his jacket and hands it to her. 'Put this on.'

'I don't need it.'

He crouches down in front of her. 'You'd prefer to freeze?'

He's right. Her pride will be useless if she's only going to harm herself. She takes the offered coat from him and wraps it over her shoulders, but the warm leather has no effect on the cold.

'Any injuries?'

'Seriously, I'm fine. You don't have to babysit me.'

'Take off your shirt.'

'Excuse me?'

'Your ship crashed. I want to check for injuries.'

She pulls back and crosses her arms. 'I'm perfectly capable of checking myself.'

'You're almost as stubborn as a Nomad,' he says as he pulls his t-shirt over his head.

'What exactly are you doing?'

'Whether you like it or not, you can't get warm without me. I didn't waste fuel and ammunition saving you just for you to die of the cold.' He sits beside her and leans back against the wall. 'I'm just going to hold you against me so you don't freeze to death. Nothing more.'

She quietly studies him for a moment, then nods. She'll do anything to feel warm again, even if it means being close to Gryffin.

Terra peels her wet clothes off and lays them out, not that they'll be doing much drying. Once finished, she probes her sore ribs and hisses in pain. Gryffin looks at her and his frown deepens. 'What?'

'I think I have a few bruised ribs.'

'Wouldn't be surprised. It was an impressive crash. You can get checked out properly on *Ares*.'

Gryffin gestures for her to sit in between his legs. She manoeuvres herself into the spot and instantly feels the warmth coming off his chest.

He hesitantly wraps his big arms around her and pulls her close so her back is pressed firmly to his chest. She nearly moans in pleasure as his warm skin touches her icy back. Her teeth chatter loudly as she struggles to get warm.

He suddenly moves her to sit on his legs so most of her weight is on his flesh thigh. 'Curl up against my chest.'

'Sorry?'

'Pull your legs to your chest, tuck your arms in and lie on me.'

She does as she's told and snuggles against his warm flesh. The hard metal on his chest presses against her as Gryffin curls his big body around her, effectively encasing her in a very cosy Gryffin blanket. Just when she thinks it can't get any nicer, his temperature increases. His breathing seems to become strained and she can feel his body tensing.

'Are you alright?'

'I'm fine.'

'Why did you leave Ultar without saying goodbye?'

'Rest.'

'But—'

'Rest,' he orders, ending any possibility of a conversation. She shuts her mouth and snuggles in against his hard chest, just listening to the sound of his heart beating. There is no chance she'll be able to sleep and isn't even going to attempt it. Sitting on him with bare skin touching may not affect him in the slightest, but she can't say the same for herself.

She moves her face towards his chest to stop the buckles of the knife holster strapped to his bicep from digging in to her — then stops moving. Even that small action awakens her body. Her chest feels like it's going to explode. Everywhere his skin is touching hers tingles, like the nerve endings are on fire.

After holding her position rigidly for a few minutes, she allows herself to relax slightly. It is either that or endure muscle cramp from tensing her limbs. His arms loosen slightly as she makes herself comfortable, then encase her again when she settles. She's angry with her body for not getting on board with her emotions. She's not meant to have these feelings for him. She can't allow herself to. Terra takes a deep breath and instantly regrets it as his familiar and intoxicating scent adds more torture to her predicament.

It feels like she's been here for hours, but guesses it's only been a few minutes. She closes her eyes, and lets Gryffin's warmth work into her icy skin and sore muscles.

∞

Gryffin grits his teeth and puts all his energy into not frying Terra. He thought his body heat would help her, but the shock of the crash mixed with the cold and rain had done a real number on her. So, he did the only thing he could think of. He lets a little extra power go to his implants to warm them. A fine balance exists between warming Terra and killing her by releasing too much energy.

He turns his head away from her, hoping to stop her scent from affecting him, but it's not doing any good. This is the last situation he needs right now. They may have been intimate only a few times, but the feeling of her bare skin against his is driving him crazy and he's having a bloody difficult time keeping his body from betraying him. She is the only person he's ever been with, but he can't imagine how anyone else could have such a powerful effect on him. Holding her like this without being able to actually be with her causes a tight feeling in his stomach. Still, anything is better than the hollowness he's had since he left Ultar.

Terra moves slightly then settles again. He resists the urge to open his tightly clenched fists and stroke her skin. Before he can stop them, Terra's words crash into his head. 'I'm with someone else.' He hits his head against the stone behind him. He's such an idiot. He can't have her. The wind howls around the mouth of the cave. The cold air works its way around the corner so, even though he doesn't want to, he holds her tighter against him. She needs him to keep her warm and safe — nothing else.

Besides, after what he did to the colonies and his Nomad, he has no right to any comfort or calm. The only thing he should be focused on is putting his mess right. If he can somehow bring his... the Nomad back together, they can protect the colonies again under Chayse's leadership. It's not going to wipe the slate clean, but it's all he can do.

He sucks in a deep breath and slowly exhales through his mouth. He's wound so tight he feels like he's about to snap. Terra snuggles in closer to him. He bites back groan of pain as she presses against his sensitive metal thigh. Her rear inadvertently rubs against his groin through his boxers. The sensation flies straight to his brain. Stay focused. Stay focused. *Ares* should be back for them in a few hours. Then she would be — damn it. She's going to be stuck on *Ares*.

He clenches his fists even tighter and focuses on the dart of pain as his fingernails tear into his skin. There's no way he can afford to just let her have a transport. Especially not with so many Rogues in the area. That means until they get back to the rest of the fleet, Terra is going to be on *Ares*... at the same time as him... on a ship that's suddenly going to be far too small.

Terra wakes up with a start. Her foggy brain tries to make sense of where she is, but she's still half asleep. A warm body presses tight against her. Terra cuddles in closer, not in any rush to get up.

'Terra, *Ares* is on the way.'

Ares? What's *Ares* doing here?

A metal hand brushes against the side of her face. 'Terra, get dressed. They'll be here in three minutes.'

Suddenly the events come back to her. She's in a cave with Gryffin. She opens her eyes and is met by the man himself, his brow wrinkled as he intently watches her. The soft red and blue glow is coming off his implants again, lighting the dark cave. 'You okay?'

She stretches her stiff limbs and nods. Clearly, her plan to stay awake had failed miserably. 'How long was I asleep?'

'About twenty minutes.'

She's still cold, but not nearly as bad as she was earlier. Gryffin reaches behind him and hands her his t-shirt. 'Put this on, your clothes are ruined.'

Without arguing, she pulls his shirt over her head. The material is warm and dry against her cool skin. He helps her to her feet and she's relieved to see his t-shirt reaches down to cover the tops of her legs. He puts on his trousers and sleeveless jacket, then tucks his gun into its holster. He gathers her in his arms again — presumably to keep her warm rather than out of any form of affection. After a minute or so, she hears *Ares* coming. The sound of her engines gets louder as she breaks the cloud cover and drops out of the night sky. Unlike most ships Terra has seen, there are no lights showing. No landing lights, nothing from the crew quarters. 'Why are there no lights?'

'You can't raid if people can see you coming. We usually go dark for things like this.' The large vessel settles above them and a steel ladder drops down in front of the cave opening. Terra looks in horror at the swaying ladder, dangling about ten feet from the ledge. Gryffin walks to the edge of the cave and looks up, his hair blowing around his face. He signals to someone on the ship before he walks back to her and holds out his hand. 'We're going to have to jump.'

She stares at him in disbelief. 'I can't jump that.'

'You hang on to me and I'll jump.'

She looks down at his hand, out at the ladder and back down at his hand. 'Gryffin—'

'Trust me.'

Just like that, she knows she's going to do it. Like every other time he's told her to trust him. He's never let her down, not in those situations anyway. She meets his eyes and nods. He grabs her around the waist with his flesh hand. 'Wrap your arms around my neck, your legs around my waist and hang on tight. Keep your eyes closed. I promise I won't let you go.'

She silently nods and wraps her arms around him, clenching his leather jacket in her hands for extra anchorage. He lifts her legs up and tucks his shirt around her to keep her covered. His grip around her waist increases as he runs and leaps from the mouth of the cave.

Terra squeezes her eyes shut and feels their bodies flying through the air. They jolt to a stop and Terra swears she hears Gryffin grunt in pain, but his grip never falters.

Not able to stop herself, she opens her eyes and looks down. The bottom of the ladder trails away into darkness below them. 'Look at me, Terra.'

She pulls her gaze from the nothingness below them to his face. His purple eye locks on to her and immediately grounds her.

'Just focus on me. We'll be on board in a minute.'

The sound of voices above her gets louder. Strong hands grab on to her arms. She looks up to see Desyl above her, leaning over the railing. 'Terra, we've got you. Let go of the captain so we can pull you up.'

She is helped over the side and lowered gently to the top deck. Desyl crouches over her and wraps a blanket around her shoulders. 'You okay, Terra?'

She nods, never more grateful to be lying on a cold metal deck than she is at that moment. Terra tightly cocoons herself in the blanket and watches as Gryffin hauls himself onto the deck. He stands and looks at her for a moment before he walks away without a word. He drops down the hatch and disappears from sight, leaving her alone with Desyl.

Desyl frowns and turns to face Terra. He clearly forces a smile onto his face. 'Let's get you cleaned up and into some warm clothes.'

∞

Gryffin shouts and shoves his metal fist through the centre of the training drone. The large machine shudders for a moment before collapsing in a heap on the floor at his feet. Frustrated that his opponent surrendered, he savagely kicks the drone, over and over, until the metal shatters. He spins quickly when he hears footsteps behind him. Desyl raises his hands in surrender as Gryffin levels his gun at him.

'Want to explain what you're doing, sir?'

Gryffin lowers his gun. 'Not a good time.'

'You don't say. Can I ask why another drone is dead?'

'She okay?'

'Terra? Yes, sir. She's in the med bay at the moment being checked over. She's going to be sore for a bit, but it could have been a lot worse.'

'Did you find out anything else about the group that attacked her ship?'

Desyl shakes his head. 'Apart from the fact they're Rogue — nothing.'

'Get three teams ready. I want both ships salvaged.'

'Yes, sir. Where should I put Terra? I mean, she can't stay in the med bay and the general crew quarters probably isn't the best place for her to stay.'

Gryffin forces his metal fist to unclench at the thought of her sleeping anywhere near any of his crew. 'My room. I'll stay in here.'

'But you're the captain. You can't sleep in here.'

'Why not? No point putting someone else out just so I can get an hours sleep.' He turns away and rubs along the side of his chest implant, trying to ease the twinge of pain.

'What's wrong?'

'You have your orders. Get back to work.'

Desyl takes a step closer and shakes his head. 'Not happening.' He pulls a scanner out of his pocket and runs it over Gryffin's body. Not in the mood for company, Gryffin decides to pull the scanner from Desyl and send it on a one-way trip across the room. Desyl looks at the remains of the equipment before he leans back against the wall. 'Anything else you fancy breaking, sir? We don't have much back up or support out here. Broken equipment will be difficult to replace.'

Gryffin raises his eyebrow and silently looks at Desyl. His new second-in-command is as stubborn as Chayse.

'Sir, you don't have to fight me. I'm on your side. I'm just trying to do my job the best way I know how.' Desyl purses his lips and looks up at the ceiling for a moment. 'Sir, I get why you don't trust me.' He snorts and laughs. 'Hell, I seriously doubt I'd be able to trust again if I were you. All I can say is that I'm not Klay. If I have to, I'll spend every minute of my time as your first officer proving that to you. I've got your back, sir, if you'll let me.'

Gryffin lets his head drop and closes his eye. Another person he's been a complete ass to. He never thought about how Desyl is coping with everything. He doesn't even remember thanking him for getting *Ares* back from Klay in the first place. If it wasn't for him, *Ares* could very well have been lost.

Finally feeling in control of himself, he turns around to face him. 'I know you've got my back, Desyl. You've shown me and the Nomad that every single day.' He just doesn't trust himself.

That's basically what it comes down to. He doesn't trust himself, doesn't trust his abilities to get the Nomad back, and doesn't trust that the thing in his head won't take him over again.

The silence stretches on until Gryffin finally shakes his head and turns away. 'Sort Terra out.' He stops a few steps from the broken drone and looks over his shoulder. 'She'll need to be marked. It's not safe for her otherwise.'

Desyl's mouth drops open. 'Sir, she won't be happy about that.'

Gryffin climbs the stairs to the upper level. 'She doesn't have a choice.'

Desyl hurries after him, trying to keep up with his long strides. 'Maybe the request should come from you.'

Gryffin ducks under a support beam in the corridor. 'It is coming from me.'

'No. I mean personally.'

Crew step to the side as he storms past. 'Just tell her.' The last thing he wants to do is go anywhere near her. Being alone with her in the cave was difficult enough without seeing her again. *Ares* had arrived to collect them both too soon and too late. He would have given anything for even five more minutes holding her, protecting her. On the flip side, the longer he was with her, the harder it was for him to let her go again.

Luckily, there is enough going on to keep him busy and well away from her while she is on board. He'll confine her to his room until they meet with the rest of the fleet. Desyl can bring her food and anything else she needs. If he lets Desyl look after her then he doesn't have to see her. He nods to himself as he climbs the stairs to the command platform. It might just work.

∞

'This is some kind of joke, right?'

Desyl shakes his head. The look of unease on his face does nothing to help. 'It's for your own protection. It's protocol for anyone joining the crew, which is what you're doing until we meet the rest of the fleet. Once it's done you'll be protected by the Nomad.'

'So, he ordered you to do his dirty work for him.' That's the bit that's annoying her more than the actual request. The last time she saw Gryffin was when she was pulled back on to *Ares* a few hours ago. He didn't even have the decency to come and see how she is or to make this request — no demand — himself.

He shrugs. 'As you say, he ordered me. He's the captain, I'm not about to ignore his orders. He wants you to see Ryder to get it done by the end of the day.'

'Does he now?' Terra isn't stupid. It's impossible not to notice the tattoos on each of the crew. Black swirling marks cover various different body parts ranging from arms and chests to backs. It doesn't matter where it is, they all have one. Well, all except Gryffin himself who just has his pretty massive griffin. What she didn't know is that the tattoo marked each crew member as Nomad. Although each one is different, there are certain parts of the design unique to the Nomad.

Everyone serving on *Ares* also has purple colouring added, which marks them as being under Gryffin's protection.

Desyl opens the door and gestures for her to follow. 'So, you're telling me the Foundation doesn't have a similar system?'

Terra ducks to avoid hitting her head on the low hatch leading from the med bay. Even after working on *Ares* for months, she still can't help but notice how different the Nomad ship is to any ship she's ever been on before. Foundation ships are light and airy, the corridors are tall and wide, allowing crew to pass through without incident. *Ares*, however, is dark and cramped. They repeatedly have to pause to give room to other crew passing by. More than once, she has to duck to keep the top of her head intact. She has no idea how someone as tall as Gryffin copes.

'Of course we — they do. We each have a miniature data chip embedded in the underside of our arms. It contains all our information.'

Desyl laughs loudly. 'You telling me a tattoo is worse than a chip?' He shakes his head. 'Personally I wouldn't be too keen on any government embedding anything in me, thanks all the same.'

Terra opens her mouth to argue, but can't find a reasonable response. She snaps her mouth shut, infuriated that perhaps Desyl has a point. 'So, if I agree, I'm part of the crew?'

Desyl smirks at her over his shoulder. 'Won that one, didn't I?' A tall Nomad openly stares at Terra as she walks by. He only stops after Desyl glares at him. 'You won't be joining the crew. As you can probably tell, you stand out on *Ares*. Safer for you to stay in your assigned room.'

He climbs a small set of metal stairs and stops at a large door. Her eyes are instantly drawn to the deep impression of a fist in the plating. Only one person she knows could have done that. 'Why are we here?'

Desyl opens the door and steps inside. 'Your room while you're on board.'

She slowly follows him across the threshold and her heart instantly speeds up. She was expecting a small guest room or even just a room with a bunk. Never for one second did she expect to be in this room. 'But this is Gryffin's room.'

Desyl nods. 'He insisted. Don't worry. It's all yours while you're here. The captain will bunk down in the training room.'

'He can't do that.'

Desyl shrugs. 'He doesn't sleep much.' He walks over to a small door against the far wall and turns the light on. 'Besides, it's the only room with a bathroom.' Desyl stands in the centre of the room and shoves his hands in his pockets. 'I'll bring you some food and clean clothes.' He points to the comms panel beside the low bunk. 'You need anything, just call me. Now, about what we discussed earlier. You agreeing?'

She lowers onto the bed, grimacing when she feels the thin, hard mattress. 'No.'

Desyl crosses his arms and his expression darkens. 'We're going to some remote places to find Nomad. Unless you're marked as—'

'His?'

He sighs, suddenly looking like he'd rather cut off body parts than be here having this conversation with her. 'To put it bluntly — yes.'

'So, where is he? Why isn't he here asking himself?'

'I don't know what Foundation captains actually do, but Gryffin is an active member of the crew. He's busy.'

She lets her head drop. 'Of course he's busy.' She has a feeling he'll be pretty busy until they re-join the rest of the fleet.

Desyl's face softens. 'It's the truth, Terra. He's not—'

'Avoiding me,' she finishes. 'I'm not as naive as I look, Desyl. It's very clear what he's doing. What... what exactly are we talking about, tattoo wise?'

'The captain doesn't believe it's necessary to permanently mark your skin. He's suggesting a temporary one you can remove when you get back to *Infinity*.'

Even though the idea of getting a tattoo, temporary or not, doesn't sit well with her, she can't deny the fact that Gryffin is trying to make it as easy on her as possible. She's still not happy, but she supposes she can live with something down her neck. At least with her long hair loose it will be hidden. 'Fine, but if I do this I want him to use me.'

Desyl's face flushes red as his eyebrows shoot up in surprise. 'What?'

'Relax. I mean on the crew, Desyl. I get this done, he puts me in comms. I'm a good officer and he'd be mad to keep me locked up in here.'

His eyebrows head back south and he shakes his head. 'I really don't think the captain will go for that.'

She crosses her arms. 'Tattoo and comms. That's the deal. Your choice.'

'Damn it.'

Smiling widely, Terra lowers herself to sit on her bed again and crosses her legs. 'I'll also need a uniform.'

Cursing her loudly, Desyl leaves and slams the door behind him.

21

Aleena gasps and covers her mouth. 'Is Terra all right?'

Roman nods. 'Ryan wasn't so fortunate. Gryffin said he'll try to recover his body, but until *Ares* gets back to the surface, he won't know if it's possible.'

'What happened?' Lucan asks.

Roman sighs and rubs his eyes. 'Rogues must have got wind about the rendezvous. Either that, or they just got lucky.'

Lucan curses, then smiles apologetically at Aleena. 'Luck has nothing to do with it. I'm not saying Rogues are stupid, but the odds of a ship being in the same area as the transport is slim. We all know it.'

Aleena takes a sip of her water before she speaks. 'Are you suggesting the base is compromised?'

'We'd be fools to not consider it.'

Roman nods and takes a deep breath. 'Lucan is right. The population on the surface has exploded. We have no system, nothing we can use to verify the identity of the refugees.'

'You believe the Foundation or the Rogues have planted a... What is the term?' Aleena asks.

'A mole.'

'Thank you, Lucan. Is that what you believe?'

'I'm just saying we have to be careful.' Roman stands in front of the Sector map on the wall. He points to a location on the map. 'They were on their way to meet *Ares* here when their transport took heavy fire. Terra managed to take it down. Unfortunately, Ryan died when they crash landed.'

'Why didn't *Ares* help sooner?' Lucan asks.

'They got there as fast as they could.' The very abrupt message delivered by Desyl left no doubt in his mind that Gryffin blames Roman for the delay. Gryffin may have a point. Foundation rules and procedures have no place out here. 'Gryffin actually saved Terra from being taken by the Rogues.'

Lucan blows out a breath. 'Terra should be banned from ever leaving the surface again. All she seems to do is attract trouble. Good thing Gryffin was there to save her yet again. It's becoming a regular thing.'

'Yeah, well I think it's a tradition we can afford to break.'

'We going to go and get her?'

Roman shakes his head. 'I'd love to, Lucan, trust me, but we can't afford to send another transport at the moment. We need all our ships here. As much as I never thought I'd say this, the safest place for Terra is on *Ares* with Gryffin.'

Lucan laughs. 'Can't see the boss being overly keen about that.'

'You don't think he'd kick her off the ship do you?'

Lucan shakes his head. 'No way. It's just going to be interesting having her on a Nomad ship.'

Roman nods his head. Interesting is putting it mildly. Having Terra and Gryffin cooped up on the same ship with no way to escape will force the two of them to talk. It'll either work or be a disaster.

∞

Terra looks at her reflection in the cracked mirror. It clouded after her shower, but she's not going to risk wiping the shattered glass. She knows the glass was replaced after *Ares* crashed, so clearly Gryffin had fought with it at some stage since he left. She pads across the floor with her bare feet back to the bed. His bed. She still can't quite believe he gave up his personal space for her.

She wraps the small towel tightly around her and sits on the edge of the bed. She looks around the room again, trying to find some clue, some extra information that will help her understand Gryffin better, but all it does is raise more questions.

There's nothing bar the basic furniture. No trinkets, no souvenirs of visits to other worlds. Nothing. The only things that give any insight into him are the shattered mirror and the numerous dents in the walls. Those two things disturb her more than she'd like to admit.

Feeling slightly more human after her shower, she dries her hair with a towel she borrowed from his bathroom before slipping into a fresh pair of fitted black trousers and a red vest. When Desyl escorted her back from dinner in the mess, she had found her bags from the shuttle waiting for her. He may claim to know nothing about emotions or people's feelings, but every now and again, Gryffin does something that completely contradicts his claims. The way he was with her in the cave earlier was one of those times. Even after everything that had just happened, she felt safe with him in the dark cave. For a short time at least, the anger she held dissipated slightly.

With nothing else to do in the empty room, she climbs onto his hard bed and buries her face in his thin pillow. His smell immediately ignites a fire deep within her. She's furious at Roman for forcing this situation on her. Things were going just fine. Gryffin was far away from her and that suited her. Or so she thought. When she saw him in the shuttle, she had to stop herself from throwing her arms around him. The feelings she had for him came rushing back. It's not real though. She knows that. The ship had just crashed and he saved her. Of course she got carried away in the moment. It's only natural.

She rolls onto her back to get away from his scent, but it doesn't do any good. She closes her eyes and tries to shut down her brain, but sleep continues to evade her. She throws the cover aside, climbs off the bed and lowers to the floor. Terra manages one sit-up before her ribs convince her to stop. She lies back on the cold floor and stares at the ceiling. Maybe a few glasses of Ultaran ale will help knock her out. She'd give anything to sleep until they reach Ultar again and she can get off this ship.

∞

'Over my dead body.'

Desyl steps back as Gryffin's facial implant glows red. 'Sir, she's insisting.'

'I don't give a damn if she's insisting. She's not joining the crew.' Gryffin paces his office, trying to keep the irrational anger from taking over. How can she even suggest something like that? It's ridiculous!

'Sir, with all due respect, you can't really keep her locked in... well, locked in your room. It's not fair to her.'

'Fair? I'm trying to keep her safe!'

'Yes, sir, I know that, but maybe if you explain it to her in person, she'll understand better?'

Gryffin shoves his hand into the wall beside him. He doesn't want to see her. Why does she have to be so stubborn? He runs a hand through his hair and squeezes his eye shut. 'Damn woman.'

Without another word, he storms from his office and along the corridor towards his room. Desyl races after him, presumably to make sure he doesn't hurt Terra. The thought only serves to add fuel to his anger. He's still not trusted.

He manages to rein in his temper long enough to give Terra a chance to open the door instead of barging in. Her eyebrows shoot up when she sees him at the door. She recovers quickly and crosses her arms as she leans against the doorframe. 'Captain. I appreciate you taking time out of your busy day to see me.'

He feels his eye change as her comment grates on his already irritated nerves. He places a hand at either side of the doorframe, more to stop himself from entering the room than anything else. 'You have a problem following orders?'

She squares her shoulders and doesn't back away from him. 'I'm not part of your crew, so your orders mean nothing.'

'You are a guest on my ship, so you do what I say.'

She laughs sharply. 'Guest? I'm a prisoner, Captain.'

'You're ungrateful.'

'Really? I thanked you for helping me. You're clearly the one with the problem. You go out of your way to save me then just dump me on Desyl at the first available opportunity. Why did you even bother to help me when I'm clearly an inconvenience for you?'

Gryffin ignores Desyl fidgeting beside him. 'I gave you one simple order to follow.'

'Simple! It's far from simple and you did not order me. You had your poor lackey beside you do it.'

The metal doorframe groans as he squeezes it in his hand. 'I've more important things to do than deal with you.'

As soon as the words leave his mouth he knows he's gone too far. Her eyes harden and she clenches her jaw. Without a word, she pushes past him and storms down the corridor. He bangs his head against the wall and curses himself. 'Go after her.'

Desyl doesn't need to be told twice. He chases after Terra as she hurries away from Gryffin. There's no point going after her himself. He'll just make a bad situation even worse. Hopefully Desyl can convince her to stay without a fight. She can't leave, she's got nowhere to go. He doesn't want to lock her in his room, but if he has to in order to keep her safe, he'll do it.

∞

'Terra, wait!'

Terra ignores Desyl's shouts as she continues towards the cargo bay. She doesn't have a plan at the moment. She just knows she needs to get as far away from Gryffin, his ship, and his crew as she can. Maybe she can follow in true Nomad style and steal one of Gryffin's transports.

'Terra. Stop walking. Please!'

Desyl catches up and grabs her arm. She jerks her arm away from him and spins around. 'What, did your esteemed captain order you to come after me?'

He rests his hands on his hips and takes a deep breath. 'Listen, I get why you're upset. I'm just asking for a few minutes. Please, Terra.'

She can't explain why, but she allows him to lead her back down the corridor to a side passageway. The corridor ends in a large door. Terra steps through and gasps as she finds herself in a vast, double ceiling-height training room. The Nomad may not be as affluent as the Foundation, but this is probably the best equipped training room she's seen. 'This was an empty shell when *Ares* left. How did you do all this?'

Desyl smirks as he climbs down the metal stairs and leads her to the back corner. 'All the equipment was in the cargo hold. With the structural damage repaired, all we had to do was put the final touches to it.' He walks around a large metal partition blocking off the back section of the room. When she steps around the corner, she gasps in shock.

The walls look like someone has taken a sledgehammer to them. Broken metal sparring sticks are piled into the corner and two large training drones lie in pieces on the floor. That's not what shocks her though. It's the large patches of blood covering the dents in the walls and splattered on the floor are what gets her attention. 'What happened here?'

Desyl leans against the partition and folds his arms, one foot resting against the wall. 'This is Gryffin's training space.'

'Training? It looks like someone's been beaten up here.'

'Yeah. Gryffin.'

'I don't understand?'

'We may have got Gryffin back, but he's not the same. He spends every minute either on the command deck or in here. He barely sleeps, eats next to nothing, and trains until he bleeds.'

Terra realises the bruises she saw on his chest in the cave must be as a result of his excessive training. 'Are you saying he's hurting himself... intentionally?'

Desyl lowers his head and sighs. 'I don't know for sure. All I know is that he's going to kill himself if things don't change. It's like he's punishing himself for something.'

'Is the mod still working?'

Desyl nods. 'From what I can tell. He avoids or reschedules examinations whenever he can. Can't blame him after what happened.'

'Why are you telling me all this? What do you expect me to do?'

'I'm not telling you this to try and guilt you into staying voluntarily. I just don't know what to do. I've tried talking to him but... well, you can guess how that went.' He rubs a hand over his neck and Terra notices the faint outline of a bruise.

'Did he hurt you?'

Desyl smiles sadly. 'He had his metal hand a little too tightly around my neck. I did question his orders, but I wasn't expecting that reaction. I honestly thought I was finished. I'm really worried about him, Terra.'

After hearing all that, she can't blame him. If what he says is true, which she can't really dispute given what she's seen, it sounds like he is in trouble. That still doesn't mean that she's going to be able to do anything about it. 'I agree it's worrying Desyl, but I really don't see what I can do. He clearly doesn't want me here and, to be honest, I don't want to be here either.'

Desyl pushes away from the wall and takes a few steps closer to her. 'Can you not try to get through to him?'

'I'm the last person he'll listen to.' The truth in her statement turns her stomach. She wishes more than ever that she could get through to him, but if she couldn't convince him to fight on the freighter, she has less hope now.

Desyl steps closer to her, the concern plain as day on his face. 'I'm not above begging.'

Terra waves her arms in the air. 'What good will it do? Unless he's willing to face what's going on, nothing is going to change. He knows what the Foundation is doing to the Sector. He's seen what's happening to the colonies. If that doesn't force him to get his head back on what he needs to do, I don't know what will. So many people worked their backsides off to give him medical attention and help him get back to full health. The expense of his treatment alone nearly crippled the group. He's just throwing it all back in their faces by heading on this rampage of his. He owes it to the group as well as himself to get it together.'

Desyl's face suddenly drops and he stands to attention. A feeling of dread hits her. There's only one person who would have that effect on him. Turning slowly, she faces Gryffin's purple glare. 'So, that's all I am — a damn investment?'

'Gryffin, I didn't mean that like it sounded.'

'Who decides when I've paid off my debt? When do I stop being property?'

'Please, Gryffin—'

'Desyl,' Gryffin cuts her off. 'Escort Commander Rush back to her room and make sure she stays there.' Without waiting for Desyl to acknowledge him, Gryffin turns and leaves.

Terra feels like she's going to throw up. She can't believe he heard all that. The conversation replays in her mind and her queasiness increases. She made him sound like a commodity.

'Well, I think we're both in for a few fun filled days.'

'I should apologise.'

Desyl grabs onto her arm as she takes a step away. 'Hang on there. That's the worst thing you can do. Trust me, when he's angry at you, the only, and safest option, is to hide.'

'You can't be serious? We're all adults here. He's deserves an apology.' She walks away and climbs the steps. 'You're coming too.'

'Not happening.'

She reaches the top and leans over the railings. 'Are you really going to let me roam the ship without supervision? I don't think he'd be too happy about that.'

Desyl groans and slowly follows her out of the room.

22

Gryffin stands in the doorway and watches as Terra sleeps. He had forgotten how beautiful she is. Trying to be as quiet as possible, he moves closer and crouches down beside his bed. He hadn't intended on coming back to his room, but he couldn't stop his feet. The last few hours were spent on the surface trying to salvage what they could from the ships. After what he heard in the training room, he had to get off the ship and get away from her. He'd even refused to speak to her when she came with Desyl to apologise. They have nothing to apologise for. He realises that now, but at the time, it... hurt that she would think that about him. He is property. Since the day the first piece of metal was put in him, he became property of the Foundation. Until he dies or the Foundation is destroyed, he'll remain like that.

A few hours on the surface helped calm him down. Thanks to the still raging storm, salvaging the Rogue ship had taken longer than planned. They came back two hours late, soaked, covered in mud, and exhausted. It was worth it though. The spare parts, leftover ammunition and residual fuel will come in handy. Terra's ship and the remains of her pilot have also been brought back to *Ares*. There isn't much left of the ship, but maybe she can put some of the parts to use.

Terra mumbles in her sleep. Her mouth is open slightly, her chest rising and falling with each breath. The small vest is doing nothing to help distract him from the body hiding under it. Her dark hair is loose and spread over his pillow. She looks so perfect. He could definitely get used to seeing her on his bed, in his bed, under him... He doesn't care where she is as long as he can have her. He wipes his muddy hand on his leg before he slowly reaches out to her. He gently brushes a wayward strand of hair from her face. She moans in her sleep and smiles. Terra curls up more and pulls his pillow towards her chest.

His hand retreats like it's been struck. She must be dreaming about her man — on his damn bed. What the hell is he doing? He pushes himself up and steps back from her. His stubble rasps loudly under his fingers as he wipes a hand over his face.

She's not his, can never be his. He looks down at himself — muddy, wet, bleeding, bruised, pretty much the worst he can possibly look. She has no place with him. She seems so small and delicate. Too pure for his world. Too pure for him.

He walks towards the door as quietly as he can and closes it behind him. Without paying attention to where he's going, Gryffin quickly finds himself in the small bedroom area at the back of the training room. He pulls off his sodden clothes and dumps them in the corner. With no one around, he doesn't hide the limp that's been plaguing him lately.

His new leg hurts like hell and is only getting worse. It's always hurt, but the dull throb is quickly increasing to a burning fire in the living tissue under the metal. The red, angry flesh joining the metal itches like crazy and makes sleep next to impossible. If the control implant didn't help to dull the pain, it would be damn difficult to walk. He probably should get Desyl to look at it, but he doubts there's anything he can do. He's lived with the modifications long enough to know what's happening. His body is rejecting the new limb. It's only a matter of time before something drastic will have to be done. Something else to look forward to.

He practically drags himself and his dying leg into the shower and rests his head against the side of the stall. Exhaustion clouds his mind and dulls his senses. His body feels far too heavy and hunger twists at his gut. He tried to eat when he got back from the surface, but couldn't stomach anything. He's too tired to eat, yet sleep continues to remain firmly out of his grasp. He got used to losing consciousness rather than falling asleep when he was in the lab and he's struggling to break the cycle. He knows he's losing weight, but he doesn't have the energy or interest to do anything about it.

He works his shoulders under the hot water as he tries to get rid of some of the tension — from fighting the Rogues and from knowing that she's only a few floors above him... in his room... on his bed.

He looks down and frowns. Clearly his brain isn't the only part of him that needs a release of tension. Willing his body to calm down doesn't do any good either. If anything, the damn thing gets harder. He grits his teeth as he reaches down and strokes himself. He really hates touching it but he has no bloody choice. There's no way he's going to be able to go anywhere until he's sorted himself out.

He closes his eyes and tries to forget it's his own hand down there. The image of Terra kneeling in front of him pops into his head, instantly ramping up the tension that's ready to burst out of his body. He grips himself tighter as he imagines Terra's wet hair clinging to her back as her mouth moves along his length. The water tracing its way down her spine as her lips grip him tightly. He curses under his breath as his release hits, rocking through his body. Drawing a shaky breath, he opens his eye and crashes back to reality. No Terra. Just his own hand. He turns the water to cold, wincing as the icy spray hits him.

He's having a hard time stopping the dreams and fantasies he lived in while he was in prison. It's too easy to retreat into his head, to be with her over and over again, but in truth all he's doing is torturing himself. He needs to get his head focused back on his job. He's meant to be the big hero, coming back to save the Nomad and the colonies, but at the moment he isn't doing much of that.

Feeling completely disgusted and ashamed, he hobbles from the shower and crashes onto his bed. He closes his real eye, but the new eyepiece refuses to shut down. He covers the optic with his hand, but it doesn't work. Can't sleep if one eye is still open.

His radio sounds from the pile of wet clothes in the corner. He groans out loud and uses some of his dwindling energy to get to his feet and retrieve his radio. 'What!'

'Sir, the Rogue computer is ready for you.'

He shuts down the radio and gets dressed on autopilot. The last thing his body needs right now is to connect with a computer, but it's the quickest way to access the system. At the moment, finding out what the hell is going on with the Rogues and the Foundation is far more important than his health.

∞

With one flick of his chin, Gryffin clears the room. The half dozen well-built, tough, tattooed Nomad scatter like rabbits. Looking at Gryffin, Terra can't really blame them. His nostrils flare and his muscles bulge as he keeps his arms firmly crossed. She knows the anger is directed solely at her. She's disobeying his ridiculous orders again. At least he can't complain about the tattoo. A scary looking, very heavily tattooed Nomad called Ryder had done the deed. Ryder had been the perfect gentleman, even though he was slightly argumentative when she told him exactly what design she wanted. Apparently, he thought the small griffin climbing up her neck in the centre of the Nomad design might rub Gryffin the wrong way — not that she could have cared less.

'What the hell are you doing here?'

Terra throws the rope on the ground. 'I needed to get out. I couldn't bear to be cooped up in that room any longer.'

'So, you just decide to wander around my ship and do whatever you want?'

She puts her hands on her hips and looks at the large fan spinning on the ceiling as she tries to calm down. Whatever small semblance of manners Gryffin may have had months ago is well and truly dead now. 'I'm working off some of the pent up aggression I have towards you. I either train or I take it out on you.' She takes a few steps closer to the fuming Nomad captain. 'I didn't ask to be stuck here. Trust me, I'd rather be anywhere else in the Sector than on *Ares* with you.'

The anger in his face ebbs to be replaced by the flash of something she's never seen him display before. Hurt. She hurt him. While she is still angry at him, the fact that she can hurt someone like Gryffin with mere words doesn't sit well with her. She pushes the feelings aside to focus on being angry at him and his infuriating silence. She grabs her towel off the bench and decides to call an end to the too short training session. 'Well, as much fun as this has been, I think I'll go back to my cell.'

He waits until she gets to the bottom of the spiral staircase before he speaks. 'Damn it. You're on the crew.'

That stops her in her tracks. Although she made the demand, she didn't expect him to agree. She only said it to annoy him and prove that he can't push her around. 'This some sort of game?'

'No.'

She takes a step closer to him. 'So, you're saying that I can work in comms. That I can "wander around your ship" as you put it.'

He turns slightly towards her and nods. 'Yes.' His large shoulders drop slightly when he looks at her face. 'You're still angry.'

'What do you think? I know me being here isn't what either of us wants, but you don't have to be such a... such an ass about it.'

He furrows his brow. 'I'm a what?'

She prods him in the chest with her finger. 'An ass. An idiot. A jerk.'

He brushes her hand away and crosses his arms. 'You're right. I must be an idiot to risk my ship, my crew, and my life to save you. Again.'

'I didn't ask you to,' she shouts. He mutters under his breath and turns away. 'Don't you dare walk away from me again!'

He doesn't even look in her direction as he replies, 'I'm walking away before I do something you'll regret.'

'Nice, Gryffin. Threatening me too.' He briskly walks towards the steps leading to the upper level. 'Walking away is what you do best, isn't it? When things become too difficult or emotional, your first reaction is to turn your back.'

He spins quickly and levels his purple gaze on her. 'What the hell are you talking about?'

She waves her arms in the air and turns away. 'Forget it!' Terra wraps her arms tightly around her torso and glares at the remains of a training drone in the corner. She's a stupid fool for letting him get to her like this again. Why didn't she just leave as soon as he arrived? Now, not only is she trapped on his ship, but she's also angry and embarrassed at her outburst.

He picks up a sparring stick and crosses the space between them quicker than she thought possible. He holds the stick out to her. 'Hit me.'

Terra frowns, sure she's misheard him. 'Excuse me?'

'I said hit me.'

Terra frowns. 'Let me get this straight. Your answer to this conversation is for me to hit you with a stick.'

'Yes.'

Serves her right for expecting something a little more explanatory. While hitting him is incredibly tempting, it's not going to address the reason behind her anger. Her walls crumbled slightly in the cave and she's furious with herself for allowing it to happen. Without knowing it, she had offered her heart to him just to have him stamp on it with one of his large boots when he brushed her away again. He had saved her life, kept her safe, then just left again.

After everything that she's been through with him and his commitment issues, this shouldn't be a surprise to her. Something happens to her when he's around that makes her forget all the hurt he's caused her. She forgets the raw pain he leaves every time he brushes her aside.

She eyes the sparring stick in his hand and makes her decision. Maybe it's high time she shows the Nomad captain just how upset she really is. 'Are you any good at sparring?'

His eyes narrow. 'You want to fight me?'

She throws her towel back on the bench and takes a few steps closer. 'You're not afraid you'll be beaten by a woman, are you?'

He lowers the stick slightly as he examines her. She can see him trying to figure out if she's being serious or not. Just to prove her point, she walks around him and picks up another stick from the holder against the wall. Terra circles him as she turns the stick in her hand to get a feel for the weapon. She comes to a stop in front of her opponent again, takes up a fighting stance and waits for him to make a move.

Gryffin stands opposite her and mutters something under his breath about her and a death wish. She's under no illusions that he's going to win, but she'll do her best to make sure she doesn't make it easy for him.

She started sparring over the months he was missing. Anything to occupy her mind, keep it away from thinking about him and wondering if he was still alive. Without wanting to blow her own trumpet, she is actually getting pretty good at it. She'd even managed to beat Chayse on one or two occasions. Looking at her current opponent, she has a feeling he's a whole scenario entirely.

∞

So much for keeping away from her. He fully intended to stay as far away from her as he could. It had worked. For twenty-three and a half hours he managed to go about his daily routine and not bump into her once. On a ship the size of *Ares* that was a bloody good trick. Pity his luck hadn't extended past day one.

All he wants to do is train. Try to work off some of the tension and frustration ready to erupt from his body. A few hours alone to pound the hell out of a drone, maybe even a few crew members if they are stupid enough not to get out of his way, is just what he needs. He didn't think he'd see her here. She's supposed to be in his quarters, not in the training room with him.

Dressed in black cargo pants and a white vest, her long hair braided down her back, the loose strands secured under a red bandanna, she hadn't noticed him walk in. He noticed her though. Noticed the way her damp skin glistened under the lights, the way the muscles in her arms moved as she jumped the rope again and again. Then he noticed the way his crew was looking at her. Saw the want in their eyes and that's when things took a turn.

Something primal inside him roared to the surface. He doesn't want anyone to look at her like that. He doesn't want anyone else lusting after her. Doesn't want anyone else imagining being with her. She is his.

Except she isn't and she never will be.

She turns around to wipe her face on the towel and her braid falls over her shoulder to expose her neck. He drops his sparring stick on the ground when he sees a griffin crawling up the back of her neck. The design is exactly the same as his one. In fact, they could be a matching pair with the same pose and the same purple eyes. It's not quite what he had in mind but she does have the Nomad design around it creeping a short distance across the back of both shoulders.

The griffin will probably work better than most of the designs she could have chosen. Still doesn't explain why she went for one exactly like his. She hates him.

He picks up the stick and takes up a fighting stance as he waits for her to make the first move. She suddenly lunges, and he manages to block her attack. Not fazed at all, she moves again and again, gaining confidence with each blow. He didn't know she would be such a good opponent. Of course, he's holding back quite a bit, but even so, she is showing remarkable skill. He smiles to himself. He might just enjoy this.

Terra examines her opponent as she steadies her breathing. Gryffin may be a lot bigger and stronger than her, but that doesn't mean he's automatically won. She's quicker and hopefully can change positions faster than he can. It's a weak strategy, but it's all she has. Gryffin returns her silent scrutiny, but his face gives nothing away as usual.

Terra lunges at him. He swiftly spins and avoids her stick. Gryffin turns to face her again and holds his position. She attacks again. Clearly expecting the move, he sidesteps neatly, leaving her stick slicing through thin air instead of contacting with his shoulder. Terra regains her footing and turns to strike him again but he ducks.

'You going to join in or just dance around me?'

A small smile flashes across his face briefly before he reins it in. 'Just giving you a chance to warm up.'

'Stop stalling.'

He moves faster than she thought possible and lunges at her with several short slices. Terra parries all but one, which strikes her across the back of her legs. She curses and steps back away from him.

'Better?'

Terra smiles and brushes her braid off her shoulder. 'Not bad, Captain.'

'Been training?'

An image of herself and Bray training together flashes across her mind before she shoves it away. 'Less talking.'

Gryffin nods and instantly presses the advantage, thrusting and slicing with his stick, backing Terra up against the wall. He slams the stick against the metal to the side of her head, then retreats.

She glances at the deep dent beside her ear and raises her eyebrows. That could have been her head. Gryffin silently watches her as she catches her breath.

Without giving him any notice, she lunges. Gryffin ducks and jabs his own stick into her thigh. He withdraws as she curses, unable to keep the concern from creeping onto his face.

'You okay?'

She brushes away his concern. 'It's a bit late for you to be worried for me.'

Gryffin's jaw tightens and his face loses all signs of any emotion. He holds his arms out to the side in a silent invitation to attack. Terra goes crazy, but it's the crazy of a fighter. She drives him back with thrust after thrust, taking risky chances, yet retaining just enough speed to stay in control. She knows he's letting her win. There's no way she can physically drive someone the size of Gryffin back. She shouts in victory as he slams against the metal wall, but her elation is short lived.

With her concentration broken, he swings his stick in a circle and swipes at the back of her legs. She falls to the floor, rolls and tries to get to her feet, but Gryffin knocks the stick from her hand. Terra lies on her back and stares up at Gryffin looming over her. She reaches out and grabs her stick lying beside her to fight back. Gryffin is on top of her before she can lift her stick off the ground. He takes hold of her wrist and pins it to the ground.

'You lose, Commander.'

∞

They stare at each other, nose to nose as he holds his position on top of her. She's having difficulty catching her breath and it's not all because of the match. Staring into his deep purple eye, she feels like she's drowning, being pulled deeper into his gaze as his body holds her firmly to the mat. Her heart races as she breathes him in. The smell of leather and soap wrapping around her senses like a familiar blanket.

Following closely behind her heart, her body joins in the fun, the heat rising through her. She swallows past the lump and clears her throat. If she doesn't put some distance between them fast, she's going to do something stupid and more than likely very humiliating. 'I should—'

'Why my mark?' he demands.

'Um, Desyl said I needed to be marked as a member of your crew, so that's what I did.'

'You know what he meant. I'm bloody sure he never mentioned getting a smaller version of mine. It's like a target on the back of your neck. People will think you are actually mine. Why'd you choose that?'

She shrugs as much as she can with him pressed on top of her. 'People can think what they want — we both know the truth. As for the design — I've always liked it. If I'm going to be stuck with it for now, I should at least—'

That's as far as she gets before Gryffin presses his lips to hers. His calloused hand finds her skin and moves up her body as his tongue drives in and out of her mouth. Something nags at the back of her mind. Something which stops her from holding on to him and taking this a lot further, but she can't think of what it is and gives in to the moment.

She's an idiot. Top of her class all through the academy, youngest serving crew member on *Infinity*. That took some serious intelligence. It's just a pity she can't access any of it right now. What she has to do is stand up. Give Gryffin a piece of her mind and then leave the room. But no. Her hands betray her and take on a life of their own. She's angry and upset at him, yet she still wants him. Right now. She traces the firm ridges of his abdomen and drags a nail gently along the edge of his chest implant. If she wants to cool things down, that's not the way to do it. As soon as she touches the sensitive skin joined to the metal, there's no going back.

Before she can fully register what's going on, she's naked on the floor of a very public training room. Gryffin rests a hand to either side of her head and leans over her. She's never had anyone look at her the way he does. Without saying a word or doing a thing, he can make her feel like the most important person in his world. His robotic eye glows brightly as he looks at her. He wants her, it clearly shows on his face and she's not going to stop him.

His metal hand lifts from the floor and moves down her body. He runs a finger along her jaw and down her neck to her chest. Terra feels like she's submerged. Her heart races loudly in her chest as he slowly examines her. He swallows and the griffin pendant moves against his neck, catching the light. She wants to touch him, but the way he's looking at her changes her mind. The need to be with her is still on his face, however there's also sorrow. He focuses on his hand, which has found its way down her body. The sorrow instantly disappears as raw need takes over again.

He kisses her as he pushes a finger inside her. She moans and arches her back to push him deeper into her. The smooth metal finger is joined by a second, making her writhe in pleasure against him. She can't explain why his metal hand does that to her but she can't get enough of it. It's been too long since she'd been with him, and right now she honestly doesn't know how she survived for so long.

He holds her wrists over her head, firmly pinned to the floor in his flesh hand as his metal hand drives her over the edge. Gryffin kisses her to stifle the scream she can't hold back. He suddenly pulls out of her as the door bursts open. Gryffin growls and covers her with his body as Desyl enters the room. 'Sir, you're— Shit, sir. I—'

'Get the hell out!'

Desyl blushes and turns around, but doesn't leave. 'Sir, we need you on the surface. It's urgent.'

Gryffin's whole body tenses above her and she really wishes Desyl would leave, for his own sake more than anything else. 'I said get out of here, Desyl.'

Getting the hint at last, Desyl leaves the room and stands just outside the door stopping it from closing. Gryffin lets out another string of profanities before grabbing Terra's clothes and handing them to her. With his body still blocking her from sight she quickly gets dressed trying not to let the mortification drive her to tears. As soon as she's dressed Gryffin stands up and helps her to her feet. Without a word he follows Desyl from the room.

∞

'Don't say it, sir.'

Sayber holds his hands up and smiles innocently. 'I wasn't going to say anything.'

Bray steps onto *Perses* and immediately feels his stress and worries leave. This is home. Since his grandparents died, *Perses* was the first place he actually felt comfortable. It's where he belongs. He thought staying on Ultar as the Hunter representative was the right thing to do. Even though he joined the Hunters as a Foundation sleeper agent, he considered himself a Hunter. He stayed behind to make sure they were being fairly represented. Then things changed with Terra and it gave him another reason to stay. Deep down, he missed the Hunters, he just thought he had to be on Ultar.

He now realises that was the wrong decision. Sayber quietly

watches as Bray familiarises himself with the inside of the cargo bay. The Hunter captain sits on a wooden crate with his arms crossed. He is just how Bray remembers. His hair is a little longer and tied in a tail at the base of his neck and his neatly trimmed goatee is tarnished by a new small scar.

Bray points at Sayber's face. 'Still learning how to shave, sir?'

Sayber shakes his head and looks down at his worn brown boots. 'Not going to work, Commander.' He gets to his feet and saunters towards Bray. He stops in front of him and looks him in the eye. 'I. Told. You. So. There, I feel so much better now.'

Bray grimaces. He deserved that. Although Sayber supported him when he said he wanted to stay on Ultar, his final words to Bray had been, 'Keep away from her. She's Gryffin's. It won't end well for you.' Of course, Bray had brushed the warning aside. He knew better. Gryffin was dead. Terra was available. What could go wrong? People don't just come back from the dead. This is real life, things like that don't happen.

Well, until it did happen and it ended badly for him, just like Sayber predicted.

'Thanks, sir.'

Sayber slaps him on the back. 'I think you need to say something to me now.'

Bray clenches his teeth. While he likes this new, less stressed Sayber, he could do without the attitude. With the uneasy truce forced on the Nomad and Hunters, mentality had changed among the group. Things may change if Gryffin convinces the rest of the Nomad to join again. At the moment, the Hunters hold the biggest hand. That gave Sayber peace of mind. With the Nomad reunited, the balance of power would shift back to the Nomad. 'You were right.'

Sayber grins. 'Now that's all out of the way, welcome back. Quinn will be glad to get back to his position. Don't think he warmed to the second-in-command role.'

'You get the message I sent?'

Sayber nods. 'Sounds interesting. It'd be nice to give our fighting skills a bit of a workout. Avoca sent through the details for six of the prisons. That still leaves four we know nothing about.'

'Six is a good start. We got room for the inmates?' Sayber leads him along the small corridor towards his room.

'We've got twelve ships with us. We split the crew once we get to the prison. Leave some crew there while the prisoners are shipped to Ultar.'

'We're going to take the prisons?'

Sayber shrugs. 'Why not? Each prison holds a pretty good position on the border. If we can take the locations, we will. If we can't, we'll blow them to pieces. The last thing we need is the Foundation populating them again.' Sayber is quiet for a moment. 'So, I guess I should ask, how's my old mate Gryffin?'

Bray snorts.

'Ah, touchy subject?'

'Let's just say, I'll be glad when this truce is over.'

'Ouch! Is he in one piece?'

Bray nods. 'Some new mods, but nothing that'll do him any long term damage.' He sighs. 'I know he's going to be a bonus, but...'

Sayber unlocks the door to Bray's quarters. 'You don't need to explain. Can't say I'm looking forward to our reunion. I'll leave you to get settled in. Meeting in ten.'

Bray sits down on his bed and takes a deep breath. It's good to be back.

'I told you so!' Sayber shouts back down the corridor.

Bray groans.

∞

Terra knows she shouldn't go in. She should respect his privacy, but her body has other ideas. There's no way she can just walk away knowing Gryffin is in there wet and naked. Ever since Desyl's unwelcome interruption, she's been unable to get Gryffin out of her head. She silently navigates around the various exercise equipment and stops as she gets to the back of the room. From what Desyl showed her earlier, the large partition houses a few showers and the broken machinery waiting for repair after Gryffin's training sessions. She takes a deep breath and carefully peaks around the corner.

Gryffin has his back to her, the glass door of the shower giving her an unobstructed view of his naked body. He is perfect — every muscle, line and curve exactly as it should be. His head is bowed, allowing the water to run off his hair and down his back. His thick arms are braced against the wall. His biceps bulge as he leans against the metal wall. The heat grows in her body as she watches the water run down between his strong shoulders, over the large griffin wing and down his spine before trailing to his powerful thighs.

He drops his arms and turns suddenly. Terra gasps and ducks back behind the wall. After a few tense seconds of only the sound of falling water, she risks another look. She whispers a silent prayer of thanks when she sees him again. He's turned to face the shower door, his head down as he rolls his big shoulders under the spray.

She forces her eyes away from temptation and follows the thin lines of metal that run across his groin. He didn't have those modifications when they were together on Ultar. The new additions must have been given to him on the freighter. The thin metal trail leads from the top of his metal thigh, across his groin and down his left leg to join with a thick metal band in his skin above his left knee.

Her heart sinks when she realises there is quite a lot about him that she doesn't know — physically, but more importantly, emotionally. Looking at him as he is now, all of his scars, the metal, and tattoo, the quenched heat rises again. Even though her heart is breaking at what had been done to him, it only makes him all the more appealing to her. He's been through more than anyone else she knows, but instead of letting what happened defeat him, it just makes him stronger.

Feeling more courageous, she positions herself behind the broken drones in the corner. She crouches down and watches as Gryffin steps out of the shower and wraps a towel around his waist. He runs a hand through his hair to brush the wet locks from his face. Terra can hear her heart beating loudly in her chest. She's never seen him like this before. The man in front of her is just Gryffin. No weapons, no uniform and no image to uphold.

He walks with a very pronounced limp over to the small bunk serving as his bed. He lowers onto the bed and rests his right leg on a box in front of him. Gryffin grimaces as he pulls a panel off the side of his mechanical thigh. Terra watches in morbid fascination as he inserts a fine metal pin into his leg. After digging around for a minute he curses in pain then relaxes a little. He pulls his towel off and wipes it along his leg before throwing it in the corner. Gryffin slowly lifts his leg onto the bed and lies down. He rests his arm over his face while he massages the flesh above his leg with his metal arm.

Terra suddenly feels uncomfortable watching him. She quietly makes her way out of the room. The large overhead fans hide her footsteps from Gryffin's sharp hearing. She leans back against the closed door of the training room and wipes a hand over her face. Her heart wants to go back inside and stay with him, but she has no right. He doesn't want or need her hanging around him.

After staring at a blank spot on the opposite wall for a few minutes, Terra finally connects with her brain again. She wanders through the gloomy corridors on her way back to her room. Seeing him like that unsettled her. He seemed vulnerable. That's a word she would never use to describe him. She's embarrassed to admit she's never thought about how he lives day-to-day with his implants. He does a great job hiding it, but they clearly cause him pain. Her father has a lot to answer for.

Terra eventually reaches her room and locks the door behind her.

She pulls a crumpled piece of paper from the inside pocket of her toolkit and stares at the small folded square. It's caused her nothing but trouble, yet she can't bring herself to throw it away. It's been months since she's looked at it, but feels an uncontrollable urge to change that right now.

She lies back on the bed and unfolds the worn page. Her eyes swim as she looks at the drawing of Gryffin. It's the very first one she ever drew. It's the drawing that brought the Foundation to Gryffin in the first place. She traces her finger along the side of his face and sucks in a deep breath as the tears flow freely down her cheek and onto his pillow. She'd give anything to go back to that time. At least Gryffin could bear to be in the same room as her back then.

Gryffin turns to face Terra. 'You sure I can't convince you to stay on board?'

She shakes her head. 'Unless you're going to stoop to a new low and lock me in my room.'

'Don't tempt me,' he mutters under his breath.

Gryffin stares out the window at the crowded docks around the space station. He hasn't got the first clue what to do. The last time he united the group, they had come to him, ship by ship, requesting to work with him. He didn't have to actively get everyone together. Judging by the traffic at the docking area, there should be more than enough people here that he can target so hopefully it won't be too difficult. He just hopes they don't try to kill him as soon as they see him. It's his fault they're scraping the bottom of the barrel in this hell hole in the first place. The once fierce ships have been reduced to a run down jumble of scrap.

He scratches the skin beside his ocular implant and frowns. How is he supposed to fight against the Foundation with run down ships?

'We're here,' the pilot informs them.

No time to back out now. 'Let's move out.'

He takes a deep breath and brings the control implant out to play. As soon as the door of the transport opens, the humid air hits him. It brings along the aroma of stale sweat, old beer and rotten food. Terra covers her nose and mouth. He can't blame her — this place smells like everything in it is rotting or dead.

'Everything I'm wearing is going out the airlock when we get back to *Ares.*'

Desyl chuckles. 'You just need to toughen up, Commander. Too much for your delicate Foundation sense of smell?' He takes a deep breath and coughs loudly.

Terra crosses her arms and laughs as Desyl retches. 'Oh, what's wrong, Commander. Too much for your delicate Nomad sense of smell?'

Desyl sneers at her as the rest of the team join the laughter.

'Enough!' Gryffin's command instantly silences the group. He pulls up the hood on his brown jacket and steps off the loading ramp. Fluorescent tubes flicker above them as they push out of the bay. The irritating lighting continues in the corridors. Artificial lighting is harsh enough on his enhanced eyes without the flickering adding to the fun. He's going to have one hell of a headache later. He roughly shoves a drunk aside when he gets too close. He hates crowded places like this. People get too close and there's not a lot you can do about it.

He stops as a large group of loud men push past. More than one of them bumps into Terra. Gryffin takes her hand and pulls her closer to him. She squeezes his hand and smiles at him. Now that his possessive side is satisfied, he pushes his way towards the bar, still firmly holding Terra's hand.

He weaves through the rancid, sweaty crowd until the corridor opens up into a large, badly lit, noisy bar. The four walls are lined with small private booths, which run all around and up the seven floors making it seem like they're standing in the centre of a large honeycomb. Gryffin has a bad feeling about this. The room is so cramped full of people there's barely enough standing space left. Finding anyone in the crowd is going to be next to impossible. Gryffin directs the group over to a relatively clear corner.

He leans over to speak to Desyl. 'Find an empty booth — preferably at the edge of the room and not on the bottom floor.'

'What are we going to do?' Terra asks.

'You're going to stick to my ass like your life depends on it. That's your one and only job.'

'I'm not just an accessory. I'm here to help. You point out familiar faces and I'll get them to meet. That way you'll stay hidden until the last minute.'

He clenches his jaw. It doesn't matter how many times he tells her, she insists in undermining him in front of his crew. He opens his mouth to put her back in her place, but is cut off by Desyl. 'Makes sense, Captain. It'll help speed things up.'

He turns to Desyl. 'What are you still doing here — you've got your orders.'

Smiling apologetically at Terra, he disappears into the crowd.

'You follow my lead Terra.' She nods and opens her mouth to speak, but he cuts her off. 'Don't mess with me on this one, Terra. If I even think there's going to be any trouble, I'm hauling your ass back to *Ares*, no arguments. Understood?'

He waits for the argument, but she surprises him by agreeing. 'Okay. Lead the way, Captain.'

He quietly looks at her before he shakes his head, takes her hand again and leads her into the swarm.

∞

He must be going soft.

There's no other reason for him to be in a bar full of ex-Nomad, ex-Hunters and Rogue fighters with Terra. Not exactly the perfect location for a first date — not that they're even close to being on a date. He mentally kicks himself. What the hell is he doing thinking about first dates? He must be malfunctioning.

He directs her towards the bar and tells her to order two drinks so they don't stand out. Gryffin feels really uneasy. The effect of the Nomad split is evident everywhere. While the station was never luxurious, it was far from the dump it is now. Seeing his people like this angers him. This is what's left of them. They're in a worse state than they were before he joined them. It makes him all the more determined to put things right. They saved him years ago. Now it's his turn. He just hopes he can find someone willing to help before it's too late to turn things around.

He pivots around to check on Terra and sees a man standing next to her. The man moves his hand towards her rear. Gryffin quickly grips the man's wrist. He squeezes hard with his mechanical hand until bones break. The man's screams are swallowed up by the loud music blaring throughout the bar. Gryffin hits him on his head, knocking the man unconscious as Terra continues to get their drinks, completely oblivious to what has just happened. He goes back to scanning the room and spots a familiar face in the crowd. He motions for Terra to look across the room at a large man in his late forties sitting at a table with a group of four men. 'Who is he?' she asks.

'Vance. He is the captain of *Styx* — or was the last time I saw him.'

'Friend or foe?'

'Was a friend.'

'I'll go talk to him.'

Gryffin grabs her by the arm. 'No. It'd be better if Desyl gets him. You come with me.' He leads a confused Terra through the crowds to the booth his team secured. Vance is old-school Nomad. Women have no place on a Nomad ship or crew. They're only good for one thing and Gryffin is damned if he's going to put Terra in a situation like that — willingly or not. He nods at the Nomad standing guard and shuts the door behind Terra.

'What happened to me helping out?'

Gryffin checks out the small window of the booth. Any attack would be severely hindered by the crowd below them. 'My rules, Terra. You got a problem, I'll escort you back to *Ares*.'

She makes a face and slumps into the chair. Gryffin ignores her attempt at a glare and paces the small booth while he waits for Desyl to convince Vance to meet. Then it's all up to him — if Vance doesn't kill him first. Probably best he doesn't think about that too much. The first few minutes will be the decider.

His thoughts are interrupted when he hears a knock on the door. Gryffin pulls up his hood and takes out his gun. He moves to the far corner where he can see the whole booth then nods at the crew member with him. The young officer opens the door to let Desyl and Vance into the room.

Vance looks around the booth. His gaze settles on Terra for a bit too long before moving back to him in the corner. The year hasn't been too kind. Vance is just shy of fifty with long blond hair tied in a ponytail. His contrasting brown beard is streaked with grey and braided half way down his chest. His brown eyes still hold a mischievous glint that always gets him in trouble — mostly when there's alcohol involved.

Desyl pulls out a chair and motions for him to sit.

'Well, you've certainly got my attention.' He sits on the nearest chair, turns to Terra and licks his lips. 'Especially you.' He slaps his knee and winks at Terra. 'Care to keep me company sweetheart? It's been a hell of a long time since I had a sweet ass like yours on my lap.'

Terra turns her back to him and gestures at the mark on her neck. 'Are you really sure you want to go there?' she asks.

Vance's face drops when he recognises the mark. 'Bloody hell, you're part of *Ares*?' The smile creeps back on his face. 'Now, you don't really expect me to believe that the *Ares* crew suddenly decided to break tradition and let one lone woman on their crew, do you? I'm sure they won't mind sharing you. I'll be gentle, I promise.'

Gryffin can't hold back the irrational emotional side of himself. It roars to the surface as he clears the distance between himself and Vance. He lifts the older man off the chair and slams him against the wall. He tightens his metal hand around Vance's neck and lets the power course down his arm. He pulls down his hood as he holds Vance off the floor. 'You talk about her like that again and you'll be eating the barrel of my gun. Understood?'

Vance's eyes open wide. 'What the hell is going on here? You're dead!'

'Not yet. You understand what I just said? It doesn't matter if I'm around or not, that mark protects her. It protects all Nomad, no matter what. You're no better than a slaver talking like that!'

'I apologise, sir.' Vance's face turns purple as Gryffin continues to squeeze his neck. He slams him against the wall one last time then drops him to the floor. Gryffin quickly glances at Terra, but she breaks eye contact and drops her gaze to the floor. He swallows deeply, knowing he completely overreacted. Attacking Vance like that wasn't in the plan. He's here to convince the captains to join with him again, not threaten to shoot him for talking about Terra. He has to rein in these dangerous emotions for Terra. At this rate, he'll destroy things before he's had a chance to fix them.

Vance pushes up into a sitting position and rubs his bruised neck. He coughs and tries to catch his breath as he looks over at Gryffin. He only hopes he didn't push his point too much. Vance slowly gets to his feet and walks up to Gryffin. He braces for the blow he deserves, but Vance does the last thing he's expecting. He laughs loudly and shakes his head.

'My God, it really is you.' Vance slaps him on the back and smiles. 'Welcome back, High Commander.'

∞

Terra sits back on her chair and tries to process what just happened. Gryffin had nearly choked Vance because of what he said about her. She's going to go mad trying to figure him out. No one has ever stood up for her like that. She's more than capable of handling Vance and his advances, but it was still nice to have Gryffin do it for her. In true Gryffin style he had completely blown it out of proportion. While she thought his actions would surely have put an end to the meeting, she'd been surprised when Vance had laughed the whole thing off.

Vance takes a swig from his bottle and sits back down, crossing his long legs at the ankle. 'So, Gryffin, what's this cloak and dagger meeting all about? Where have you been for the last year?'

She notices the pained look on Gryffin's face. 'I was stuck on one of the prison moons.'

'That where you got your new eye?'

'I want to reunite the Nomad,' Gryffin replies, ignoring the previous question.

Vance looks at him for a moment before laughing out loud. 'You're ambitious I'll give you that.'

'You don't think it's possible?' Terra asks.

Vance glances at Gryffin before answering her. 'No offence, but no, I really don't.' He turns his attention back to Gryffin. 'You may have *Ares*, but it'll take more than that to inspire us to join forces again.'

'Why?' she asks again. Gryffin frowns at her, but she ignores him. This affects her just as much as him.

He must notice the look on Gryffin's face. This time he addresses him. 'With the greatest respect, Commander, you killed many of our colonists. Thanks to that, we're being hunted like animals. We've lost half of our ships with many of the ones left turning Rogue just to survive. We've been forced to go back to the old ways even though it's against everything we fought for under your command.'

'But now that Gryffin's back surely you can all work together to put it right?' Terra says, again ignoring the daggers coming at her from Gryffin's direction.

Vance leans forward and looks at Gryffin. 'Sir, I fully supported you in your work to make the Nomad into more than they were. I was amazed at the way a young man could command our unruly group. It was a massive hit to us when you were taken. When you were declared dead it was as much a relief as it was a loss to the group. No one wanted to see you being used in that way. But we have long memories, sir. I'll fly with you again—you have my word on that. As for the others...' He lowers his head and looks at the ground.

'What?' Gryffin asks.

'Well...' He blows out a breath. 'Sir, you may be fighting a losing battle. Don't get me wrong. I'm not saying the answer will be no from everyone else. All I'm saying is that trust, or lack of, could be a problem. You're a damn powerful ally, sir, but you're an equally powerful enemy.'

Terra can see the truth in Vance's eyes even before he speaks. 'You believe the others will refuse, don't you?'

Gryffin looks down at the ground and Terra's heart sinks. He's giving up. Vance leans forward and clasps his hands together. 'I don't want to kick you when you're down, sir, but it'll take a lot to convince the others. Regaining that trust is key to getting the rest of the fleet on our side.'

'There isn't time for me to earn that trust back.'

Vance shrugs. 'Not saying I have the answers. Just advising you that it'll take more than a quick chat to get them back. Especially after what's happening to your allies.'

'What?'

Vance grimaces. 'Afraid you're a liability. People are still being targeted because of you.'

Gryffin quickly looks at Terra. 'What's he talking about?'

She lowers her gaze. 'It's nothing, Gryffin. Forget it.'

'No! I want to know what he means.'

She doesn't want to have this discussion with him, especially with Vance in the room. The older captain frowns at the glare she throws in his direction. 'The Rogues that attacked the transport I was in, were looking for you.'

'But why attack your ship?'

'Everyone knows you were working with the crew from *Infinity* and that you have a soft spot for one of their women.' He nods and smirks at Terra. 'I get the impression from your reaction this is the woman in question. Anyway, after what happened on the freighter and on Ultar, all your allies are targets. If a Rouge group suspected your lady friend, or any of *Infinity*'s crew was on that transport, they would attack. They wouldn't want her dead, just alive enough to talk.'

Gryffin's purple eyes burn brightly as he looks at a spot of the wall behind Vance's head. Vance looks down at his clasped hands and takes a deep breath. 'It's not been easy since you...'

'Turned?' Gryffin finishes.

Vance grimaces, but nods once. 'Exactly. It's been damn hard on us. The word Nomad leaves a bad taste in many mouths. I hope you've got something special up your sleeve. You're gonna need it.'

25

Gryffin wipes the blood from his eye and attacks the drone with everything he has. The fighting machine deflects the blows, landing its own across his chest. Gryffin swings the metal sparring stick down on the machine's head, splitting the hard metal shell, but not doing anything to slow it down. He grits his teeth and shoves his foot against its legs to knock it off balance. On its way to the ground, it grabs Gryffin's boot and twists his leg violently. Luckily, he sees what's about to happen a split second before it does, giving him a chance to flip his body in the same direction as his foot. He slams his boot into its chest and tries to get to his feet before his opponent does. The drone strikes him across the chest with its sparring stick, forcing him back to the ground again. It gets to its feet and rams the stick against Gryffin's side, breaking the already bruised skin. He curses in pain as blood weeps from his wound.

'What do you think you're doing?'

He ignores Terra and rolls onto his uninjured side. The drone pauses before it turns and moves away from him at Terra's instructions. 'Hey, get back here. I wasn't finished!'

Terra takes the place of the drone. Her long hair is loose, probably to hide the Nomad tattoo on her neck. He can't blame her. It isn't exactly going to offer her any protection. Not anymore.

Her bare arms are crossed over her chest, the tight black vest hugging her curves — not that he's looking. Neither is he looking at her lower half, which was nicely encased in a pair of leather trousers. No, he definitely isn't looking.

She taps her booted foot against the floor and clears her throat. 'I asked you a question.'

'And I said I wasn't finished. I'm trying to train.'

'Is that what you call it because it looked a hell of a lot different to me. If you're intent on killing yourself, I'm sure there are easier ways of going about it.'

With no grace whatsoever, he manages to sit up and leans against the wall, smearing blood across the metal plating. 'You offering to do the deed, Commander?'

Her face softens slightly. She crouches in front of him and the trousers tighten around her thighs. He seriously needs help. How many days until she's off his ship?

'Do you want to talk about it?'

'What would you like me to talk about?'

Terra opens her mouth to say something but stops and looks behind her. It's only then he notices the dozen or so crew working out in the training room have literally frozen to the spot. Before he can order them to leave, she jumps right in. 'Get out!' Within seconds they're alone.

'You after my command too?'

'Well if you acted like a captain every now and again, I wouldn't have to.'

'Sayber and Klay tried to take my command. You could be lucky number three. Join the long list of people who screwed me over.'

Terra thumps him full force in his already bruised face, the blow impacting under his right eye. 'You're pathetic and a coward. You enjoy letting a machine beat the crap out of you? Does it help you sleep better at night?'

'What I do with my free time has damn all to do with you.'

'It's my business when you're taking the Nomad down with you. I don't understand you. You should be fighting to get the Nomad together so we can get rid of the Foundation. How exactly is... whatever this is, helping you do any of that? Get up to the command deck and do your job.'

He pulls himself to his feet, irritated that he needs to support himself against the wall for a moment. 'I'm done listening to you. Get back to your quarters and stay there until we get back to Ultar.'

She shoves him back against the wall. 'That's your answer — to lock me away? Confining me to quarters won't make your problems go away.'

'It'll make you go away.'

'Knock it off, Captain. Stop feeling sorry for yourself and deal with what's going on,' she says, shoving him against the wall again. 'Deal with whatever is making you hurt yourself like this. Have you even seen yourself? You look like you've fought a war single-handed. Do you realise how out of control you actually are?'

'Terra...' he warns.

'No, it's about time someone tries to get through your thick skull. You need to listen. I can't sit back and watch you destroy yourself one piece at a time. You're unpredictable, moodier than usual, not sleeping or eating, and there's barely any skin left that's not bruised or cut. You nearly killed Desyl in front of the command crew for no reason. The Nomad deserve a captain who wants to lead them – not beat himself up.'

'Appreciate the vote of confidence.'

'I know you're more than capable of reuniting the Nomad and

leading this crew. The problem is you don't believe you can. Not anymore. I'm worried about you...' Her breath hitches for a moment. A small amount of guilt creeps in, but he dismisses it. 'Your crew is worried about you. Maybe if you spoke about-'

'No!'

'But you clearly need to get it off your chest.'

'I don't need to get it off my chest. I need to forget about it.'

'You can't just forget about it. You went through hell for ten months. Maybe you came back to *Ares* too soon. It's only been a few months since you got out of the med bay.'

'Give it a rest, Terra. I survived five years of fun when I was a kid. Ten months is nothing. Now, get the hell out of my way.' He clenches his fists as he resists the urge to shove her out of the way. Instead, he moves to the side, trying to get around her. He needs to put some space between them before he does hurt her.

'Where are you going?'

'Anywhere you're not. This conversation is done.' She holds up a sparring stick to stop him from passing. 'Don't tempt me, Terra. Get the hell out of my way.'

She stands firm so Gryffin grabs the stick out of her hands and launches it against the wall. 'Last time – back off.'

'I'm sorry, Gryffin.'

He hears movement above him, but his reflexes are messed up thanks to all the abuse he's been throwing at his body. The tranquiliser dart hits him in the chest, followed by one to his upper arm and another to his neck. He looks up at the walkway surrounding the room and can make out the shapes of four or five people holding guns. His vision continues to swim as he looks back at Terra.

'You left us no choice.'

He opens his mouth to reply but nothing comes out as he crashes to the ground.

∞

Terra winces as Gryffin kicks at the door to his cell. The bars don't give under the abuse. Desyl said it was designed to hold him and, so far, he hadn't been able to break out. She never thought she'd be the one to lock him in it like this, but they'd run out of options.

Gryffin's purple eyes never leave her as he prowls back and forth the small space. She hasn't seen him like this before. For the first time since she met him, he's scaring her.

Gryffin beats his fists against the bars of his cell. 'Open the damn door, Terra. Now!'

She crosses her arms, more so to hide the shaking, and stands firmly in place. 'You're wasting your breath, Captain.'

'So you do remember that I'm the captain of this ship! I'm ordering you to let me the hell out!'

'I can't, Gryffin.'

He barely contains the growl as he targets his first officer instead. 'Desyl...'

He lets the unspoken threat hang in the air. Desyl clears his throat but doesn't flinch away from Gryffin's purple eyes. 'You can glare at me all you want, sir. This has to end, and if keeping you in there for a bit helps, I wouldn't be doing my job as your first officer if I let you out.'

'What has to end?'

Terra clasps her hands in front of her and focuses on them instead of his furious expression. 'Since I joined *Ares*, I knew there was something different about you, something not quite right, but until today, I don't think I fully understood what's going on.'

He crosses his arms and leans against the bars. 'Care to share this... epiphany with me?'

'Your eyes.' Something changes in his face as she says those two words. The almost over-confident air surrounding him drops, which just serves to prove it to her. 'You've been using the control implant non-stop since I got here.'

'That a question or a statement?'

'The latter. Do you have any idea how much damage you're doing to yourself by using it continuously?'

'Why am I in here?'

Desyl gestures wildly. 'Because you're killing yourself! The implant was designed to give you an edge when needed. It wasn't designed to be used like this. I've been on *Ares* for years. You've never needed to use it this much before. If something is going on with you... If you feel you can't... I don't know, function without it, we need to deal with it.'

Gryffin pushes off the bars and goes back to his prowling. 'So everyone's still worried about their investment.'

'It's not like that, Gryffin, and you know it.'

'I'm back in a damn cage, Terra!'

She turns away from him and looks to Desyl for help, but he shakes his head. He's at a loss too. They both know Gryffin well enough to know it will be impossible to get through to him when he's like this. He's angry and falling into an argument isn't going to help anyone — least of all him. 'Okay. Fine. Stop using the implant. Right now. Show me, show all of us we're wrong.'

'You don't give me orders.'

'You're right. But he does,' she replies as she points at Desyl. 'He's taking command of *Ares* until you're ready to admit you have a problem.'

Gryffin slams his metal fist into the bars. 'Not so different from Sayber and Klay, are you?'

Desyl storms straight up to the cell. 'You haven't got a clue what you're talking about, sir. I'm doing this because I have your back. I'm doing this because, believe it or not, I actually do give a damn what happens to you. You're so dependent on the implant, we're losing you to it. You're completely unpredictable and that makes you dangerous – to the crew and yourself. The implant is changing you, sir.' He sighs and shakes his head. '*Ares* is loyal to Gryffin the man, not Gryffin the machine. Break the link, sir.'

Instead of threatening or shouting, Gryffin lowers onto the cot, lies back and closes his eye. Desyl curses and turns away from his captain. He calls the four security guards closer. 'He doesn't leave that cell for one minute without my say so. I don't care how much he threatens you. He stays. Got it?'

They nod in unison as Desyl storms from the room. Terra watches in silence as he charges through the door and down the corridor. Well, that went exactly as she thought it would. She looks at Gryffin once more before she follows Desyl from the room. She just hopes Gryffin sees sense and severs the connection before they lose him for good.

∞

Terra stands against the railings and looks down into the training area. Gryffin is either asleep or ignoring everyone again. In the three hours since they locked him in the cell, he hasn't backed down or said anything beyond their initial discussion. His irritating stubborn streak only seems to be exaggerated by the implant.

She clutches her bag of medical supplies to her chest and pushes her shoulders back. The thought of walking down the metal stairs fills her with dread, but his injuries need seeing to and she's put it off long enough. At least his body will have time to heal if he's restricted to the cell. This self-destruct path Gryffin is on, is not only taking him down, but it's also destroying any chance of reuniting the Nomad and fighting against whatever the Foundation has planned. If he doesn't snap out of it soon, they could all be in trouble. Unless he breaks from the implant and deals with what happened to him, the Nomad will never be a group again. In the space of one meeting with Vance, Gryffin had managed to double their fleet — she prefers to look at the bright side. Convincing a certain brooding Nomad to do the same is going to be a tiny bit harder.

Taking her fifth deep breath she descends into the training room and cautiously approaches the cell at the back of the room. It may be foolish on her part, but she hasn't brought any additional security with her. Desyl has stationed someone outside the door just in case, but she insisted on going to tend to Gryffin alone. She has to show him that she trusts him.

She stops at the cell and knocks on the metal. A minute goes by without any response, which doesn't surprise her in the least. 'Open it.'

The guard frowns but does as he's told. He locks the door behind her. 'Leave us.'

'Commander-'

'Now!'

Once alone, she places her bag on the ground and turns to face him. Gryffin is sitting on his bed, silently watching her. The blood from the wound the drone gave him still covers his shirt.

'Thought I confined you to quarters,' he snaps.

'I'm insubordinate, remember.' She moves to the end of the bed, ignoring the venom coming from him. She opens her bag and takes out a couple of towels, a small bowl, sterile swabs, ice-packs, gloves, a bottle of water, and a suture pack. Doing her best to dismiss the icy stares from behind her, she fills the bowl with water and places it on the floor at his feet. She kneels in front of him and snaps on the gloves. 'Strip.'

He raises his one, very bloody eyebrow. 'I'm not in the mood, Terra.'

She pokes a finger into the wound on his side and he hisses in pain. 'I don't really care. Now strip. Or do I have to call some of your crew in here to restrain you? Don't think I won't,' she confirms at the look of disbelief on his face. They stare each other down for a few seconds until he finally relents and pulls his t-shirt over his head. Terra blows out the breath she was unconsciously holding. That was easier than she thought it would be. He may not believe her, but she does actually have a team ready to restrain him. Seems his foul mood has rubbed quite a few of them the wrong way.

'Trousers too,' she says when he sits down again. He unfastens his boots and pulls them off before pushing down his trousers. Trying to remain emotionless becomes increasingly difficult when he's standing in front of her in just a pair of black boxer shorts, but this isn't about her. It's about trying to help Gryffin who, by the look of the injuries on his body, is well overdue for some help.

Both legs are covered in large bruises and cuts, the skin joined to his metal leg is torn exposing some of the wiring underneath and she can't see any flesh that isn't bruised on his torso. The large wound from sparring seems to be the worst of the cuts, but it's certainly not the only one. His tattoo is barely visible on his arm and chest through the bruises, and his right eyebrow has a large gash across it, thanks to the drone and her. His bottom lip is split and swollen as is the skin around his eyepiece, but that's not what upsets her the most.

His ribs are more pronounced and the large dark ring under his eye stands out in stark contrast to his pale skin. She shouldn't have let whatever this is go on for as long as she has. He clearly isn't well. 'I thought the drones have safety protocols built in?'

'Dismantled it. It's no fun unless there's a real threat.'

'Sit down,' is all she can say. What else can you say to a reply like that? She starts by cleaning the large hole in his side before he bleeds out. 'It's going to need stitches.' He just nods without looking at her. She checks the gauge on the anaesthetic but he stops her before she injects it into him.

'Don't bother. My implants will neutralise it.'

'What can I use?'

He shakes his head. 'Nothing will work. Just stitch it.'

Terra presses her lips together in a tight grimace. She opens the suture pack and pauses with the needle next to his skin. She's never sutured anyone while they were conscious before. Forcing her hand to move, she pierces his skin and pulls the thread through. To his credit, Gryffin barely flinches while she places ten stitches in his side. 'When did you last eat?'

'I don't need you to look after me.'

She snorts and shakes her head. 'Someone needs to. I can count your ribs.'

'Then don't look if it's bothering you.'

She cuts the thread and places a dressing over it. 'Sometimes you have the mentality of a five-year-old.'

His only response is to glare at her for a few seconds before he looks away again. Turning back to the job at hand, she focuses on his wounds. 'So, have you thought about what we said?'

He refuses to answer, which doesn't surprise her in the least. He's in a difficult mood, even for him. Unfortunately, the next most severe wound is the one over his eye. She pulls the chair around, sits in front of him and carefully moves his hair out of the way. 'Right, so if you're not willing to talk about your use of the control implant are you ready to tell me what's bothering you?' It's futile at best, but she can't bear the silence any longer. 'Tell me what's going on in that head of yours.'

'Why don't you hook me up? I'm sure you can download some juicy info. Share it with the rest of the fleet. They must want to know how their investment is doing.'

She pulls away, hurt by his words. This isn't going to work. He's too wound up in his own problems to care about what he's doing to himself and everyone else. He needs a swift, sharp kick — and fast. She pulls off her gloves and stands up. 'Very well, Captain. You win. I'm not going to waste my time and perfectly good medical supplies on someone who doesn't want to be helped. You say you're only here to reunite the Nomad and bring the colonies back together, but you're not.'

He looks up at her and his purple gaze glows through locks of his hair. 'What?'

She leans down and looks him straight in the eye. 'You clearly couldn't care less about any of that. If you did, you wouldn't be giving up. You're nothing but a hypocrite. You claim to hate the mechanical side of yourself, yet here you are, hiding behind it because you're scared.'

'I'm what?'

'You're scared and angry, and instead of dealing with those feelings, you're hiding like a coward.'

He quickly pushes to his feet. 'I'm not a damn coward.'

She prods him in the chest. 'Prove it! You never needed the implant to command the ship and fleet before. Are you really going to let the Foundation win by becoming exactly what they want you to be, an emotionless robot?'

His nostrils flare as he takes deep breaths.

'I don't have time to waste on this. Desyl needs everyone on this ship focused on the Nomad fleet.' She shakes her head and turns away from him.

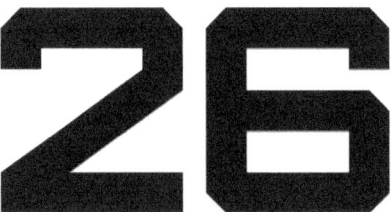

Damn it.

She's right. He is a coward hiding behind something he hates. Gryffin wants to say something, anything to get Terra to stay, but she's gone before he gets his mouth to work. He briefly considers seeing if there's anything in the bags that can help him escape. It'd be a waste of time. She's too smart to bring anything like that into the cell. He ignores the pained protests from his injured body and pulls his clothes back on. He leans against the bars and glares at the guards stationed with him. One of them catches his eye, but quickly turns away again.

They don't understand. No one does. If they did, he wouldn't be in this cage again. When he broke out of the Scientist's lab, he swore he'd ever be in a cage again. He sure as hell wasn't expecting Terra and his own crew to imprison him. He kicks the bars and runs his hands through his hair as he paces the small section of floor assigned to his prison. He may be a coward for using the implant, but there's not a lot else he can do. Without it, he'd be worse than useless. He's a mess.

Not sleeping. Not eating. Not able to function without a lump of metal in his head. He's a disgrace to the Nomad.

The implant is the only thing keeping him from being a total loss. Once the Nomad are reunited, he'll stop using it. He'll never use the damn thing again if that's what people want. He can't turn it off until then. But how can he make them understand? It's not as black and white as they all think.

He grabs onto the bars and pushes back against them. He needs to get out of here. He needs to get back on the command deck. His throat closes and he reaches up to make sure the collar hasn't suddenly made a reappearance. As if that's not bad enough, the hollow feeling in his chest increases. Seems it wants nothing to do with the implant either. He gives the control implant a little more freedom. It does the trick. A cold numb feeling takes over. He breathes steadily as he gets used to the strange out of body sensation. He knows he should be worried about what the control implant is doing to him. At the moment, keeping the horrible emotions and sickening hollowness at bay is more important.

With no distracting unfamiliar emotions to deal with, the old reliable anger pops to the surface. Anger at being a prisoner again. Anger at his crew for locking him up. Anger at being helpless, yet again.

Gryffin's body tenses as he focuses on the bars separating him from his freedom. Something clicks in his head. An irrational surge of rage leaves his body and focuses on the bars. He roars and throws his body against them, again and again. The security team races over to the bars, but are unclear what to do. They'd better get the hell out of his way if he breaks out. He'll have no problem ploughing through them. They're in his way. A small part of him actually hopes they stay. He wants to hurt them, to hurt someone. He wants to fight.

His torn fist leaves blood on the bars, but he doesn't feel the pain. He rams his shoulder into the door over and over. The cage vibrates under his attack but doesn't yield. The damn thing was designed to hold him — even in an implant-controlled rage.

His guards shout at him to stop. The horror on their faces only spurs him on. The bitter tang of blood fills his nostrils as he punches, kicks and throws his body against the metal. 'Open the door!'

As one, the guards shake their heads. Damn them. He'll take them out once he gets out of here. Sweat stings his eye and plasters hair to his face. He opens his mouth to give another useless order. The words stop in his throat. Pain like he's never felt before tears out of his new eyepiece. A gargled scream rips from his throat. He presses his hands to the eyepiece and falls to the ground. Blood fills his mouth as he continues to scream.

∞

Terra feels sick. Waves of dizziness threaten to bring her to her knees. Gryffin's screams ring in her ears to keep her pounding heart company. The sour taste in her mouth doesn't help her queasiness. She loses her footing at the bottom of the stairs, but Desyl is there to catch her. He helps her to her feet and holds her hand as they race to the training room. What they find when they step onto the mezzanine level will stay with her for a long time. Gryffin is writhing on the floor with his head firmly gripped in his hands. Blood is smeared on the floor and bars of his cell.

Desyl roars orders at the guards but Terra doesn't hear anything. She's already charging down the spiral stairs. She grabs the bars to slow down and skids to a halt. 'Open the door!'

The guards look at Desyl for instructions. He joins her at the cell and shakes his head. 'It's too risky, Terra.'

'Open the door!'

Desyl crouches down beside her and looks at Gryffin. 'He's still using the implant.'

She shoves his hand off her arm. 'I don't care about that. He's in pain.'

'Shoot me.'

They both quickly look at Gryffin. 'Gryffin, can you hear me?' Terra reaches through the bars, but can't quite reach him.

'It won't... let... go.'

She sits on the floor and presses her face against the bars. She can barely see his face behind his hands. 'What can I do? Let me help.'

'Shoot me. The pain... will help. Like on Ultar.'

Her mouth opens and closes. Desyl pulls her away from the bars. 'He's right. Roman said Gryffin gained control again when he was shot. It's worth, well, a shot.'

Terra can't believe she's hearing this. 'Desyl, this is crazy.'

He shrugs and pulls out his gun. 'You want to do it?'

She looks back at Gryffin and gasps. His purple eye is locked on to her. Blood seeps from his nose and the corner of his mouth. His face is a mask of pain as he breathes through clenched teeth. 'Please.'

Without a word, she takes the gun from Desyl. Terra points it at Gryffin, targets his arm and fires. He grunts in pain. 'Again.'

She pauses for a second then does as ordered. The bullet grazes the side of his arm and Gryffin suddenly stills. Terra lowers the gun and slowly approaches the bars. 'He's not breathing!'

Desyl places his palm against the lock and punches in his code. The door clicks and she rushes to Gryffin's side. Desyl is quickly beside her with the med kit. He pulls the portable oxygen from the case and fixes it over Gryffin's nose and mouth. 'Gurney!'

'What's wrong with him?' Terra wants to remain calm and composed, but is seriously struggling. Calm and composed are a distant memory. His blood stains her clothes as she reaches over to check his pulse. 'There's no pulse. What's wrong with him?'

Desyl ignores her. At some stage he attached a small monitor to Gryffin's chest implant. He frowns at the screen.

'What is it?'

'Just shut up for a minute!'

Terra forces her mouth closed and focuses on Gryffin. His clammy skin is pale. He looks dead. 'Is he...'

Desyl finally acknowledges her. 'Not yet.' He jumps up and steps aside as the gurney finally arrives. The security team carefully lift the captain off the floor and strap him down. Desyl pulls her to the side as the gurney disappears up the lift. 'His implants have shut down. We need to hook him up to a temporary unit while I figure out how to reboot them.'

'What does that mean?'

'It means I have to go. Come with me if you want, but keep out of my way.'

Before she can respond, he steps into the lift with Gryffin. Terra stares after him for a few seconds. She feels numb. Her legs wobble so she slumps onto the bed in the cell. She stares down at her hands. Gryffin's blood covers her palms. This is her fault. She suggested the cell. What was she thinking? She knows nothing about his implants and how they work. He's in system failure and she's to blame.

∞

He's never been drunk. In his thirty something years, he's only tasted the stuff once. One mouthful of Ultaran ale had been enough to turn him off for life. The stuff burnt like liquid fire. If that wasn't bad enough, something in the alcohol affected his implants. His implants neutralised the effect, but only after a few minutes of his heart racing and blindness. Nothing could convince him to try ale again. Why anyone would voluntarily drink something that gives them little control over themselves is beyond him. Control is the very thing he fights to keep a hold of on a daily basis

Years of Ultaran parties has given him plenty of experience with hangovers. He's heard enough crew members complaining about the aftereffects of the stuff. Even so, he's sure the headache currently clamping and squeezing his skull tightly, would give any hangover headache a run for its money. Nausea twists his empty stomach and he really wishes someone would remove the large spike from his artificial eye. He moves his head slightly and groans as a fresh wave of pain courses through him.

'Gryffin?'

Terra's voice echoes loudly in his head. He wants to tell her to turn the volume down, but he can't find the energy to move his mouth, let alone speak.

'Can you hear me?'

He groans in pain and manages to force out a desperate plea. 'Loud.'

Someone, hopefully Terra and not Desyl, brushes a hand through his hair as he lies in the blissful silence again. Once he gets used to the pain, he realises the implant is silent. He feels... empty. Even though he hates the implant, over the last few weeks it protected him from everything, both emotionally and physically. With nothing to block them, memories of the months in captivity break out of their hiding places. A large aching cavity seems to open in his chest. Something blocks his throat, restricting his airway. He grabs his head as memories of his assault on Ultar join in the mix. The dam has finally broken free.

Terra's voice manages to break through. 'Gryffin, please, you're scaring me. What's wrong?' She tries to lift his head, but he pulls away.

He holds his head tighter as more and more memories push out of their hiding spots. Pockets of pain erupt over his body to add a more realistic feel to the memories. A horror reel of death plays in front of him — deaths of innocent Ultarans at his hands, deaths of prisoners as part of the experiments. It's all his fault. Terra's voice echoes in the background, but there's too much painful interference for him to get a hold on it.

The memories and the locked away feelings reach the pinnacle of their assault causing Gryffin to lose his final weak grip on everything.

He tries to link with the implant again. Tries to build the dam again, but it's a lost cause.

Strong hands hold him down on the bed. Terra takes his face in her hands. 'Look at me!'

He struggles to do as she asks.

'Get control of this, Gryffin.'

Easier said than done, but he wants to do as she says. He focuses on her green eyes and tries to. He doesn't know what to do... how to control it. A stab of pain shoots through his arm. The pain increases, but he welcomes it. He grits his teeth and opens his eye as fingers dig into his arm in the same spot where he was shot.

Terra looks down at him and smiles. 'I've missed that.'

'What?'

'Your blue eye.'

'Can you let go of me now — that hurts.'

She gives his arm one more squeeze for good measure and leans over him. 'How are you? You scared us all.'

He frowns and blinks a few times. 'Fine.'

'You're not getting away with fine.'

'I'm not using the implant, that's what you wanted, right? Nothing else matters.'

'How can you say that? Of course it matters. You asked me to shoot you. Twice. Whatever's in your head isn't going to just go away. Is it memories you're struggling with?'

'How I deal with my feelings is my business.'

She sits back and a satisfied grin covers her face. 'So that's the core of the problem.'

He curses his slip of the tongue. 'I'm tired, Terra. Just go.'

'Oh no. That's not going to work. You're not going to ignore me, or this. Why are you so angry?'

'I'm not angry.'

'Really, you could have fooled me.'

'I'm just a little...' Frustrated. Pissed off.

She moves closer, her face neutral. 'A little what?'

He really doesn't want to do this, but he has no choice. Short of shooting her, she's not going to leave. He's not really convinced that he actually wants her to leave. He's having a hard time focusing on anything other than the images in his head. Arguing with her is giving him a welcome distraction. He never thought he'd need someone in his life, but he needs Terra. She's the only small spark still visible through the choking darkness that surrounds him.

'Lost.'

Her brow wrinkles slightly. 'Why?'

'I knew there was a chance they wouldn't follow me again. After everything I did, I expected it. But hearing it from Vance... it threw me.'

She nods and gestures for him to continue. No easy escape for him. When he doesn't speak she crosses her arms over her chest. He sighs and focuses on the wiring peeking out from his torn leg. Anywhere is better than looking at the disappointment on her face. 'Using the implant helped me focus on what I needed to.'

'In other words, helped you ignore your feelings.'

'I shouldn't have taken it out on you and the crew.' He looks up at the ceiling and sighs loudly. 'All I seem to be doing is making things worse.' He scrubs a hand over his face. 'I need to fix this mess, but I haven't got a clue how. All I've ever known is the Nomad. I owe them my life. I have to get them flying together again. I don't care what I have to do. As long as they're united... well, that's all I want.'

She reaches out towards his face, but pulls her hand back before she makes contact. Instead, she slips on a pair of gloves and begins cleaning the two wounds on his arm. 'You can't depend on the implant to help you get through this. If you can learn to talk about and to deal with what's going on in your head, it will make you a stronger person.'

'The implant does that.'

'Artificially.' She pulls back and looks him in the eye. 'I can't imagine what's going on in your head. I'm struggling with the little I know about what happened to you. I do know one thing, however — using the implant as you have been will destroy you. You're not a machine, Gryffin. Don't lose yourself to what they tried to make you. You're so much more than that.'

Hearing her say that helps to dull the ache in his chest. He spent years trying to prove he's more than what the Foundation and Rayde tried to make him. It's been years of trying to juggle the machine side of him as well as the unfamiliar human emotions. He doesn't want to be what he is, but when things got too tough, he ran and hid behind the very thing he hates about himself. Not exactly the actions of someone who hates not being fully human. All his life he's been stuck in the middle somewhere — never accepting the unpleasant aspects of each side of himself. 'I am a coward.'

Terra grimaces and brushes some hair off her face. 'I apologise for saying that.'

'No, you're right.'

'Well, there's never a recorder around when you want it. Okay, so, what's your plan?'

'For what?'

She scrunches her nose up as she concentrates on his arm again. Gryffin resists the urge that suddenly comes over him to kiss her nose. He really needs to get a hold on himself.

'For fixing what you did. How are you going to get the Nomad back together? And before you jump down my throat — yes I did hear what Vance said.'

'Then why are you asking me if you've just answered the question?'

She picks up a dressing, places it on the wound and reaches for the tape. 'So, you're just giving up? You fought to get out of the facility. Why bother going to all that effort if you're just going to walk away?'

'It's not that easy. Other than forcing them, there's not a lot else I can do.' As Terra examines his face, he keeps his eyes firmly on a spot of rust on the ceiling.

'Well, how did you get them together the last time?'

'They came to me.' She wrings out her cloth and wipes it carefully over his face. The cloth comes away stained rust-brown. He must look a state after his episode in the cage. She moves down to his chest. He closes his eye and swallows deeply, relieved that her focus is elsewhere. The large lump in his throat is making swallowing difficult and his pulse seems to be all over the place.

'Why did they come to you?'

He never really thought about it before. It just sort of happened. He took command of *Ares* and over the next year slowly tried doing things differently. Within the first year he'd signed up five colonies. It wasn't a lot, but he had chosen well. The colonies each offered the Nomad something different in return for their protection. They went from having a far from reliable ship, hardly any weapons or medical supplies and fighting each other for scraps of food, to actually living for the first time in years.

He'll never forget the first meal Aleena invited them to on Ultar. Although initially embarrassed when his starving men had all but inhaled the food, Aleena had just smiled and kept the food coming. There were more than a few ill Nomad the following day, but no one complained.

Word had quickly spread through the rest of the fleet and within a few months there were three additional ships aligned with *Ares*. Over the next year another twenty-three ships joined, while the final six had signed up early the following year. Everyone prospered from the deal — more than just having food and medicine. For the first time in years they were actually a group. Safety came hand in hand with that.

Terra looks at him strangely.

'What?'

'You zoned out for a minute. Maybe you should get some rest.'

'No!' he replies a little louder than he planned. The last thing he wants is to be alone with all this confusion. He's never wanted company, but now the thought of being by himself freaks him out.

'It's okay, I'll stay. So, why did they join with you?'

'I guess the security brought them into the group. Instead of being out there alone, they had something to belong to.'

She meets his eye and smiles. 'Sounds a little like you, doesn't it?'

It does sound like him. The Nomad gave him security after what happened, both when he was a child and recently. It may not be the group as a whole, but *Ares* supports him. The crew didn't turn their back on him. They had even rebuilt *Ares* so she could lead the fleet again. 'Doesn't help with the Nomad issue.'

'The Nomad came to you because you offered security and somewhere to belong. Seems like that's needed now more than ever.'

'Because of me.'

'Because of the Foundation.' Her piercing green eyes lock onto his stopping any further argument. 'People will believe whoever shouts the loudest. At the moment nothing is shouting louder than the devastation in this Sector. People need something to believe in again.' She pauses. 'There have been so many stories flying around since you... left.' He can't help but notice the way her eyes gloss over towards the end of the sentence. 'Very few people actually talked about you being dead. Most of the talk revolved around speculating where you were, when you would come back, how you would 'kick some Foundation ass' when you got back,' she adds with a smile. 'You just need to give them something to believe in, something to fight for.'

27

Terra smiles as she climbs out of the transport and looks around the cargo hold of *Ares*. She was only gone for three days and was surprised at how much she missed the ship. Possibly her temporary captain too. Like the rest of the crew, she spent most of the time over on *Styx* trying to make her fighting fit. The smaller vessel had taken quite a few bad hits over the months and, with colony support thin on the ground, Vance had been unable to give her the attention she needed. While she hadn't expected to be on the list of crew being sent to *Styx* for the repairs, she had been delighted to see her name included. Maybe Gryffin is finally realising she has more to offer.

Vance had been nothing but a perfect gentleman with her, as were the rest of his crew. Desyl did let it slip that Gryffin had done his usual diplomatic threatening to ensure everyone behaved. Some things never change.

Terra hasn't spoken to Gryffin in the three days since she patched him up. She would have given anything to spend all her time making sure he was all right, but they couldn't afford the luxury. Desyl assured her that he'd be fine. *Ares* is Gryffin's family and each member of the crew would look out for him — whether Gryffin wanted it or not. She fully trusts the Nomad are more than capable of dealing with him. She just wishes she could help him more than she has. It's probably for the best. Being so close to him, watching over him while he was unconscious, and tending to his wounds hasn't helped her get over him in any way. She's still in love with someone who doesn't know how to love.

Terra tries not to get too upset about her predicament. She hauls her small bag through *Ares* and dumps it in his quarters. After a quick shower and change, she makes the short trip to the bridge to report in with her captain. She can't help the small smile that crosses her face. Gryffin is her captain. Initially, she didn't want to be anywhere near *Ares* — or her captain. The ship is dark and cramped, the Nomad act completely differently to Foundation crew and Gryffin is stubborn and rude, but after spending some time with them, she realises she's actually rather fond of them all. They may approach things differently, but that's not a bad thing. The Foundation could hardly be used as a good example of how to run a group.

Terra stands at the bottom of the steps leading to the command deck and attempts to steady her racing heart. In spite of her best efforts, she is excited about seeing Gryffin again. The longer she's on *Ares*, the stronger her feelings for Gryffin get and that's not good. His mixed signals are enough to drive anyone insane. The best thing for her is to restrict contact with him to only ship duties. Not exactly easy on a ship the size of *Ares*.

It's not going to get any better if she delays. She straightens her shoulders and climbs the steps, staggering at the top when she sees Gryffin. It may only have been three days, but it could have been a year judging by the difference in him. Even without saying a word, one look from him tells her volumes.

His big, broad shoulders are back, his posture strong and sure as he stands at the front of the command deck. The bruising on his face is fading and she is even more thrilled to notice the very obvious lack of new ones. He turns to face her and holds her gaze. The coldness that has been present since they got him back from the dead has vanished. His dark blue eye is alive and vibrant. Their quiet staring is drawing attention so she moves to her station.

Clearly hiding his own smile, Desyl takes his place next to Gryffin. 'Everything's done. *Ares* and *Styx* are ready and awaiting your orders, sir.'

Gryffin leans on the metal railing circling the upper command deck. 'We're going back to the station where we found Vance.'

Desyl raises his eyebrows. 'But, sir, no one else there was interested.'

She feels him looking at her so lifts her head to meet his blue eye. She may be imagining it, but she's convinced she can see a small smile on his face. 'It's up to me to convince them.'

∞

'Who the blazes are you?'

Bray steps into the cell with his gun raised in front of him. He immediately gags at the suffocating smell of stale sweat and human waste clouding the warm, damp air. A hulk of a man rises to his feet and examines him. Bray leaves his gun trained on the prisoner. One look at the man tells him the prisoner could snap him like a twig if he wants to.

His attention is drawn from the man to the room he occupies. The cells in this place are worse than he remembers. Prisoner wellbeing only exists in the facilities closer to Earth. No one checks the outer prisons. Why would they? They're well outside the safe travel distance from Earth. Who in their right mind would risk an encounter with Rogue groups just to check on some prisoners?

What was once a gleaming, seamless metal wall is now rusting and has been patched up so many times it's hard to tell what pieces are original. The lavish toilet consists of a hole dug in the ground. By the sounds coming from it, you risk offering your flesh to the hungry rats if you get too close. Distant relatives of the Earth cockroach share the prisoner's wafer thin mattress. A chipped cup full of thick, brown liquid sits on the floor next to the bed. At the moment, one of the cockroaches is taking a dip in whatever is in it. If all the cells are like this one, he's not going to have a hard time convincing them to come with him. Just standing in the room is making him itch.

Bray slowly lowers his gun. This guy will be a massive asset to the group — literally. His large biceps bulge as he crosses his arms. He takes one step closer to Bray. The light from the corridor hits him and Bray is tempted to lift his gun again. Bray is tall, but this guy would give even Gryffin a run for his money. His massive chest is bare apart from three large scars across his torso and a tattoo of the Foundation logo with a red target covering it on his left pec. Another Foundation fan by the looks of it.

The man squints against the light entering the cell behind Bray. He frowns and clenches his fists. 'Cyborg, you've got one minute to leave before I kill you.'

Not for the first time Bray curses the implant beside his eye. 'I'm not a cyborg. I'm a Hunter.'

'Really, because you sure look like one.'

Bray points his gun at the man. 'Let's get one thing straight. I am not a cyborg. I want their creator and every one of the things dead. Now, do you want out of here or not?'

The man's brown eyes bore into Bray. He frowns and scratches his jaw. 'I don't have a lot of other options right now, Hunter. What's the catch?'

Bray ducks back into the corridor as gunfire and shouting echoes through the facility. Time is running out. He needs to get him on his side, and quickly. It'll make the rest of the isolation prisoners easier to convince. 'Hunters and Nomad have joined. We're fighting against the Foundation occupancy. This is their next target. They want to experiment on all the prisoners here.'

The man grunts. 'You've convinced me.' He grabs a small box off the shelf attached to the wall. 'I'm all packed and ready to go.'

Bray steps back out into the corridor and gestures to the neighbouring cells with his gun. 'How about the rest? Will they be on board?'

The man pushes matted blond hair off his face and smiles, surprisingly showing an intact set of teeth. 'Given half the chance, they'll bite your hand off as quick as the blasted rats will bite your arse off.' He sticks a large hand out. 'Garvan.'

Bray clasps his hand and shakes it once. 'Bray.'

Garvan shakes his head and chuckles to himself.

'What so funny?'

'Things are just slotting into place. You escaped here years ago. Still a legend among some of the older residents.'

Bray freezes. He's a legend? That's news to him. Probably best he doesn't let slip that he had help from a Foundation admiral. Might tarnish his reputation. 'I am?'

Garvan nods. 'You were the last. Security stepped up after that.'

'How about we change that and get out of this shithole.'

Garvan slaps him on the back and approaches the neighbouring cell. Bray contacts the crew as Garvan sees to the locks. 'How we doing up there?'

Sayber curses a few times as gunfire explodes near him. 'Ah sure, we're having a party up here. What's keeping you? Don't want you to miss out on the fun.'

Bray keeps a close eye on Garvan as he speaks to another inmate. They're a long way from trust. Bray is offering a way out. Only time will tell if trust can develop from that. 'Just collecting a few strays. We'll be at the transport in ten.'

'Make that five. We'll be dead in ten.'

Bray closes the connection and gestures at Garvan. 'Pick up the pace.'

'Right you are.' He moves to the next cell and frees the locks as Bray deals with the cells to the right. Instead of having a heart to heart with the twelve in isolation, Bray ushers them out of their cells with his gun and lets Garvan do the introductions. He's shocked when women step out of two of the cells. Looks can be deceiving but he can't imagine they're the deadliest criminals in the Sector.

As expected, the inmates don't need time to mull over the offer. They help themselves to weapons from the downed guards and, after stopping to repay a few of them for their hospitality, obediently follow Bray to the end of the corridor. He meets with the rest of his team and they lead the new recruits up through the levels to the main prison.

The acrid smell of smoke fills Bray's nostrils the higher they climb. He wipes the sweat from his face as the heat builds. The sound of their boots on the metal staircase is quickly drowned out by the screeching of alarms. They reach the door that opens to the main facility. Bray carefully peers through the bars and signals to the Hunters behind him. He slowly opens the door and two Hunters step out, their weapons at the ready. They quickly sweep the area and give the all clear.

Bray scans the level. The Hunters have been busy. Foundation and cyborg guards litter the concrete floor. Their once pristine uniforms darkened with blood. Bray's boots squelch as he steps over the bodies. He glances back at the inmates. Some of them are smiling. He can't blame them. The guards weren't here to make the prisoners lives pleasant. Sayber's voice crackles in his ear. 'Shift your arse, Bray!'

He doesn't need to be told twice. 'Move!'

The newly formed team quickly clears the level and climbs up another flight of stairs to meet with Sayber. Empty cells line the corridor. If all these people agree to work with them, they'll have a fairly healthy army. Bray leads the team through the next door.

'Down!'

As one, the mismatched group drops to the ground. Rounds punch into the concrete wall above his head, showering him in dust and debris.

'Where are they?' Garvan asks.

'Damned if I know. Must be above.' He risks a quick look and spots a cyborg on the mezzanine level. 'Cyborg. I can see the red eye.'

Garvan curses and grips his gun tighter. 'Hate those wretched things. Any bright ideas?'

'I'll keep him busy. Take everyone to the next level.' He doesn't wait for a response. Bray slams the door open and dives behind the metal staircase. It should offer him a little cover but not much. He fires at the cyborg, keeping his attention away from the open doorway. 'Now!'

Garvan sprints across the open floor with the rest of the team. Bullets fly past Bray's head. One of them hits an inmate in the head. They don't stop to check on him. He's dead. Bray's next shot hits home. The cyborg tumbles over the railing and lands on the concrete. Bray sprints after the team and reaches Sayber. The Hunters and any remaining guards are each trying to hold the floor. Upturned metal tables provide little cover from the bullets flying in their direction. The smell of cordite and blood assaults him along with the sounds of gunfire. Sayber brushes blood stained hair off his face. He smiles widely in spite of the situation. Bray can't help but to smile back. He's missed this. Missed being on *Perses* and working with Sayber. The man is just the right side of crazy to keep things interesting. 'Having fun, Commander?'

Bray shakes his head. 'Not especially, sir. Time to go?'

'Couldn't agree more. The ones I got out are already on their way to the transports. They're just waiting for us to get a move on.' Sayber speaks quickly into his radio. The rest of the Hunters will rendezvous back at the transports. Bray turns to his new recruits. Garvan is holding his own against the onslaught. 'Ready to move on my mark?'

Garvan pauses long enough to nod. Bray fires a few rounds, and gets to his feet with Sayber. 'Move!'

The team breaks cover and races towards the door as the Hunters provide covering fire. They burst through the door and Sayber skids to a halt. He tears the control panel off the wall. The light over the door blinks once to confirm it's sealed. Bray herds the group ahead of him towards the waiting transports. The tang of blood in the air lessens as they leave the main facility behind. He'll be glad to get out of here. Memories of the years he spent here are far from good. As angry as he is about Avoca's lying, he'll be in his debt forever. He'd still be rotting in this dump if he hadn't helped him escape.

They enter the main hangar and Bray allows himself to relax a little. The five ships are loaded and ready to go. He ushers his team into the nearest one and once everyone is in, seals the door. Sayber orders the ships off the ground immediately. With only standing room, the occupants bump against each other as the ship takes off. One by one, the ships turn around and move towards the cargo doors.

A large hand slaps him on the back. He turns to face Garvan. Blood is splattered over his face and torso, but he's still smiling widely. 'Haven't had that much fun in years. You live up to your reputation, Bray.'

28

'I blame you for this.'

Terra glances sideways at Desyl as she straps her holster around her waist. She wants to come back with a smart remark, but deep down she agrees with him. She really doubts Gryffin would be doing this unless they'd had their talk a few days ago. While she's relieved he stepped off his destructive path, she's not so sure about his latest plan.

Ares and *Styx* are on their way back to the station at full speed. Long range scanners show thirteen old Nomad vessels there and he's desperate to arrive before they leave. Having so many in the same place at the same time is the stroke of luck they need right now.

Ignoring Desyl, she turns to look at the other crew in the cargo hold. Gryffin had divided the crew up between the two ships. His own crew have been in constant training since the fight at the Port, but Vance and his men haven't used the time as wisely. Months spent wallowing in alcohol has dulled their skills. Due to this, the crews have been mixed — with some *Ares* and *Styx* crew on each ship so both are covered. He ordered everyone to dress in their black leathers, leaving as much of their markings as possible on display. He doesn't want anyone mistaking who they are when they attack the station.

That's the bit she still can't quite get her head around and the bit that Desyl is blaming her for.

At the briefing two hours ago, Gryffin gave everyone clear orders on what's expected of them, beyond that he hasn't said what his overall plan is. She doesn't doubt he has one, she's a little anxious about what it actually is.

The Captain strides into the bay, instantly silencing the murmurs of disquiet and uncertainty among the crew. He stops just inside the room and casts an eye over the people gathered in front of him. Every available Nomad has been pulled from both crews for this mission. He's only leaving a handful on each ship so they can be ready to leave in a hurry if needed.

He meets her eyes and holds them for a moment before turning back to the room. All eyes are on him — hers included. He's wearing his uniform like everyone else, but instead of the shirt, he's wearing a sleeveless leather jacket, which shows off his tattoo and implants in all their glory. He nods at Desyl who opens a comms channel with *Styx*.

'We're docking in six minutes,' Gryffin says. 'The team on *Styx* is going to take the ships docked at the station. The thirteen Nomad vessels are priority, but once we have them, secure as many of the other vessels as you can. We'll take whatever we can get. *Ares* crew will lock down the station. Terra, your job is to shut down comms to and from the station. Unless the transmissions are on our channels, they don't go anywhere.'

She nods at him. 'Yes, sir.'

'Remember, these are our people. I need them alive if this is going to work. If you have to take a shot, do it. But be damn sure you can justify it to me later.' He pauses for a moment, his brow crinkles as he frowns. 'I know this is going against what we've done for the last few years and I know that you're all a bit unsure about what I'm ordering you to do. The truth is, the Nomad are dead if we don't do this. I'm sure as hell not ready to let us die. If that means going back to how we were then that's what we have to do. We need ships. They have ships. We're going to take them. It's that simple. Get into position.'

Terra moves to the small team assigned to help her with the comms on the station. 'You all set?' Gryffin asks from behind her, startling her.

She nods. 'We all know what we're doing.'

'Good, just make sure you stick close to me. The rest of the team will clear the way, but we're not sure how many people will be guarding the comms room.'

'Stick close to you?'

He guides her away from the group. 'If they get a comms signal out we could have trouble coming at us pretty quick from who knows how many different directions. Your part is key to everything else going according to plan. Also, I don't trust anyone else to get you there in one piece.'

'Are you confident you can use the implant without it taking control again?'

He shrugs. 'I've got no choice. If we're going to have a chance I have to use it.'

Terra takes a deep breath. 'I don't want to see you in a cell again. Please promise if you feel it taking over you'll shut it down.'

'You just focus on your job and let me worry about everything else.' After wiping the smiles from the faces of the rest of the team with an icy stare, he turns to face the door as they near the station. 'Let's go.'

∞

Gryffin looks out the hatch window as *Ares* docks with the station. Twenty-one ships sit alongside her. Thirteen are Nomad and they're the ships he's going to target. He braces as *Ares* shudders. The locking clamps slam into place and the engines shut down.

Each of the Nomad coming with him are armed, but for now, their job is to blend in with the locals. Until they're in position, he doesn't want to attract any attention. As soon as the hatch opens, Gryffin and the Nomad teams merge with the locals and move towards their targets. He veers off down a small access corridor and stops beside the maintenance terminal. He punches his fist through the cover to expose the unit. Gryffin turns to Terra. 'Find the connection. See if I can link.' She quickly connects her scanner. He's hoping that he'll be able to control the system himself and shut down the comms. Anything is better than having her wandering through this place.

After examining the information for a moment, she shakes her head. 'No good. The system is severely outdated. It looks like everything is run by one central computer. If you connect, the power surge will kill you.'

'Any of the main systems accessible from this panel?'

She frowns and shakes her head. 'It's all controlled from the primary engineering section.'

Just perfect. 'Looks like you're up then. Ready?'

She packs away her kit and nods. Before they step into the corridor, Gryffin links with the control implant. His stomach churns as his vision swims. The control implant fights for dominance, but he keeps it under a tight leash. He ignores Terra's concerned look and leads the team into the busy corridor to join with the other four Nomad assigned to his team. They get to the door leading to the stairs without any problems. He even manages to ignore the various people bumping into him along the way. He'll find them and kill them later. Gryffin glances around before he pulls sharply on the door. The tired lock gives way. He slides the door back and holds it open as the team squeezes through. After putting the metal back in place, he follows them down the stairs. Less than two minutes later, they reach engineering. He opens the door and checks the interior. They're alone. He gestures for Terra to go inside.

'How long do you need?'

Terra doesn't immediately respond. She's too busy looking in horror around the dark, cramped, and noisy room. 'How am I supposed to find anything in this mess?'

Gryffin orders two Nomad to keep watch. The other two step inside with him. His purple eyes scan the room. He nods towards the far corner. 'There's a big unit over there. Could be it.' He taps his gun against the nearest Nomad's arm. 'Eyes on her.'

Gryffin leaves Terra to her work and contacts Desyl. 'Well?'

At first, all he can hear is a burst of conversation on the other end. Desyl must have reached the main bar. 'We're all ready to go, sir.'

'We've reached comms.' He closes the connection and scans the room. The other Nomad with him is checking the ventilation system while Terra curses and mutters to herself in the corner. 'You okay?'

She shakes her head, before realising he's not actually looking at her. 'No.'

Gryffin joins her beside the lump of machinery. 'What's the problem?'

'I'm not familiar with this system.' She pulls the panel away from under the screen and gasps in shock. 'It's a keyboard control!'

'And?'

'I'm not trained for this. This machine is older than I am.'

'Yeah, well unless you figure it out quickly, you won't be getting any older.'

'Helpful.' She quickly pulls out her tablet and hooks it into the port on the side of the machine. 'Please connect,' she mutters to herself as she waits for the machines to link with each other. As the systems argue about connecting, Gryffin stands up and rolls his shoulders. He's itching for a fight but it's the last thing he actually wants. Fighting his own people will truly shatter any chance they have at a happy reunion.

He lifts his gun when Terra suddenly shouts. She smiles sheepishly. 'Sorry. They've connected.' She breathes a sigh of relief and wipes her arm across her sweaty forehead. 'Is it just me or is this room as hot as a sauna?'

'What's a sauna?' Terra throws a look at him that tells him he's asked a bloody stupid question. 'Just get a move on.'

'Thanks,' she replies sarcastically.

'Sir!'

Gryffin silences Terra with a look and hurries over to the guards outside the door. They gesture towards the stairs and hold up two fingers. They've got company heading their way. They duck back inside the room and close the door. 'How long, Terra?'

She glances down at the screen. 'Just under a minute.'

Gryffin sends two Nomad to stay with Terra at the back of the room. Her work is a priority. He stands to one side of the door with the last Nomad to the other side. They'll each take one, if they decide to come inside. He presses back against the wall and strains to hear what's happening outside. The footsteps approach and stop outside as the door is pushed open.

The men don't have a chance to voice their surprise. Gryffin drags one inside the room and the other Nomad takes care of the second. They're not Nomad. Gryffin nods. They knock out the two men and drag them into the corner of the room.

'Out of time, Terra.'

She packs up her kit and joins him at the door. 'I'm done. Comms are under Nomad control. Everything is rerouted through *Ares*.'

He nods and contacts Desyl. 'Good to go here. Comms are secure.'

Over the shouting and cursing in the bar, Desyl shouts his reply, 'All set.'

'One minute.' He shuts down his radio. 'Right, masks on.' He pushes the button on the device behind his ear and the metal mask covers his face. It's been a long time since they've used their masks.

They used to be part of day-to-day life — worn to protect their identity, and his of course. For the next part of his plan, the masks are vital. He looks down at Terra. Her green eyes are distorted behind the purple shielding over their eyes.

He quickly checks everyone is ready and then leads them from the room. The signal comes through from Desyl. It's starting.

∞

Terra follows Gryffin out the door and waits as he speaks to Desyl. It will take two minutes for the anaesthetic to work through the ventilation system and into the air supply. After that, depending on the individual's condition, probably another two for everyone to be knocked out. Initially, when he spoke of attacking the station, she feared the worse. The longer she is with the Nomad, the more she is learning about them, and Gryffin. He isn't going to send his men into a situation where they can be killed if there's a better way of doing it. 'How do you know this will work?'

Gryffin glances quickly at her. 'We've done it before.'

'You've knocked colonists out as part of your protection?'

'You know we do more than that.' His exasperated expression is hidden behind his mask but she knows it's there. She always hoped the other side to the Nomad was exaggerated. She doesn't want to think of Gryffin acting as a hired killer. She can't really criticise him. Life is tough out here. She fully understands how locals would and have been driven to doing things they may not agree with. Survival topped everything else.

'Time to round them up.'

Gryffin leads them back up the stairs and towards the crowded areas of the bar. They need to find the Nomad personnel among the other occupants and separate them. Gryffin will be happy to take anyone who wants to join, but the Nomad are the first task. There's only one tiny flaw to his plan. Gryffin may know each of the Nomad, but he's the only one. The only way to tell the Nomad apart is their tattoos. The ink they use has a certain composition. They'll have to scan each tattooed man to see if the ink matches. Terra can't think of a more unsettling way to spend the evening. They're also against the clock. Everyone needs to be contained before the anaesthetic wears off.

They enter the main floor of the station and are met by the strangest sight Terra has ever seen. Masked Nomad and unconscious bodies fill the corridor. Some of the Nomad are already slicing the material covering arms, backs and chests of the unconscious men to check for tattoos.

Desyl steps over a portly, half naked man and stops in front of Gryffin. 'Nomad in the bar?'

Gryffin nods. 'Everyone else in the bedrooms along this corridor. Make sure the locals and the rooms are cleared first.'

Desyl nods and hurries away. He steps closer to her. 'Make sure you're with a Nomad at all times.'

She knows her glare is lost behind the mask. 'Where are you going?'

'I need to check the other levels. Stay here. If any of them wake up don't deal with them yourself.'

He disappears with his security team along the corridor. Terra continues her useless glare even though he's long gone. She looks down at the large man at her feet. No visible tattoo, but that doesn't mean it's not on his back. She crouches beside him and watches his clammy, filthy chest rise and fall as he sleeps. Why didn't she bring gloves with her?

'It's really all or nothing with you.'

Bray looks up and smirks at Sayber. The Captain is leaning against the door frame with his arms crossed. The Hunter working on Bray's tattoos stops what he's doing and nods at Sayber.

'I figured I've put it off long enough,' Bray replies. Like the Nomad, Hunters use a particular design of tattoo to mark them. It wasn't compulsory, more a tradition than a set rule. Since he joined *Perses*, Bray considered himself a Hunter, but his connection to the Foundation had stopped him from taking up this tradition. He didn't want to dishonour the Hunters by getting the tattoos while still reporting to the Foundation. Things are different now. With ties cut to the Foundation, Bray no longer feels conflicted.

'You don't have anything to prove,' Sayber says.

Bray nods at the Hunter in front of him and the man continues his work. 'You let me stay on the crew. You didn't have to do that.'

Sayber nods. 'It's done, Bray. Whatever happened is behind us.' He walks around the Commander and whistles. 'You could have started small.'

Bray smiles. Getting the black swirling marks over both arms and his chest is probably overkill. Usually, only long serving Hunters go for the full artwork. 'Makes me look tougher than you.'

Sayber slaps him across the side of his head. 'You wish, Commander.' Sayber sits back on a chair and stretches his legs out in front of him. He strokes his goatee as he watches the Hunter finish his design. 'So, where's your new friend?'

'Garvan's training with some of the men. He's eager to prove himself.'

'Is he Hunter material?'

Bray shrugs. 'Could be. He's fitting in with the other guys. Someone with his recent life experience would be a plus.' Bray twists his arm so the Hunter can work on the other side. 'He'll need some intensive training to bring him up to everyone else's level. I think he's worth the effort.'

Sayber nods. 'I agree. We'll give him a few weeks and see how he gets on. I'll consider his future once I see what he can bring to the group.'

The Hunter working on Bray finishes his task, slaps the Commander on the back and leaves the two officers alone. Bray gets up and examines the results in the mirror. The thick black swirls run from each wrist and down his chest to his waist. There's no mistaking which group he flies with. 'I'll set out a training schedule for him.'

Sayber shakes his head and stands beside Bray. 'You're going to do more than that, Commander. You will stick to him every single minute of the day. You eat with him and you train with him. Everything. If he's going to have a chance at getting accepted into the group, he should have the chance to learn from the second best Hunter.'

Sayber laughs and slaps Bray on the back before he turns to

leave the room. 'Second best, Commander. You'll never be tougher than me — doesn't matter how many tattoos you get.'

'Yes, sir.' Bray grabs his t-shirt off the bed and carefully puts it on over his tender skin. He's got about an hour free before his shift starts — plenty of time to start some training with Garvan.

∞

Gryffin and Terra stand side-by-side outside the sliding door leading to the main bar area. He freezes and just stares at the metal plating on the door. 'Are you alright?'

He looks down at her. 'I give orders, not motivational talks.'

'You've negotiated with colonies. This is the same.'

He shakes his head. 'The future of the Sector never depended on me convincing a few farmers to sign up with me. I screw this up, we've just cost ourselves a fortune in fuel for nothing.'

She touches his arm, giving it a gentle squeeze. 'Stop over-thinking this. You just took an entire station without any casualties. Get in there and finish this.'

He takes a step towards the door, but stops again just before it opens. 'You coming?'

'You want me to go with you?'

He nods. 'You're part of my crew. I want you by my side.'

She nods, not able to stop the smile that spreads across her face. 'Of course.'

'Just stick close to Desyl. You're going to attract some attention in there.'

'Are you sure it's a good idea to bring me in with you? This is about you and them. If bringing a woman in there with you is going to cause problems-'

'Might as well throw it all at them at once. I've already betrayed and drugged them. What's a woman on top of that?'

He opens the door and walks into the room as if he owns it. As soon as he enters the bar, the room erupts. Angry shouts and curses drown out every other sound in the room. The crowd surges forward as Gryffin stands in front of the bar. If not for the wall of armed Nomad between them and Gryffin, she has no doubt they'd gladly rip him apart. She swallows past the large lump closing her throat.

Gryffin quietly watches the angry mob, thirsty for his blood. She's not sure he's delaying for effect or if he's having second thoughts himself. Either way, she doesn't envy him. Not quite getting the attention he wants, Gryffin fires a bolt of electricity at the ceiling to silence the group. Terra suddenly feels like all the eyes are on her. A female Nomad standing with the rest of the command crew is certainly getting attention. Desyl takes a barely noticeable step closer to her and she can't help but feel grateful. She does her best not to fidget and takes her lead from Desyl. Holding her gun in her hand, she pushes her shoulders back to show more confidence than she feels. Easier said than done. Especially when more than half the group look ready to attack at any minute. Perhaps this wasn't the best idea.

∞

'I can see from your faces some of you know who I am. For those that don't, I'm Gryffin.' The rumble of anger works through the group again causing Gryffin's security team to stand protectively in front of him.

One of the Nomad pushes to the front of the group. 'We heard you were dead.'

'Not yet. I've come here to talk to you.'

The man snorts. 'You don't talk — you kill. So, High Commander, you going to finish what you started?'

Gryffin inwardly grimaces at his words. This is where he's meant to convince them to work with him. Pity he can't think of a damn thing to say. He's a fighter, not a talker. Unfortunately, this situation will need a bit of both if he's going to get everyone out in one piece. 'I'm not going to kill you.'

The man scoffs. 'Sure.' He raises a gun and directs it at Gryffin.

Another five men emerge from the crowd, weapons raised. So much for checking the unconscious men and the room for weapons. If he survives someone is heading out the airlock for this. 'Well, we ain't putting our guns down, so what now?'

With no other option, Gryffin steps out from behind his detail and stands in front of the men. He slowly lowers his gun. 'I'm not here to fight you. I'm here to get the Nomad back together and flying as one again.'

The leader of the small group laughs. 'Right. Now why would we do something as stupid as fly with you again? You're the one we need protection from.' Murmurs of support ripple through the room. 'You may have convinced Vance, but that's as much as you're going to get.'

'Down!' Terra's scream pierces through the other shouting in the room. He drops as a bullet shatters the glass display case behind the bar. Shards rain down on him as the room erupts. He looks up and panic grips him when he can't find Terra. Where the hell is she? He jumps to his feet and charges his arm. His men are holding the crowd back but the armed Nomad are still in the throng somewhere. He scans the angry faces and spots her. She's gaining ground on the leader. His artificial eye zooms in on her. The damn fool is going after him.

He checks the bodies between them and curses. There's no way he can get to her before she reaches the man. He tries to aim at him, but he's still taking pot shots towards Gryffin. Seems he's not a fan. Gryffin lurches to the side as the bullet skims by his ear. He hisses in pain as the next one grazes his upper arm instead of hitting his chest.

All of a sudden, another weapon sounds in the crowd and the shooting stops. His team finally steps back from him and he looks at where Terra should be. The angry Nomad is on the floor at her feet and her gun is pressed against another armed man. She has her arm tightly around his neck as her weapon pushes so tight against his head the skin on his temple crinkles.

Gryffin stares at Terra as she commands the crowd. 'Put you weapons down or he dies!'

The female voice seems to cut through the angry male ones like a knife. Everyone stops what they're doing and turns to face her. Gryffin wants to step in, but she appears to have control of the situation.

She forces her weapon against him harder. 'I'm not asking. Put them down. Now!'

Gryffin tenses his arm, ready to shoot, but the men do as she commands. One by one, they lower their weapons to the ground. Gryffin nods and some of his men go retrieve the guns. Terra nudges her captive forward. The man slowly walks to the front of the group and, once out of the throng, Terra pushes him away from her. Gryffin stares down at her, but she keeps her gun and eyes trained on the crowd.

He shakes himself out of his daze as Desyl deposits the unconscious leader at his feet. He takes restraints from Desyl and fastens them around the leader's scrawny wrists. When he commanded the group before, he demanded all Nomad be trained and trained well. Every Nomad had to train daily to keep up to his standard. The man he's looking at hasn't seen a sparring stick or a weight for months. His movements were sluggish and his shots sloppy. The stale beer wafting from his body and clothes probably didn't help. Gryffin's stomach drops. If they're all like this, then the future of the Nomad could still be in trouble.

Gryffin checks on the rest of the team. Apart from a few minor grazes, they got through it in one piece. Gryffin wipes the blood off his arm. He clenches his fist as his hand trembles. His first reaction is to use the implant to steady himself. Instead, he turns to Terra. 'Where did that come from?'

She smiles. 'Is that a thank you?'

'Thanks.'

'No problem. So, it's three to one now. Nice to finally be able to save you for once.' She nods towards the uneasy crowd. 'Don't you have something to say?'

He faces the men and tries again. 'I'm going to keep this short because we don't have a lot of time. Last year I was taken by the Foundation and used to destroy the only two things I give a damn about: the Nomad and our colonies. While I was their guest, they copied some of my cybernetics and created soldiers to fight for them. I want to get the Nomad back together so we can destroy them.'

'Yeah, and we told you we didn't want anything to do with you,' one of the men shouts from deep in the crowd.

'And I'm choosing to ignore you,' Gryffin responds. 'The Foundation are attacking and taking over colonies along the outer edges. If we don't do something now, we'll lose this Sector. We're not dead yet. The crew from *Ares* and *Styx* stand with me. They're going to fight for us and wear our colours and markings with pride. I'm giving you a choice now. Stay and wallow in your own vomit for the rest of your short lives until the Foundation arrives and wipes you all out or fly with *Ares* again and take these bastards down once and for all.'

'You can't stop this!'

Gryffin is silent for a moment. Terra looks up at him and gasps along with the rest of the crowd as electricity courses over every inch of his body. His implants glow blue and red as he directs his purple eyes at the crowd. 'Maybe not, but I'd prefer to die trying than accept what's coming and do damn all about it. This station is on lock down for six hours. Get sober and think about it.'

He shuts the electricity off and exits the room with his team. The metal doors shut behind them, sealing the crowd inside. After leaving instructions with his team, he turns and walks away down a side corridor.

∞

Sitting on the floor in a dark, smelly corridor isn't exactly how

Gryffin thought he'd celebrate surviving that room. He hadn't planned on using his implants to that extent either, but he needed something to show that he can handle this. Some way of proving to them that he's still leader material and has something up his sleeve that can help them.

He leans back against the wall, ignoring the foul smell of rotten food around him. Hopefully, they'll have signed up all the men in six hours. Having those thirteen ships with their full crews would be a massive help. He just needs to stay awake long enough to talk to them again.

'What is that smell?'

He groans to himself as Terra pulls up a crate to sit beside him. That would have been a better idea than just slumping to the ground. Bit late to be worried about it now. 'I don't want to know.'

She looks down at him. 'How bad is it?' He raises his eyebrow in a silent question. 'The pain from using the implant twice.'

He looks away from her, preferring to examine the pile of rubbish in front of him than look at the pity on her face. 'Are the comms between the ships set up?'

'Yes and stop deflecting. Just for once try to answer the question. On a one-to-ten scale.'

'One,' he replies quickly, hoping to shut her up.

She frowns and shakes her head, a few strands of dark hair falling by her face. 'So, that's an average person's eight. Why don't you go back to *Ares* for a few hours? Get some proper rest.'

He rests his head back against the wall. He will never admit it out loud, but that sounds like a great idea. He knows his body needs rest and by denying it what it needs, he's only causing more problems for himself. 'I've got things to do here.'

She snorts and shakes her head. 'Yeah, right. Is there anything I can do to ease the pain?'

He shakes his head. It's his own fault for overdoing it. His new internal implants may help with the day-to-day pain, but it seems nothing can help with the aftereffects. 'I have to go.'

She puts her hand on his shoulder to hold him down. 'No you don't. Everything is under control for the next few hours. We all know what we're doing. Take the time to get over this.' She tucks a lock of hair behind her ear. 'Don't bite my head off. I thought the mod is supposed to help with the pain?'

'Seriously, Terra. Drop it.'

'Gryffin—'

'It's not blocking the pain anymore, okay!' he shouts, before he can force his mouth shut. He closes his eye and wishes she would leave him alone. He's too tired and sore to deal with her at the moment. 'I'll be fine in a few minutes. Get back to your station, Commander.'

He nearly sighs in relief when he hears her stand up and move the crate, but instead of leaving, he feels her body press against his side. He opens his eye to find her sitting on the ground beside him with her head on his shoulder. She slowly traces circles on the flesh part of his arm. 'You have a real problem with orders.'

'You looked after me in the cave when I was cold. Now it's my turn to look after you while you rest.'

'I don't need looking—'

'Rest,' she orders in her best authoritative voice. 'I can be as stubborn as you when I want to be. I'm not going anywhere so stop wasting your breath. I'll make sure you're at the meeting in six hours. I promise.'

She silently glares at him and he realises it's no good. She's not going to back down and he really doesn't have the energy to keep arguing. In spite of being irritated by her stubbornness he gives in. 'Fine. I'll stay, but I'm not sleeping.'

'No problem. I'll stay with you.'

Gryffin groans and gives up. His implants are hurting enough without banging his head against the wall with Terra. Some time out won't do him any harm. His meeting with the Nomad will turn out to be a success or a total disaster. Either way, he'll find out in six hours.

Terra sniffs the air around her and grimaces. She sat with Gryffin for about an hour until he was strong enough to get back to work. An hour on the ground in the rancid corridor allowed the aromatic odour to infuse with her clothes. If the captains cause problems, she can just waft her arms in the direction of the group to drive them back. Even though her bottom had been completely numb and her sense of smell attacked by the rubbish, she had been more than happy to sit there with him as long as she could. Weeks spent abusing the implant will take time to get over. He really needs a few days off to give his body the rest it desperately needs. It's not an option though. She seriously doubts he's ever taken a day off.

The group of Nomad fidget and pace outside the room. Everyone is on edge. There's a lot riding on the next few minutes. Terra honestly doesn't know how Gryffin can be so relaxed. He's the picture of calm as he leans against the side of the corridor with one leg bent, his foot against the wall and his arms crossed over his chest as he silently looks at the door waiting.

Desyl wanders over to her. He opens his mouth to talk but pauses and wrinkles his nose. 'What happened to you?'

'Don't ask.'

He grunts and takes a step away from her. 'That'll keep the men away from you. Effective.'

She glares at him but can't argue. She does stink.

'He okay?'

She refuses to look at him. 'Now's not the time for an argument, Desyl.' Gryffin glances over at them. His eye narrows as they talk.

'Hey, I'm not here to argue with you. You're not the only one worried about him.'

He's right. 'Sorry. I'm just a little stressed about... well, everything. How is he so calm about this?'

Desyl glances over at him but turns when he sees Gryffin's still looking at them. 'It's what he does. It's what he's designed to do.'

She checks her gun again. There's no need. She's already checked it about a dozen times in the last few minutes. Even after training with the Nomad and Hunters, situations like this still make her anxious. She fully trusts Gryffin and the Nomad to keep everyone safe, but a lot can still go wrong. They're seriously outnumbered. It'll be up to Gryffin to keep everyone under control. His robotic eye glows in the dim light and is focused solely on the door in front of him.

'So, how do you think this is going to go?'

Desyl sighs and shrugs. 'Hard to say. If Gryffin had told them he commandeered their ships, it would be a straight yes.'

'Why didn't he tell them?'

'He wants them to join because they want to, not because he's holding their ships hostage.'

'And if they say no?'

'Let's take this one step at a time.'

Gryffin pushes off the wall and squares his shoulders. 'It's time.'

∞

Bray spins on the balls of his feet and lands a forceful blow to the back of Garvan's legs. Garvan grunts and retaliates with an impressive move that leaves Bray on his back on the mat. Bray jumps to his feet and rolls his shoulders. 'Not bad. Ready to go again?'

Garvan blows out a breath. 'Just give me a few seconds to catch my breath.'

Bray swings his stick and Garvan narrowly avoids a serious headache. 'Your enemy won't give you a few seconds. Keep going until I kill you or tell you to stop.'

Garvan makes a face. 'That's encouraging.'

'Not supposed to be. Why are you holding back?'

Garvan laughs. 'Holding back? That was my best move!'

Bray snorts. 'I've seen you do better. Push yourself.'

Garvan wipes his forehead with his arm. 'Not that I'm complaining, but why is a commander personally training a nobody like me?'

Bray pushes damp hair off his face and lowers onto the bench attached to the wall. 'You've got potential. I just want to make sure it's not wasted.'

Garvan joins him on the bench. 'I appreciate that, but getting me out of Foundation custody was enough.'

Bray leans forward and rests his arms on his legs. 'There is a chance you could be offered a permanent position on *Perses* — if you're interested.'

Garvan's eyebrows shoot up. 'You mean I would be a Hunter?'

Bray nods. 'We're a little away from that right now, but I've told Sayber you have the makings of a Hunter.'

Garvan looks down at the ground for a moment. 'Thank you.' He looks back at Bray with a large smile on his face. 'I really thought I'd die in the place. Being a Hunter would be an honour — if I'm accepted.' The smile drops slightly and he looks back at the ground.

'What?'

'I heard you're working with the Foundation. They took my life from me. I'm not sure how I'll fit with that dynamic.'

Bray gets up and holds out his hand to pull Garvan to his feet. 'Nothing to worry about. The *Infinity* crew want as little to do with the Foundation as we do. Besides, the partnership is a temporary one. As soon as things settle, we'll go our separate ways again.' Bray gets into position. 'We've got another prison raid coming up and I want you on my team.'

Garvan smiles and stands opposite Bray. 'You do?'

'Best of three. You take me down and you're on my team.'

Garvan's grin gets bigger as he lunges at Bray.

∞

The door opens in front of Gryffin and he confidently walks back into the bar. He primes his arm and grips his gun firmly in his hand. He's fully expecting a fight. After destroying their life it's the least he deserves. As a precaution, he ordered Desyl to stick to Terra no matter what. If this goes wrong, he doesn't want her hurt in the crossfire.

Surprisingly, the bodies part as he walks, making a clear path for him and his crew. He scans the faces, but instead of anger and hatred, he sees acceptance. No weapons are raised and he can't sense any hostility. He may just make it out of here in one piece. He vaults on to the bar top again and stands tall. The silence continues for a moment, not for effect, but to give himself time to steady his breathing. Addressing a group of Nomad never intimidated him before. Seems the Foundation took his confidence along with his freedom.

'You've all had time to think about my offer. Now it's decision time.' He catches Desyl's eye and nods. Desyl opens the double doors and steps aside. 'I'm not going to force any of you to fly with me again. This has to be your choice.' He gestures to the door. 'If you're not with me, leave. Just get out of the Sector before things get worse.'

Gryffin stands rigid. Every muscle in his body tenses as he waits for the room to clear. Three minutes later, the room is still full. He looks down at Terra to see a huge smile on her face. She winks at him and nods once. They're all staying. So many different scenarios have gone round and round in his head since he decided to come back here, but none that involved all of the Nomad staying. He suddenly hasn't got a clue what to say or do. A few of his crew look in his direction, so he gets back on track.

'Captains with me. The rest of you go with Desyl. Try to rummage up some food.'

He drops off the bar and relaxes slightly. As the Nomad file from the room, Terra moves closer to him. 'Congratulations, Captain.'

'I need you to check the comms links on each of the ships. Make sure they're up to scratch before we leave tomorrow. Take a security team with you.'

He fully expects an argument, but she smiles and nods. 'Yes, sir.' She gestures at two of Gryffin's security and they follow her from the room. Gryffin watches her walk away. He doesn't realise he's still staring after her until he feels the eyes of the other captains on him. Luckily, one of his crew interrupts, saving him from the looks. 'Sir, three Rogue ships have just arrived. The captains are requesting a meeting with you.'

'So they can kill me? Tell them to leave before we shoot them down.'

'Actually, sir, they want to join the group.'

That gets everyone's attention. Gryffin glances at his comrades to see the same confusion on their faces. 'Bring them over.'

∞

Gryffin sits back against the edge of the table in the bar as Desyl leads the three Rogue captains into the room. He manages to hide the look of shock on his face when a man and two women stand in front of him. Seeing two female captains among the Rogues throws him off for a second. Times have changed since the Foundation took him.

The taller of the two women brushes her long red braid behind her shoulder and crosses her arms as she regards him with distaste. Her dark green eyes pick him apart as she sneers at him. The large scar that runs from the left corner of her mouth to her ear helps add a serious touch of fierceness to her face. 'That's him?'

He doesn't know what to say in response to her attitude. Terra, Milla, and Aleena are the only women he's dealt with and they're as different from each other as they can be. Doesn't give him much of a basis for dealing with women in general. 'What do you want?'

The red haired woman takes a step closer. His security immediately move to intercept her. 'Hey, take it easy. We really need your guard dogs here? You afraid of us, Nomad?'

Gryffin slowly rises to his feet. 'They're here to stop me from killing you, Rogue. I'm only entertaining this meeting because I'm curious. We've shared this Sector for years, but this is the first time you've requested a meeting. Why now?'

The blonde woman puts her hand on the red haired woman's arm. 'My name is Baila. This is Rua,' she says, gesturing to her female companion. 'And Dare.' The man nods once at Gryffin, but says nothing. 'We're as uncomfortable with this meeting as you are. Don't have much choice though. The Sector is at war and we have to pick a side.'

Gryffin clenches his jaw to stop it from falling open. Rogues are well known for being more reclusive than the Nomad. They have no structure and no order. They rarely travel in groups and survive by taking what they want, when they want. They actually make the Nomad seem like a fleet of angels. 'Thought you picked your side?'

Rua faces Baila. 'Told you this is a bloody waste of time. He's not interested.'

'Rua. Just shut up and let Baila speak,' Dare commands. The redhead looks like she's about to argue, but takes a step back and nods.

Baila pushes her shoulders back as she faces him. 'Usually we don't take sides. I admit, some ships are working for the Foundation, but apart from the payment, they don't care what the Foundation does. We don't share their thinking. The Sector won't be much good to anyone if it's overrun with Foundation ships. We heard rumours you were back and decided to see if anything can be worked out.'

'Heard rumours. You been attacking ships that may be linked to me?'

Baila glances at her two companions and they both shrug. 'No,' Dare responds. 'I've heard of something like that going on. Nothing to do with us.'

Gryffin narrows his eye as he examines the Rogues. They seem to be telling the truth — not that it means a damn thing. His track record with recognising lies ranks up there with his experience with women. 'Let me get this straight. You want to fly with the Nomad. You know we're working with the Hunters and a few ex-Foundation ships, right?'

Baila nods. 'That's why we're here. Seems like all the groups are involved. All you're missing is a few Rogue ships.'

Gryffin crosses his arms and looks down at the group. He's not going to instantly dismiss their offer. Three extra ships will help, but can he trust them not to shoot him in the back at the first opportunity?

Rua shakes her head. 'Waste of time, Baila. No Nomad will be seen dead working with a weak female. They think they're better than us.'

Gryffin pushes past his security and stands in front of the trio. 'I don't give a damn if you're male or female. As long as you know which end of the gun to point at the Foundation, I couldn't care less. I don't have much faith that you won't turn things to your advantage though. I'm not keen on a Rogue bullet in my back.'

'You outnumber us. There's a higher risk of a Nomad bullet going astray than a Rogue one.' Baila glances at her comrades. 'We wouldn't risk our lives by meeting with you unless we were serious about this.'

Gryffin nods at Rua. 'Can you keep her under control?'

Rua bares her teeth and Dare holds her back. Baila smiles and shakes her head. 'No promises. So, Nomad,' Baila holds her hand out to him, 'do we have an agreement?'

Two hours ago, if someone told Gryffin he'd be thinking about flying with Rogue ships, he probably would have shot them. But here he is — seconds away from creating another uneasy alliance. First the Hunters and now the Rogues. To survive out here you have to adapt or die. If working with the Rogues means the Nomad will survive for even one more day, as a leader, he has to agree.

Gryffin grits his teeth and forces his hand to take Baila's. 'It's Gryffin, not Nomad.'

Baila nods and releases his hand. 'Whatever you say. So, Gryffin, what's your great plan to destroy the Foundation?'

'I just came to see how you are after today.'

Gryffin moves forward to block her entry with his body. 'I'm fine, Terra.'

'Can I come in?' While he left the meeting with what he wanted, the process had taken its toll on him. He may be able to hide it from the rest of the crew, but she can see the tension rolling off his body. When he came back to *Ares*, he was wound so tight she thought he was about to snap. She saw the order he placed on the system two hours ago. He wants the training room to himself so he can work out. He's come so far over the last two weeks — there's no way she's going to let him blow off steam by fighting with a drone.

After an extremely painful wait, he finally backs away from the door and disappears into the room. She takes that as a yes and follows. By the time she catches up with him, he's on the edge of his bed and looks like he wants to kill something. The muscles in his arms and neck strain as he clenches his fists together. 'I'm busy.'

She slowly lowers herself onto the other end of the bed. 'You don't need to have a sparring session, Gryffin.'

His eyes bore into her. 'You keeping tabs on me now?'

'I'm not going to apologise for being concerned about you.'

He stands up and walks to the other side of the room. 'I don't need or want your concern.'

'The mission was a fantastic success. You should be with the rest of the crew celebrating, not planning on getting beaten up.'

His eye narrows. 'Thanks for the vote of confidence.'

She sighs and resists the urge to roll her eyes. Trust him to focus on defending his macho pride. 'What's got you so wound up?'

'I didn't think it would be that difficult to convince them! You saw what they were living in. I messed things up so badly they had to seriously think about whether to stay in that shit hole or to work with me again.' He turns his back to her and runs both hands through his hair, resting his palms on his head.

'Everyone wants to work with you again. You even got three Rogue ships to join. Focus on that part.' She moves slowly and closes the distance between them. She places her palms on the centre of his back. Fully expecting him to dive away from her touch, she is pleasantly surprised when all that happens is the tensing of the muscles in his back. She pushes her hands up to his shoulders and massages the thick cords of muscles along his neck. Gryffin lets his arms drop to his side and lowers his head. Terra hesitates for a second at his reaction. She gently works her fingers further up his neck into his hair.

Her heart races in her chest as she brushes her fingers down his back. She moves closer to him as her hands travel around the edge of his waistband. She slowly unzips his jacket and pushes the leather down his arms and onto the floor. Terra runs her hands back up to his shoulders and gently massages the tight muscles.

Gryffin takes a deep breath and groans.

'Lie face down on your bed.'

He looks over his shoulder and raises his eyebrow.

'Just humour me. Give me ten minutes. If you still want to beat the drone, I won't try to stop you.'

He studies her for a moment before complying. Terra pulls the first aid kit out from under his bed and takes out the bottle of antiseptic gel. Not quite massage oil but it will do. She climbs onto his bed and straddles his waist. She squeezes some gel into her hands and rubs her palms together. Terra starts on his shoulders and works each of the large knots until they surrender. Her fingers travel over the numerous rough scars scattered over his back as she does her best to ease some of his tension.

This massage is another first for him if the knots she can feel under her fingers are anything to go by. She just hopes it will do the trick. The last thing she wants is to have to patch him up after another fight with the drone. She leans on him as she works on a large knot. He really has to learn how to deal with his emotions in a less violent way. If he keeps working through his problems by beating something or allowing something to beat on him, he's not going to last much longer.

Her fingers press against the raised 35 burnt on his skin. The identifying brand was forced onto him by the Foundation... by her father. She directs her anger at them into dealing with the tension in Gryffin's shoulders. 'That okay?'

He grunts into his pillow so she takes that as a yes. To keep her mind firmly focused on her task, she concentrates on the series of scars on his back, wondering about the story behind each one. She pushes some unhelpful thoughts from her mind and gets to work again. Her fingers dig into the muscle under the griffin wing across his back. Not even the tattoo managed to escape injury. A large scar runs the length of its wing. The wound, newer than most of the other ones, must have been inflicted while he was missing.

She wipes a lone tear from her eye and curses herself. To protect herself, she needs to stay angry at him, but the longer she spends with him, the more she notices her anger ebbing away. She's actually turned on and sad at the same time. This is what he does to her. How can she possibly know what's going on between them when he's causing such conflicting emotions in her? As if to prove her point, the heat rises through her body as her groin rubs against him. A small gasp escapes her lips and she instantly freezes.

'You okay?

Terra climbs off his back and smiles. 'Of course.' She grabs a towel off the floor and briskly wipes her hands. Gryffin turns onto his side and props himself up on his elbow. 'I'll get a dressing for the cut on your arm.'

'It's just a graze. Don't worry about it.'

'It's no problem. I'll just be a few minutes.' She hurries from the room and walks to the med bay on autopilot. Putting distance between herself and Gryffin isn't working. Giving him a massage is way off plan. He may be giving her mixed signals, but she's no better. What was she thinking? Time to get back on track. She'll dress his arm, then politely excuse herself.

Feeling a little more in control of the situation, Terra marches back to the training room. She comes to an abrupt halt at the end of his bed when she sees him. Gryffin is asleep. She smiles and tiptoes closer to him. He must have been exhausted and the massage helped push him over the edge.

Terra tidies the small space and fills a glass with water and places it beside his bed. Unfortunately, he's fallen asleep on the thin blanket, so she hurries back to his room and gathers another blanket and a packet of rations. Sleep is a great start, but he needs to eat too. She's no fool. She figured out a few days ago his rations have been redirected to her. He may not need to eat as often as she does, but that's no reason to starve himself. That's all changing today. Even if she has to force the food down his throat, he will eat.

Terra carefully drapes the blanket over his body. His metal arm is hanging over the side of the bed, but she dare not touch it in case she wakes him. After making sure he has everything he might need, she leaves him to his desperately needed sleep. Once the training room door is firmly shut, she contacts Desyl. Within two minutes, the whole ship is forbidden to go anywhere near the training room until Gryffin comes out.

Terra smiles as she makes her way back through the ship. Hopefully, this will be the first step on his road to recovery.

∞

Garvan knocks the guard out and moves him aside as Bray leads the others out. They load the prisoners on the transport and Bray gets them on their way. Once Garvan ensures everyone is disarmed, he joins Bray in the cockpit. The prisoners may have worked with Bray to get out, but that means nothing now they're free. A bullet to the back of his head isn't at the top of his thank you present list.

'That was fun.'

Bray smiles and shakes his head. 'You're not all there, you know that, right?'

Garvan laughs. 'After surviving that place, I intend to enjoy every minute out here.'

'I have to ask. What were you in prison for?'

Garvan leans back in the seat and smiles. 'Guess.'

Bray sighs but goes along with him. 'You picked a flower from a protected parkland.'

Garvan laughs again. 'Not quite. It's nearly that ridiculous though. I'm an architect.'

Bray frowns. 'And that's a crime?'

'It is when you're the head designer for the new Foundation colony.'

The craft sweeps to the side as Bray loses concentration for a second. 'What new colony?'

Garvan shrugs. 'Beats me.' He crosses his thick arms over his chest and glares out the window. 'They've been planning it for years. They didn't tell us any more than we needed to know.'

Bray enters a course to take them back to *Perses*. 'They imprisoned you for that?'

'My team and I worked on it tirelessly for two years. Every minute was spent fine-tuning every single detail. We went through months of simulations to make sure it all fit together.'

'Fit together?'

He nods. 'It's like a large construction kit. Everything was built ahead of time so it can be quickly shipped and built on site. Anyway, once the last of the t's were crossed, we had reached the end of our usefulness. The final meeting came to an end and we were escorted by armed guards into a transport. Next thing we know, we're the newest inmates of the prison moon.'

Bray takes a deep breath. The Foundation really doesn't care what lives they destroy on their way to domination. 'What about family? Do you have any?'

'Wife, son, and daughter.' He shakes his head. 'Don't know what bull they were fed. I probably committed an act of treason. Seems to be the most common crime.'

'How long have you been there?'

'Heading towards three years when you got me out.'

'Hang on. Three years? No offence, but you look and act like you've been there a lot longer.'

Garvan flashes him a wide smile. 'Survival of the fittest, my friend. After being beaten up countless times in the first few days, I decided I'd had enough. Instead of letting the attacks happen, I fought back. Any spare time was spent in the training room. The Foundation discarded me, but I wasn't going to curl up and die. The two women and six of the men you found with me are the rest of my design team.'

Bray is lost for words. He fought his way out of a high security prison with a team of architects.

Garvan glances at him and laughs loudly. 'You're impressed. Go ahead. You can say it.'

Bray laughs loudly. 'Yes. I'm impressed.'

'Can I ask you something, Commander?'

Bray nods. 'Go for it.'

'You trust the Foundation and Nomad? Hunter and Nomad relations are well known. How do you know they won't stab you in the back? Each group could very easily destroy the other two without flinching.'

'Common enemy.'

'It'd take a lot more than that for me to trust my enemy. I'm not questioning you — just don't want you to die before I pay you back for saving me.'

Bray sighs and looks out at the landscape as they fly by. 'We're family.'

Garvan frowns. 'I don't get it.'

'Gryffin is my brother.'

His frown deepens. 'Brother-in-arms you mean.'

Bray shakes his head. 'Same mother. Different father. Just keep it yourself. Don't want it common knowledge. Gryffin still doesn't know we're related.'

Garvan blows out a deep breath. 'That's cosy. Couldn't make this stuff up. Hold on. Gryffin has a brother and father — I thought he was made?'

'No.' Bray takes a deep breath and concentrates on the controls. 'He was taken when he was ten and modified. I found out who he really is last year. I thought he was dead. Anyway, we don't fully trust each other, but not a lot else we can do. Roman's people are great planners, Gryffin's are the best on the surface and Hunters excel in the air. For the moment, it works well.'

'Impressive family you have there, Commander.'

'You know what would be even more impressive?'

'Yes, but you have to ask.'

'Really?

'The last few years weren't filled with queues of people asking me for my help. I don't need to tell you what the prison is like. Taking is the golden rule.'

Bray knows exactly what Garvan means. 'Garvan, do you remember the design of the colony?'

Garvan smirks. 'Yes, of course I remember the design. Thanks for asking. I lived and breathed that blasted thing. Won't do you much good unless you know where they're putting it.'

'Would you be able to figure out possible locations based on the design?'

Garvan pauses then nods once. 'If I can sit down with the rest of the team we may be able to narrow it down for you.

'Sounds good. We'll also need you to give us as much information as possible about the facility.'

Garvan nods. 'Whatever you need, Commander. Hey, does this mean payback?'

Bray looks out the window as *Perses* appears ahead of them. 'It means payback all right.' Bray touches the metal on the side of his face. Garvan will have to get in line behind him.

32

Gryffin wakes to the feeling of a hand gently running through his hair. A familiar scent hits his nose, but he can't place it. Not that he could care less at the moment. He doesn't care where he is or who's touching him. All he knows is that he feels... relaxed. His body aches, but not in a bad way. He can't remember the last time he woke up without serious pain somewhere. Then again, he can't remember the last time he actually slept.

'Morning.'

Terra's voice helps to bring him out of his sluggish stupor. He finally convinces his eye to open, but the mechanical one refuses to wake up. 'Morning?' He takes in his surroundings. Terra is sitting beside him on his bunk. A small computer rests on her knee, while she runs one hand through his hair. He immediately feels embarrassed and sits up quickly. 'What happened?'

Terra laughs and shakes her head. 'Nothing, Gryffin. I gave you a massage and you fell asleep. I promise.' She frowns and leans closer to him. 'What's wrong with your eye? There's no light coming from it.'

He shakes his head. 'Nothing.'

Terra pushes him back onto the pillow and pulls her kit off the floor. 'Stop being stubborn.' She leans over him and unclasps the cover from the eyepiece. 'So, did the sleep help?'

'Yeah. How long was I out?'

Terra doesn't reply for a few seconds as she works on his eye. 'Em, it must be about thirty hours or so.'

He sits up suddenly and yelps in pain as Terra's screwdriver pushes into his eyepiece. 'Why the hell did no one wake me!'

She pushes him back onto the bed and wiggles the screwdriver until it comes free. 'Don't jump up like that again. I can fix your eye, but I can't replace it. Desyl and I banned anyone from coming in here. I don't care if you're angry about losing a day. If you didn't get some proper sleep, you would have keeled over.'

'That's not your decision to make.'

'Yeah, well, someone had to. This wiring is appalling. No wonder it keeps failing.' She leans closer and frowns. 'Okay. Right, that should be it.'

His eye comes back online. 'Expert in cybernetics now?'

She shrugs. 'We've all had to adapt in the last few months. The more you can do, the better.' She sits at the end of the bed and holds out an energy bar. 'Time for breakfast.'

He glares at the bar. 'I'm not hungry.' To prove him a liar, his stomach growls loudly.

'Sounds to me like you are.' She folds her arms across her chest and he instantly knows she's not going to back off. 'You've done so well over the last week. What's wrong with you now?'

He pushes to his feet, but has to hold onto the wall to stop his legs from collapsing.

Terra is immediately at his side, but he moves out of her reach. 'I don't have time for this now. I've got to get to the command deck.'

'No, you don't. Desyl has everything under control. We're a day away from meeting the rest of the fleet. I've upgraded the comms units on each of the Nomad ships. The Nomad as well as the Rogue crews are training to get back in shape, and we've done a full weapons run through with everyone. We're all set.'

'You've interacted with the Rogues?'

'Of course I have. Actually, Rua isn't too bad once you get to know her. It appears having me on board has eased some of their issues with the Nomad.'

'You? Why?'

She openly stares at him as if he is slightly crazy. 'Because I'm a woman and so are two of their captains. Seriously, please tell me you noticed that small detail.'

He quickly looks away, feeling like an idiot. 'Yeah, well, are they behaving themselves?'

Terra nods. 'So far. Baila thinks she may be able to convince a few more ships to join you. Roman has arranged for us to drop in at Taldor to resupply the fleet.'

'Thought the Foundation took that colony?'

'They did. We took it back about six months ago, but we're on the verge of losing it again. We use the underground tunnels to store supplies, so we need to clear it out.' She gets up and throws the energy bar at him. 'We'll reach Taldor in a few hours. The plan is to land the fleet. It'll take about two hours to get everything together. The Rogue's have a few repairs they need to carry out and five of the Nomad vessels could do with being refuelled. After that it's on to Ultar.' She suddenly freezes and looks at him. Terra stands to attention and clears her throat. 'With your permission of course, Captain.'

Gryffin grunts in response and focuses on a panel on the wall opposite him. While it sounds like everything is sorted, he's still angry. He's the captain. He should be organising everything, not sleeping. How is he supposed to gain the respect of his people if he can't even stay awake?

'The fact you slept won't undermine your authority,' Terra says, somehow reading his thoughts. 'If anything, it will help. We need you in top form, sir,' she adds with a small grin on her face. 'Now, eat that bar, have a shower, and get dressed. No time to laze in bed, sir.'

Without another word, she leaves him with his energy bar.

∞

Roman watches as *Perses* and another three Hunter battleships lower onto the surface. The long grass waves violently as the powerful engines disrupt the otherwise peaceful evening. It's been a long time since Sayber's been anywhere near the base. He placed his re-earned trust in Bray to speak for the Hunters. Like Gryffin, Sayber is more comfortable on his ship. The routine of day-to-day life on the surface holds no excitement for him.

While Roman was studying for his placement, he yearned for a life on a ship. The thought of being able to travel anywhere in the Sector and beyond was appealing to a young cadet. Up until a few months ago, he was still under that impression. He loves *Infinity*. The ship is everything he could ever have asked for. She was the start of his planned illustrious career in the fleet. Stealing her hadn't exactly been in that set of plans.

His old plans were that of a Foundation captain. He's not that person anymore. He doesn't mourn his old life. Outer Sector living agrees with him. This new Roman will be quite happy to spend the rest of his days on Ultar with Aleena. He'd give anything to explore a future with her. With little quality time available, their relationship has not progressed as far as he would like. Until the power struggle in the Sector is resolved, their other commitments must take priority. It's a fact he accepts, but deeply regrets that he has to make the choice at all. He has to be the commander of *Infinity*. Once the Sector is secure, he'll be handing *Infinity* over to someone else.

Sayber saunters down the ramp from *Perses*. His long braid hangs over his shoulder and hides the top of the large scar that runs up his arm. He slaps Roman on the back and nearly sends him toppling forward. 'Still a traitor I see.'

Roman shrugs. 'I guess you could say the lifestyle is growing on me.'

Sayber rubs his goatee and smiles. 'It has a nasty habit of doing that. *Ares* back yet?'

Roman shakes his head. 'On her way. They just have a quick stop off at Taldor first. You must be looking forward to your reunion with Gryffin.'

Sayber grimaces and looks back at *Perses*. 'Not top of my to-do list, but common enemy and all that.' He looks back at him and smiles again. 'That's my mantra at the moment.' He claps his hands together and turns to face *Perses*. 'Well, we got everyone we could. There were a few that seemed to enjoy the hospitality too much to leave. Weren't going to force them.'

'How many did you get?'

'Three hundred and twelve in total.'

Roman is surprised. He didn't think there would be that many prisoners. They must have been shipping prisoners through the old Port for years without informing the citizens. 'Do they know what's happening?'

Sayber nods. 'There's a fair few useful bodies among them. I'd say about a third of that number could be utilised in the fleet or on the base. The rest can be helpful on the surface. We also took all but one of the prisons.'

Roman frowns. 'You didn't mention that in your report?'

Sayber grins and hold a finger up to his mouth. 'Eyes and ears everywhere, Roman. There's something, or should I say someone else, I left off my report. Call a meeting.'

'Roman!'

He flinches as Lucan's voice threatens to rupture his eardrum. 'What's wrong now?'

'The Foundation fleet are moving towards the Nomad!'

∞

'How many?'

Desyl looks up from the screen. 'Ten ships, sir.'

Gryffin slams his fist against the railing. 'Damn it! Foundation must have moved in sooner. How the hell do they know we're here?'

Desyl shakes his head. Terra climbs up the steps and joins him on the command platform. 'The transports are ready to go, sir.' When he doesn't immediately respond, she moves to face him. 'Sir, what's wrong?'

'Foundation coming our way.'

Her shoulders drop. 'How many?'

'Ten ships, six minutes out,' Gryffin replies.

'I'll go with the transports.'

Desyl and Gryffin turn to look at her. 'What?' Gryffin asks.

'You need everyone on *Ares*. Let me go with Vance to get the supplies.'

Gryffin shakes his head. 'No way.'

'Why not?

He steps closer to her. 'Because I'm the damn captain and I say you're staying here.'

She laughs and jabs him in the chest with her finger. 'You know it's a good idea to send me so stop being stubborn, sir,' she adds.

Poking him in the chest is bad enough without everyone on the command deck witnessing it. They fall silent as they wait to see how he reacts. He lowers his voice and leans over her. 'At this rate, you'll be lucky if I don't kick you off the crew, Commander.'

Desyl takes his life into his own hands by interrupting, 'Sir, time's getting on. We need to move. Commander Rush has been on Taldor before, perhaps she is the best one to lead the party?'

Gryffin hears the logic in his words, but he still wants to knock Desyl to the other side of the room for pointing it out. He doesn't want to send her to the surface, but he's not thinking as a captain. He doesn't know what his problem is. All he knows is that something in his head is screaming to keep her close to him. 'You okay to do this?'

She doesn't bother to restrain the large smile. 'Yes, sir.'

He opens a connection to Vance. 'I need you to get the supplies with Terra. The rest of the fleet will cover you.'

'Copy that.'

Terra climbs down the steps to the lower platform. Before he can stop his legs, he hurries after her. He guides her over to a corner, out of prying eyes. 'No chances, okay?'

'Just do your job and keep them away from us. You do that and we'll be fine.' She squeezes his arm, then races down the corridor. His breathing seems to quicken with her fading footsteps. He's getting tired of these weird sensations. They make it difficult to focus on anything else.

He climbs back up to the command platform and leans on the railings. A small beep signals Terra's transport leaving the cargo bay. *Styx* moves in to protect it and they turn towards the surface. He swallows past the lump in his throat and forces himself to sit down. Hopefully, blowing up some Foundation ships will help. He pulls a cable from his pocket then hooks into *Ares'* weapons system.

The rest of his fleet falls into position to either side of *Ares*. He can't help but be a bit apprehensive. It's the first time the reunited Nomad and the Rogues will fight together. It could either go really well or end in a bloody disaster.

Once everyone is in position, he gives the order to intercept the ships. He doesn't need to say anything else. They've all worked and survived out here long enough to know the rules. Kill or be killed. It's that simple. He loads *Ares'* guns and slows his breathing. He's not wasting any time by vocalising orders to fire — he's going to control that part himself. He wants this over and done with fast so he can go to the surface.

The Foundation fleet comes into range and his fleet break formation. Desyl expertly pilots *Ares* while he targets the oncoming ships. The Foundation ships may be more manoeuvrable than some of the larger Nomad ships, but they're still coming out on top. The Nomad and Rogues act on instinct. He locks *Ares*' guns on the largest Foundation ship, targeting her engines. His aim is true, but he doesn't stop there. Once the ship is incapacitated, he fires again and again until she is nothing but debris.

Desyl guides *Ares* through the remains of the ship and they go after the next one. Gryffin smiles as another ship falls to a combined Rogue and Nomad attack. Eight left.

33

Roman ignores the angry words directed at him as he pushes a man aside in the tunnels. He bursts through the door and skids to a halt beside Lucan. 'What's going on?' Lucan nods towards the screen at the line of Foundation ships. Roman leans closer and notices there are a lot fewer ships at the location than earlier in the day. 'Where have the rest of them gone?'

Lucan zooms in on the area of space surrounding Taldor. 'They're exactly where we don't want them. The signal is weak so I can't tell you how live this data is. But, it does look like Gryffin has company.'

Roman glares with contempt at the cluster of dots, slowly crawling across the screen towards Taldor. There's nothing he can do to help. By the time he launches *Infinity* or *Epsilon*, the battle would be over. 'There's no reason for the Foundation to go anywhere near Taldor.'

'They're going to take it back though, aren't they,' Lucan says.

Roman leans on the desk and examines the fleet on the screen. 'What are the odds they decide to move in at the exact same time that *Ares* arrives. I don't buy those odds.' He stands up and crosses his arms. 'No, they knew *Ares* was coming.'

'Insider?'

He spins to face Sayber and Bray along with another well-built man. 'I'd like to say no, but I'm not convinced.'

Sayber joins him at the screen. 'Guess we can't rule it out. Ultar has opened its doors to a lot of people. It wouldn't be difficult to sneak someone in under the radar. What's *Ares* facing?'

Roman nods towards the screen. 'Ten.'

'How many with Gryffin?' Sayber asks.

'According to Terra, *Ares*, fourteen Nomad vessels, and three Rouge ships are making their way to meet with us.'

Lucan frowns. 'Rogues. Seriously? What the hell is he thinking?'

'That we can do with every ship we can get.' Roman pushes a picture of the new Port across the table. 'We have no idea what's going to come through that. I don't care if our fleet consists of Rogues, Nomads, Hunters and New Foundation. As long as we have a common goal, we can all work together.'

Lucan and Sayber glance at each other. Roman doesn't miss the look that passes between them. 'Any word from *Ares*?'

Lucan shakes his head. 'Nothing. The Foundation has taken up position between Ultar and Gryffin. He'll have a fun time getting to us through all that.'

Sayber snorts. 'What the blazes are you worrying about? *Ares* can take that alone without all the others there for support. She'll be grand.'

'These are highly manoeuvrable Foundation ships.'

'Yeah, and they're up against a fleet consisting of people who have trained and fought nearly every day. No competition. It's just what Gryffin needs to get himself back in the zone.'

Roman glances at the screen again, not in the slightest bit convinced. 'We need the extra supplies from Taldor. The Foundation must know that. Why else would they suddenly take an interest?'

'Hold on one minute,' Lucan says. 'Gryffin is going to Taldor? You sure that's wise?'

'There's no other option. The Foundation are about to take the colony back. If we don't clear the supplies, we'll lose the lot.'

'I understand, but the last time he was there with *Ares*, he attacked them and destroyed half the village.'

Roman scratches his jaw. 'He can handle it. Doubt the locals will kick up much of a fuss with an armada of Nomad ships.'

Lucan leans back in her chair and blows out a breath. 'Ah sure why would they have a problem with Gryffin and a pretty big armada landing on their colony? Don't know what I'm worrying about.'

Roman's eyes narrow. 'Thank you for that, Lucan.' He's right, but that's not going to help anyone at the moment. 'I have to ask this. The mod Chayse designed for Gryffin...'

Lucan crosses his arms across his broad chest. 'Last scan was just before he bailed on us. Everything seemed to be operating as designed. No saying if that's still the case. Wouldn't do any harm to check him as soon as he gets here.'

'Right. Make sure that's done.'

'And if he refuses?' Lucan asks.

'Let's just cross that bridge when we come to it. Dismissed.' He waits until the room clears before he leans back in the chair and closes his eyes. They're so close to gathering the numbers they need to realistically give the Foundation a run for its money. If Gryffin can't get his fleet through the blockade, their rebellion will be finished before they've really started. He can't accept that. There is no other conceivable outcome for him. The Foundation have to be pushed out of the Sector and back to Earth. They have to know they can't just take what they want.

He rises to his feet and wanders back through the tunnels. Warm sunshine hits his face as he steps out onto the surface. He looks up at the cloudless sky and sighs deeply. As irrational as it sounds to him, he wants revenge. The single-minded focus scares him a little. He's barely spoken more than a few sentences to his son, but the connection is there for him and there's not a thing he can do about it.

The Roman clan is a large one. Even though his parents knew he was destined for a role on a Foundation ship, they never gave up on him having a family. He may be nearly fifty-three, but they still live in hope.

What he wouldn't give to tell them that he actually has a son. But it's impossible. They would never understand what Gryffin is. They would focus on his record and the metal. He clenches his jaw as anger tightens his throat. The Foundation took a son and a grandson. What gives them the right to play God like that? What right did Callum have to tear his son apart? The Foundation and his former best friend will pay for what they did to Gryffin, and to his life. It's probably the only thing he can do for him as a father and there's no way he's going to let him down.

∞

Terra examines her handheld unit and frowns. 'It should be around here somewhere.'

Vance snorts. 'Why don't you try to narrow it down. Sooner or later, the Taldorans will get wind we're here. Don't fancy meeting them without serious back up.'

Terra takes a few steps away from Vance. She likes the man but hurrying her isn't going to help. She checks the coordinates again and smiles. 'Found it!'

He hurries to her side while the rest of the Nomad stand guard. Terra drops to her knees and quickly clears the dirt from the floor of the cave. Once Vance decides to actually help instead of just watch her, they uncover the large steel hatch in the floor. 'The main storage unit is about a mile from here. Which should give us time to get everything moved to the main cargo doors by the time Gryffin and the others arrive.'

Vance gestures to his team. 'Two of you stay here with the transport. The rest with me and the commander.' Terra turns on the light on her gun and slowly descends into the dark. Creatures scurry away from her as she walks deeper into the tunnel. The last time she was on the surface was when the Taldorans signed the treaty with the Foundation. That particular visit ended in Gryffin attacking the surface and destroying most of the town. She nearly lost her life in one of these tunnels, but he had stepped in at the last minute and saved her from falling to her death. It seems like such a long time ago now.

'How much further?' Vance asks, startling her.

'Should be just up ahead. Any word from *Ares*?'

'No. Doesn't mean anything. We better get a move on.'

Terra doesn't bother responding. No point talking to him about her worry. She pushes the nagging concern aside and concentrates on the maze of tunnels ahead. They come to a fork so she stops to check the screen. 'This way. The storage unit is around the corner.'

Three minutes later, they reach a large metal door. Terra types in the code and steps aside as Vance and another two Nomad push the door open. Rows and rows of boxes, bags, and pallets greet them. Vance whistles. 'Well, would you look at this. Where'd this lot come from?'

Terra shoves the handheld back into her pocket and powers up a heavy duty trolley. 'Combination of sources. Some come from attacks on Foundation ships and outposts, some from Rogues, and the rest we picked up and stockpiled from lost colonies.'

'Impressive. And the Taldorans are on board with you leaving it here?'

'Aleena worked her magic after we got the colony back. I'm not sure how happy they'll be to have the Nomad here again.'

'Best get this sorted before they find out. Right lads, move everything up to the cargo doors. We got to get out of here before we're noticed.'

∞

Gryffin can't help but smile as Rua's victory cheer travels through the intercom. He'll have to watch that one. She's more vicious than he is. 'How are we looking?' he asks.

Desyl grabs onto the railing as *Ares* is rocked by a lucky Foundation shot. 'Three left.'

'Take us down. I'll take two teams and meet with the recovery team on the surface. Desyl, *Ares* is yours.' Gryffin uses his link with the system to contact the other ships. 'Rogues, clear the area surrounding Taldor. I want the rest of the fleet to cover our path to Ultar. Keep the way clear.' One by one, the ships acknowledge and break away from the group.

'Sir,' Desyl says, 'your transport is ready and your bike loaded.'

Gryffin looks up at him. 'Bike?'

'It's about time you took it out, sir. Shame to leave it under a tarp in the cargo bay.'

Gryffin smiles and gets to his feet. Desyl is right. It's a waste. 'Don't crash my ship, Commander.' Gryffin walks away, ignoring the look of horror that crosses Desyl's face. He races through the ship and meets with the teams in the cargo bay. After arming himself from the armoury he steps up the loading ramp of the nearest transport. The young Nomad beside him instantly tenses as he lowers onto the bench. 'Let's go,' he commands.

The ships lift off and move towards the bay doors. Gryffin sits back and stretches his legs out in front of him. His boot brushes off the large black and chrome motorbike taking up the centre walkway of the transport. The fierce looking griffin painted in front of the worn, brown leather saddle is a welcome sight. He should have taken the bike out long before now. What does it matter if the last time he rode it, Terra was clinging tightly to him? He has to stop thinking about her or he's going to drive himself crazy.

To take his mind off her, he runs through the plan, over and over in his head. Ten minutes later, the transport shudders as it lands on Taldor. The moonlight bathes the inside of the craft as the back lowers. Gryffin swings his leg over the bike and settles into the saddle. He keys in the security code and the engine roars to life. A large smile spreads over his face at the familiar sound. He rubs his hand over the griffin painted on the side. 'Let's go have some fun.'

∞

Gryffin pulls his bike to a halt at the top of the cliff. He leans forward on the handlebars and looks down at the town. The last few months haven't just been rough on him. Taldor is a wreck. The Foundation must be desperate for colonies if they want this one. His attack nearly a year ago hadn't done the town any favours, but that doesn't explain the derelict buildings, overgrown town square and general air of misery that hangs over the place. Maybe all the locals cleared out when the Foundation showed interest in the colony? Maybe they left because of what he did?

He brushes the pang of guilt aside. If he dwells on all the shitty decisions he's made in his life, he'll still be sitting here in a few years. He checks in with the team guarding the transports. All quiet there too. It's not going to last. Word will spread from the ships in orbit. He left the Nomad and Rogues dealing with the final three ships. He needs all the supplies off Taldor. And Terra. There's bound to be a few Foundation personnel embedded in the village. With no firm intel, he hasn't got a clue how many possible threats they're looking at. He can't help but smirk to himself. Just like the good old days.

He pushes those feelings into the box along with his regret. Time to focus, instead of reminiscing. Another five minutes goes by until it all kicks off. He straightens in his saddle as lights spread through the village. Seems everyone got the news at the same time. He clicks his radio on. 'Vance, status.'

His radio crackles then Vance's voice cuts through. 'We've just started loading the transport. Hell of a lot of stuff here.'

'Things are heating up out here. I'm moving in to intercept. Make sure you get as much as you can.'

'Understood.'

Gryffin turns in his saddle. The three transports behind him power up and leave. They need to keep everyone away from the tunnels. He doesn't give a damn what happens to the village — it's too late to stop the occupancy. Gunfire echoes in the distance. Gunfire directed at his ground crew. It takes a lot of restraint for him to resist sending the fleet in, but he's caused the Taldorans enough trouble. The last thing they need is him levelling their town for a second time. Terra must be rubbing off on him.

A cold gust of wind blows his hair across his face. He quickly ties a bandanna over his hair then turns his bike around. He accelerates down the dirt track towards the town, the tyres kicking up gravel and dust as he speeds along the path.

He slows down as he approaches the village and pulls out his gun. The town sits to either side of a straight road. It's perfect for what he needs. It's also perfect for the locals to launch a counter attack. He'll be a sitting duck. Well, a duck sitting on a motorbike as it speeds through the town. He's a relatively easy target for anyone with even the most basic weapons training. That just makes things more interesting for him.

He smiles as he revs the engine. Lights appear in more of the windows. Seems he's getting attention. Transport lights sweep the town, getting closer to him. He releases the brake and charges towards the town. His robotic eye makes targeting a lot easier. It's like having a gun sight built in to him. He fires at the derelict buildings, trees, transports, anything without people. He wants to distract, not kill.

He gets to the end of the road and spins around in a cloud of dust. The transport above him is joined by a second as he kicks the bike up a gear and repeats the process.

34

'Where's Gryffin?'

Vance shouts orders at the newly arrived transport crews before he glances quickly at her. 'Running interference.'

Terra looks past the transports towards the town. The glare from the Taldoran transport beams cuts through the darkness. 'They're looking for him?'

He nods and pushes past her going back into the tunnels. Terra can just about make out the sound of his bike engine. She follows Vance back into the gloom, dodging the sea of bodies briskly hauling the cargo out and onto the ships. 'How are we looking?'

'Another few runs back into the cavern should do it. You stay here. I'll give them a kick. Gryffin won't be able to keep them running around after him for long.'

He disappears into the tunnels with more speed than she thought possible from the slightly overweight Nomad. With nothing to do inside, she races along the corridor and back to the transports. She busies herself by checking the cargo straps on all the boxes as the rest of the Nomad continue to load up. The sound of an approaching engine brings her out of the back of the transport. She rubs her sleeve across her forehead to brush her sweat soaked hair from her face. At first she thinks it's Gryffin, but as it nears, she realises the sound is wrong. It's something much bigger than a bike engine. She withdraws her gun and contacts Vance. 'Wheeled transport approaching.'

She ignores his reply and presses tight to the side of the ship. The grey, all-terrain vehicle charges over the brow of the hill, it's front wheels crash back down to the dirt as it reaches the level platform at the top. Before the vehicle has even slowed, the occupants open fire. Terra jumps back into the cargo hold. Her gun is no match for their weapons. 'Vance! I'm taking fire. Do not come out!'

In direct conflict to her statement, she hears rounds coming from the direction of the tunnels. Why is she not surprised? She opens the far side hatch and crawls out, keeping the ship between her and the truck. Vance draws their fire as she targets the main gunman. She slows her breathing, pauses and takes the shot. His head rocks to the side as the round enters just above his ear. She dives behind the ship as attention now focuses on her. Vance commences his assault and another shooter loses a piece of his head.

Terra breaks cover and fires on the final man in the cab, but her timing is off. Instead of focusing on Vance, he's facing her. She falters for a split second then takes the shot. She hits him in the chest, but his round grazes her leg. Vance races out and, after placing another bullet in the shooter's head for good luck, drops down to his knees in front of Terra. 'You okay?'

She nods. His bullet just grazed her leg. Vance helps her up and brings her back into the entrance of the tunnel. 'Gryffin's on his way.' She closes her eyes and groans. 'Sorry, did I hurt you?'

'No. Why did you call him?'

'He'd want to know. My neck would be on the block if I didn't tell him.'

Terra settles back against the dusty ground as a Nomad wraps a bandage around her leg just below her knee. 'Who were they?'

Vance stands at the entrance with his gun at the ready. Clearly, he's expecting more trouble. 'Locals.'

That explains the shoot first — don't bother asking questions attitude. They heard Nomad were on the surface and wanted revenge. 'You better finish loading up before he gets here.'

Vance nods behind her at the crew coming out of the darkness. 'Way ahead of you.'

Terra sits back against the rock wall. Blood seeps through the bandage. She'll be glad to get back to *Ares* and have it looked at properly. 'Did he lose them?'

'Not when I spoke to him. He'll ditch them before he comes here though.'

Terra nods and looks out in to the dark night. She really wishes Vance hadn't called Gryffin. She wants to prove herself as part of the crew while she's on board. Calling in the captain after a graze won't help her do that.

∞

Gryffin's bike roars up the incline towards the tunnel. He reaches the transports and skids to a stop. Before the dust has even settled, he kicks out the stand and dismounts. Terra frowns as Gryffin charges into the tunnel like a man possessed. He shoves aside any Nomad unfortunate enough to get in his way. The crew member applying pressure to Terra's wound retreats hastily before Gryffin barrels into him. 'What the hell happened?'

Terra pushes up onto her elbows. 'Whoa, Gryffin. I'm fine. A bullet just grazed my leg.'

He crouches down beside her and his glowing purple eyes examine her wound. He carefully peels the material from the wound causing Terra to hiss in pain. His eye instantly locks on her. 'Sorry.'

She frowns, certain she's misheard him. That's only the second time she's ever heard him say that word. 'No need to apologise. Just stings a little.'

Gryffin rises to his feet and stands in front of Vance. 'What happened?' he asks again. Vance quickly runs through the events. 'Is anyone else injured?'

Vance shakes his head. 'No, sir.'

His reaction to her injury confuses her. The anger is expected. She's been on board long enough to know he'd be angry if any of his crew was injured. It's the concern that's throwing her. He's usually so good at hiding what he's feeling, but not right now. He is genuinely concerned about her and is doing a really bad job at hiding it. 'This isn't serious. I'll be on my feet in a few hours.'

He grunts and pulls the bandanna off his head. His hair falls over his face to hide his pained expression. He gently wraps the bandanna around her leg and secures it over the wound. He lifts his head and looks at Vance. 'We ready to go?'

'One minute, sir.'

He turns to face her again and surprises her by gently brushing a lock of hair off her face. 'I'll take you back to *Ares*.' Gryffin carefully slips his arms under her and lifts her from the ground. Terra doesn't care that the six Nomad personnel are staring open-mouthed at the out of character compassion displayed by their leader. His reaction to her injury may be unfamiliar to them, but she knows this side to him. This is the side he usually keeps firmly under wraps. Every now and again, he lets his wall down. He let it down in the cave and is doing the same now.

She honestly thought he would never be like this with her again. Since the first fumble in the training room, he's kept his distance from her. Ever since that moment, she's been trying unsuccessfully to convince herself that she's happy about it. But, being cradled in his arms, she realises she can never be happy about him ignoring her. It hurts and he's the only one that can make it stop.

Terra tries to keep her own wall up around her heart, but she knows the structure is failing. His strong, warm body hugs her close. She decides to make the most of it and snuggles in against the side of his neck. She smiles as his breathing hitches for a second.

Without letting her go, he straddles his bike. 'I need both hands. Hang on tight.'

She wraps her arms around his torso as he enters his code and starts the engine. The large machine roars to life and, after checking she's not going to fall off, he turns it around and accelerates down the road back towards *Ares*. Every bump jars her injured leg, but she really couldn't care.

All too soon, he calls *Ares* in to pick them up. She hears the ship's powerful engines approach from somewhere above them. The noise increases as *Ares* drops out of the clouds and moves into position about a mile ahead of them. Gryffin pulls his bike to a stop and shouts instructions into his radio. She can't make out much of what he's saying, but the words 'jump' and 'bike' don't help put her at ease. She risks a quick look and is horrified to see *Ares* hasn't actually landed on a road. Instead, her loading ramp hangs suspended in the air beyond the edge of the sheer drop ahead of them.

'What are you doing?' she shouts, but her question is lost under the sound of *Ares*' engines and the roar of his bike as he accelerates towards the ship. Terra buries her face against his chest and tightens her grip around his torso. All she can do is hang on and hope they don't plummet to their death. She focuses on the steady and reassuring beat of his heart, trying to keep her own under control. His bike gathers momentum as it races down the hill towards the cliff edge.

'Hold on,' Gryffin shouts over the growl of the engine. She tightens her grip around him, sure that she'll have to peel her fingers out of his skin if they survive this. The sound of the dirt track under them disappears as the tyres leave the ground. She holds her breath, only releasing it when a sudden jolt rocks her as they land. The tyres screech along the metal floor as Gryffin pulls the bike to a stop. The engine noise from *Ares* is muted as the large bay doors slam closed. Gryffin gently peals her arms from around him and looks at her. 'You okay?'

She nods quickly. 'A bit of warning before you do something like that again would be great.'

His frown softens. 'Where's the fun in that?' He kicks down the stand and gestures to the tall Nomad on the platform above him. 'Transports are just behind. Get us out of here as soon as they're on board.' He leans back in the saddle so he can look at her again. 'You want a gurney?'

'Of course not. I'm perfectly capable of walking.' She slides off the saddle with every intention of doing as she said. Unfortunately, her leg has other ideas. As soon as she puts weight on it, the pain makes standing difficult, let alone walking. Gryffin catches her before she makes a bigger idiot of herself.

Without a word, he gathers her in his arms again, and briskly walks to the med bay. Gryffin gently lowers her onto a bed and cuts her leathers to expose the wound. He turns to search through various drawers and cupboards, gathering everything he needs. Terra watches in silence as he expertly cleans the wound while clearly avoiding looking directly at her. After a few minutes, she has to break the silence. 'You know, you're pretty good at that.'

He grunts as he carefully covers the wound with gauze. 'Loads of practice.'

'I'll bet.'

He finishes with her leg and takes out a syringe. He carefully examines the line of bottles on the shelf and takes one from the centre. He passes it to her. 'You want to check the label? Make sure it's the pain killer.'

She shakes her head. 'After everything you've done for me, I doubt you'd try to kill me now.'

He takes her hand and puts the bottle in it. 'I can't read. I recognise the label, but I need you to check to be sure.'

Her eyes open wide. 'Don't be ridiculous. You read the reports we record for you. You hook into the system and can control it. That's just not possible if you can't read.'

He leans on the bed beside hers and crosses his arms. 'Desyl usually verbally records his reports. I can recognise numbers and some letters on the other reports.'

She sits up straight on the bed and purses her lips. 'And connecting to the system?'

He looks away and shrugs. 'As I said, I recognise numbers.'

It takes Terra a moment to realise exactly what he's saying. 'You recognise the code?' She slides further down the bed and swings her legs over the side. 'You can read computer code?'

'Yes.'

She can barely form any thoughts, let alone words. She knew he could connect to the system, but she assumed, as Roman and Milla had, that he accessed what he needed because he could read the file names. The fact he can read computer code never entered her mind. 'That's amazing, Gryffin. Why haven't you told anyone?'

'Why should I? You don't discuss how you read. Why should I?' He rises to his feet. 'Ready to go back to your room?'

Even though she'd love to ask more questions, she knows he's done answering. 'I'm fit to work.' She does fill the syringe with the recommended dose of pain killer, however. It may just be a graze, but it hurts.

'Rest first. We have a few hours until we get to Ultar.' Terra opens her mouth to argue, but he jumps in before she can speak. 'I'm ordering you to rest for a few hours.' Instead of letting her walk to her room under her own steam, he carries her through the corridors again and gently sits her on the bed. He turns the shower on and hands her a towel. 'I'll organise some food for you while you get cleaned up.'

Ten minutes later, Terra steps out of the shower feeling much better. She wraps the towel tightly around her and freezes at the door when she sees Gryffin walk into his quarters with a tray of food. Real food. Her mouth instantly waters at the smell that hits her. 'Where did you get that?'

He carefully places the tray on his desk. 'Helped ourselves to some of the local's food. Payment for shooting at my crew.'

Terra doesn't bother pointing out that they were only shooting at his crew because he destroyed their town last year. She grabs a pair of shorts and a vest, gets dressed quickly in the bathroom and then sits down to eat. 'Are you not having any?' she mumbles around a mouthful of potato.

'Already ate.'

'Hmmm. Of course you did.' She swallows and takes a long drink of water. 'Everything go well with the rest of the resupply?'

He leans against the wall and crosses his arms. 'We got what we needed. How... how's your leg?'

She waves away his concern. 'Nothing to worry about. Nice shower, amazing food, and some pain killers are a great combination.' She resists the urge to lick her plate clean and leans back in her chair. Her eyelids close as the painkiller works into her system. 'Sorry, I'm just a little sleepy.'

Without a word, Gryffin carries her to the bed and drapes the blanket over her as she falls asleep.

35

The meeting room falls silent as Roman and Aleena enter. Roman feels bone weary. He can't remember the last time he had more than three hours sleep in one go. Watching the Foundation's attack on the Nomad had taken its toll. It was difficult to sit and watch the attack, helpless to offer assistance of any kind. Lucan had been right. The Foundation proved no match for the Nomad fleet. They fiercely attacked without hesitation. Explosions were still working through the targeted Foundation vessels as the Nomad moved away and targeted the next. They were ruthless. The old saying *never wound an enemy* must be learnt by all Nomad from an early age. He's just glad they're on the same side. For the moment at least.

He sits down and reaches for the cup of coffee like it's a long sought after lifeline. 'This is your meeting Sayber. What do you want to say?'

Sayber leans back and drapes his arm on the back of the chair. 'As I explained to Roman earlier, we secured all but one of the prisons. We haven't given up on that one yet, we just need some reinforcements.'

Lucan nods and smiles. 'Great. *Epsilon* can come and help if you Hunters aren't up to the challenge.'

Sayber grins. 'Not worried about friendly fire?'

'I'll try to control where I shoot.'

Sayber shakes his head and looks back at Roman. 'Anyway, Bray discovered a little something that could prove to be very useful.' He nods out the window to a giant of a man standing beside Bray in the main hangar.

'Little?' Lucan snorts.

'Who is he?' Roman asks.

'His name is Garvan. Don't know if that's his full name. He was in the isolation wing of the second prison along with a few other colleagues of his. From what he says, he worked as the head architect on a secret project for the Foundation. They wanted him to design a new colony.'

Roman lowers his cup to the table. 'What new colony?'

Sayber shrugs. 'Need to know apparently, and he didn't. They worked for two years then were thanked by being hauled off to prison.'

Aleena gasps and shakes her head. 'That is terrible.' She looks out at the man and frowns. 'Forgive me for saying this, he does not look like an architect.'

Sayber laughs. 'Absolutely not. Prison life changed him, I guess. So, Roman, any idea what's going on?'

'No, and that worries me. Does he have any more information?'

Sayber looks at Garvan. 'He sat down with his team and redrew the facility. Apart from what it looks like, he's at a loss.'

'What about the man himself, do you trust him?'

Sayber glances at Roman. 'About as much as you trust me. Bray questioned most of the inmates from the prison. Information about his arrival is sketchy and I'm sure you know time doesn't mean much inside. They agree he's been there a long time. Years at the least which fits his story.'

'So he predates *Infinity*'s arrival here.'

Sayber nods. 'Unless the Foundation knew you were going to bump into the Nomad and all this was going to happen, they wouldn't have a reason to plant him. No, he's genuine. So are his less than happy feelings for the Foundation.'

Roman looks to Aleena. She purses her lips and nods once. 'Bring him in.'

'Bray!' Sayber shouts, startling everyone at the table. 'Get your ass in here!'

Roman rolls his eyes, Aleena shakes her head, and Lucan just laughs. Things are never quiet with Sayber around.

Bray and Garvan step into the room. Roman stands up and holds out his hand. Garvan doesn't hesitate and firmly shakes his hand. 'Welcome to Ultar, Garvan. Glad to have you here.'

'Not half as glad as I am to be here.' He bows at Aleena. 'I appreciate your hospitality.'

She smiles. 'Do not mention it. You are welcome. Please, have a seat.'

He sits beside Roman, dwarfing the Foundation captain. 'So, you're Foundation.'

Roman shakes his head. 'Not anymore. We are all united by one factor. We all want to bring an end to the Foundation. Sayber says you have information on a new facility.'

Garvan nods. 'Any enemy of the Foundation.' He pulls a chip out of his pocket and tosses it to Bray. He loads it onto the screen after he closes the security shutters in the room. An image of the facility fills the screen. Lines of cuboid buildings, some linked and others standing alone, sit to either side of a perfectly straight road. Approximately one hundred buildings make up the main colony. At the end of the road, a large building sits alone, towering above the other much smaller ones. 'As you can see, we designed it so most of the work and fabrication can be undertaken by drones on Earth. The wall panels simply slot together to form the dwelling.'

'And that's what they requested?'

Garvan nods. 'They wanted something lightweight but durable, easily erected and dismantled, and it had to be transportable. Building the units on site would be far more cost effective than shipping them to the site, but they insisted.'

'Can you hazard a guess as to what they wanted it for?'

Garvan takes a deep breath. 'Well, I seriously doubt anyone from Earth will be living there.'

Aleena rests her hands on the table. 'Why do you say that?'

'The houses are small. One main living space, a bathroom and one or two bedrooms. No one I know of on Earth would lower themselves to live in something like that. Whatever they want it for, it's built for practicality instead of luxury.'

Lucan crosses his arms as he glares at the screen. 'You reckon the inhabitants will be forced to live there.'

Garvan shrugs. 'Don't know. Seems likely though.'

'We need to tell Gryffin.'

Garvan blinks and looks at Lucan. 'Is he here?' The room falls silent and everyone looks at Garvan. 'Hey, listen, I'm just curious. I don't have an ulterior motive. Difficult not to hear about someone like Gryffin, especially if you're a resident of a prison.'

'No offence, Garvan, but trust needs to be earned first.'

Garvan nods at Roman. 'I understand. So, what do you want from me. How can I help?'

Roman points to the model of the facility. 'I know you've probably been told to do this already, but go over everything. Make sure you've noted down every detail you can remember.'

'Sure.' He gets to his feet and leaves with Bray closely behind.

Sayber waits until he's gone to speak. 'Well?'

Roman rubs his forehead as he considers his response. This group of architects came into their lives at the right time and he'd be crazy not to take advantage. 'Seems genuine. You happy to keep a close eye on his team?'

'He's been working with Bray. I'll leave it like that for the moment.'

'How is Bray?' Aleena asks.

Sayber makes a face. 'Seeing her again will be tough on him. He's strong. His fellow Hunters will look out for him. Have to admit, I was relieved to see you didn't soften him with your Foundation rules and regulations.'

Roman smiles and shakes his head. 'He was never truly part of the Foundation. As soon as he stepped onto *Perses* he was a Hunter.'

'Foundation's loss, Hunter's gain.'

Roman nods slowly. He just hopes Bray's new friend is a gain for the group and not their undoing.

∞

Terra groans as she tries to hold on to sleep. She's too comfortable to consider moving. After putting it off for another few minutes, she finally peels her eyes open to see a large metal hand hanging over her shoulder. She follows the line of the hand to the arm it's attached to. Her breath freezes in her chest when she suddenly realises there's a large body pressed tightly against her back.

She rubs her eyes with her free hand and looks back at the arm, but it's still there. She rolls onto her back and winces as her injured leg protests. Terra hesitantly turns her head and comes face to face with Gryffin. He's lying on top of the covers, clothed and still wearing his fully loaded holster. It doesn't look like he left her room after he brought her back from the surface. His real eye is hidden in the crook of his arm, but as far as she can tell, the robotic eye is shut down.

She can't believe he stayed with her while she slept. There was no need, it's not like she was in any medical danger. He must have stayed because he wanted to. There was no other reason. Her heart hammers loudly in her chest. The intense feelings she buried for months break through the badly constructed wall around her heart. A lone tear rolls onto the pillow under her head as she reaches out and gently brushes his hair back from his face. She loves him and feels utterly disgusted at herself for trying to deny it. Her thumb traces along the edge of the new eyepiece and his artificial eye comes to life, but he doesn't pull away. He turns his head slightly, uncovering his other eye.

She runs her finger along the old wound that stretches from his forehead, across the top of his nose and down his cheek. His mouth parts slightly as she trails her finger across his lips. 'You didn't have to stay.'

Gryffin shrugs. 'I wanted to. How's your leg?'

'Good. I was lucky to receive first class treatment.'

He frowns slightly. 'I'm sorry.'

'For what?'

'It's my fault you were hurt. I screwed up the last time I was on Taldor. That's why they attacked.'

'Well, I can't argue you may have been a bit heavy handed the last time, but my injury isn't your fault. We're up to our neck in conflict. Bumps and scrapes are to be expected. Are you like this every time a member of your crew gets a minor graze?'

Gryffin rises to his elbow and looks down at her. 'You're more than just a member of my crew.'

Terra freezes and stares at him. 'I am?' He nods once, but instead of moving closer, he pulls back from her. 'What's wrong?'

He wipes a hand over his face and gets to his feet. 'I have to get back to the command deck.'

She quickly pushes up to her elbows and hisses in pain as her wound protests.

He lowers onto the bed beside her again. 'You okay?'

Terra looks him straight in the eye and takes the plunge. 'Do you want me or not?'

His artificial eye zooms in on her. 'I never said I didn't want you. I always want you, that's the damn problem.'

She can't help the enormous smile that spreads across her face. She never thought she'd hear those words from him. 'So, why are we avoiding what's between us?'

'I heard you on Ultar. You were talking to Milla about being with someone.'

Terra pauses and her heart sinks a little. She can't believe he overheard that conversation. Her breath catches in her throat. What else did she say to Milla? She tries to remember the conversation, but it's a blank. If she mentioned her father, he would have said something to her by now.

'You're in a relationship, with someone. That's what you meant, right?'

'Well, yes, but I'm not with anyone, Gryffin. Not anymore. I haven't been since before I left for *Ares*.'

'You haven't?' Gryffin frowns as he looks at her. 'Ever since I got back you've been acting like you can't stand to be in the same room as me.'

She inwardly winces. When put like that, she realises she has been a little harsh. 'After I thought you died... I guess I was angry.'

'At me?'

She nods. 'I thought you had given up too easily on the freighter.'

'Easy?' Gryffin laughs once and shakes his head. 'It was anything but easy. There was no choice and no time.'

His flippant reply pushes her to her limit. She leans back on the pillow and crosses her arms. 'That's exactly my problem. How do you know that? There might have been time to get you off the ship, but you just decided to crash the freighter. I could have found a way to remove your collar. There was a team of people who could have figured out another solution. Instead you ran head first into a suicide mission.'

She looks up at him as she wipes away a tear. 'The last image I had was of you sitting on the floor with a large hole in your chest. It didn't have to be you facing the enemy alone like a hero. It didn't have to be your life. You offered yourself up without even thinking about me, about us.' She takes a deep breath at the end of her unplanned outburst and silently watches for his reaction.

He leaves the silence hanging for a painful minute before his gaze leaves her face and turns towards the floor. 'You were, or are, angry at me because you think I wanted to be the big hero and save the day alone?'

When he says it back to her, it sounds like a pathetic argument. 'Well, yes, but—'

'You really think I wanted to die alone on the floor of that ship?' he interrupts. Gryffin looks back at her, his expression blank. 'Like you said, I had a hole in my chest, the Foundation was about to launch another fleet through the Port, our defences were stretched to their limit, and I couldn't leave the freighter with my head attached. I was trapped and there was no time to figure out a way to get the collar off me. The best option was to use the freighter to destroy the Port and stop the Foundation in their tracks.

'I honestly thought I was going to die, Terra.' He laughs harshly. 'But I didn't. I woke up back on his table staring at myself in the mirrored ceiling as he worked on me. I tried so hard to get out of there and come back to you, but I wasn't off the table much during the first few months.'

He frowns and Terra knows he's gone back there. She touches his hands and Gryffin jumps slightly.

'I am sorry you spent all that time thinking I was dead, but I need you to know I came back as soon as I could. I never stopped thinking about us.' He taps the side of his head. 'You were always in here. Whenever they'd strap me to the table, I'd switch off. I got good at disconnecting from my body over the years.' He turns to look at her. 'I'd go somewhere with you.'

His admission surprises her. 'Where would you go?'

He looks away and shrugs. 'Anywhere. It didn't matter. Thinking about you got me through ten months in that place.'

'I've been such an idiot. I'm so sorry.'

'For what? You were alive and happy. My plan worked. I'd prefer you alive and hating me than the alternative.'

She reaches up and runs a hand along the side of his face. 'I never thought you'd come back.'

'You and me both.' He looks at the blanket and frowns so deeply, the top of his ocular implant seems to disappear. 'Yesterday, when I saw you in that tunnel, bleeding, I lost it.' He looks back at her and his blue eye is glistening. 'I don't want to stay away from you any longer. I want you.'

She nods and smiles, relieved that she managed to restrain herself to just a nod. 'So, what happens now?'

Gryffin leans forwards and kisses her. Terra lies back on the pillow, pulling him down with her as their kiss becomes more desperate. They've got nearly a year to make up for.

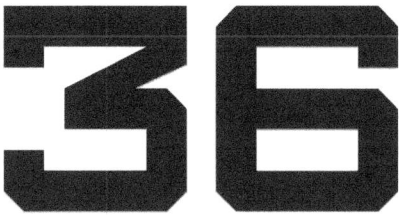

'You're naked.'

Gryffin frowns at her. 'That usually happens when I take all my clothes off.'

She punches him playfully on the arm. 'That's not what I mean. I've just never seen you fully naked in the light before.'

He rolls over onto his side and props his head up on his metal arm. 'That your final answer, Commander Rush?'

Terra's cheeks redden slightly and she looks away. 'Of course.'

The corner of his mouth twitches slightly.

'Why do I get the feeling you're hiding something, Captain?'

'I know you saw me in the shower.'

The slight blush turns to a full red face. 'That was all an act because you knew I was watching you?'

He shakes his head and a lock of hair falls over his face. 'Trust me, if I'd known earlier that you were there it would have played out differently. I only realised when you left the training room. I know every creak and groan this ship makes — including the top step of the stairs. I heard you leave.'

She sits up and brushes her hair off her face. 'I'm so sorry, I didn't mean to invade your privacy.'

He shrugs. 'Enough people have seen my body. I gave up on privacy a hell of a long time ago.'

'That doesn't help me feel any better about spying on you.'

'Don't worry about it. I checked on you one night after you came on board.'

Her eyebrows shoot up. 'Oh, really? Spying on me while I was asleep. Well, I think we're even.' She wraps the blanket around her shoulders. 'So, why has this happened now? You've done nothing but push me away since I got here.'

He sighs and looks up at the ceiling. 'What I said to you about not being safe with me still stands. But, I've wanted you like this since that night on Ultar a year ago. Being with me will put a target on your head. That's why I flipped when I saw my griffin on your neck. It just put you with me even more.'

'Gryffin, you can't live your life assuming the worst is going to happen.'

'It did happen though, Terra.'

'So, why the change of heart if you believe the threat to me is still there.'

'The way you were on the station. You fought like a Nomad. You saved me from a bullet to the head and helped the rest of the crew. It was the same on Taldor. It hit me that, maybe, you can handle yourself. Yes, the threat is still there, but I have to accept that you're not completely helpless. I'm still not happy about you being anywhere near me...'

'But?'

He looks at the blanket and frowns so deeply, the top of his ocular implant seems to disappear. 'When I saw you in that tunnel bleeding, I lost it.' He looks back at her and his blue eye is glistening. 'I don't want to stay away from you any longer. I want you.'

She nods and smiles, relieved that she managed to restrain herself to just a nod. 'So, what happens now?'

He smiles at her and she feels like a ridiculous teenager again. 'Well, I don't know about you, but I'm getting into the shower.' He gets up and walks towards the bathroom, not in the slightest bit embarrassed about showing her all of his body. He gets to the door and turns back to look at her. 'You want to watch from there or get a bit closer?'

∞

After being delayed in the shower twice by Gryffin, Terra finally extracts herself and gets dressed. As she ties her hair back, her attention is caught by the patchwork of scars covering Gryffin's torso. 'Can I ask you something?'

He pulls on his trousers and glances up at her. 'What?'

'What are all the scars on your body from? Did... did the Foundation do... that to you?'

He shakes his head. 'What good will knowing do?'

'I need to know Gryffin. There's so much about you. So much to you and I've barely scratched the surface.'

'And you start with my scars?'

She nods. 'They're part of your history. Each one of them helped to make you the man you are today.'

He scoffs and shakes his head. 'Right.'

He lowers onto the bed and she sits beside him. Terra turns his head to face her and gently traces the jagged line that runs from his forehead, across his nose and down his cheek. 'How did you get this one?'

He sighs. 'I was attacked with a broken bottle.'

She swallows deeply. 'Okay, and the one on your cheek?'

'Knife attack a few years ago. And before you ask, the one across my neck was Sayber. Damn bastard nearly took my head off.'

'And you're okay to work with him?'

He shrugs. 'I nearly took his arm off. Besides, we need to work together for the moment.'

It's upsetting to hear how he's been hurt, but she's relieved her father had nothing to do with the scars on his face. He lowers his head and the light catches on his metal ocular implant. He may not have given Gryffin the facial scars but he did give him something worse — his metal eye.

'What about the rest. The ones on your chest and back.'

'Terra...'

'Please.'

'Some of them. Will you shut up now?'

'Some of them? I don't understand. You've got dozens and they look like precise cuts.'

'There's just no shutting you up is there?' He rubs his forehead. 'I got the rest from Rayde.'

'Rayde? Did he cut you when you were on the freighter?'

'When Rayde captained *Ares*, he ran a tight ship. Everyone on board had to pull their weight, including me. It took a long time for me to recover from my time with the Foundation, so I had to work extra hard to catch up. It was his way of giving me a kick when I needed it.'

Terra's mouth drops open as she dumbly stares at Gryffin. 'Giving you a kick? You mean he hurt you. And you were okay with that?'

Gryffin shrugs. 'He just saved me from a living hell. A few cuts is nothing compared to that.'

She gets up and paces the floor. 'When exactly would you need a kick?'

'His vision for me was as an enforcer. I had to do things most other people wouldn't want to. Initially, I took some convincing.'

'So he tortured you to turn you into a thug? I can't believe I'm hearing this?'

'I'm only alive because of him. That training served the Nomad over the years.'

'You're justifying what he did? You wouldn't hurt someone so he sliced your skin open as punishment?'

'Of course I'm not justifying it. But he taught me that we have to do things we don't want to, for the good of the group. If I have to hurt or kill someone to help the Nomad, I'll do it. No question.'

'My God. The stories they tell about you are correct. You kill for money, don't you.'

Gryffin stands up and pulls a t-shirt from the chair. 'How the hell do you think I paid for *Nemesis*? I don't have a vault of credits hidden away. I had to work damn hard to get her off the ground.'

'You're actually proud of what you do?'

He nods. 'I'm proud of the Nomad.'

'That's not what I mean.'

'You think I'm proud that I can easily kill?' He steps closer to her. 'You think I'm proud that the man I thought of as a father, helped make me into this? I'm not, okay! I didn't have any choice.'

'Don't try that excuse — of course you had a choice. You could have walked away.'

'To what! Look at me, Terra. Whether I like it or not, I was modified and conditioned to kill. I can't change that.'

'You're in charge of your own life, Gryffin. You can do whatever you want!'

He stands in front of her with his arms out to the side. 'Looking like this? I can't go anywhere without a mask on or my face hidden. You really think I can just quit, buy a farm on Ultar, and tend to cattle for the rest of my life?'

'You can try.'

He laughs and turns away. 'You need to get your head back in this Sector. This is what I do and I'm damn good at it. It's a fact.'

'It's not who you are though.'

'It is, and Rayde saw that.'

'He exploited and tortured you. I don't understand you. Why is Rayde even a factor in how you view yourself. You hate him.'

'I killed him because he lied to me, not because he hurt me.'

Terra's stomach twists at his words. She licks her suddenly dry lips and tries to gloss over his comment. 'Excuse me?'

'Without his training, I wouldn't have survived as long as I have.'

'So, would you have been able to forgive him if he'd told you the truth from the start?'

Gryffin shrugs then pulls the t-shirt over his head. 'I'm not saying that.'

Terra tucks her legs under her and cuddles the pillow to her chest to hide the fact she's trembling. 'Have you ever wanted to do something else with your life?'

Gryffin can't hold back the laugh that breaks free.

'I'm serious. Rayde only wanted to use you.'

'For the good of the Nomad.'

'He hurt you.'

'That's your view. I see it differently.' He fastens his holster around his waist. 'The Foundation tore me apart every day for years. Every damn day their scientist would strap me to a table and drill or weld or cut. You may hate Rayde, damn it I hate him too, but he saved my life. He took me from that and spent years putting me back together. I couldn't walk. Couldn't talk. Nothing. You may not like what he conditioned me to do, but he just finished what your people started.'

∞

'Sir,' Desyl's voice sounds from the comms unit beside Gryffin's bed.

'What?'

'We should reach the rest of the fleet in about four hours.'

'Understood. I'm on my way.' He shuts down the connection and turns to face her. He's hoping she'll let him get back to work without commenting, but he isn't that lucky.

'So, what happens to us when we get back to Ultar?'

Just the question he was hoping she wouldn't ask. He runs a hand through his hair and sighs. 'Nothing.'

She turns to face him. 'So that's it, we just go our separate ways? Forget everything that's happened between us?'

'We don't have a choice.'

'Is any of this affecting you?'

'Damn it, Terra. Of course it is.' He tucks a lock of hair behind her ear. 'I'd give anything to be able to take you away from all this mess, to be able to give you the life you deserve, but I can't.'

'It's not about what I deserve, I just want to be with you.' She sighs heavily and rubs a hand over her face. 'I don't understand why you went out of your way to get Milla and Chayse onto the same ship, but don't seem willing to give us the same chance. They want to be together, we want to be together. What's the difference? If you really want this to work you'll fight for us instead of just walking away!'

'It's not that simple and you know it. Chayse doesn't have a bloody big target painted on his back. You know as well as I do that the Foundation won't leave me alone until they have me in chains or I'm dead. There's no other option for them.'

'Then we deal with it together as a couple.'

Gryffin snorts. 'What do couples usually do when one of them is half machine and being pursued by the Foundation?' She turns away from him and wraps her arms tighter around her body. He sighs and stares up at the ceiling, hoping for some sort of inspiration, some clue on how to make this better for her. He knew heading into this that he'd just end up hurting her. Why didn't he stay away?

'Listen, you've already been taken once as a way of getting to me. If Bray and Sayber hadn't been there, who knows how it would have played out. I can't risk that again. I can't risk you again.'

'I'm not just someone you have to look after. Stop insulting me by constantly referring to me like I'm some damsel in distress.'

'I know you're capable.'

'Then stop treating me like a child! I'm a grown woman who has found someone she wants to be with. Stop hiding behind what's happening and tell me the truth.'

'I want to be with you, that's never been an issue. I have never let anyone get as close to me as you are. Desyl tried to drag me in for testing because he thought I was malfunctioning. That's how out of character all this is for me. But, as much as I want you here, you need to get back to *Infinity*. It's safer for you there.'

'You really need to come up with a better excuse. Rayde is dead and the Scientist is gone.'

'There's more to worry about than them.'

'We'll handle the Foundation. They can't get you if we all stick together.'

'Terra, don't make this harder than it already is.'

'But that's what I'm trying to say! It doesn't have to be hard. There is nothing stopping us from being together.'

He's clearly fighting a losing battle. 'Terra—'

'Just give us a chance. That's all I'm asking.'

He wants to continue the argument, but they're just going around in circles. Terra is adamant and he doubts there's anything he can say to change her mind. Not that he really wants to. He would have walked away — no question, but he wants to stay. He knows a happy life isn't what he deserves. Someone like Terra wants to be with someone like him. It doesn't make sense.

'Fine.'

That one word makes Terra squeal and throw her arms around him. He hopes he hasn't just signed her death sentence.

∞

Gryffin silently leans back in his command chair as *Ares* completes her final descent to Ultar. His gaze lands on the scarred landscape.

Every downed tree, every missile crater, every additional headstone in the graveyard is because of him. Nothing he does can ever make up for that. His stomach clenches at the thought of setting foot on the surface again. He took the coward's way out when he left as abruptly as he did. He had no right to run, but he couldn't face a conversation with Aleena or see the look of disgust in the locals' eyes. No running for him anymore.

Ares jolts as she touches down in an open field just outside the village. He groans and wipes a hand over his face when he sees the very people he wants to avoid, step out of the tunnels — Aleena and Roman.

'Sir?'

He glances up at Desyl. 'What?'

Desyl steps closer to him. 'Sir, we've landed. What are your orders?'

Gryffin can feel the eyes of the entire command crew on him as he stalls. 'Get the fleet on the ground and unload the supplies. Once that's done, everyone take twelve hours off and get some rest.'

Desyl's eyebrows shoot up. 'Really?'

Gryffin resists the urge to shout at him. 'Yes, really. If you don't all move now, I'll change my mind.'

Less than a minute later, he is alone on the deck with Terra. 'You can't put it off forever.'

He looks up at Terra, leaning against the railing in front of him. 'Put what off?'

She points over her shoulder at Aleena and Roman, still patiently waiting in front of *Ares*. 'I'm pretty sure they're not waiting so they can attack you.'

'You think I'm afraid of them?'

She slides on to his knee and traces her finger along the scar on his neck. 'You're still blaming yourself for what happened. It's only natural you'd be anxious about coming back here.'

'What about you? I thought you'd be the first one off the ship.'

'Stop deflecting.' She looks at the welcoming committee. She rises to her feet and holds out her hand. 'Come on, Captain.'

He glares at the pair waiting for them, then at Terra, but her smile only gets bigger. She has a point and that just irritates him. He has to meet with them face to face at some stage. Best to get it over and done with. He shakes his head and takes her offered hand. Before they leave the command deck, he pulls his gun and knife out of his belt and hands them to her. 'Just in case.'

∞

Roman can't help but smile when Terra steps off *Ares* and hurries towards him. She throws her arms around his neck and hugs him tightly before she composes herself and pulls away. 'Sorry about that. I'm just really glad to see you again.'

Roman laughs. 'Hey, no need to apologise. It's been a long few weeks.' He looks over her shoulder at Gryffin. The captain stands a few steps behind Terra with his arms by his side. He looks like a very different person to the one that left in such a hurry. He still could do with more meat on his bones, but he appears stronger and healthier than he was. Something about his posture and the way his eyes dart between the members of the group catches his attention. If Roman had to guess, he'd swear that Gryffin is nervous about being here. Roman steps forward and holds his hand out to his son. The awkward moment stretches on a bit longer than he would like, but eventually Gryffin takes his hand and shakes it briefly before breaking contact. 'Good to see you, Gryffin. I can't thank you enough for bringing Terra back in one piece.'

'We've got the body of your pilot in the med bay.'

Terra spins to face him. 'You do?'

Gryffin shrugs. 'I don't leave people behind — dead or alive.' Gryffin nods towards Desyl who is waiting at the base of the ramp. 'He'll help you with the body.'

Roman calls for med support to collect the body. 'Now, I'm sure you could all do with some rest before we debrief.'

Gryffin nods. 'I've got some things to see to on *Ares*. Twelve hours enough time?'

Aleena steps forward. 'We have plenty of available room here, Gryffin. There is no need to stay on your ship.'

Terra takes Gryffin's hand and turns him to face her. 'You need a break, Gryffin. *Ares* will still be there in a few hours. Please.'

Gryffin nods and allows Terra to lead him by the hand into the facility. 'Did you see what I did, Jensen?'

'You mean did I see Terra and Gryffin holding hands. Yes. You don't think they're a couple, do you?'

Aleena shakes her head. 'I cannot hazard a guess. In all the years I have worked with him, he has never been that close to anyone. He hates being touched. Had I not seen their display myself, I would not believe it happened.'

Roman's heart sinks to his stomach. If Terra and Gryffin are together, it just makes an already messy and emotional situation even worse. Too much can go wrong at any second. 'She can't have told him about her father.'

'No. Nothing good can come of all these secrets. Gryffin is far from stupid. If he stumbles upon the information himself, it will be so much worse for everyone. Both you and Terra need to, have to, speak to him.'

Roman sighs and rubs the back of his neck. He was hoping Aleena wouldn't say that. 'We need him focused on the Nomad. If I tell him now, what's to stop him from leaving again? It's just not the right time.'

She crosses her arms and scowls at him. 'You are being a coward. There will never be a right time. Just like there will never be a right time for Terra to tell him about her father. I have known Gryffin for many years. He keeps a wall around himself to prevent people from getting close, to prevent people from hurting him. The only way he can live with his past is to keep firm control over his present. For so long, every minute of his day was controlled by someone else. He may seem harsh and appear hostile, well, all the time, but that is how he copes. He expects things to be done his way or, how did he put it, "you should get out of his way." Rayde's betrayal has deeply affected him. I do not mean any disrespect, but Gryffin thought of Rayde as a father. Learning that Rayde was only interested in him because of what he is was devastating.'

'You're not expecting me to step in and make everything better. Replace one father figure with another.'

She shakes her head. 'Of course not. That is the last thing he wants.' She paces in front of him, her full attention on the grass under her feet. She finally stops and looks back at him. 'I am about to break a confidence, but I believe it is necessary. Gryffin was told by the Scientist that he was given to the project, that his parents didn't want him so they sold him.'

Roman tries to swallow, however all moisture has disappeared from his mouth. 'He told you that?'

She nods. 'It was many years ago during one of his rare talkative moods. That is why it is vital you tell him the truth yourself. He will need you to explain what happened between you and his mother, otherwise he will believe you both sold him without a second thought.'

Roman rubs the back of his neck as the tension builds. He's never been an aggressive person, but the more he learns about what the Foundation and Callum did to Gryffin, the more he wants them dead, and that scares him. 'Any idea how he'll take the news?'

Aleena shakes her head. 'There will be fallout and I cannot say how bad it will be. All I do know is that the longer you leave it, the worse the situation will get. Both you and Terra risk damaging your relationship with him permanently. Tell him before he learns the truth himself.'

She turns abruptly and walks away.

37

Terra lowers into the seat beside Gryffin and looks around the room as the others file through the door. Amazingly, Gryffin had slept for nearly ten hours. He may deny it, but his body needs rest. Weeks of forcing himself to stay awake has well and truly caught up with him. She glances sideways at him and isn't put at ease by his expression. The muscles in his face are nearly pulsing as he clenches his jaw. She resists the urge to take his hand or offer some other form of comfort — he made it clear before they left the room that he's a captain and she's a commander. The lines can't be blurred while they're with the rest of the group. It took her nearly an hour to apologise for taking his hand when they first stepped onto Ultar. She didn't bother to point out that he hadn't refused her touch. He needs to take back control of the situation and she doesn't have the heart to deny him.

Besides, at the moment she has bigger things to worry about. Her stomach tightens when Bray enters the room and sits down opposite her. Well, this definitely makes an awkward situation even worse. Bray glares accusingly at his brother while Gryffin barely even acknowledges the Hunter. His attention is solely focused on the Hunter leader. Sayber nods at Gryffin as he sits beside Bray.

As the unofficial leader of the group, Roman takes his seat at the head of the table and clears his throat to start the meeting. 'I have to say, it's good to have a full house again. I'd like to welcome *Ares* back. Things have certainly shifted in our favour with the addition of the Nomad and Rogue ships. We may actually have a good chance of holding the Foundation back now the Nomad are reunited with Gryffin at the lead.'

'I'm not going to lead them,' Gryffin replies.

'What?' Terra asks at the same time as Roman.

Gryffin rests his elbows on the table. 'The Nomad have come together, but it's only temporary. They're working with me because they don't have a choice. It's either me or spend their lives wandering the Sector. I killed any trust they had. It's only a matter of time before they decide to take their chances alone. They need Chayse to take command and lead them. He's the safer option.'

'This isn't about safe options,' Roman says. 'This is about winning. The Nomad need you at the helm. We need you there.'

'I'm not stepping back from the Nomad, just the High Commander role.'

Bray laughs and shakes his head. 'Pressure too much for you, Nomad?'

Roman stands up and places a hand on Bray's shoulder to silence him. 'There's no need to make any rash decisions, Captain.'

'This isn't a rash decision. You need the Nomad fleet. Without them you're all dead and so is the Sector. But there's no fleet with me at the lead. It's that simple.'

'But you have reunited the fleet,' Roman argues.

Gryffin shakes his head. 'Out of fear, not loyalty. They used to trust me with their lives, now they're just worried I'm going to kill them if they say no. I can't lead them like that. I've got them all together in one place, but that's as much as I can do. I've spoken with all the captains. They agree Chayse should succeed me. After *Ares*, *Nemesis* is the stand out ship in the fleet. It makes sense. They'll support him.'

'You're being an idiot,' Sayber says. 'I've called you many things, but never that. Stand down if you want, but not now. There's enough shit going on without messing with leadership within the group.'

'I haven't been here. It's not going to mess up anything.'

Sayber curses and leans back in his chair with his arms crossed. 'You've always been too damn stubborn for your own good. It'll bring you down one day.'

The hair lifts at the back of Terra's neck as Gryffin smiles back at Sayber. Something about his response sets alarms bells ringing in her mind, but she can't put her finger on what it is.

∞

Terra grabs Gryffin's arm as he storms away from the meeting. He suddenly stops and looks down at her. 'What exactly are you doing?'

He gestures down the corridor. 'Going back to *Ares*.'

Terra stands in front of Gryffin to block his escape. 'No, I mean about stepping down? You just got the Nomad back.'

He glances around him, then grabs her by the arm and pulls her into the store room behind her. 'I'm doing what I have to.'

'You're running away again! We need you and you're just going to abandon us.'

His eye quickly melts to purple. 'You really think that's what I'm doing?'

'What else would you call it?'

'I told you that I need to fix my mess. This is the only way of doing that. You really think I want to step down? There's no other choice if I want to help the Nomad.'

'Of course there is. Yes, it will take time to earn their trust back, but it's possible. The mod Milla fitted to you should help with that.'

He leans against the wall and runs his hand along the scar on the side of his head. 'It'll take more than that. I killed a lot of people.'

'But that wasn't your fault! Why can't you accept that?'

'You don't get it. The Nomad all know how easy it was for the Foundation to turn me into their weapon. They witnessed what I can do first hand. Up until then, what I am was a plus for the Nomad. Now...' He takes a deep breath and shrugs. 'Having a... cyborg leading them is too much of a risk. I killed people I would have given my life to protect. How are they expected to ever trust me again?'

'Milla and Chayse fixed the control implant.'

'For now.' He leans back against the wall and shrugs. 'It's done, okay. I'm not going to change my mind.'

Terra hates to admit that he may have a point. For the moment at least, they need to be united against the Foundation. If even one piece was out of place, they wouldn't have a chance at winning. 'I wish there was another option.'

He leans down and rests his forehead against hers. 'There isn't. You know that as much as I do.'

She closes her eyes and sighs. 'Damn it.'

He pushes back from her and smiles. 'Get used to it. I have to.'

Terra lays her head against his chest and wraps her arms around him. She has a horrible feeling he's giving up. In the short time she's known him, leading the Nomad was his life. He would have given up his arm rather than the High Commander role. She buries her face into his t-shirt and tries to ignore the nagging doubt that something is seriously wrong.

∞

Gryffin makes his way to the med bay in a bit of a daze. Milla wants to check his mod and now is as good a time as any. It's not like he has anything else to do. He doesn't regret his decision to step down as High Commander. Chayse will keep the future of the Nomad secure.

Gryffin knocks on the door to the med bay and Lucan stands to attention. Milla looks at him and blinks a few times. 'Well, well, High

Commander. Thought you'd put up a bit more of a fight. I'm impressed.'

He doesn't have the energy to correct her on his title. She'll find out soon enough. 'No point putting it off.'

'Well, wonders never cease.' She gestures towards the nearest bed. 'Hop up. This shouldn't take too long.' She leans on the bed behind him and taps on a tablet. 'So, any problems with the new mods?'

'No.'

Milla crosses her arms and looks at him. 'Try again, Captain. I'll just find out when I run the scans anyway.'

He sighs and decides to actually tell her the truth about the pain. 'The eyepiece and my leg.'

Milla leans over and gently prods the plate over his eye, making Gryffin grunt in pain. 'I'll remove it and see what's going on. Can I see your leg?'

He pulls his trousers down and sits on the bed. Milla turns back to face him and frowns at his leg. 'The flesh attached to the metal looks a little red. I'll need to see inside.' She looks up at Lucan. 'Care to do the honours?'

'Sure. Lie down, sir.' He gently probes the skin above and below Gryffin's metal thigh.

Gryffin grinds out a curse as fire bursts through his leg. 'It hurts, okay. You can stop poking it.'

Lucan smiles sheepishly. 'Sorry, sir. I'll make this as painless as I can.'

Gryffin stares at the ceiling as Lucan unfastens each of the screws holding the top piece of metal in place.

'That's the top layer off. Ready for the next bit, sir?' Gryffin nods. 'I'm going to apologise in advance. This is going to hurt.'

Lucan unscrews the next level of metal and the pain explodes through Gryffin's limb. He clenches his teeth as Lucan exposes the inside of his leg. Milla leans over and takes a deep breath. 'That's pretty unpleasant. It's a mess. How long has it been giving you trouble?'

'Since I got back to *Ares*.'

Lucan's eyes narrow. 'Damn it, sir. Your heroics are going to kill you some day. I know your implants make you more resilient, but you're still human. This should have been seen to weeks ago.'

'I don't need your opinion. What the hell are you even doing here? Are you not a captain now?'

Lucan straightens and smiles. 'I am. *Epsilon* is grounded at the moment. Her main engine took a hit from a Rogue transport. Until it's repaired I'm at a loose end. Thought I'd help out in here.'

Gryffin looks away but doesn't reply. It's not his place to order Lucan around anymore — they're at the same level now.

'So,' Milla says as she pulls on a pair of gloves, 'did something specific happen to it?'

'No. The more I use it the worse it gets. Think it's failing internally.'

She sits down on the chair beside the bed and frowns. 'I think you might be right. I had hoped you'd get a few years out of it before this happened. I suppose it's a waste of time telling you to keep weight off it.'

'Not practical.'

Lucan crosses his arms and peers over Milla's shoulder. 'Any bright ideas, Milla?'

She scrunches up her face as she stares at his leg. 'All I can do is clean it and give you an increased dose of antibiotics. Hopefully some of it will work into your system before your implants neutralise it. I'll contact Chayse and see if he has any ideas. In the meantime, no training.'

'What?'

'C'mon, Gryffin, surely that's common sense. You need to rest it. Unless we can figure out some way to fix the mess the Foundation made of your leg, there may be no other alternative but to amputate.'

Nausea twists in his stomach at her words. 'You mean I'd lose my whole leg?' That's all he needs to hear after losing command of the Nomad.

She nods slowly. 'It's a possibility. We'll do whatever we can to stop that from happening, but it's not looking good. I'll take some scans of your leg so my team can examine the entire limb.'

'I don't want anyone to know about this — especially Terra.'

'It's not my place to tell her. It might be something you have to consider at some point. It's not going to get better overnight. You could need some help to walk in the not too distant future.'

'No one.'

Milla nods. 'It's your call. We'll give it a good clean and see if that improves things for you at all.'

He nods once and closes his eye. His throat tightens when he thinks about what Milla said. A sudden coldness travels through his body. He hates feeling helpless, unable to fully control what's going on with his own body.

Lucan stands beside Milla and she points to something inside Gryffin's leg. 'We'll start here and work down. Minimal contact, okay?'

Lucan nods and they both begin working.

'Why are you still here?' Gryffin asks Milla. 'I thought you were moving to *Nemesis*?'

Milla looks at him over the rim of her protective glasses. 'Ah, that's on hold for the moment. *Nemesis* is tied up at the far side of the Sector. I'm stuck here until she can make it even half way back to Ultar to collect me or meet a transport. I've waited this long, a few more weeks won't hurt. And, it worked out well for you. You get the pleasure of my company again.'

'Damn it!'

Milla pouts. 'Hey, I'm not that bad.'

Gryffin sucks in a breath. 'That was for my leg, not you.'

'Sorry, sir,' Lucan replies. 'My bad. It's a bit difficult to know what I can touch without hurting you.'

'You're inside my leg, how about you assume everything hurts.'

'Yes, sir. Milla, any idea what that is?'

Milla shakes her head and leans closer to examine whatever Lucan is pointing at. 'It looks like it's been fused to the bone.'

Gryffin slams his metal fist down on the bed. 'I don't need a running commentary.'

They both stop talking and work in silence for a few minutes. The sounds coming from inside his leg are nearly worse than them describing what they're doing.

'So, sir, did Aleena give you a hard time for planting me among her people?'

Gryffin shakes his head. He knows Lucan is trying to distract him and he's grateful. 'Hasn't mentioned it so far. Was she upset about it?'

Lucan frowns and shakes his head. 'Surprised more than upset.' He touches a sensitive spot and Gryffin curses in pain. 'Sorry. To be honest, I think she was glad I was here. Having a Nomad on the surface helped when Nera attacked and tried to take Ultar.'

Gryffin rises to his elbows and instantly regrets it. He's got a strong stomach but seeing the inside of his leg pushes it to its limit. He lies back down again. 'Nera? What did he do?'

Lucan fills him in on Nera's attempted take over as they steadily work on his leg. Gryffin never liked Nera, but never thought he'd try to take Ultar. At least Lucan was there to help Aleena. 'Aleena fought with you?'

Lucan smiles widely and nods. 'Hell yes, sir. She did me proud.' His smile fades slightly. 'The kills took their toll on her. Even had to stop her from ending Nera.'

Gryffin can't quite believe that bit. She was so against killing, it shocked him to hear she was eager to end someone's life.

Milla steps back and pulls off her soiled gloves. 'You okay to put him back together?'

Lucan sets to work reattaching the internal pieces while Milla steps closer to the head of the bed.

'Not good?' Gryffin doesn't know why he asked. He can see the truth on her face.

She shakes his head. 'I'm afraid not. I can treat the infection, but it won't fix the problem. Unless something can be done internally, it's not going to get better. You need a new leg.'

'But you can't do that, right?'

She shakes her head. 'I wish. If we were in Foundation space in a state-of-the-art facility, I probably could grow new tissue and rebuild your leg.'

'You mean without using metal?'

'In theory, yes. Out here, that's not an option, I'm afraid.' She rests her palms on the bed and leans over him. 'I promise, whatever happens, I will sort that leg out for you. You have my word.'

Gryffin nods, feeling slightly more reassured by Milla's confidence.

Lucan screws the cover plate back on his leg. 'Eye now.' Lucan leans over and unscrews the cover while Milla hooks up the monitors to check his internal components.

Lucan frowns. 'Terra wasn't wrong about this wiring. Bloody disaster.' Lucan removes a damaged piece of wire, glares at it then throws it over his shoulder.

'That better not be important.'

'It wasn't actually attached to anything.' He shakes his head. 'We can do better than this, sir. I'll talk to Bray and Chayse. It's just blind luck it's worked as long as it has. No pun intended.'

Gryffin doesn't bother telling him that Chayse isn't going to help fix his eye. He has bigger things to deal with now. Gryffin yelps as a small spark jumps from his eyepiece. Lucan's only response is to mutter a few choice words and shake his head.

'Right, I've tightened the connections. There has to be a better alternative than this. I'll take some scans and try to something else out for you.' Lucan sits on the bed opposite him and sighs. 'Ready for us to check your programming?'

Gryffin nods although he's far from ready, especially after hearing what he just did. He needs to know that everything is still as it should be. No telling what else the Scientist or Rayde had done to him. Alterations might have been missed when he came back.

Gryffin lies back on the bed and studies the ceiling as Milla checks the monitors attached to his chest and ocular implant. Gryffin's mind wanders as they carry out the examination. Without even realising, he connects to the system through the monitoring equipment and explores. After spending months working through the system on the station, it's nearly second nature to him. He follows the lines of code around the base system, easily breaking through any and all firewalls. While Lucan and Milla work on his body, his mind unlocks the files detailing everything that's happened with the group since the incident at the Port. He learns about *Ares* crashing to the surface and the work that was involved in putting her back together. He clenches his jaw when he finds out about the series of attacks the Foundation and Rogue ships have carried out against the defenceless colonies.

Curiosity gets the better of him and he delves into his own file. He never asked what the Scientist did to him while he was gone. He knows that his implants were taken off line for a few hours, but it never occurred to him to ask what they found. From what he can decipher, it was just some programming changes. Nothing that Chayse struggled to rectify.

He's about to pull out of the system when some code catches his attention. Something seems to be linking his file to Roman's and the Hunter called Bray. He concentrates on the information and he finally figures out what it's telling him.

'Why does my file have Roman and Bray's name in it?'

Milla's mouth opens and closes a few times before she composes herself. 'Your file? When did you read your file?'

'There's a DNA match. What the hell is going on?' He sits up and pulls the monitors off his chest as he sorts through the information in his head. 'My DNA matches theirs?'

'Just lie down for a minute, please.'

'No. What's going on, Milla?' He stands up and closes the gap between them. Lucan pauses for a moment then pulls his gun out and points it at Gryffin.

'Sir, back away.'

Gryffin ignores Lucan. 'Tell me what's going on?'

Milla shakes her head. 'It's not my place to tell you. Let me get Roman.'

Gryffin takes another step closer and is mirrored by Lucan. 'Back off, sir.'

Gryffin wants answers more than a bullet to the chest, so does as he's told. 'Get Roman in here now!'

Milla activates her radio and makes the call, while Lucan's attention stays on him. The only thing he can think of is that Roman and Bray had something to do with the project. Why else would their DNA be on his record? None of this makes sense. Then again, not a lot of anything made sense since he got back.

Lucan and Milla quietly watch as he paces in front of the door. After a few minutes of tense silence, Roman bursts through the door slightly out of breath. Gryffin faces him. 'Why are you listed in my file? Talk.'

Roman nods. 'Will you please sit?'

'I don't need to damn well sit. Tell me what the hell is going on!'

'I'll tell you. Lucan, stand down. Get Milla out of here.'

Lucan doesn't move for a few seconds, then finally gestures for Milla to walk over to him. He takes her by the arm and, without taking his eyes off Gryffin, guides her out of the room.

Roman nods again and sighs. He looks up at Gryffin. 'Yes, our DNA matches.'

'Were you involved in the project?'

Roman's mouth drops open. 'No! Absolutely not.' He pauses for a moment and takes a deep breath. 'You're my son.'

Gryffin hears the words, but they don't quite make sense. He waits for Roman to laugh or do something to brush away his statement, but he doesn't. If anything, he looks like he's about to throw up. 'You're serious.'

Even though it's not a question, Roman nods.

Gryffin doesn't know what to do with the news. What is he supposed to do? 'So, why is the Hunter listed?'

'Bray is your half-brother. You have the same mother, but different fathers.'

'So, you're not his father?'

Roman shakes his head. He's gone from having no blood family to having a father and brother in the space of a few seconds. 'How... how is that possible. I'm from...' He falters. Where is he from? The life he remembers starts chained to the floor in the lab. He always assumed he came from the Sector, but he never really gave it much thought. There wasn't any point. 'I'm from Earth?'

'Yes. Your real name is Daegan Sawyer. Both you and Brayden were born on Earth. Your mother was Irish, hence your names, but we met in the Academy.'

As much as he wants to deny it, the name Daegan does sound familiar. 'When did you do the test?' Gryffin asks, trying to take the focus off his past life.

'Gryffin, please—'

'When!'

'Milla ran the sample from the bullet Terra dug out of your chest.'

His eye locks on to Roman as his pulse races. He absently touches the bullet wound in his upper chest. Terra gave him the lasting present after he saved her from some slavers. It was the first time he saw her and she had certainly left an impression. 'But that was over a year ago. You knew who I was when we met on Taldor, on Ultar?'

Roman at least has the decency to look ashamed. 'Yes.'

'We spoke one-on-one for nearly ten minutes. It didn't cross your mind to say something to me? Damn it! I was on your ship for days before you handed me over to Balfe. Why did you keep this to yourself?'

'I was wrong, okay! I hold my hands up. I made a massive mistake not telling you. Please, all I'm asking for is the chance to explain things to you.'

'You had over a year to speak to me. It's too late now.' He quickly pulls on his boots and leaves the med bay. Dud leg or not, he needs to beat the hell out of something before he targets Roman.

38

Bray viciously attacks the training drone, pretending it's Gryffin instead of a faceless robot. He stupidly followed Terra out of the meeting and caught the two of them kissing. Even though their relationship ended, knowing she ran straight back into Gryffin's arms drives him crazy. She could just move on from him in the blink of an eye? Did the few months they shared mean nothing? He breaks his stick across the drone's head and gives it a vicious thump for good luck. He's just relieved that Gryffin had the sense to stand down. There's no way he could ever work with him.

He spins to hit the drone again and freezes when he spots Gryffin at the door. Perfect, just who he wants to see right now. The two brothers silently look at each other until Bray breaks the stalemate. 'Walk away Nomad. This room is in use.'

Gryffin's head tilts to the side and his eye narrows. 'You're Bray. You're my... half-brother?'

Bray slowly faces Gryffin and crosses his arms. Great. So the truth is finally out. 'I'm Bray, but I'm sure as hell not your brother, half or otherwise.

Gryffin frowns. 'I remember you. You were on the freighter.' He touches the scar on the side of his head. 'You designed the mod?'

'Yeah. One of the admirals involved in the project hired me to help you. Didn't know who you were though.'

Gryffin's arm drops to his side and he clenches his fists tightly. 'It would have made a difference?'

'Guess we'll never know.'

'I know I've been out of it for a while, but I don't remember doing anything to you. Why the attitude?'

Bray launches the remains of his stick against the wall. 'You're really that wrapped up in yourself you can't see the problem.' Gryffin silently watches him and the optic replacing his eye stares unblinking at him. 'I've got better things to do than explain it to you.'

He takes a few steps towards the door, but trips on the stick Gryffin throws at his legs. Bray crashes to the floor, the impact knocking the air from his lungs. Gryffin roughly pulls him to his feet and shoves him against the wall. 'What the hell is your problem?'

Bray tries to untangle himself from Gryffin's grip, but it's like trying to move a tank. Electricity races down the Nomad's arm and stops at his wrist. 'I asked you a question, Hunter.'

Bray struggles against Gryffin's grip. 'So, you're going to kill your own brother, huh?'

'You said it yourself — we're not brothers.'

Bray kicks out at Gryffin's metal leg, hoping that he hits the seam where the flesh and metal meet. Gryffin's curse tells him he's found his target. Gryffin drops him and takes a step back. His purple eyes glow brightly in anger as he massages his leg.

Bray ignores the wooden training sticks and pulls a metal one out of the rack. He spins it in his hand and, without waiting for Gryffin to arm himself, attacks.

Gryffin ducks and avoids the first blow, then sidesteps to miss the second. Luckily, the third hits home. Gryffin glances at the blood trickling down his arm. 'You seriously want to fight me?'

Bray smiles. 'Damn right I do. You need to pay for what you did. No time like the present.'

Gryffin's shoulders drop slightly. 'Fine.' He pulls a stick out of the rack and takes up position in front of Bray. Before Gryffin can prepare, he launches his attack. Bray lands blow after blow on the Nomad. Instead of making him feel better, the lack of reaction from Gryffin just angers him more. 'Fight back!'

Gryffin sidesteps, saving himself from a blow to the head. 'I fight back and you'll die.

Bray snorts. 'Lofty opinion of yourself, huh?'

'You've got serious problems, Hunter.'

Bray sees red. He's not the one with the problems. 'She was mine!'

Gryffin falters, allowing Bray to jam his stick into his chest. 'What?'

Bray wipes his arm over his face and takes a deep breath. 'Terra and me. Before you came back from the dead, she was with me.'

'You?'

Bray shoves Gryffin hard in the chest. Gryffin takes a step back and stares at his brother. 'Yes, Nomad. Me. She was happy with me, but then you had to show up again and turn things on their head. You destroyed her with your stunt on the freighter. The mighty Gryffin sacrificed himself for the good of the Sector.' He shrugs and smiles. 'Best thing you could have done. Pity you didn't think about how it would affect Terra. I helped her out of that mess. I was the one she came to for comfort. I was the one to make her forget about you. I was the one she slept with every night.'

Gryffin's arm glows as he clenches his fist.

Bray snorts. 'Go on! Hit me. Prove me right.' Bray steps closer to his brother and looks up at him. 'Sooner or later, she'll see you for what you really are. Then she will leave you. And I'll be there to pick up the pieces, brother.'

∞

'Hey! Watch where you're going!' Terra shouts as she is pushed aside. The man mumbles an apology as he rushes down the corridor.

'You okay?' Desyl asks.

Terra rubs her shoulder. 'Yeah. Wonder what his problem is.'

Desyl pushes her aside as another man races past, followed by a third. Terra manages to grab the next woman before she gets away. 'What's going on?'

'It's Gryffin and the Hunter Commander. They're fighting in the training room.'

Terra releases the woman. 'Oh, that's not good.'

Desyl hurries down the corridor before she has a chance to say anything else.

Terra runs after him while she calls Roman on her radio. She gets to the training room and pushes through the gathering crowd. 'Come on people! Don't you have work to do?' Evidently, watching Gryffin and Bray fight is far more exciting. She finally reaches the front of the crowd and gasps when she sees the two brothers. They are literally beating each other. She takes a step into the room, but Desyl holds her back. 'Not so fast, Terra.'

'We can't just let them kill each other.'

'You step in to that, they could hurt you. Suppose it was only a matter of time. Who's winning?'

Terra glares at Desyl. 'This is serious.'

He brushes away her concern. 'It's just a fight, Terra. Pretty much a daily occurrence on Nomad ships.'

She grimaces as Bray hits Gryffin's face, drawing blood. 'They're going to kill each other!'

'Of course they're not. Gryffin isn't fighting. Trust me, if he was, Bray would be dead already.' Desyl nods towards the men as Gryffin quickly sidesteps one of Bray's blows, but doesn't retaliate. 'See. The captain is just letting Bray vent.'

Terra pushes her hair off her face and sighs. 'This is ridiculous. So we just do nothing while he vents on Gryffin. There are other ways to vent than beating each other like cave men.'

Desyl shrugs. 'Whatever works.'

Roman pushes through the crowds and sends everyone scattering back to their posts with one look. He turns to face the room and shakes his head. 'Any idea what it's about, sir?' Terra asks.

Roman rubs the back of his neck as he sighs deeply. 'Gryffin found out about Bray and me. I can only assume it has something to do with that.'

Terra's heart sinks. Even though most of the aggression is coming from Bray, she knows Gryffin well enough to see that he's not in a good place either. She's just grateful he is actually holding back.

'I should have told him,' Roman says. 'I could have stopped this from happening.'

Desyl sucks in a breath. 'Doubt that. This is a Hunter/Nomad fight. They need to blow off some steam.' He leans against the wall and folds his arms. 'My money's on Gryffin.'

Terra glares at him. 'Oh for goodness sake. We're not betting on this.'

Desyl shrugs. 'Suit yourself.'

∞

Gryffin ignores the stabbing pain from his leg and forces himself to his feet. The Hunter just won't back down. Not that he's too keen on finishing this just yet. His brother was with Terra. The thought keeps his anger well and truly fuelled. How far had they gone? Had he touched her? Gryffin can't help the growl that escapes.

Bray paces in front of him and twirls the stick in circles. 'Jealous, Nomad?'

Of course he's jealous, but he's not going to give Bray the satisfaction of responding.

Bray shrugs. 'Don't know why you're so surprised. You did leave her after all. Leaving has consequences — for everyone, not just you. Did you ever stop to think about the people you left behind?'

Gryffin ducks Bray's stick and attacks, swiping at the younger man's legs. Bray crashes to the ground, but rolls quickly and springs to his feet. 'I had no choice but to stay on the freighter.'

Bray's stick whistles past his ear when he dodges at the last second. 'I'm not talking about the freighter!'

'Stop acting like children! Stop this!'

Gryffin ignores Terra's protests from the doorway. Roman is standing in front of her, blocking her from entering the room. 'What are you talking about?' Gryffin asks.

Bray slams his stick into Gryffin's already struggling leg. The limb picks that precise moment to give in. Gryffin lands heavily on his knee and his vision swims as the pain vibrates through his metal leg. He manages to avoid a full force blow to the head, but Bray's stick tears a gash on his cheek. The Hunter lowers to one knee and leans on his weapon as he examines his opponent. 'This is about our home. Our family.'

Gryffin doesn't say anything. He wasn't expecting that.

'What? Nothing to say.' Bray kicks Gryffin in the chest. His vision swims as his head hits the floor. Bray presses his stick down on Gryffin's throat and puts his foot on his metal leg.

Gryffin grinds out a curse. His leg might as well have a target painted on it. It's meant to help him, not be used as a weakness. 'What do you want me to say?' Gryffin asks. 'I haven't got a damn clue what you're talking about.'

'We were a regular family until you just had to go on that school trip. Mom said you begged her for weeks to let you go and eventually she gave in. By pushing for that yes you managed to destroy everything. You killed our family!'

Gryffin's chest tightens and it has nothing to do with Bray's weight on him. The Scientist told him his parent's didn't want him. That they willingly gave him up to the project. He's believed it all his life. Did his family — did Roman, actually want him? 'Is that what happened?'

'You know it is!' Bray shoves the stick tighter against his neck.

Gryffin doesn't fight back. He's stupidly allowed himself to live his life believing another lie. Has anyone told him the truth? 'They wanted me?'

Bray sneers down at him. 'This isn't about you. Why did you keep on at her to let you go? The least you can do is answer me. You owe me that!'

He owes him? Gryffin's anger flares to the surface. He doesn't owe anyone anything. Before Bray knows what's happening, Gryffin forces his way out of Bray's grip. He locks legs with the Hunter and flips him onto his back. With their positions swapped, Gryffin wraps his metal hand around Bray's neck. 'What makes you think I owe you anything?'

'You made my parents life a misery. Made my life a misery. They spent every minute of every day looking for you. It killed them in the end. I grew up an orphan because of you!'

'That's why you hate me?'

'Of course it is!' Bray tries to pry Gryffin's metal hand open, but it won't budge. Bray's cold hazel eyes glare at him. 'You should have stayed dead. All you do is destroy everything!'

Nausea twists Gryffin's stomach. He's right. His plan to reunite the Nomad, protect the colonies and drive the Foundation out hasn't really got off the ground yet. All he's managed to do is drive Chayse away and gain a father and brother that want nothing to do with him. Not exactly a success.

He glances over his shoulder at Terra. Tears stream down her face. Tears he's caused, no doubt. 'Gryffin, please let him go.'

And now she's asking him not to hurt Bray. She's clearly chosen her side. He applies more pressure to his hand and leans closer to Bray. 'I know you're not going to believe a damn thing I say, but I haven't got a clue what you're talking about. The first memory I have is waking up chained to the floor in a lab. I wish I could remember our parents, but I can't, so there's no point having a go at me about it. If you want to hate me — fine. There's enough people who feel that way, one more isn't going to keep me up at night. Now, I think it's probably best you keep away from me.'

He releases Bray and uses his sparring stick to push himself to his feet. Without looking at Terra, he limps out the door. Just before he turns the corner he glances over his shoulder and his heartbeat seems to slow down. Terra is kneeling on the ground with her hand on Bray's face.

∞

The sharp slap she gives Bray does nothing to help Terra's mood. 'What the hell was that for?'

Roman and Desyl take that as their queue to leave. They briefly glance at each other and quickly disappear down the corridor.

'Seriously? What exactly did beating each other achieve?'

Bray licks his split lip. 'Made me feel a bit better.'

She gets to her feet and paces the floor in front of him. 'Well, that's great. I'm so glad you feel better. The Foundation are breathing down our necks and we need everyone working together to defend the area. How exactly is fighting the leader of our biggest ally going to help?'

Bray sneers as he gets to his feet. 'He's not the leader anymore. You still have him on a pedestal, huh?'

'Grow up, Bray. Listen, I get there are unresolved issues between you both, but you could have talked about it instead of beating each other. Being honest with him surely would have been preferable to this.'

'That's rich coming from you.'

Terra's eyebrows squish together. 'What does that mean?'

'Have you told him about your father yet?'

She crosses her arms to try and hide the fact they're shaking. 'That has nothing to do with this.'

He laughs and pushes his hair of his face. 'Of course not. Telling him the truth would ruin the little bubble you're both in. How exactly do you think he'll react when he finds out that — firstly you've been lying to him, and secondly, who your father is?'

'He'll understand.' The loud laugh from Bray confirms the stupidity of her comment. Of course Gryffin won't understand. 'Are you going to tell him?'

Bray quickly meets her eyes. 'You really think I'd do that? You made your choice, Terra. I get that. I'm not happy you've gone back to him and I'm not convinced he won't screw this up and hurt you. But I have to respect your decision.' He steps closer and drops his chin to meet her eyes. 'You keep out of my business with him. It's got nothing to do with you. Just like this thing with your father has nothing to do with me. Deal?'

She nods quickly. Bray glances over his shoulder as he walks away. 'I will say one last thing though. Tell him, Terra. It's not going to go away.'

∞

39

Bray storms into his old room and kicks the door with his boot. He leans against the wood and attempts to talk himself out of his rage, but he's struggling. Since he re-joined *Perses*, thoughts of Terra have been pushed to the back of his mind. He'd made the decision to leave her, right or wrong, and he had to live with it. But being back here, seeing him with Terra... it's just too much. Every time he sees Gryffin, he wants to hit him.

Bray curses loudly and kicks the side of his bed. The wooden frame moves under the impact to uncover a leather binder peeking out from under the bed. He pulls it out and sits at his desk. He flips through the pages and his anger flows more freely. It's Terra's drawing pad and the damn thing is full of pictures of his brother.

Terra flat out refused to pick up a pencil since Gryffin died. He never realised why until now. Page after page of Gryffin's face and body assault him. No wonder she gave up drawing. The Nomad seems to be her only inspiration. He can't stomach any more of the images. He leaves the binder on the desk and contacts his ship. 'I need everything Sayber downloaded from Balfe's unit.'

'Commander, the Captain locked those files.'

'I'm ordering you to send them to me. I suggest you do what I say.'

The Hunter pauses for a moment before answering. 'Yes, Commander. Give me five minutes.'

Bray paces as he waits for the files to come in from *Perses*. He doesn't know why Sayber locked them, but he's too angry to think about the consequences of disobeying his captain. He's hoping there's something in the files to lead them to the Scientist and the Foundation stronghold in the Sector. Sayber checked them months ago, but maybe he missed something. It's worth a shot. Anything is better than having to work one more day with his brother.

He finds the files from the freighter and loads the first one. A list of subfiles opens on his screen. Schematics, scan data, test stats and test subjects. Without thinking, he opens the test subject folder and his eyes instantly lock on one labelled #35. His finger hovers over the file. He knows that's the designation given to his brother. He should try another file but curiosity wins. He opens the folder and scrolls through the data.

There isn't much — just a few basic schematics of his implants, some test data and a sub-folder of video files. Bray opens a video file and watches as the Scientist appears on the screen. He runs through data from his last set of scans then steps aside to give Bray a clear view of his brother strapped to the operating table. Bile rises in Bray's throat as the Scientist walks to a trolley holding medical instruments. His brother begs and pleads to be released as he struggles to get free. Blood drips from his bonds as he cuts his wrists in his desperation to escape. Through all the pleas, the Scientist completely ignores him. It's almost as if there's a mannequin on the table instead of a living, breathing person.

The Scientist picks up a bone saw and holds it to Gryffin's wrist. Bray is frozen to the spot. He wants to shut the screen off but he can't move. If he could reach for his gun he'd shoot the screen. The sounds of his brother's screams echo in his head as the saw digs into his flesh.

After spending an hour with the Scientist on the freighter, Bray knows first-hand how horrific his methods are. The implant on the side of his face throbs in sympathy as he remembers being helpless to stop what the bastard was doing to him.

The clip ends and another automatically loads. The Scientist again runs through some data then moves aside. This clip must be from a few years later. His brother looks about thirteen or fourteen and is again strapped to the table. Instead of pleading for his release, he lies perfectly still. His thin, pale body is covered with incisions and smeared with blood. A thick collar is wrapped around his scrawny neck. Numerous implants are attached to his neck, chest and legs. The Nomad must have been able to remove those when they found him.

The camera focuses on the remains of his arm. He's been around enough combat injuries to recognise gangrene. That explains why most of his lower arm is now gone. Bray holds his breath and digs his fingers into his legs as he watches the Scientist take some connectors and wiring from the table. He begins to fit them to the remains of Gryffin's arm. Bray watches in horrified silence for a few seconds before he realises something. Gryffin is completely silent. The Scientist cuts, drills and screws bits to his flesh, but Gryffin barely flinches. That's more disturbing than the procedure.

Bray pushes the unit off the table. As it crashes to the ground he jumps to his feet and races for the bathroom. He kicks the door open and barely makes it to the toilet in time. He drops to his knees and empties his stomach. Once he finally gets control of himself, he splashes water on his face and examines his reflection in the mirror. The small implant beside his eye throbs, but he relishes the pain. It's the least he deserves. He squeezes his eyes shut and leans over the sink. He was so caught up in hating and blaming his brother, he never once thought about what happened to him. Bray's stomach churns again as the images from the video play over and over in his head.

∞

Roman enters the hangar and circles *Ares*, following the sounds of banging and cursing to *Ares'* loading ramp. Gryffin limps up and down the ramp, loading boxes of ammunition and supplies on to the ship. He must have ordered the rest of the crew to leave or they noticed his foul mood and left him to it.

Gryffin stops what he's doing as Roman approaches. 'I'm not in the mood for you. Get out of here.'

Roman tries to pick up one of the boxes Gryffin is loading, but can't even lift it off the ground. He moves to one of the smaller boxes and follows Gryffin into the ship. 'You should get your leg seen to.'

Gryffin dumps the crate he's carrying in the far corner of the cargo deck. 'So, you've come here to talk?'

'I've come here to see how you are. I know finding out that I'm your father must come as a shock.'

Gryffin turns to face him. 'You think I give a damn that you're my father or that the Hunter is my brother? I couldn't care less. It's not going to change my life one bit.'

Roman hides it, but Gryffin's words hit him like a physical blow. He knew they'd never have a typical father and son relationship, but a part of him was hoping for a miracle. 'I see.'

Gryffin slowly approaches him. 'You should have binned the data or told me. It shouldn't have been something that everyone else knew except me.' His blue eye changes to match his mechanical purple one. 'I've had enough people betray me and keep things from me. I thought all that was behind me.'

Roman grimaces at Gryffin's words. 'I didn't hide the truth to betray you. I honestly didn't know how to tell you I'm your father. I made a mistake keeping this from you and I can't undo that. I know I'm asking for a lot, but can we try to work through this?'

Gryffin kicks a crate against the wall and runs a hand through his hair. 'Work through what? I've seen families on Ultar and the other colonies. I have a vague idea what it means to have a father and a mother. You really think we can talk about our problems or reminisce about my childhood? You want to talk about the time my eyes were removed or when my hand was cut off? Or how about last year when I had half my leg replaced?'

Roman slumps back on to the crate behind him. 'Please, Gryffin, don't—'

Gryffin looms over him and his robotic eye zooms in on him. 'Did you know about the experiment?'

Roman rises to his feet. 'No. Of course not!'

'You didn't know that your son was being modified by your own people?'

'If I knew, I would have got you out. I swear. I didn't even know you were my son until we ran the test on the bullet.'

Gryffin examines his metal arm. 'Little consolation. Why did you sell me?'

Roman shakes his head, unable to form any words for a moment. 'Whoever told you that was lying.' Roman forces himself to meet Gryffin's stern gaze. 'If I could turn back time, I would. All we can do is continue from this point.'

'You think some sort of relationship is going to come out of this? You handed me over to the Foundation. I told you the Foundation changed me, but you made a decision to ignore the results. You stood back and watched as Balfe led me away in chains.' Gryffin looms over him as Roman shrinks away from his glowing purple glare. 'You're worse than Balfe and the other admirals. At least they had the guts to face me and tell me the truth.'

Roman feels the bile rise in his throat. 'Gryffin—'

'You knew what they were going to do to me!'

'Balfe said you'd be taken back to Earth for a trial.'

Gryffin laughs harshly and turns away. 'You're a bloody idiot.' He looks back at Roman. 'So, you thought I was born like this?'

'Of course I didn't.'

'You think the Nomad changed me?'

Roman shakes his head. 'We ruled that out after the meeting on Ultar.' He can't say any more. Gryffin is right. He knew deep down that the Foundation had done this to him. The thought had never been allowed to surface, but it had been there. 'I thought I was doing the right thing.'

'For who? Because it sure as hell wasn't for me. They did this to me while I was awake.'

Roman closes his eyes and breaths through his nose.

'Look at me!'

He opens his eyes to find Gryffin's furious face right in front of his. His attention is immediately drawn to the new eyepiece and the robotic optic in the centre. The optic narrows as it zooms in on him.

'You can't have it both ways. You gave me up to be worked on again. Fine, you followed your superior's orders. But that doesn't mean I'm going to forget what you did. You may not have held the drill, but you sure as hell put me in its path.'

Roman nods. He can't blame Gryffin one little bit. 'I understand.'

Gryffin studies him in silence for a moment before he turns away. 'Get off my ship. Now.'

Roman wants to stay and try to make amends, but it's clearly a lost cause. He nods, walks down the ramp and weaves through the bay on autopilot, only stopping when he reaches a small storage room further along the corridor. Once away from prying eyes, he slumps onto a crate. He squeezes his eyes shut as spots flash in his vision. Roman buries his head in his hands and forces himself to take slow, deep breaths. It doesn't help. His imagination runs wild, throwing images at him of Gryffin being tortured.

Until Gryffin rejected him, he didn't actually realise how much being a father meant to him. Now, he's managed to lose the connection before he even had a chance to enjoy it.

∞

Terra enters Gryffin's room to find him pulling up his trousers. Her heart immediately races when she sets eyes on him. He's fresh from the shower, his wet hair falling over his face. His chest is bare, the bruises and cuts from the fight stand out clearly on his skin.

He sits down on his bed and his leathers creep dangerously low. Gryffin picks up a piece of his gun that's dismantled on his bed and cleans it. He looks up at her briefly before he turns his attention back to what he is doing. 'You come here to stare?'

She tucks a lock of hair behind her ear. 'No, sorry, I just want to explain.'

'Did you know about Bray and Roman?'

She nods once. 'It wasn't my place to say anything. We were under orders to capture you and Roman knew it would cause problems if the Foundation found out. He deleted the report and we were ordered to forget about it.'

He grunts once and concentrates on his gun. Terra lowers into a chair and rests her tool kit on the ground. She takes a deep breath to steady the butterflies in her stomach. She's come so far with him over the last few weeks on *Ares*. It will destroy her if he decides to pull away from her for good. Not that she can really blame him if he feels that way. 'I should have told you about me and Bray.'

'Yeah, you should have.'

'I know I've handled this badly. I was trying to save you from getting hurt. I guess that backfired.'

He shrugs and looks down the barrel of his gun. 'You mean it would save Bray from getting hurt.'

'Both of you. What happened today was completely unnecessary.'

He puts down the barrel and picks up the next piece. 'You and my brother were, or still are, in a relationship. I should have known.'

'We're not in a relationship anymore. It ended before I came to

Ares.'

'Why?'

'Why?'

He scrubs his hand over his face. 'Damn it, Terra. Stop answering my questions with questions! Why did it end?'

'It ended because I'm not in love with him and we both knew it.' She gets to her feet and cautiously lowers next to Gryffin. The muscles in his arms are strained as he polishes the handle of his gun. Now that she's next to him, she realises he's not actually angry. His brow is scrunched and his eye is still blue. If anything, he appears confused. 'I'm in love with you, Gryffin.'

His hands instantly freeze and he turns his head to face her. He looks at a spot on the wall behind her, draws in a deep breath and slowly releases it. 'You don't have to say that.' He looks back at the gun again. 'I saw you with him after I left.'

'You mean when I slapped him?'

Gryffin's eye locks onto hers. 'You slapped him? Why?'

'I was tempted to slap you too. There was no need to do that to each other. Ever heard of talking?'

He shakes his head. 'Wouldn't have worked.'

'Perhaps, but surely it's worth a try. I'm not keen on seeing the man I love being hurt.' She reaches for his hand, but he pulls it back.

'I'm not an idiot, Terra. I understand why you were with him.'

She jerks her head back. 'So, you're not angry about me being with your brother?'

'I didn't say that,' he growls. 'The thought that he... touched you in any way makes me want to drive my fist through his chest and out the other side.'

She wrinkles her nose. 'Nice imagery.'

'I understand why you were with someone else. Even if he is a Hunter. I'm angry that the relationship with him ended.'

Terra frowns. 'What?'

'You had a chance to be with someone normal. Well, normal for a Hunter.' He stands up and walks to the far side of the room. 'You and Bray can have a life like that. Marriage, children, a house. I know how important those things are to people. Those things aren't in my future.'

'That doesn't matter. We can—'

'Of course it matters! Our futures are not linked. We're too different!'

'If this is about your implants, I don't know how many times I have to tell you, they're not a problem for me.'

'What I am is only going to get worse.'

Her eyes narrow. 'What do you mean?'

'My body is struggling with the implants. I'm dependant on the cybernetics, but my human body is in constant battle with them. It's only a matter of time before I'll need more work done just to keep me going. My future is too unpredictable.'

Terra thinks back to when she saw him working on his metal leg in the training room. 'What's wrong with your leg?'

He scrunches his brow, confused by her change of direction. 'Where did that come from?'

'I've noticed you limping more over the last few weeks.'

His shoulders drop slightly. 'Thought I was hiding it better. The metal is only on the outside. Most of my limb underneath is organic. The Scientist thought it would work. It's not.'

The bile rises in Terra's throat at the mention of her father and what he did to Gryffin. 'What can be done?'

Gryffin shrugs. 'I'm managing for now. Or was until the Hunter used it as a punching bag. Probably need a whole new leg at some stage, unless someone figures out how to keep my real lower leg with my metal thigh.' He looks down at Terra. 'That's what I'm talking about. The best thing for you is to be with someone else. My brother can give you what I can't.'

Terra laughs. 'Don't be ridiculous.' She shuffles closer to him. 'I want to be with you.' She traces her finger along the back of his metal hand. 'I need to show you something.' She takes her work bag off the floor and pulls a small notebook out. 'When you died at the Port, I stopped drawing. I couldn't pick up a pencil without thinking about you.' Terra opens the first page and hands it to Gryffin. 'I drew that yesterday.'

He looks down at the pencil sketch and a small, barely noticeable smile pulls at the corner of his mouth. The urge to draw had completely taken her by surprise when it hit. Since he was torn from her life, even thinking about drawing made her feel uneasy. But since Gryffin came back, so did her passion for drawing. She watches as he traces a metal finger along the pencil lines. The sketch shows two hands: Gryffin's metal one clasping her smaller flesh one.

'You're my inspiration. You have been since I ran full force into you.' She takes his metal hand in hers and runs her thumb along the solid plating. 'I don't want to lose you again. I know what you are. I've never shied away from that and I understand things may become difficult in the future, but we can handle it. I don't care if you have one metal limb or four.' She taps her fingers against the side of his head. 'As long as you are still you where it counts, we'll be fine.' He opens his mouth to say something, but she presses her finger to his lips. 'Yes, I know there's metal in there too. Stop ruining the moment and shut up. All that matters is how I feel about you. I love you.'

His glowing purple eye locks onto her. 'I don't want anyone else to touch you. Ever.'

Terra can't help but smile. Not quite an I love you, but it will do for now. 'Can you promise me something?'

He frowns slightly. 'What?'

'Can you please keep your fist out of Bray's chest?'

He sighs loudly. 'Fine.' Gryffin looks back at the drawing and smiles again. Not the usual whisper of a smile this time, but a full smile.

Terra runs her hand along his leg. 'What you said about other people touching me...'

The possessiveness she sees in his lone eye when he turns back to face her, sends shivers through her body. He picks her up in his arms and brings her into the bathroom. He puts her down in the shower and, before she can take any clothes off, turns the jets on. She doesn't protest as he rips her shirt open along with her underwear. Terra pushes his wet trousers down his legs, only breaking their hungry kissing long enough for him bend down to remove his boots. She kicks off her own boots, and her trousers soon join the other ruined clothes on the floor. Gryffin lifts her off her feet and forces her against the back of the shower stall.

She wraps her legs round his waist as he thrusts into her, over and over. Gryffin claims her mouth, his tongue matching each thrust of his hips.

She missed this, missed being with him. It surprises her how someone who has had the life he has, someone who has been hurt so badly by so many people, can be so gentle and attentive. The Gryffin she sees in times like this is a complete contradiction to the Gryffin that exists the rest of the time. She doubts many have seen the person under the impenetrable shell. Terra's eyes drift close as he increases his pace.

'Look at me, Terra.'

She smiles and does as asked. For whatever reason, he needs her to look at him when they're together. His glowing purple eyes hold her firmly in their grasp as his metal arm wraps around her, keeping her firmly in place as she screams in pleasure.

Her head drops onto his shoulder as she concentrates on the simple task of breathing. If it wasn't for his metal arm, she's sure she'd be sprawled on the floor, unable to move.

'You okay?'

She laughs onto his shoulder. 'Just breathing.'

He nudges her head up and meets her eyes. His hair is plastered to his face, the purple glow from his eyes shining through. 'Breathing is good.' He brushes her wet hair back and nods at the tattoo on her neck. 'You can get that removed now.'

She shrugs. 'I'm used to it being there. I don't think I want to have it removed just yet.'

His eyes glow brightly as he frowns at her. 'Really?'

'Really.' She frowns. 'Should I be worried that your eye is purple?'

The purple seems to grow more intense. 'It doesn't just go purple when I'm angry. This has nothing to do with the implant.'

'So, how do I tell the difference?'

He moves inside her and she bites back a groan. 'I think you know the difference. Or do you need another demonstration?'

She laughs again. 'Give me a chance to recover first.'

He gently traces a finger down her jawline. He frowns slightly, as if having an argument with himself. 'You're really mine?'

Until he says those words, she didn't realise how much she needed to hear them. He's willing to give them a chance instead of giving up. He's hers. She looks deep into his swirling blue and purple eyes. 'Always.'

He smiles and her she feels her heart trip over itself. He really needs to smile a lot more. Gryffin pushes her tight against the wall and places a hand to either side of her head. 'So, recovered yet?'

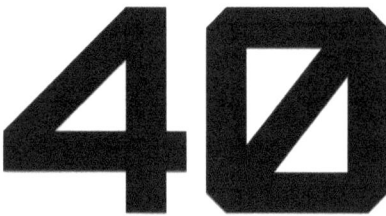

Bray straightens his shoulders. He'd rather be facing the Scientist's knife again than standing here, but it's something he has to do. He forces his hand up to the door control panel and steps into the engine room. He follows the sounds of metal against metal and finds Gryffin working on a unit at the back of the room. 'Lost your way, Commander.'

'No.'

Gryffin pulls out from under the unit. 'I wasn't asking, I was telling.'

'Can we talk?'

Gryffin raises his eyebrow, but silently stands up and wipes oil off his metal hand. Bray leans back against the auxiliary engine and gets himself together. He's about to eat a shed-load of humble pie. Better get this over and done with. 'I apologise for attacking you.'

Gryffin's eyebrow shoots up, but other than that, he doesn't say or do a thing.

Bray swallows deeply. 'You going to say anything?'

Gryffin tilts his head to the side. 'What's the catch?'

Bray shakes his head. 'Straight up.'

Gryffin moves closer to Bray. 'Up until a few hours ago, you wanted me dead.'

'I can go back to wanting you dead if you'd prefer.'

Gryffin's robotic eye zooms in on him. 'You can't use me as a punching bag one minute then apologise the next.'

Bray sighs and looks up at the ceiling. 'Whatever is going on between us, stays here. You have my word.'

Gryffin examines him for a long moment. Not a lot can make Bray feel uncomfortable, but being locked in Gryffin's purple gaze really unnerves him. He is finally released when his brother turns away and stands in front of the unit. 'You or your Hunters mess with me on this, and I'll bury you all.'

'Agreed.' He's finished the planned part of his conversation, but he doesn't move.

Gryffin glances over his shoulder at him. 'What?' It's more of a growl than a question.

'I need to ask you something.'

Gryffin plugs into the console to check his repairs. 'Ask. Then leave.'

Bray silently approaches the screen and watches the Nomad scroll through the schematics without saying a word or touching the system. 'Nice trick.'

Gryffin grunts. 'Has its uses.'

Bray's fingers run across the small implant at the side of his eye. At least Gryffin can do something with what the Scientist gave him. He's just left with a useless piece of metal that serves no purpose. Milla can't even remove it as the Scientist connected it to his brain. Any attempts could put him at risk.

'Aching?'

Bray glances up to find Gryffin looking at him. The Nomad crosses his arms and waits for Bray to respond. It takes him a few seconds to kick start his brain. He wasn't expecting anything like that to come from Gryffin. 'A little. Can't wait for that side effect to end.'

'Still waiting myself.'

Bray nods solemnly as the truth sinks in. 'Figured as much. How do you...' He doesn't finish the sentence. He's not ready for a deep and meaningful with Gryffin yet. He looks back at the screen — anything to distract him from Gryffin's steady gaze. Instead of getting the hint, Gryffin surprises him by leaning back against the console to block his view.

'You just deal with it. Some days are good. Some are bad. Ignore it.'

Bray laughs. 'Yeah. Sounds easy when you say it like that.'

Gryffin shakes his head and looks down at the ground. 'Never said it's easy. You let that rule your life,' he says, while he points at the metal on Bray's face, 'you let him win.'

'So, every day you're fighting, huh?'

Gryffin shrugs. 'Better than huddling in a corner.' Gryffin turns back to the screen. 'It could be a hell of a lot worse.'

Bray squeezes his eyes shut as an image of the Scientist looming over his brother pops into his head. He's right. What is he doing complaining about a small piece of metal on his face and another piece on his chest. At least he has all his limbs. Bray rubs the back of his neck. 'Listen, if you want... if there's anything you need to know about... our mother—'

'No,' Gryffin replies, cutting him off. 'I don't ever want to know about that.'

Bray scrunches his brow. 'Why not?'

Gryffin pushes him back against the wall. 'I don't have to explain myself to you, Hunter.'

Gryffin dismisses Bray and slides back under the console. Bray massages his neck and swallows deeply a few times. He's never going to be able to figure out Gryffin.

He walks towards the door, but Gryffin stops him. 'Bray.'

'What?'

'You wait until Terra is out of the way before you shoot me in the back.'

Bray glances over his shoulder, but Gryffin is buried under the unit. He shakes his head and walks away.

Bray leaves the room and the threat behind. He walks purposefully to the cargo bay. He needs to get off this ship. Needs to get away from Gryffin. The images from the videos are firmly stuck in his mind. All he could see when he spoke to Gryffin was a young boy being tortured.

He shouldn't have watched the footage. All it did was blur things. Instead of seeing Gryffin as a Nomad enemy, he sees his brother, broken and bleeding. It's part of the reason he changed his mind about the plan. He feels guilty. All these years hating his brother for disappearing had transformed into a type of survivor guilt. However difficult he thought things were for him, it is nothing compared to how life has been for Gryffin.

He's spent most of his life blaming his brother for what happened and now he's feeling lost. As much as he wants to keep blaming Gryffin, he believes him when he says he doesn't remember anything about his previous life. Instead of being angry, he feels a little sad. At least he has the memories. He remembers going to the park with his parents, being read to before he went to bed every night, his mother cleaning his knee when he fell off his bike. All the things regular kids remember.

After hearing about his brother's first memory he actually starts to consider himself incredibly lucky.

∞

As soon as Bray's footsteps fade away down the corridor, Gryffin drops the tools and sighs deeply. He pushes out from under the console and leans against the unit. He doesn't want Bray in his life.

Or Roman. Things were so much simpler when he just had the Nomad to worry about. Once you have people in your life, people close to you, they became a threat. Roman, Bray and Terra might as well have a large flashing sign on the heads saying 'Take me to get to Gryffin'.

He may not give a damn about Roman and Bray, but he doesn't want their deaths on his already bloodied hands. He never asked for any of this family shit. What is he supposed to do? Talking about the good ole days is out. He doubts they'd be interested in hearing about his childhood. It's not exactly a cheery conversation. Pretending to be concerned about their lives isn't something he's interested in either. Small talk and chit-chat irritate him. Say what you have to say then shut up. Useless conversation about weather and other things no one has any control over is a complete waste of time.

Why did Bray have to bring up anything to do with their parents? He doesn't want to know anything about them. Even knowing they existed, or still exist in his case with Roman, is too much. It's almost easier for him to accept what the Scientist told him. He had been given to the Scientist by his parents. End of story. It took him a long time to believe it, but the facts were hard to hide from. No one came for him. No one looked for him. He didn't have much choice, but to accept he wasn't wanted.

He's not surprised it was all a lie. The truth just makes everything he experienced, what he is, that much worse. His mother actually did want him and died while searching for him. For years, he believed his life started in the lab. There was nothing before, or at least, nothing worth remembering. That's all changed though. There were ten years of normal life before he woke up with the Scientist. Occasionally, he's had dreams about people he doesn't know and situations he doesn't remember. He always ignored them. Now he knows those images are probably of his past life — he's glad he did ignore them.

After accessing his file in the med bay, he knows he's thirty-four years old — a bit younger than he thought, but at least he knows now.

Not that it makes any difference to his life. Working back from how long he's been with the Nomad and how old he was when he disappeared, he was with the Scientist for five years. He remembers every single minute of his time there as if it happened only yesterday.

He struggles with those memories every day. He's learned to live with it. To survive. Until Terra.

He grips the edge of the unit and pushes back against it. The metal groans under the pressure. He clenches his metal fist and slams it into the console. The twisting, gut-wrenching queasiness is nearly impossible to ignore. His concentration is non-existent. The only thing keeping him from latching onto the implant and not letting go is the promise he made to Terra, and that's one promise he's going to keep. It's always like this when she's not with him. She's the only one who can bring him comfort. He can't lose her. Remembering the past will only bring more problems for him, and for her.

∞

Terra leans against the door and watches Gryffin train with Rua. She smiles as the Rogue captain gains the upper hand and strikes him across the side. It's about time he found someone to give him a bit of competition. For the first time in weeks, he seems almost content. Her heart drops at the thought of potentially destroying all of that. She needs to tell him the truth about her father, but she's terrified of his reaction. What happened to Gryffin isn't her fault. She knows that, but that doesn't mean Gryffin will agree. He's still trying to come to terms with his emotions. This might be the breaking point for him.

She considers putting it off. All she wants to do is take him back to the room, curl up in bed with him and forget everything to do with her father. But she can't. Whatever small chance there is that he'll forgive her will instantly vanish if he hears the news from someone else. It's a miracle he hasn't already been told.

Rua dances around Gryffin and swipes at him with no rhyme or reason. 'C'mon Nomad. I thought you were good at this?'

Gryffin twirls the stick in his hand. He may not say anything, but Terra knows he's not happy about being bested by a woman, let alone a Rogue woman.

Gryffin rolls his shoulders and faces Rua. She laughs. 'You want more? You got it! I've got no problem taking you down in front of your girlfriend.'

She attacks, but completely misses her target. Her over confidence results in a sloppy move. Gryffin easily ducks her stick and Rua crashes to the floor. Before she can get to her feet, he pushes the tip of his sparring stick against her shoulder and pins her to the ground.

'You talk too much. If you're talking, you're not concentrating on the fight.' He releases her. 'Keep practising.'

He ignores Rua's more than colourful language and walks towards Terra. The hollow ache in the pit of her stomach increases with each step he takes. His deep blue eye instantly locks on her and she forces a smile. All she can think about is the fact that her father was the one to give him his new severe looking eyepiece.

'You okay?' he asks.

With those two little words he manages to show her just how much in his own way he cares for her. 'Yeah. Can we go somewhere? I need to talk to you.'

He leads her into a small storage room down the corridor. She closes the door behind them and turns to face him.

Gryffin leans against the wall and crosses his arms. 'So, talk.'

'Okay.' She gestures to the crates lining the wall. 'Can we sit?' He pulls down two wooden crates and places them on the ground. She faces him, but can't bring herself to look him in the eye as she speaks. 'Jensen and my father were best friends growing up. They both joined the academy together and were like brothers. When my father died, Jensen looked out for me. He sort of became a surrogate father.'

'You trying to convince me to talk to him?'

'No, no. Well, yes, that would be great, but that's not what I'm trying to say.'

'Stop trying and just say it.'

'Right. Um, last year, Milla patched into the comms system on *Omega*. It was just before it hit the Port. She only managed to access one of the transports as it was leaving. Jensen... he heard my father's voice.'

Gryffin sits up. 'What?'

'We've confirmed it was him. My father was definitely on that transport.'

'As a prisoner?'

'Bray—'

'What does he have to do with it?'

'Please, Gryffin. We showed Bray pictures of my father.' She takes a deep breath. 'Gryffin, he confirmed that my father is the man known as the Scientist.'

She knows it's not possible, but the air temperature in the room suddenly plummets. Gryffin's now purple eye looks at her in disbelief. 'He's your father?'

Terra nods slowly.

'How long have you known?'

'Does it matter?'

Gryffin slams his metal fist against the side of the crate. 'Of course it damn well matters! How long have you been lying to me?'

'It wasn't lying exactly.'

'Don't, Terra. You honestly think that makes a difference?'

'I found out just after the conflict at the Port. I—'

'You knew the whole time you were on *Ares*? Is everyone on this base lying to me? Why didn't you tell me?'

'Gryffin, please, just sit down and I'll explain.'

He punches the wall. 'I don't want to sit down. What's to explain? Just like everyone else I've ever trusted, you've screwed me over.'

'I was too scared to tell you.'

His shoulders drop as he turns quickly to face her. 'You're afraid of me?'

'What? No, of course not. That's not what I mean. You had just come back to us. There was so much going on with you. I didn't want to add to that.'

'That's the whole damn problem — people thinking for me! You're all convinced I'm going to go crazy at any second. That I can't make decisions for myself. I need you all to back off and let me think for myself.'

'So, you would have been fine if I'd told you sooner? You would have put it to the back of your mind and reunited the Nomad anyway?'

He glances at her briefly.

'Exactly. You wouldn't have been able to let it go. I had a hard enough time convincing Bray to drop it. I wouldn't have been able to stop you from doing something that could have gotten you killed.'

'You told him, but not me. Am I the only idiot being kept in the dark?'

'Gryffin, I honestly didn't keep the truth from you to hurt you.'

'You didn't have to keep the truth from me at all! First the 'you and Bray thing' and now this?'

'Yes, I know it looks bad, but just for once can you try to see things from someone else's viewpoint. How do you think I feel knowing that my father is still alive and that he's this horrible person? I don't want anything to do with him.'

'What else have you been lying about?'

'That's the part you're focusing on? Seriously. What's wrong with you?'

'What else have you been lying about!'

She steps back and her shoulders slump. 'Do you care about me at all?'

'What does that have to do with it?'

The anger builds in her body. She stalks up to him and pushes him roughly in his chest. 'Everything!' she screams at him. She beats her fists against his chest. 'Why can't you see that? I am in love with you, Gryffin. When something affects you, it affects me too. That's the way it works.'

'And the lies? That how it works too?'

'I didn't want to tell you! I feel physically sick at what he did to you. At what my father did to you. My father! Don't you get that?'

He spins around and pins her against the wall. 'I get it. Your father made me into this!'

Tears pour down her face. 'I know he did. Believe me, if I could somehow undo all the pain and hurt he caused you, I would in a heartbeat. If I could give you back the life he stole I would... but I can't.'

'You expect me to believe anything you say?'

As his cold purple gaze bores into her, she comes to a frightening realisation. She's lost him. He isn't in the least bit interested in listening to a word she has to say. He's solely focused on himself. 'You know what? I can't do this.' She slips out from under his arms and walks towards the door.

'Where are you going?'

She looks over her shoulder. 'Far away from you!'

41

Aleena stands at the door to the training room and watches Gryffin at the far end of the room below. The captain is sitting on the small bunk against the back wall with his head in his hands. The large overhead fans spin noisily above her. Aleena didn't realise it until now, but she missed their droning hum. No matter what anyone tries, the fans always rattle. Even the new fans that were fitted after the crash, rattle. It is part of the ship's personality.

She takes a long, deep breath and walks down the spiral staircase. She may be upset with Jensen and Terra for keeping the truth from him for so long, but she also sees it from their side. It was always going to be a difficult situation.

She stops in front of Gryffin and realises it is worse than she thought. She has come to within touching distance and Gryffin still has not realised he has company. 'Gryffin?'

Gryffin jumps slightly and lifts his head from his hands. He scowls at Aleena. 'Not now, Aleena.'

Aleena clasps her hands in front of her. 'I think we need to talk.'

Gryffin snorts and his purple eye locks onto Aleena. 'Just get the hell out of here.'

Aleena instantly notices what Gryffin is doing. 'So, you are hiding behind your implant again. Desyl mentioned that you did the same on *Ares* quite a bit. What were you thinking using it all the time?' Gryffin takes a deep breath, but doesn't say anything. Aleena is at a loss. She has never seen Gryffin like this and has certainly never known him to use the implant just to function. 'So, is it your plan to ignore me and hope I go away?'

'I either ignore you or throw you over the railing. Your choice.'

Aleena moves from the bed to a chair, which she places in front of Gryffin. 'Look at me.'

Gryffin glares at Aleena.

'I never saw you as someone who would quit so easily. You survived everything you did just to let the Foundation and Scientist win now? I thought you were stronger than that.'

'So now you want me to be an emotionless robot?'

'I did not say that. You survived a much worse situation with less support. Jensen, Terra, Chayse, Desyl... there are so many people willing to help you. Why would you step down when the fleet needs you the most?'

'I stepped down so Chayse can lead them.'

Aleena scoffs. 'Chayse does not want to lead them. *Nemesis* is more than enough. You are the High Commander. Take your position with Terra at your side.'

'That's not going to happen.'

'There is no reason why not. Apologise to her for your reaction. She will forgive you and you will forgive her.'

'Don't, Aleena. I will shoot you.'

'You cannot blame her for the actions of her father.'

'Drop it, Aleena. I've had enough of this to last me a lifetime.'

'No, I will not. Someone has to make you listen. Do you really think the answers you are looking for are here? I know what you did to yourself a few weeks ago. Non-stop brutal training. Hurting yourself. Is that why you are here now? Were you going to fight all the drones until there is no one left to take out your anger on.'

'Aleena,' he warns. Gryffin rises to his feet and does his best to intimidate Aleena into ending the conversation. It nearly works, but as usual, Aleena ignores him.

'I will not let you hide from this. Answer the question! Is it easier to have a fight than to deal with what is bothering you?'

'I just want everyone to leave me the hell alone!'

'Have you got a short memory?

Gryffin frowns. 'What are you talking about?'

'The last time you pushed us all away and decided you did not need help, it nearly killed you. Stop being stubborn and let us help you.'

'This is different.'

Aleena waves her arms in the air. 'How? Please enlighten me.'

'It just damn well is.'

'Language, Gryffin. You are fortunate enough to have good people behind you, and all they ask is that you fight.'

Gryffin gets right in her face and glowers down at her. 'Back off.'

'If you are trying to scare me it will not work. This anger, this self-pity, it is not you. The Gryffin I care about is a fighter. I was under the impression the Nomad and the colonies mean everything to you. No matter what got in your way, you ploughed through and fought for us. What happened to that person? Did the Foundation finally win and break you?'

'Save me the psycho babble. Things are different.'

'True, but that is a good thing. There are so many people supporting you. Give them a chance.'

Gryffin steps closer to Aleena, pushing her back against the wall. 'I gave them a chance and they lied to me.'

'And they know it was a mistake, but it was done for the right reasons. They care about you, Gryffin.'

Gryffin takes a step back. 'Why does everyone think that's an excuse?'

'Because it is. I struggle to understand you, Gryffin. You know Rayde lied to you from the day he found you. He spent years forcing you to ignore your emotions, repeatedly told you they make you weak and that you should not let anyone close to you. You know he was wrong, yet you still believe him.'

'What the hell do you mean?'

'How else would you explain what you are doing now? You are more than just a weapon or a fighter. You are a brother, a son, a friend, and a lover, if you just accept it.'

Gryffin turns to walk away, but Aleena firmly grips his arm. 'No running! For once in your life, take advice from someone else.'

Gryffin shakes Aleena off. 'You're really pissing me off now. Get out of my way.'

Aleena steps in front of him and shakes her head. 'I said we need to talk.'

'I'm done talking.'

'What are you so afraid of?'

'I'm afraid of myself!'

Aleena freezes at Gryffin's outburst.

'I'm afraid if I let all these... feelings out I won't be able to control them.' He hits the side of his head. 'There's so much in there, locked away... I don't know what to do if it all comes out.'

'Keeping it inside may destroy you. Perhaps, if you talk maybe it will help you deal with those feelings.'

'How the hell can I deal with it? I hate what I am, Aleena. I hate what they did to me.'

'I know, Gryffin.' Aleena is more than aware of Gryffin's daily struggle with what he is and what was done to him. 'Let us help you deal with it. He may be the last person you want anywhere near you, but Bray knows some of what you are going through. You have a lot in common with him.'

Gryffin snorts. 'Two brothers altered against their will. Great conversation starter.'

Aleena grimaces. 'Perhaps you are right. It does not sound great when you say it like that. You are correct, you are brothers—'

Gryffin slams his metal arm against the wall with such force it leaves a dent. 'Bray's brother and Roman's son was killed a long time ago. Whatever he was before, it's long gone. They turned me into something to be feared. People are scared of me, Aleena. Scared of what I look like, scared of what I can do. I hate the whispers. I hate the way they look at me like I'm a freak. What did I do to deserve this?'

Aleena is at loss for words. She was not expecting this level of openness from him. 'I truly wish I had the words to make this better.'

Gryffin runs a hand through his hair as he paces the metal floor. 'That's the damn problem. Nothing can make it better. It is what it is. But Terra...'

'She makes it better?'

Gryffin nods. 'She doesn't hate what I am.'

'Of course she does not hate you. She accepts you for who you are. Terra has always accepted you. She loves you, Gryffin.'

Gryffin rubs his chest and closes his eye. 'It hurts here — deep inside, but she makes it go away.'

Aleena frowns. 'Milla has checked you implants?'

Gryffin nods. 'Using the control implant helped, but I don't need them when I'm with her. This thing with her father... I don't know who to trust. I can't even trust myself anymore.'

'She knew the truth would hurt you. Hurt your relationship. Her feelings for you are more important to her than her father. He contacted her a few weeks ago asking that she hand you over, but she refused. She would never put you in a situation where you could be hurt again.'

'The lie is nearly as bad.' He glances over his shoulder at her. 'I can't believe she's related to something like the Scientist. What he did to me... to the others... We were kids. We should have been having a life instead of being cut open.'

'Terra did not know what he was doing. No one that really cared or cares about you knew the truth. Terra loves you, Gryffin. Let her help you. Let her close to you, please.'

He frowns and looks down at her. 'Her father contacted her about me?'

Aleena nods. 'Yes, but as I said, she refused to listen to him.'

He leans back against the wall and studies the large fan spinning above him. 'Chayse here yet?'

'*Nemesis* is due in the next few hours. I know that look. What are you thinking, Captain?'

'Get everyone together when he gets here.'

'What are you going to do?'

'Maybe it's time we give the Scientist exactly what he wants.'

Gryffin walks away from her, ignoring her protests

∞

Chayse yelps as Milla leaps from the ground and throws herself at him. He loses his balance and lands on his back on the cargo ramp. 'Whoa, Milla.'

She pushes back from him and smiles. 'Sorry, I didn't break you, did I?'

'I think I'm in one piece.'

She gets up and holds out her hand to him. 'I'm so glad to see you.'

'I got that.' He looks down at the bag sitting on the ground at the base of the ramp. 'Going somewhere?'

She smiles widely and nods. 'Too right I am. Doctor Collins

reporting for duty, Captain.'

The smile disappears from his face as he holds out his hand. 'I need to see your transfer order first.'

Milla nods and skips down the ramp to her bag. She rummages in the side pocket, pulls out a tablet and races back up to him. 'Here you go, sir.'

Chayse slowly reads through the entire report, enjoying the annoyance building on Milla's face. 'Well, this all seems in order.' He holds out his hand. 'How about I show you to your room.' She coughs loudly. 'Sorry, I meant *our* room.'

He takes her hand and leads her up the ramp. 'So, any news since I left?'

Milla blows out a long breath. 'I'm not sure where to start.'

He looks down at her. 'Why do I have a bad feeling about this?'

'Because like me, you are not an idiot. Care to guess?'

'Gryffin?'

Milla nods. 'It's all gone a little off kilter. Gryffin found out about Bray and Roman being related to him. Bray and Gryffin beat each of other up. Gryffin found out about Terra and Bray. Gryffin and Terra made up. Then Gryffin found out about Terra's father and now they're not talking. Oh and Gryffin's leg is failing and his new eye is less than reliable.'

Chayse stops and turns to face her. 'Is that it?'

'Yep, well apart from Gryffin standing down as High Commander.'

'What? I was only gone a few weeks.'

'Never a dull moment.'

Chayse shakes his head as he leads her around the corner and up a flight of stairs. He opens the door to his room and steps aside to let her in. Milla walks around the large room as Chayse places her bag on the bed. 'Is Gryffin okay?'

Milla sighs as she sits down on the bed. 'He was a bit of a mess, but I think Aleena managed to get through to him.'

Chayse shakes his head as he sits down next to her. 'She's one of the few he'll actually listen to.'

Milla lies back and rests her head on her arm. 'Someone needed to give him a good kick. He's been moody, argumentative and a real pain in the ass. Ever since he killed Klay he's been on a self-destruct path.'

Chayse lies down beside her. 'Have to admit, I'm glad he took Klay out.' Chayse plays with the leather cuff around his wrist and sighs. 'Klay made my life hell on *Ares*. Since the day I stepped foot on the ship, I was treated like I was diseased. Not only was I the new guy, but I also reported directly to Gryffin so no one trusted me.' He meets her eyes briefly and smiles sadly. 'I wanted to be an active Nomad so badly. I'd watch teams leave the ship, follow Gryffin into raids and negotiations, and wish I could be part of that.' He looks back at the ground again and swallows a lump in his throat. He thought he was over everything that happened on *Ares*, but talking about it just brings the feelings back. Night after night alone in his room while the rest of the crew ate in the mess. Conversations ending whenever he was around. Being the target of too many pranks to count.

He understands why Gryffin kept out of it, but instead of doing something, Klay actually encouraged and joined in. He now knows Klay was afraid he was getting too close to Gryffin. Any chance he had to discredit or shun Chayse, he sure as hell took it. 'Klay hated me from day one. Nothing I ever did was good enough.'

Milla rolls onto her side and traces a finger down Chayse's face. 'But you answered to Gryffin. What could Klay do?'

'He was second in command. There was a hell of a lot he could have done to help instead of nothing.'

'We've all had good and bad things in our lives. They make us what we are. I'm not taking away from what Klay encouraged, but it made you tough. Gryffin saw that strength.'

He smiles and kisses her wishing he had her confidence in his abilities. 'So, what's the plan now. Gryffin's called a meeting.'

She shrugs. 'No idea. Gryffin isn't a fan of talking. I'm sure we'll all know our parts when he wants us to.'

'What do you think of her?'

Gryffin doesn't know what to say. He steps out of the hangar and slowly approaches the large battleship in front of them. *Nemesis* is impressive. Aleena and the team on Ultar managed to build one hell of a ship and he's damn proud of them. While *Nemesis* is his life's work, he knows nothing about her. If he had been involved in her creation, the Foundation would have used that information against the Nomad when they had control of him. He examines the ship and manages to hide the smile. 'She looks vaguely familiar.'

Chayse smiles. 'Yeah, blame Aleena and the engineers for that. It's fitting though — *Ares* is our flagship, makes sense *Nemesis* should take after her.'

Gryffin's robotic eye zooms in on the finer details as he walks under her hull. 'Captain's seat working out for you?' Chayse doesn't immediately respond. Gryffin glances at him and tilts his head. 'What?'

Chayse takes a deep breath. 'It's not easy.'

Gryffin laughs briefly. 'It's not supposed to be.'

'You make it look that way. How do you cope with all those lives resting on every decision you make — both good or bad?'

Gryffin runs his flesh hand along the grey hull. 'You do what you have to do. There's no room for regret or doubt. Make the decision and move on.' He pulls his hand away and faces Chayse. 'Are you ready for what's coming?'

Chayse purses his lips as he thinks. '*Nemesis* and the crew are ready. We'll fight to the end. That's all I know.'

Gryffin nods. 'Good answer.'

'You know that if we attack the Foundation colony, they'll make a move on Ultar, right?'

Gryffin doesn't answer. Ultar has suffered too much. The last thing they need is another Foundation attack. He's got a plan though. Well, the bare bones of a plan, but it's a start. The problem he's having trouble with is the mix of people and groups. If they're to come out of this with minimal losses, it means Nomad, Hunters, ex-Foundation, and Rogue's will have to put all their issues aside and work as one. There's a first time for everything, but it's a lot to ask.

There's also a risk of one of the groups forcing control once the Foundation is taken care of. They could quickly find the ship next to them is an enemy with their guns pointing in their direction. He knows the Rogues and Nomad can work together. While on the way to Ultar, the groups mixed in the ships, training together, so they can be a more effective team. Even though the relationship is new, he has more confidence in the Nomad and Rogue partnership than the Nomad and Hunter one.

Sayber is still on his list. He's been there for a long time and it would take a bloody miracle for his name to move. Gryffin's also sure Sayber feels the same way about him. The time will come when they have to act on it. But not until the Foundation is out of the picture — for good this time. If it means Gryffin has to go to Earth to personally put a bullet in each and every member of the Council, that's what he'll do. That has to be his priority. Nothing else can get in the way of it. Nothing.

Gryffin holds his metal arm up in front of him. He flexes his fingers and watches the plates of metal shift as he moves. 'Call a meeting with the leaders of each group. I want everyone else training, and I mean everyone. Use the base, the fields, ships. I don't care. We need to step it up so we're ready. Get the maintenance team together. Make sure every ship is serviced and ready to fly.' He walks back towards the base, and calls back to Chayse.

'Meeting in five.'

∞

Garvan looks up from the screen when Bray knocks on the door. 'You got that information ready?'

Garvan nods and holds the tablet out to Bray.

'You're not off the hook that easily. He's going to need to talk to you first.'

Garvan grabs his jacket from the back of the chair and follows Bray out the door. 'Who?'

Bray doesn't answer as he gestures for Garvan to follow him. Feeling slightly uneasy, the ex-prisoner pulls his jacket on and hurries to catch up with Bray. 'Where are we going?'

Bray stops at the meeting room and pauses with his hand on the door. 'As much as it pisses me off to say this, you're going to have to sell yourself. If he doesn't buy into you and what you know, we're all screwed.'

Garvan frowns. 'Why do I get the feeling I might not come out of this in one piece.'

Instead of trying to put him at ease, Bray opens the door and leads Garvan into the room. A man in his mid-thirties sits at the head of the table examining a tablet. Garvan freezes as the man looks up at him, but it's not his face that he recognises, it's the metal arm.

'You're Gryffin?'

Gryffin raises his eyebrow. 'Disappointed?'

'Surprised.' He tilts his head as he looks at Gryffin. 'No offense, you're just a little younger than I imagined.'

'And you don't look like an architect.'

Garvan laughs. 'It's been a while since I was called that.'

Gryffin nods towards the seat beside him. Garvan pushes past the other chairs and slowly lowers into the one assigned to him. He looks up at the man he's heard so much about. He's surprised how young he actually is. The infamous Nomad can't be much older than his own son back on Earth.

Bray sits opposite him and Garvan smiles as he notices the similarity between the two men. Bray frowns at him and the smile disappears. 'So, what can I do for you?'

Gryffin pushes the tablet across the table to him. 'My former second-in-command picked out these planets as possible Foundation sites. Any of these work for the structure you designed?'

Garvan places Gryffin's computer next to his and examines the data.

'You trust the data from Klay?' Bray asks.

Gryffin leans back in his chair and folds his arms. 'Damned if I know. He's got history of lying.'

'Can you get him in here?' Garvan asks. 'Maybe if I can ask him about some of these locations—'

'He's dead,' Gryffin interrupts.

Garvan raises his eyebrows and looks down at the screen. He doesn't need to ask who killed Klay. Garvan checks through each of the requirements on his list and compares the data to the list of locations offered by Klay. His heart races as one of the locations stands out from the rest. He points to a cluster of small worlds at the far right of the screen. 'There. Surface seems a fit, right atmosphere and close enough to the Port for supply runs.'

'Can you find anything on the planet?' Gryffin asks Bray.

The Hunter takes Gryffin's tablet and puts the coordinates in. 'Think you may be on to something, Garvan. It's an old mining colony. Been deserted for decades but the underground structure is still intact.' He slides the computer up the table to Gryffin. 'The Foundation could bring in Garvan's cubes for the surface and have a series of service tunnels underneath.'

Gryffin looks up at Garvan. 'Guess it's the best target we have. I just hope you're right.'

∞

Roman looks around the room as Gryffin, Sayber, Bray, Chayse, Milla, Garvan, Lucan, Aleena, Desyl, Rua, and Terra take their seats. If not for the direct order, he doubts Terra would be here. Her red-rimmed eyes stand out in harsh contrast to her pale skin. Roman looks over at Gryffin. The Nomad captain doesn't look much better than Terra.

Aleena briefly filled him in on her discussion with Gryffin earlier in the day. He's grateful for Aleena's interference. At least she managed to somehow convince Gryffin to remain as their leader. Aleena refused to give Roman many details, but did say Gryffin had opened up to her a little. It's a small start and his son's future with Terra is clearly still debatable. Hopefully, once the Foundation is confronted, some of the ghosts can be put to bed once and for all.

'Right, well, Gryffin called this meeting so I'll hand the floor over to him in a moment.' He rests his clasped hands on the table in front of him. 'I'd just like to say something first, if I may. There's been a lot of upset within the base recently.' He looks up at Gryffin, but as usual, the Nomad's face is unreadable. 'Revelations have come out, much later than they should have. I know it is difficult for some here to work with others at the table, and I understand the part I have personally played in that.' Gryffin looks away from Roman and focuses on the centre of the table. 'What I'm trying to say is, as difficult as it may be

— there are bigger issues here. We need to perform as one, work together as one, and bring the Foundation down as one.'

He takes a few seconds to look at each face sitting around the table. Gryffin is still showing the centre of the table too much interest, Terra is looking at her hands, Sayber is focusing on Bray, while Bray is looking at Terra. Chayse and Milla are smiling at each other, Garvan, Lucan, and Desyl are focusing on the map at the head of the table and Rua is looking at Bray, which surprises Roman. His eyes fall on Aleena last. She smiles widely at him and nods once.

'Okay, now that is out of the way, Gryffin?'

The Nomad nods to Chayse. Chayse loads data onto the screen. 'Garvan found a site for the new Foundation colony,' Gryffin says. 'We think it's already being built.'

'How do you know that?' Roman asks.

'Over the last few weeks, activity has increased around the new Port,' Chayse explains. 'A lot of cargo vessels have been coming through. *Nemesis* has tried to track them, but within a few seconds of entering the Sector, the ships cloak.'

'I didn't know the Foundation had cloaking capabilities?' Sayber says.

'Rayde,' Gryffin replies. 'He gave details on the Nomad cloaks to Balfe. They've perfected what we adapted.'

'Where did you get your technology from?' Roman asks.

'From a contact.'

Roman doesn't bother asking for clarification he knows he won't get.

Bray rubs the skin beside his facial implant. 'There's no other way to track them to the colony. Garvan's information is the best we have.'

'Are you certain there's no way to confirm the location?' Roman asks. 'Can you get anything from the coordinates your father sent you?'

Terra shakes her head. 'It's a cloaked comms beacon. Clearly he's not stupid enough to give me the coordinates of his actual location. Without the codes for the beacon, I can't trace it back to its source.'

'I'm not keen on launching an attack with no confirmation we're even hitting the right place. There has to be some way of confirming.'

Chayse shakes his head. 'Afraid not. I've taken out as many of the ships as I can, but I had to pull back. There's just too many of them for *Nemesis* to handle alone. Besides, our attacks have only slowed them down. We take out one, and two come through next time. Whatever they're doing, they clearly don't care about the expense.'

'Why haven't you fought them before? Are you all cowards?'

Roman glances at the red-haired Rogue captain. 'The timing hasn't been right.'

She snorts. 'Timing? Just attack. Sounds like you've been hiding.' Rua gestures at everyone sitting around the table. 'Rogue, Hunter, and Nomad ships are here, ready and more than willing to fight to the death. Talking is a waste of time. We need to blow the colony to pieces.'

'Rua's right.' Bray smiles at the Rogue captain before looking back at Roman. 'I get why you're less than happy about attacking, but there'll never be a better time. We're the best of the best out here. I guarantee, the Foundation will have never come up against fighters like us.'

Roman looks over at Gryffin. 'What about you, Captain? The Nomad in?'

'The Nomad are going in with or without everyone else here.'

'We gotta find and destroy the lot of them,' Sayber says. 'It's time, Roman.'

They're right — it's time. They can't hide forever. 'Agreed.'

'So,' Lucan says, 'we attack.'

Garvan puts up a hand and Roman nods. 'Hate to be the bearer of bad news, but it's not going to be quite that easy. The colony will be shielded.'

Roman frowns. 'Why do you say that?'

Garvan transfers the blueprint of the colony to the screen. He circles the main building with his finger. 'That's the control centre. It links with all the smaller dwellings. It's set up to transfer power to the houses to shield them.'

'So we just keep firing on the surface until it loses power,' Sayber says.

Garvan shakes his head. 'Won't work. The only way to take it down is to access the controls in this building. The shielding was ahead of its time when I saw it years ago. They've no doubt improved it since then.'

'If there is something like that available, they would have fitted it to the ships,' Roman says.

Terra shakes her head. 'The amount of power needed would drain the ship's reserves.'

Bray curses. 'So, we're back at square one again.'

'We can still target the ships,' Rua says. 'Foundation ships can still fall.'

Roman shakes his head. 'A possibility, but not one I favour. We don't know how many ships they have here. Our only chance at survival is to launch a combined attack. Take out the ships and the colony. With the shield in place, we have no way of knowing how many troops or ships are on the surface.'

'So,' Sayber says, 'short of her father inviting us in, we're screwed. Is that what you're saying?'

Roman opens his mouth to reply, but Gryffin jumps in first. 'He'll invite us in.'

43

Roman stares at the ceiling above his bed. Sleep continues to evade him. He tries to go over the details of the planned attack against the Foundation, but every time he closes his eyes he sees Callum, sneaking into his room at the academy after lights out to talk until the small hours, at the hospital holding Terra just after she was born, endless talks and plans for the future. He shared all of it with his friend. First Maggie deceived him and now Callum. An unknown son and a friend back from the dead.

Logic seemed to disappear as soon as he entered this sector. Things like this just don't happen. He hasn't come across anyone else on his travels with as many issues as he has. No wonder he can't sleep. At least on Ultar, he has Aleena's company to help distract him from his own thoughts. He gets out of bed and paces his room. He's mere hours away from possibly seeing his former friend again. He misses Callum every single day, but Roman would prefer he were actually dead instead of the man he has become. He hasn't got a clue what to say to the man. And what if the Maggie he referred to in his communication is actually...

Roman shakes his head and sits on the bed. The thought is absurd. She's been dead for years. He went to her funeral. He suddenly freezes as a thought hits him. The Foundation never recovered her body. Her husband was found in the burnt wreckage but she wasn't. The officials reported that her body must have been incinerated in the crash. He gets to his feet again. What if she wasn't on the transport? He laughs loudly and paces again. Normal people don't just take bodies and keep them. He stops in his tracks. Then again, normal people also don't do what the Scientist has. From what he knows of his former friend, normal isn't a word he'd use to describe him.

If there is even a minute chance that Maggie is with the Scientist, he needs to tell Gryffin and Bray. Gryffin probably doesn't remember his mother, but Bray certainly would. Everything they've planned for could grind to a halt if the Hunter unexpectedly comes face to face with his deceased mother. He doesn't have a choice but to tell them.

Twenty minutes later, after a lot of pleading, the two Sawyer brothers are sitting opposite him in his office. Both men have so much in common with their mother, yet are so different to each other. He sees a lot of himself in Gryffin, but instead of being happy about it, the truth just rears its ugly head again. He's burnt that bridge.

Gryffin stretches his long legs out in front of him. 'Well?'

Roman clears his throat. 'You both know we eavesdropped on a snippet of conversation from the Scientist last year.'

Bray nods. 'Yeah, and?'

Roman leans back in his chair. The two brothers have definitely mastered the delicate art of conversation. 'I think it's time I play it to you.' He takes a deep breath as his pounding heart beats loudly in his ears. He's not overly worried about Gryffin's reaction, but Bray worries him. Before he can talk himself out of it, he plays the full message.

'There's been a little setback. Don't worry, Maggie. We'll get him back.'

Bray straightens in his seat. 'Maggie?'

'Who's Maggie?' Gryffin asks.

'She's your mother.' Roman watches a strange array of emotions cross the brothers' faces.

Gryffin frowns and his eye turns purple. 'He has her?'

Roman nods. 'It would appear so.' He's a bit wary of Gryffin's unexpected reaction. They don't need him to lose control now. 'Believe me, I wish I didn't know about this.'

'It's a bit damn late for that!' Bray snarls. 'You knew all this time. Why didn't you say anything?'

Roman pushes back and rises to his feet. 'What exactly could I say? That's all I know. Just three sentences. I don't even know if it is our Maggie.'

'She's got nothing to do with you.'

Roman forces his shoulders back. He doesn't want Bray to know how much that statement hurts him — however right it may be.

'Is she about Terra's height with short brown hair?'

Roman and Bray both turn to face Gryffin. Bray sits down beside him. 'How do you know that?'

'The Scientist has her in a stasis pod. She's brain dead, but the pod is keeping her body alive. She was on the freighter and in the prison. He'd talk to her while he was operating on me.'

Bray frowns. 'Talk to her how? What did he say?'

Gryffin shakes his head. 'Nothing that made any sense. Something about a trip to the beach. Doing what he did to keep them together. He planned on using my control implant to restore her.'

Bray shouts and kicks the chair across the room. 'I'm going to kill that man.'

'Settle down Bray, please. Gryffin, is there anything else you remember?'

He shakes his head. 'If I'd known who she was I would have killed her before I left.'

Bray shoves Gryffin in the chest. 'She's my mother!'

'Look at what he did to us! He wants to replace her brain with what's in my head. She'll do whatever he programmes her to do — if it even works in the first place. I don't know her, but does she deserve to live like that?'

Bray curses and runs a hand through his hair. 'At least she'd be alive.'

Gryffin spins him around and slams him against the wall. He pushes his hand against the implant on the side of Bray's head. 'Feel that pain?' Gryffin forces his brother's head up so Bray has to look him in the eye. 'Imagine that pain one hundred times over, inside your head. Imagine being powerless to stop your body doing terrible things, killing people you know, while you're locked away in there with no damn way out.'

'We could do something with her programming.'

'Look at me, Hunter!' Bray raises his head again. 'If Rayde gave me a choice when he found me, do you really think I'd choose to be like this?'

'You're alive, aren't you?'

'This isn't living and I wouldn't have picked it.'

Roman feels his throat close up. He never suspected Gryffin felt that way. He was grateful that Rayde had rescued him. If not for that, he'd never have met his son. But he didn't think about it from Gryffin's point of view.

'She's already dead. That's why he needs my implant.'

Bray turns away and runs a hand through his dark hair. He looks between his brother and Roman, the hope clear in his face. 'Maybe there's something—'

'She's dead,' Gryffin confirms again. 'I spent enough time near her to know that. You need to get any thoughts other than a funeral out of your head right now. We're going in to stop the Foundation. Nothing else.'

'Who the hell are you to make that decision!'

'He's right,' Roman says. 'She's gone, Bray.'

Bray opens his mouth to reply, but instead turns away and paces the far end of the room. Gryffin looks over at Roman, his face unreadable as usual. He may be the one that has to make the decision for Maggie. Even if Bray does agree, Roman seriously doubts he'll actually be able to make the call. Bray will never let Roman near her, so that just leaves Gryffin. The older brother wouldn't have any hesitation doing what he needs to. But would it just serve to shatter the fragile relationship between the brothers?

'You're right,' Roman barely hears the words whispered by Bray. 'I'll do it, but not there. I want to take her back with us. I'm not leaving her there.'

'I'm with you on that.' Roman doesn't want her there a moment longer either. 'We'll bring her home, Bray.'

Bray nods once and leaves the room. Gryffin stares at the closed door and crosses his arms. 'You're going to have to do it.'

Roman does a double take. 'Me? I thought you would.'

Gryffin look at him and shrugs. 'This is your battle, not mine.'

Roman nods and lowers onto his chair, suddenly feeling older than his fifty-three years. 'I can't believe I'm having this discussion with you. She's your mother.'

'And you're my father. It means nothing to me.'

Roman's lungs seem to constrict. He's angry that Gryffin's unemotional words still affect him. 'I know Maggie. This is far from what she'd want, but I don't know if I can make that call.'

'You have to.' Gryffin nods towards the door. 'He won't be making it. Turn off the pod. Put her to rest. She deserves that after what he did.'

'I need to talk to Callum, Gryffin. I need to look him in the eye and ask him what he's doing.'

Gryffin's eyes glow deep purple. 'I know he's your... friend, but I want him dead. I will kill him.'

Roman nods. 'I know. I can't blame you, Gryffin.'

The Nomad frowns. 'Thought you'd put up more of a fight.'

'He's hurt too many people to be given any latitude. What he did to you, to Bray, to Maggie, it has to stop. This all has to stop.' He wipes his clammy palms on the legs of his trousers. 'So, are you ready? Are you sure you know the plan? Do you need to go over it again?'

Gryffin frowns. 'There's a computer in my head — of course I know the plan. It's everyone else you should worry about.'

'Will it work?'

Gryffin shrugs. 'As long as everyone sticks to what they have to do, then it should.' Gryffin places his hands on Roman's desk and leans over. 'We shoot to kill on the surface. You understand that?'

Roman nods. He's far from happy about it, but it's what the group agreed. 'Of course. After everything's that happened, it's the only way.'

∞

Chayse spins on the balls of his feet and lands a forceful blow to the back of Desyl's legs. Desyl grunts and retaliates with an impressive move that leaves Chayse on his back on the mat. He lies on the ground and takes a few seconds to catch his breath. He's exhausted, but is only a few minutes in to the session. He must be out of shape.

After the meeting broke, Gryffin insisted the two men train together. He wanted to make sure everyone was ready, not that Chayse had any idea what to be ready for. No one knows what the final plan is, but that's nothing new. While on *Ares*, Gryffin always waited until the last minute before he let everyone else in on what he wants. Chayse thinks he goes over and over every little detail in his head, and only confirms once he's sure he's thought of everything.

One thing is worrying him above everything else that can go wrong; Gryffin will want to kill Terra's father as soon as he sees him. There'll be no talking and no pleading his case. Gryffin will kill him whether Terra is present or not. He just hopes, whatever the plan, Gryffin has taken that point into account.

'Should we not be getting things ready for tomorrow?' Chayse asks.

Desyl shakes his head. 'Gryffin said everyone else can handle it. Stop stalling.'

Chayse smirks. 'Just making conversation.' Desyl is right — the rest of the teams can take care of everything, but that doesn't mean he's happy to let them. Sayber and Bray are going through weapons training, Lucan is checking systems on each of the ships and the Rogue's are overseeing dividing the ammunition — under Nomad supervision. While that's underway, Terra, Roman and Aleena are checking through the system for anything suspicious. General consensus is that someone is passing information to the Foundation. Gryffin offered to hook up to the system and use his control implant to search the system, but Milla had very forcefully put her foot down. She made it perfectly clear that if anything was hooked into Gryffin and put a strain on his programming, she'd be less than happy. His leg isn't improving and Milla doesn't want any additional strain on any of his implants.

'Why's Milla checking Gryffin? Is he okay?'

Chayse makes a face. 'I think she's just giving him a once over before we set out tomorrow.'

Desyl wiggles his eyebrows. 'A once over?'

Chayse whacks him on the shoulder with his sparring stick. 'Watch it.'

Desyl smirks and holds up his hands. 'Just repeating what you said, Captain.'

Chayse opens his mouth to reply, but is interrupted when the alarms scream to life. He drops his stick when he hears the emergency radio request security teams at the med bay.

Chayse races through the tunnels closely followed by Desyl. He reaches the med bay and skids to a stop at the open door. He peers inside and meets Milla's wide blue eyes. Gryffin is facing them and has his metal hand tightly around Milla's neck. Her feet dangle above the floor as she fights against his grip. Gryffin's blank expression tells him everything he needs to know. The implant has control of him.

A security team rushes to the entrance of the room. Chayse gestures at them to stop, but it's too late. Their arrival triggers the implant's defensive mode. Chayse ducks as Gryffin fires his gun.

Chayse's heart threatens to beat right out of his chest. This can't be happening. Not to Milla. Gryffin can't hurt her. He tries to reason with himself but the horror in front of him is hard to reason away. With barely any effort, Gryffin can end Milla's life, and Chayse's life with it. Milla's blue eyes meet his. Chayse tries to reassure her but his shaking hand tells a different story. He's seen Gryffin enough times to know how this usually plays out.

'Gryffin. Please don't hurt Milla.' The words fall on deaf ears. Once locked into the implant, only Gryffin himself can break through. Milla doesn't have the hours Gryffin needs to get control of himself. Chayse tries to target Gryffin, but he can't fire without endangering her life.

Gryffin pulls Milla close to him, holding her tight against his chest. Her arms frantically move in front of her, trying to get away from him, but he's far too strong. She suddenly stills and Gryffin throws her across the room. Chayse screams as Milla flies in slow motion through the air and lands on a bed in the far corner. Her head hangs off the edge with her blonde hair tumbling over the side. Chayse hears himself screaming her name but isn't aware of his mouth moving.

Something snaps in Chayse. He locks on to Gryffin, but the security team gets there first. No one is taking any chances with Gryffin. The team remain at the door as Gryffin rocks when he is hit by shot after shot. The stun guns light up the room, and for a few seconds, they're the only sound Chayse can hear. Electricity courses over Gryffin's metal arm. Gryffin releases a pulse which hits one of the guards against the far wall. The assault continues for another few seconds until Gryffin finally falls to the ground unconscious. Chayse ignores him and scrambles across the room to Milla. He touches the side of her face. 'Milla. C'mon. Please, Milla!'

Her unblinking eyes stare at him. He feels for a pulse, but can't find one.

'No! Milla, wake up!' He holds her hand but the lifeless limb slides from his touch. He looks over his shoulder at Gryffin. The security team are busy restraining him. Chayse leaps to his feet and charges at Gryffin. 'You killed her!' He rains blows after blows down on Gryffin, not caring that he's unconscious and won't feel anything. When the security team try to pull him away, he uses his boots to deliver as many kicks to Gryffin as he can. A large Nomad pins Chayse's arms to his side and just holds him as Chayse bucks and screams to be let go. His protests increase as Lucan arrives and checks on Milla.

Lucan examines her in silence then looks over at Chayse. Even though Chayse knows she's dead, having Lucan confirm it with a curt shake of his head is too much to take.

His legs go from under him and the Nomad restraining him slowly lowers him to the ground. He beats the concrete floor with his fists — over and over and over, not caring when his fresh blood stains the floor. He can't feel it. The only pain is the chasm in his chest, ripping him in two. Lucan tries to stop him from hurting himself, but the grief is more powerful. Chayse pushes out of Lucan's grip and scrambles towards Milla again. 'Wake up, damn it!'

Lucan roughly takes Chayse's face in his hands and forces the younger man to look at him. 'She's gone, Chayse.'

'But she can't be. Check her again!'

Lucan meets his eyes and slowly shakes his head. 'She's gone,' he repeats, quieter this time.

Lucan catches Chayse as his body crumples forward. He clenches his teeth, but that can't stop the scream that tears out of his body.

44

Callum Rush looks up from his screen as Forty-Three hurries in the door. He explicitly ordered that he is not to be disturbed under any circumstances. The prisoner he's working on lost consciousness a few minutes ago. Knowing his luck lately, death will come calling for the man soon. Time is running out — for both him and Maggie. He glances over at the stasis pod nestled in the side chamber. Her last set of readings showed deterioration in her cells. Death is calling her too. If the cellular deterioration continues at the current rate, she will be lost in a few weeks. He needs the prototype.

Forty-Three stands like a mannequin in front of him. In his current mood, he's tempted to dissect the cyborg to see if he'll be of any use. 'What is it? I thought I made myself clear.'

'Our contact on Ultar has just sent a message.'

Callum pulls it from the cyborg's hand and reads through the data. His mood instantly brightens. 'It seems your dear brother is causing trouble. He killed the base's doctor.' His smile widens as the information sinks in. 'Well, well, well, your brother appears to be succumbing to his programming. Perhaps now, Terra will be more open to discussing options with me.'

'You believe she'll bring him to you?'

'I do. Think about it. If what you say is true, and she does actually have misguided feelings for him, his actions will no doubt seal his fate with the Ultarans. Even the notorious Gryffin must answer for his crimes. They may be able to excuse his previous actions. He was not in control of himself when he attacked the colony the first time.' He pauses as he remembers the success of his project.

The prototype had performed well above his expectations. His already well-honed fighting skills had been excelled by the additional work he carried out. When he faced the young man, dressed in his uniform, ready to lead the assault on Ultar, he had never felt more proud. Callum made him. It was his hard work that had forged the weak child into the formidable machine. Not for the first time, he wishes he could publish his work. The world should know what he did. Perhaps, when the project is made public, the Foundation will allow him to publish his paper.

'This is exactly what we need. The only option will be death for him. Terra will be desperate for an alternative solution.'

'What if she agrees he should die?'

Callum brushes the remark aside. It's a valid point, but one he's not willing to think about. Terra always thinks with her heart. Even as a child, she would bring home any strays she found. He smiles as he remembers a flea bitten cat she produced from her school bag. She cared for the animal every day and nursed it back to health. Terra could always see through to the true potential. No doubt she would feel the same about the prototype. If she really cared for him, being offered a way to make him fully human again would certainly appeal to her.

'Get everything ready. I don't want any mistakes this time. Once Terra gets here, I want Maggie's pod increased to its highest setting.

I need her as strong as possible before the procedure.'

'We're taking him offline?'

Callum shakes his head. 'Not initially. No, he'll need to be restrained and conscious. Any adjustments we make could cause problems with his implants. As long as we confirm everything is working as it should be, we can begin the transfer.' He checks the schematics on the screen. 'I think for safety's sake, I'll harvest everything.'

Forty-Three frowns. 'All the implants?'

Callum points to the screen. 'Just the ones in his head and torso.' He nods as the decision is made. 'Yes, we'll do that. Take everything. Better safe than sorry.' He studies the drawing and briefly thinks about Terra. Removing the implants will certainly kill the prototype, but there's nothing else he can do. Maggie and Terra may be upset at his death, but they will both be alive. Callum rubs his hands together. He'll have plenty of time to talk to them about his projects later. Right now, he has preparations to make.

∞

'I need to talk to you.'

Her stomach instantly rolls as the serene face of her father fills the screen. His wire-rimmed glasses are balanced on the end of his nose and his sandy hair is ruffled and sticking up, like he's been pulling at the locks. Not for the first time, she struggles with the truth of what he is. Callum smiles at his daughter. 'Of course. What's wrong?'

She frowns. 'What makes you think something is wrong?'

'Well, you contacted me for one. You also look troubled.'

She takes a deep breath before continuing. 'Did you mean what you said, about being able to... fix Gryffin?'

He frowns. 'Gryffin?'

'The prototype.'

His face instantly lights up. 'Of course. Forgive me, I am not used to calling him by that name. Fix him? You mean remove the implants?'

'Yes. Can you do it or not?'

'Why the change of heart? You made it abundantly clear the last time that I was not to contact you again.'

'Why does that matter? Can you do it or not?' she repeats.

'Answer me and I'll answer you.'

Terra clenches her teeth to stop her harsh reply. She just wants to get this over and done with as quickly as possible, but if she pushes too hard, he might just hang up. 'He... Gryffin... killed someone I care about.'

Her father purses his lips, but Terra sees the smile that he's trying to hide. He's actually happy about her revelation. 'And you think I can save him from what he is?'

'You said you can undo it. You made him into what he is. Every single death he committed is on your hands. She was my friend and because of your mods, he lost control and killed her. You need to put this right before more people die.'

'That still doesn't explain why you would contact me. Surely handing him back to the Foundation is the more logical course of action?'

'I want the work undone. They'll just rework him to make him worse. I've already lost my best friend, I don't want to lose the man...'

'You love.' He sighs and shakes his head. 'I understand love all too well. While I'm less than happy about your choice, I do know what you are feeling.' He sits back in this chair and runs his hand through his hair, ruffling it further. 'Very well. Bring him to me and I'll see what I can do.'

She pauses a little longer. He won't believe her if she accepts his help too quickly. 'Can you guarantee it?'

His brow crinkles. 'I cannot promise the work can be completely undone, but I will do what I can. I know him and the project better than anyone.'

'What...' She leans closer to the screen, pretending that she is concerned about someone overhearing. 'What does it involve f-for him?'

'As I said before, it will not be a quick procedure. His body has accepted the enhancements and is quite dependent upon them. Relearning how to live without them will take time.'

She rubs her eyes and shakes her head. Her reaction is real. She doesn't want to let her father anywhere near Gryffin. Ever. He's done more than enough damage to him. Even putting them in the same room as each other turns her stomach.

'Fine.'

Callum squeezes his eyes shut and nods rapidly. When he opens them again, he smiles at her, which just sends a chill down her spine. 'You have made the right decision. He will thank you for this.'

She grinds her teeth together to stop her terse reply. Her father clearly doesn't notice. He continues speaking, caught up in his excitement. 'I will send you the coordinates. An associate of mine will meet you and bring you both to me. How will you get him to accompany you?'

'That's my problem.' She shuts down the transmission before she can say something they'll all regret.

She can't accept the fact she's about to meet her father again. When she was a child, she spent so long wishing she could see him again. Now her impossible wish has come true, she is filled with dread instead of excitement. The thought of Gryffin undergoing any more procedures is unacceptable. He may never forgive her for keeping the truth from him, but the need to keep Gryffin safe will never leave her.

Terra pushes to her feet and paces the floor. She stops suddenly and curses herself. She can't believe she's going to be the one to place Gryffin in that situation again.

∞

Gryffin forces himself to sit still on the metal cot. His stomach is in knots and his heart feels like it's about to jump through his rib cage. He clenches his fists behind his back and pulls at the restraints, but they won't budge. They were designed especially for him so he's wasting his time. He tries to stretch his metal leg out to ease some of the pain, but the leg irons keep him firmly in place. He closes his eyes and takes a few deep breaths through the gag. The thick straps holding his jaw closed dig into the side of his face and push the leather, half-face muzzle tightly against his mouth.

He hates being restrained. It was part of his life before the Scientist took him back. Whenever he lost control, he would be restrained by the Nomad and locked away until he calmed down and was safe to be around again. But since his last stay with the Scientist, he can't stand the feeling of the restraints. He can't really blame them for not wanting to take any chances with him. The weird feeling in his stomach increases and he swallows deeply to stop himself from throwing up. It's bad enough being restrained without choking on his own vomit thanks to the gag. He suddenly realises he's panicking. He never panics. He opens his eyes, expecting to be back in the damp cell.

His chest rises and falls as he pulls in deep breaths. He flinches as a door slams in the corridor outside. He's half expecting Chayse to barge in with a gun in his hand. One bullet to the head — nice and quick. Chayse is entitled to revenge, it's part of the Nomad way of life. Gryffin pulls in a lungful of air and exhales slowly. He's not keen on dying in restraints in a cell.

His fists clench again as he unconsciously tries to break free. The feel of something warm and wet trickling down his left hand stops his struggles. He must have cut his wrist, but he doesn't care. He needs to get out of here. He freezes when he hears voices outside. His nostrils flare as he struggles to take in enough oxygen. His implants are doing nothing to help him calm down. The door opens and he immediately tenses. The two guards who have been guarding the cells enter the room with their arms over their heads. Terra forces them into the room and closes the door behind them. She gestures towards the bench with her gun and they both sit.

'What the hell is going on?'

Terra ignores them and pulls a stun gun out of the holster on her hip.

'Terra? What are you doing?' one of the guards asks. 'Stop this now, before you do something you'll regret.'

She points her gun at the two guards. 'It's too late for that.' She leaves her gun trained on the guards and points the stun gun at Gryffin. 'I'm so sorry, Gryffin. It's for your own good.'

Terra looks him in the eye and shoots.

∞

Terra resists the urge to race to Gryffin's side as he falls to the dusty ground. She forces herself to keep on track and stick with the plan. Ignoring Gryffin, she pulls the large supply crate away from the far wall and opens it. She gestures at the other guard. 'Empty it.'

He obediently does as she says while his companion silently watches. The guard finishes and she calls his friend over. 'Put Gryffin in the crate.'

They glance at each other. 'I said put him in the crate. Move!' One unlocks the cell door while the other wheels the crate over. They lift Gryffin off the ground and carefully lay the unconscious Nomad in the box. Terra ushers them both into the empty cell and locks the door. 'Sorry about this guys.' She seals the lid, hiding Gryffin from view.

'What are you doing, Commander? He killed Doctor Collins. He could kill you. He's not safe.'

'Just shut up! I know what I'm doing.' She powers up the trolley and pushes the crate from the room. Terra tries to act as normal as possible as she guides the unconscious Gryffin through the base. No one stops her and asks what she's doing and she's grateful for that. She seriously doubts she'd be able to have a normal conversation with anyone. Terra spots the transport in the far corner of the hangar. The back is open and ready for her cargo.

She weaves through the workers, each step bringing her closer to her target. She risks a quick glance around her, but there's no one watching her movements. Terra pushes the crate onto the transport and secures it to the floor. After another look around, she shuts the hatch and drops down into the pilot's seat. She races through the ignition procedure as fast as her fingers can go. Terra glances over her shoulder at the large crate at the side of the cargo hold. Gryffin is packed in a crate like any other piece of equipment, and that sickens her. After what seems like a lifetime, the craft lifts from the ground and she guides it through the cargo doors. After entering the coordinates her father gave her, she sets the ship on autopilot. Even though everything went as planned, she still feels more stressed than she ever has before. And this is the easy part.

Chayse picks up the bottle of Ultaran ale and takes a mouthful. The liquid burns his raw throat, but at least he can feel it. Since Lucan dragged him away from Milla, his body feels dead. Dried blood crusts his torn knuckles, but he can't feel the pain. He slams his fist against the table — nothing. The first empty ale bottle drops to the floor and he reaches for the next. He's never been a big drinker. Usually, all it took was one bottle and he would be in a drunken stupor. Another thing the Nomad crew would hold against him.

As he stretches out, the chair topples from under him and he crashes to the floor. Chayse rolls onto his back and pulls himself into sitting position. He glares at the patch of blood still on his boot. Gryffin's blood. His muscles quiver at the thought of finishing what he started. The security team had no right to pull him off Gryffin. Chayse was entitled to revenge and he was going to take it. Friend or not, Gryffin would die. Chayse would make sure of it.

The buzzer sounds on his door. Chayse ignores it and reaches for the fallen bottle. The irritating sound shrieks through his room again.

'Leave me alone!' He grinds out a curse as it goes off again. 'The captain is ordering you to leave him the hell alone!'

The buzzing at his door continues. Instead of responding, Chayse throws the bottle of Ultaran ale at the metal. The glass shatters, covering the floor with alcohol. Whoever is on the other side refuses to give up. Chase curses loudly and drags himself to unsteady feet. He wipes his sleeve across his face and stumbles across the floor. Chayse punches the door release and his terse comment freezes in his throat.

'Wow, you like shite,' Milla says as he remains open-mouthed at the door.

'What?'

'What? That's the best you can do? I've just come back from the dead.' She nods at the remains of the ale on the ground. 'Any of those left for me?'

∞

The transport enters the darkness of space without any issues, so Terra unstraps her harness and goes to check on her important cargo. She wants to check Gryffin first, but he'll have to wait. She attaches handles to either side of the floor panel, lifts the metal up and slides it out of its position. Garvan smiles up at her from his hiding space. 'Well, hello there! All go to plan?'

She nods and holds out her hand to help him up. Garvan wriggles free from the compartment and gets to his feet. He stretches to his full height and rolls his head, loosening his muscles. 'That's mighty cosy down there.' He puts a hand on her shoulder. 'Hey, you okay? You look a bit pale.'

'That was a lot harder than I thought it would be. Gryffin made it sound so easy. I fully expected someone to stop me and ask what I was doing.'

'That's good. If anyone was watching, your reaction will just make it look all the more genuine. So, we've got about three hours before we hit the target. Want to let him out?'

They lift the cover off and Garvan hauls Gryffin out of the crate. 'Do you think this will work?' Terra asks.

Garvan sits on the other bench and clasps his hands on knees. 'No reason why it wouldn't. Once Roman catches the mole, it'll be safe to launch the attack. You're all putting a lot of faith in me to dismantle the cloak. You barely even know me.'

'You know the facility like the back of your hand. There's no better person. Besides, Bray trusts you and that's enough for me.'

'You two were close, weren't you?'

She nods. 'I treated him really badly. I had no right getting involved with Gryffin's brother.'

'Bray will be fine. How bout we focus on the three of us for now.'

Gryffin suddenly opens his eye and jolts upright. Electricity surges down his arm as he rises to his feet. 'Gryffin! Stop, please relax. It's Terra. You're safe.'

His purple eyes focus on her as he breaths rapidly. 'Terra?'

She places her hand on the side of his face. 'Hey, you okay?'

He nods once and closes his eye. 'Yeah.'

'Just relax.' She gently pushes him back down on to the seat and leans close to speak quietly to him. 'You sure you're okay?'

'Just wasn't sure where I was. Did I hurt you?'

She shakes her head. 'You sure you can follow through with this?' After his reaction, she has serious doubts about introducing him to her father again.

'I said I would. It's the only way to stop this.' He glances up at Garvan and his eye narrows. Garvan takes a bottle of water from the shelf beside him and passes it to Gryffin. 'Three shots would have been enough.'

Terra grimaces. 'You told me to make it look convincing.'

Garvan holds his hand out to help him up, but Gryffin ignores it and gets to his feet alone. Terra smiles apologetically at Garvan.

'How long till we get there?' Gryffin asks.

'Just shy of three hours,' Garvan replies.

'That leaves two hours to go through everything again.'

Garvan gets up and crosses his arms. 'Hey, I've got it. I know what to do.'

Gryffin glances at him over his shoulder. 'I don't know you. We go over it. Understood?'

Terra discreetly shakes her head, stopping the argument ready to spring from Garvan's mouth. He frowns but takes her advice. 'Sure. Why not.'

∞

'Calm down! Are you bloody serious?'

Roman quietly watches as Milla attempts to calm Chayse down, but it's not going well. He glances over at Lucan, but as usual, the tall dark-haired man is impossible to read.

Milla lowers onto Chayse's bed. 'Please, Chayse. Let us explain.'

He turns to looks at Roman and Lucan. 'Us? You were both in on this?'

Roman nods. 'The three of us, and Gryffin.'

Chayse's mouth opens and closes a few times before the words make an appearance. 'This was Gryffin's idea, wasn't it?'

'Yes,' Roman replies, 'but he had good reason.'

Chayse snorts. 'It's Gryffin. That's all the good reason he'll ever give.' Chayse turns to look at Milla. 'I thought he killed you, right in front of me.'

'I know, Chayse. Listen, I'm sorry for keeping this from you, but it had to look convincing.'

'So you all used my feelings, my emotions to make it look believable?' He shakes his head. 'And there was me thinking Gryffin didn't know anything about feelings. He sure knows how to manipulate them.'

She gets up and takes his hand. Chayse tries to pull away from her touch, but Milla doesn't let him go. 'It wouldn't have worked if anyone suspected it was a ruse.'

'How did he "kill you"?'

'When Gryffin held me up to his chest, I injected myself with the drug you told me about when we first met. It slowed my heart rate and breathing down enough to make my death look convincing. Well, that and a well placed throw courtesy of Gryffin.'

Chayse wants to punch his fist through Gryffin's face, but the fact Milla is alive wins out. He cups the side of her face and smiles. 'I thought you were gone.'

She smirks. 'That part is down to my award winning performance.' Milla hugs him tightly, then pushes back to look at him again. 'We okay?'

'You're alive so we're more than okay.' He pulls her in against his side and faces Roman and Lucan. 'In the future, any plans that involve killing my girlfriend have to be run past me. Got it?'

'Of course,' Roman replies while Lucan nods.

'I'm afraid to ask, but where is Gryffin?'

Roman takes this as his cue. 'Terra took him out of custody so she can bring him to her father.'

Chayse frowns. 'And Gryffin agreed to it?'

'It was Gryffin's idea,' Roman says. 'He wasn't convinced Callum would buy the sudden change of heart. If Terra was somehow forced to bring him in, he thought it would be better believed — by both Callum and his mole. We don't know where the Foundation has eyes. Everything had to look real. Terra even shot Gryffin with a stun gun.'

Chayse's eyebrows jump up. 'She shot him?'

'Yep,' Lucan says. 'Then she took him off the base in a packing crate.'

'Sounds like something I'd have liked to see. Why Milla?'

Lucan snorts. 'Believe us, she wasn't top of Gryffin's list either. He was worried you'd get to him before Terra would and kill him.'

Roman nods. 'That's an understatement. We've watched the video feed from the cell. Every time he heard a sound, his attention immediately went to the door.'

'Yeah, I've never seen him so anxious,' Lucan says. 'He's never liked the restraints, but having to sit in the cell, waiting, with no way to stop you from exacting revenge — he was less than happy about it.'

'What now?' Chayse asks.

Roman hands him a tablet. 'Gryffin recorded your orders on that. He wants you to attack the Port.'

∞

Gryffin stares out the front window of the transport. They've got about an hour left before they reach the coordinates Terra's father gave her. He's going to enjoy every single second being out of the restraints as he can. As soon as they get close, he'll have to go back into the crate. The thought fills him with dread. Terra lowers into the co-pilot seat and checks some of the settings. 'Where's Garvan?'

'Asleep. He says he needs his beauty sleep before all the fun starts. I've to wake him up in a bit.'

Gryffin turns around to face her. 'I forgot to ask earlier, is Milla okay?'

Terra nods and leans back against the soft leather seat. 'She was just coming around from the drug when I kidnapped you. She always wanted to act. No doubt her little performance will have given her grand ideas about a change of career.'

A slight smile touches his mouth. 'Playing dead while drugged isn't too hard. How about Chayse?'

Terra grimaces and looks away. 'He's heartbroken. Are you sure he'll forgive you for the deception?'

Gryffin runs a metal finger over a large bruise covering his elbow. He hopes Chayse will understand why he was left out of the final plan. 'She's still alive.'

'True, but his grief was put on display for everyone to see. That's the part he may have a hard time moving past.'

Gryffin shrugs. 'We're all in situations we don't want to be in. She's alive and the plan worked. That's the important bit.'

'I can't believe it actually worked.'

He nods. 'Milla nearly didn't have time to inject herself. The security got there a lot quicker than we planned. So, did I hit the public enemy number one rank again?'

'Afraid so.' She looks critically at his face. 'Chayse didn't hold back.'

Gryffin slowly shakes his head. 'I got off easy.'

Terra looks down at his boots instead of his face. 'Can we talk about my father? About why I kept it from you?'

Gryffin turns back to the front of the ship. 'Not now, Terra.'

'When then?'

'Not now! Damn it, Terra, there's a time and a place and it sure as hell isn't now. Put it out of your head until after this is done. We all need to focus on the bigger picture. You and me... we don't factor into that.'

She winces at his words. 'I'm about to hand you over to my — to him, again. I'm just asking if you think we can be okay after this?'

He shrugs. 'I don't know if any of us are going to be alive after this.'

Terra nods and clasps her hands on her lap. He feels terrible for not trying to put her at ease but how can he? He doesn't have a clue what they're walking into. Their plan is full of ifs and he's having a hard enough time accepting that without comforting someone else. The first part of the plan may have gone as they discussed, but there's still a fleet of ships ready to fight, with no way to breach the shields. Unless Garvan gets into the facility and shuts the cloak down, he could very well be spending the rest of his life back under her father's knife.

He quizzed the architect for half an hour on the facility. His knowledge of the layout is pretty impressive, but things change. The

Foundation could very easily have changed the layout from the original design. Gryffin curses himself and tries to stop the doubt from creeping in. It's all stemming from his lack of enthusiasm about meeting the Scientist again. As long as their reunion ends with the man's death at his hands, he'll be happy enough.

'I'm sorry you had to go through all that.'

He turns to face Terra. 'Go through what?'

'The way you were kept in the cell. Chayse and Lucan said it's how the Nomad would do it. I didn't want to do that to you.'

He frowns, then realises what she's apologising for. 'You mean the restraints? I'm well used to them. It's fine.'

She shakes her head. 'No it's not. I saw you in the cell. I was watching on the monitor outside before I came in. You were far from fine.'

He blows out a breath as he considers how to reply. There's no way he's going to admit what happened to him while he was waiting for her to come in and get him. 'I said it's fine. I'm fine.'

She reaches across and places her hand on his arm. 'Where did you think you were when you woke up?'

He pulls his arm away. 'Damn it, Terra! Stop analysing me. Check the weapons Garvan is bringing with him.'

'He's already checked them.'

'Check them again.'

Without a word, Terra pushes past his seat and disappears through the hatch to the back of the transport. Gryffin thumps his leg in frustration, welcoming the stab of pain that erupts from the metal. Against his promise to Terra, he hooks onto the control implant. He's going to have to be restrained and stunned again in a few minutes. The way he's feeling, he's not going to be able to let them restrain him without badly hurting them. Gryffin welcomes the numbness associated with the implant. He looks at the counter on the console in front of him, but the dread and panic are pushed aside by the implant. Time to go.

.

46

Terra shuts down her transport and tries to steady her racing heart. The large stone structure looms over the landscape. The site of the new Foundation colony looks much like an old Earth. She lowers the hatch and the cyborg that guided her in, steps on board. As soon as she sees him, she has to resist the urge to shoot him. He's one of the men that was hanging around *Perses* when she was a guest. He either ignores or doesn't notice her hostility. He gestures behind him and three more cyborg enter and check the craft.

Her heart races in her chest as one of them examines the floor right above Garvan's hiding place. He scans the floor thoroughly while another checks the walls. The Nomad have been using hiding spots like Garvan's for years to smuggle people and goods. They assured her the shielding on the compartment will hide Garvan, but she's still anxious. After a long wait, the three nod at the leader, declaring the ship clear. Terra silently releases her breath. The leader gestures to the crate and they lift off the lid.

He reaches in and roughly grabs Gryffin by the hair. He turns Gryffin's head around so he can see it clearly. 'It's him. Bring them.'

The icy wind whips her hair across her face and bites into any exposed skin as she steps on to the surface. She hurries to keep up with the man who has a firm grip on her arm. The other two cyborgs carry Gryffin between them towards the large building. The large, double height doors at the front of the compound open to welcome them. Her boots crunch on the dry earth as she is pulled towards the doors. She glances over her shoulder at her transport and ignores the firm pull back to safety. There's no turning back now.

The group enter the building and the doors close behind her, trapping her inside. She is lead through a large empty lobby, unfinished offices, and out into a service corridor.

She suppresses a shiver as they walk down a set of metal stairs. Through the darkness she thinks she can hear screams, but every sound echoes around them in the empty space. About ten minutes after she left her transport, they finally come to a stop at a single metal door. The guard places his palm against the lock and the door slides open. Terra steps into a large open space. The walkway she is standing on runs the length of the wall and circles the entire room. Below her, miles of tracks weave through support pillars that hold the walkways in place. Old mining carts sit on the tracks — some empty but some with mining equipment still piled inside.

It's what's scattered among the carts and tracks that really gets her attention. Dozens of cyborgs stand to attention along the walls. Cells are fitted under the walkways and each one is occupied. Terra walks to the railing and looks directly below her. An operating theatre is set up below the walkway and is fitted with state of the art equipment.

A cold chill runs up her body when the man at the head of the table looks up and smiles at her. His glasses are a new edition, his hair is lighter and there are more lines on his face, but it's him. Her father. He waves and rushes up the steps to greet her. He holds out his arms, but she shakes her head and steps back from him, yelping as she bumps into the cyborg guard. 'Don't you come anywhere near me.'

He drops his arms. 'Very well.' He addresses the guards behind her. 'Take him below.' They push past Terra and carry Gryffin down the stairs. 'Oh, and make sure he can't escape this time.' He turns his attention back to her and smiles again. 'Come with me. We have a lot to talk about.'

∞

Garvan moves the cover off his hiding place and pauses. When he's not immediately shot at, he sits up and scans the inside of the shuttle, then breathes a sigh of relief. He's alone and the hatch is closed. He climbs out of the compartment and swings his arms to get the circulation going again. Prison life had acclimatised him to small living spaces, but the compartment is pushing even his limits. If everything goes to plan, he'll be sitting in a seat when they leave the surface. Just a few small tasks to take care of first.

He checks his gun and opens the small escape hatch at the back of the shuttle. Garvan presses tight against the side of the ship and takes in his surroundings. The transport is in the middle of a large courtyard. The main building in directly in front and looks exactly how he designed it. Row after row of modular white housing blocks sit opposite the building at either side of a large water pipe that serves the entire colony. There must be an underground well on the planet. Garvan rubs the tip of his boot along the dusty ground. No sign of any rain for a few months at least.

He turns back to the large maintenance building and chews his bottom lip. That blasted building is part of the reason he was locked away for years. Time for a bit of payback. Garvan checks for any lookouts then steps out from the relative safety of the shuttle. He crosses the open space between the ship and the building in a few seconds. Instead of using the main doors, he circles the building. The building may have been built with care, but the same attention hadn't been paid to its surroundings. He forces his way through waist high brambles and grass, wincing as the thorns pull at his clothes and tear at any exposed skin. Garvan checks the scanner and adjusts his direction.

He moves slowly and stops every few steps to check his surroundings. Time is against him. And Gryffin. Every minute longer he takes to get in, means a minute longer the Scientist has with the Nomad leader. Even though he wants to cut through the undergrowth quickly he takes his time. He'll be no use to anyone back behind bars.

Garvan checks the scanner again and crouches down. His gloved hands pull at roots, clearing the area under his feet. He brushes soil to the side and smiles as he hits metal. Garvan clears more soil off the hidden grate and works his fingers around the outline. He takes a breath and heaves the grate to the side. He half expects a Foundation security officer to jump up and shoot him, but nothing happens. He releases the breath and wipes his arm across his forehead.

Musty, damp air hits him as he peers over the edge into the pitch black. Squeaking and scraping sounds travel up the ladder to the surface and he grimaces. 'Just great, God damn rats.'

Garvan sits on the edge of the hole and, after making sure his combat leathers are securely tucked into his boots, turns on the light attached to his gun and descends into the darkness.

∞

'Anything yet?'

Lucan shakes his head. Roman resists the urge to pound his fist against the desk in frustration. Five hours have passed since Terra took Gryffin, Garvan, and the shuttle from the base. Word had spread like wildfire through the compound. He doubts there's anyone left on the surface who doesn't know what she did. As soon as Gryffin pretended to kill Milla, all transmissions to and from the base were closely monitored. It took about an hour, but the mole finally made their move. Bray and Chayse tracked the transmission back to an individual who joined the colony three months ago. He had come in with a batch of refugees and had been assimilated into one of the security teams working on the base. He had been in the team that responded to Gryffin's attack on Milla and, after he was finished, had hurried back to his room to report.

As an extra security measure, Roman and a team of Nomad had gathered everyone into the base. Until this is over, he needs to know who he can trust. Just because they found one mole doesn't mean the man is working alone.

Avoca knocks on the doorframe and steps into the command centre. 'Is there anything I can do to help?'

Roman frowns. Since Avoca handed *Epsilon* over to Lucan, the man had become a recluse. The guilt he carries for his actions in the project weigh heavily on him. 'I'm surprised to see you here.'

Avoca clasps his hands behind his back. 'I can't hide forever. I'm not going to make things right by growing vegetables, am I?'

'I need people here I can depend on.'

'I understand. I wouldn't be here otherwise.'

Roman turns and sits on the edge of the console. '*Nemesis* and *Infinity* will be moving out in the next thirty minutes. *Epsilon* is staying here with *Dannan*, Baila's ship, and *Fian*, Dare's ship. The rest of the fleet have positioned themselves near the target.'

Avoca examines the screen and frowns. 'Is it wise to have all the ships there now? Surely it will alert the Foundation.'

'Nomad cloaks,' Lucan says. 'Everyone can get into position and blow up some Foundation ships before they even realise we've arrived.' The smile leaves his face as he realises he's in the company of two Foundation captains. 'Anyway, they'll be safe enough.'

'And the Port?' Avoca asks.

'Chayse will be taking that.'

'Taking? You're not planning to destroy it?'

Roman smiles. 'No, we're not.' He looks over at Lucan. 'The

Nomad have convinced me that taking is sometimes the only thing to do.' He brings another image up on the screen. 'These are the prisons the Hunters took. Each one is in a key position along the border. Sayber has been working with the inmates and trained them. We can launch attacks on the Foundation ships near those prisons quite easily. The largest one is near the site of the new Port. *Nemesis* will work with those teams and take the Port. It's about time we control what and who enters and exits the Sector.'

'Ambitious plan, but only holding one side of the Port will be of little use. Both must be linked in order for it to work.'

Roman shrugs. 'Better than nothing. Besides, even with one half, we can control transmissions.'

Avoca glances up at Roman, wide-eyed. 'Talk to Earth?'

'It's a definite possibility. That's a little in the future. For now, we have a lot of Foundation to get through first. Aleena will be staying here to oversee, but I'd prefer if she had back up on the ground. If the worst happens, Lucan, Baila and Dare will be busy keeping you all alive.'

'And you trust me?'

His reply is cut off as Bray and Chayse come back in. Bray's sleeves are rolled up to the elbow and both arms are stained red. Chayse's shirt and blond spikes are splattered with blood. Roman stares in shock at the two men. They left a while ago to interrogate the mole. From the amount of blood on them, it was an intense interrogation. 'I'm afraid to ask.'

'He's dead,' Bray answers.

'Please tell me he gave you something before he died.'

Chayse grins. 'Of course he did.' His smile falters slightly. 'Gave it up a bit easy. I was hoping he'd hold out on us.'

'Yeah,' Bray agrees. 'Took some of the fun out of it.'

Roman is at a loss for words. He'd heard of the interrogation tactics employed by the Nomad and Hunters, but thought they were a little exaggerated. He should know by now, nothing is exaggerated out here. It is what it is. He tries to ignore the blood still on the large blade hanging from Chayse's belt. 'So, what did he say?'

'He's alone,' Chayse confirms. 'They were worried about sending more.'

'And you believe him?'

Bray nods. 'Trust me, what we were doing to him, he wasn't lying. Doesn't mean there aren't more here he doesn't know about.'

'I agree,' says Avoca. 'The Foundation would not put all their eggs in the one basket.'

Roman agrees. 'All the colonists are contained and have had their comms taken. No transmissions are leaving this base without authorisation. Speaking of which, Lucan, anything from Garvan?'

Lucan shakes his head. 'Give him a chance. He'll come through.'

Roman rubs a hand over his jaw and stares at the screen. He just hopes Garvan does what he has to do before Callum lays one finger on his son again.

Terra watches in horrified silence as her father walks around Gryffin, looking at him like he's a shiny new toy to play with. 'How did you knock him out?'

'Stun gun.'

He grunts and leaves the cell, locking it behind him. 'I must say, I am still surprised you decided to bring him to me.'

'I didn't have a choice. It was either you or the Foundation.'

He takes off his glasses and wipes them on the hem of his checked shirt. 'He is special to you?'

'What does that have to do with anything?'

He smiles and looks back at the still unconscious Gryffin. 'You're special to him. It's the reason Balfe arranged for you to be taken. It's quite remarkable really. It seems that Thirty-Five has found a way to bypass his original programming. He has feelings for you. Genuine ones. If it wasn't such a massive flaw, I would leave him as he is.'

'It's not a flaw. He's human.'

Her father tuts and shakes his head. 'Oh, Terra. He's so much more than that. Come here.'

She reluctantly follows him away from Gryffin to a bank of monitors. He points to a diagram on the screen. 'What's that?' she asks, only half paying attention. She's afraid to take her eyes off Gryffin.

'It's him.'

She frowns and studies the diagram. 'Oh my God!' On closer inspection, she realises the screen shows a three dimensional schematic of a man. 'That's Gryffin?'

Her father smiles and nods enthusiastically. 'Incredible, isn't he.' He zooms in on different areas of the diagram and Terra grows colder by the second. 'It took years to modify him to this extent, but he really is remarkable. As you can see, most of the modifications are internal. What you can actually see is merely a small fraction of the work. Unfortunately, the Nomad removed some of my original implants, but I am happy with everything they left intact.'

His voice drones on in the background as she takes in the full extent of what he did to Gryffin. Milla and Chayse spoke of his internal implants, but she never fully understood what they referred to. Her father's schematic leaves little doubt in her mind anymore. Her feet carry her closer to the screen before she can stop them. She always assumed there was maybe four or five tiny internal implants. The truth is ten times worse than that. They're everywhere. Terra's attention is drawn to Gryffin's brain. 'What's that?' she asks, pointing to his head.

Her father zooms in. 'That is what makes him work and what makes him so valuable to the Foundation... and to me. That's the control implant.'

She frowns at the cluster of pea-sized dots scattered throughout his head. 'I thought it was one implant.'

He shakes his head. 'It needs to connect with each part of his brain. It controls his ocular implant and links with the implant on his chest.

His limbs and organs are supported through that larger implant. The key to his success is making sure everything works as a whole. That's how Rayde caused the malfunctions. If you disturb the main pathway between the control and chest implant, it effects other parts of his body.'

She licks her dry lips and swallows. 'So,' she clears her throat and continues. 'when will you start to change him back?'

He splutters. 'Undo it?' He sits on the round stool at the terminal. 'I just said that so you'd bring him back to me. I have no intention of undoing it.'

Terra hates that she's disappointed by the news. She accepts what Gryffin is, but a part of her had clung to the possibility of him having a normal life as a regular guy. She'd never want her father working on him again, but if the technology existed, Milla could have done something. 'You said you'd help him.'

He balances on the edge of the seat and clasps his hands together. 'I meant that bit. Do you have any idea how much time and money has gone into your boyfriend? He literally is priceless. Unless I can figure out his control implant, he cannot be replicated.'

Terra's stomach drops. Hearing him speak so frankly about the monetary value placed on Gryffin, sickens her to her core. 'He's a living, breathing person.'

He brushes her comment away. 'You clearly don't understand.' He turns to face her and pushes his glasses up his nose. 'Let me show you something else.' She tries not to look at the man lying on the table in the centre of the room as she follows him to the far wall. 'Would you like me to explain it to you?'

Terra gasps. 'Of course not! I want you to stop it. Right now!'

He looks over his shoulder at her and laughs. 'I'm too close to stop.'

'Too close to what? You have your cyborgs. Surely you can stop any further testing.'

He sighs and mutters under his breath to the ceiling. When he looks at her again, it's like he's looking at a child constantly irritating him with stupid questions. 'You really are trained Foundation drones, aren't you? All you can see is the cyborgs. One, and the rest of the Council are so focused on copying the prototype to increase their empire they've completely missed the point.'

'What are you talking about? What point?'

Instead of answering, he saunters over to the side of the cavern and disappears into a small chamber. Terra curses under her breath and obediently follows. What she sees inside stops her in her tracks. A large stasis pod sits in the centre of the small room. Wires and tubes trail across the floor and into the pod. Curiosity draws her closer to the occupant. She leans over and peers through the glass at a beautiful dark haired woman. Something about her seems familiar, but the entire situation is throwing Terra off.

'Who is she?

He runs his fingers over the glass and gazes lovingly at the woman. Terra's stomach churns at the disturbing scene in front of her. 'This is Maggie,' he replies in a tone that suggests she's just asked the most ridiculous question.

Terra looks back at the woman and it all suddenly clicks into place. Terra stares in horror at the stasis pod in the corner of the room. 'Maggie? That's *the* Maggie. Gryffin's mother?'

He looks at the case and thrusts his chest out. 'Amazing, isn't it.'

Terra can think of quite a few choice words, but amazing definitely isn't one of them. 'Oh my God. What have you done?'

'What was necessary. Don't get me wrong, I loved your mother. I still do to a certain extent. Maggie, however, is my first love. You cannot possibly imagine how deep that bond is.'

'But she's dead.'

Terra shrinks back at the look of venom her father shoots her way. 'That's why I need the prototype. The implant in her son's head can step in and control his brain. And that is exactly what Maggie needs.

It is just fortuitous that he is also Jensen's son.'

The truth takes a few seconds to register with Terra. 'You know Gryffin is Roman's son?'

'Of course I know. Why do you think he was chosen for the project?'

'Chosen? You specifically targeted him because of who fathered him?'

'Jensen, Maggie, and I were close friends.' His gaze lands on Gryffin and he smiles. Terra looks around and notices Gryffin is lying on his side, awake and staring at the two of them. Her father leaves his seat and panic takes a grip on Terra as he approaches the cell. Callum crouches down and tilts his head to the side. 'You look like Jensen. You've got a lot of your mother in you too.' He keeps looking at Gryffin as he stands up. 'I could handle Jensen being with Maggie for a short while. They were only together for a few months before his parents took offence and enrolled him in the Foundation fleet. I forgave him for taking her away from me. But when I saw the older boy — him,' he says, nodding at Gryffin, 'at a lunch years later, I knew the truth. Maggie and Jensen may have acted dumb and tried not to draw attention to him, but Daegan was clearly Jensen's son.'

Terra squeezes her eyes shut as she tries to absorb all the information. 'You're not making any sense. What does Gryffin have to do with you faking your death to become... this twisted thing?'

His face turns serious and his attention mover from Gryffin to Terra. 'Twisted?' He laughs. 'I'm a genius, Terra.' He kicks the bars of the cell. 'He's the proof. And, yes, I faked my death. I had no choice. Jensen had to learn you don't betray a friend. A few months before, Balfe had approached me about my recent studies on cybernetics. He needed someone to work full time on pioneering a new project. Initially I refused, but after seeing that boy, I reconsidered.'

Terra meets Gryffin's eyes. The uncontrolled anger she sees scares her. 'So, just like that, you turned your back on me and Mom. Did we not enter your mind at all?'

Callum's arms drop to his sides. 'Of course you did, Terra. Balfe ensured you would be looked after. After my death, your mother received enough credits to pay for the house and for the two of you to live in luxury for the rest of your lives.'

'But you still left us! We went to your funeral. Mourned you! For what? Just so you could get revenge. Do you have any idea how crazy that sounds?' The slap to her face stings. Terra forces the tears back and faces him again.

'I am your father. Show me some respect.'

Terra laughs harshly. 'You're kidding, right? You're not my father and any respect I had for you died when I found out the truth.'

'The truth?' he scoffs. 'What do you know about the truth? All you can focus on are the details. Do you have any idea what I've achieved here? What your precious cyborg represents?'

'I know you targeted a ten-year-old boy for revenge.'

'Yes, and that boy has become so much more thanks to me. When I pointed the Foundation in his direction, I had no idea what he would become. I thought he would die quickly and Jensen could spend his life mourning him. I could never have imagined he would survive. His resilience and defiance made him perfect for the project. He is who he is thanks to me.'

'You tortured and modified him. Look at him. Do you really think he'll thank you for that?'

Her father pauses, looks down at Gryffin and sighs. 'You really do have a soft spot for him. Strange, you judge me on my past actions yet disregard his.'

'You and the Foundation were controlling him. What happened is not his fault.'

Her father laughs again. 'Oh, Terra. You think you have everything figured out. I wasn't referring to what happened recently. I meant what he did in the lab to the other test subjects.'

'What do you mean?'

Callum crouches down in front of Gryffin again. The brisk shake of his head only seems to encourage her father. 'I left for a day to get supplies.'

Gryffin shakes his head with more conviction. Whatever protests he's desperate to voice, are muffled by the gag.

Callum continues, ignoring Gryffin. 'When I got back, the twenty-two other participants were dead. Your cyborg killed them all with his bare hands.'

A cold chill runs over her skin. 'You really think I'm going to believe you?' She may have said the words, but the doubt has wormed into her. Gryffin is staring intently at her and she realises what her father said is the truth. However it happened, whatever he did, Gryffin killed them.

He shrugs. 'It's the truth. I'm sure Thirty-Five will confirm if you ask him. He broke out of his restraints and killed each of them. I didn't force him to do that. He decided to murder them. Hate me all you want but I'm not to blame for everything he's done. I simply enhanced what was already there. Perhaps you should accept the fact that your precious cyborg is actually a cold blooded killer.'

'You really think you can take attention away from your deeds by taking a shot at someone else?'

Callum gestures behind him and Forty-Three descends the metal stairs. The cyborg opens the cell and pulls Gryffin's head up. He unfastens the buckles on the gag, then drops Gryffin's head back to the stone floor with a thud. Callum gestures for Terra to come closer. 'Ask him.'

Terra stares down at Gryffin and shakes her head. She doesn't want to know the truth.

'Ask him!' Her father shoves her closer. 'Ask him!'

'Did you... What happened?'

Gryffin licks his dry lips and refuses to meet her eyes. Forty-Three takes out his gun and points it at Terra's head. Gryffin instantly struggles to get out of his restraints. 'Get away from her!'

Callum shakes his head. 'Stop being rude and answer her question.'

Gryffin clenches his jaw and finally looks back at her. 'It's true. I killed them.'

Garvan smiles as the rat flies from his boot and lands with a splash in the tunnel ahead. He eyes another one as its black eyes examine him from the ledge running along the side of the drain. 'You want to go for a swim too?'

It has second thoughts and scampers in the opposite direction. 'Thought not.' He shudders and trudges through the ankle deep sludge that fills the bottom of the tunnel. He's not even going to hazard a guess at what he's walking through. All he knows is that it's slimy and stinks. Add that to the rats, and this place runs a close second to the Foundation prison as the worst place he's been. At least he's free here.

His torch light bounces off the wet walls. The numbers stamped into the metal walls are barely distinguishable, but he finally reaches Section 22. He moves his gun in an arc and stops when the light reflects off the removable panel in the roof. Garvan bids his companions a cheery goodbye and pulls himself up the metal rungs embedded in the wall. He reaches out and grabs onto a pipe running the length of the tunnel. Once he has a sure grip, he swings out and kicks the grate. The rusted metal moves under his assault but settles back in place. 'Need a bit more convincing, huh?' He readjusts his grip and kicks out again. This time the ancient lock gives way. He reaches out and pushes the grate out of the way.

Garvan cautiously peers over the edge, his gun moving with his eyes, but he's alone. He reaches up, takes a firm hold of the edge of the hole and hauls his weight through. Years spent training in the prison has certainly paid off. Architect Wade Garvan could barely do one press up without collapsing. Ex-inmate Garvan is a very different person. He replaces the cover on the hatch and moves through the water purification room. The loud hum of the machines drowns out his movements, but will also hide any personnel. He rounds a large water tank and stops. A man in a blue overall is working at a station just in front of him. Garvan checks the rest of the room. Seems this man is alone.

He slings his gun over his shoulder and unsheathes his knife. No need to get noisy unless he has to. Garvan creeps up to the unsuspecting man, grateful for the pumps echoing through the room. He grabs the man and clamps his hand over the man's mouth as he jams the knife into his neck and twists the blade. He holds the man until he stops struggling then pulls him over to one of the large tanks. Luckily, the man weighs next to nothing, so Garvan easily lifts him up and lets him slide under the surface. He rinses the blood off his gloves and pulls his gun off his shoulder.

Garvan opens the door a crack and peers through. The corridor outside is empty. He moves out of the pump room and turns left down a small side corridor. He's leaving slimy footprints in his wake but there's not a lot he can do about them. The priority is getting to the control room. Garvan gets to the next intersection and stops. Voices travel along the corridor he needs to go down. He slows his breathing down and concentrates on the voices. They're not moving. From what he can remember, the control room is just around the corner. The men must be near, if not outside it. There's no time to wait for them to get bored and leave. He's going to have to convince them to let him pass.

He checks his gun before moving closer to his targets.

∞

Forty-Three grabs Gryffin roughly around his upper arm and drags him to his feet. His ankles are unlocked but his wrists are left restrained. It doesn't matter. He can kill the two of them with his hands tied behind his back. Terra yelps in pain and he spins to face her. Two cyborgs have her by the arms. She struggles to get free, but they're too strong. Gryffin's heart races when he sees something in her father's hands. Forty-Three shoves him roughly in the chest and he loses his footing. Gryffin scrambles to get to his feet but it's too late. The collar is fixed around her neck. The Scientist adjusts it and nods approvingly. 'Now, Thirty-Five, I'm sure you know what this is and what it can do. I'm going to need you to behave. Do you understand?'

Terra meets his eyes. She's trying to hide the panic from her face, but he sees it. He's sure it's showing on his face too. He wore one of those things for nearly six years of his life. Seeing it around her neck turns his stomach. It's part of his life — not hers. If he has to take her father apart a piece at a time, he will give up the code to the collar. He'll make damn sure of that. Gryffin forces himself to nod. Callum smiles and gestures to the table. 'Up here please.'

Gryffin grits his teeth and does as he's told. If he fights back, Terra will die. He sits on the table and swings his legs up. The Scientist unlocks Gryffin's wrists. 'You must know the procedure by now. Lie down.'

Gryffin looks at Terra as he lies back. The Scientist notices and smiles compassionately at his daughter. 'I am truly sorry this has to happen. You understand though, don't you?'

'Understand? Of course I don't understand. Why do you have to hurt him again? Just leave him alone. Please... Dad.'

The Scientist looks up at Forty-Three. 'Lock Terra in the cell and bring Maggie in please.' He moves to the base of the bed and clicks the metal locks in place, then addresses Terra again. 'To save Maggie I need some of his implants.'

Terra slumps to the dirt floor and pulls her legs up. 'So you're not going to kill him?'

Gryffin knows the answer before the Scientist confirms. 'Removing the modifications will kill him. It's a necessary sacrifice. He's on borrowed time anyway, Terra.' He roughly pushes a connector into the side of Gryffin's ocular implant.

'What are you talking about?' Terra asks. 'Is this another one of your lies?'

'I wish that were the case. I have lost a lot of promising subjects to this flaw.'

'He's not flawed.'

Her father laughs. 'His implants are.' He finishes hooking Gryffin up then sits on the stool by the head of the table. 'You see, something in my modification is killing my subjects. Those who survive the initial procedure may last for a few weeks, maybe a little longer, but they all die.'

Terra points at Forty-Three. 'He didn't.'

'My dear associate is a different model. He doesn't have the control implant. That's the vital component. Without that, there is no way to override the brain's commands.'

'Is that what you did to Gryffin when he attacked Ultar?'

Her father nods. 'Exactly.' He takes off his glasses, holds them up to the light then polishes them on his shirt. He pats Gryffin on the shoulder. 'The prototype has...' he purses his lips and pauses for a moment. 'I estimate he has weeks left at the most.'

Terra shakes her head. 'Until what?'

'The strain of the control implant will kill him.' The Scientist addresses Gryffin without taking his eyes off Terra. 'You've been having headaches, Thirty-Five?'

Gryffin doesn't immediately answer so Forty-Three holds up a remote to the collar. 'Yes,' he grinds out. It feels like a hole has opened in his chest. He hates the she's being threatened to get to him. This is why he wanted her as far from him as possible. If her father is willing to hurt her to hurt him, a stranger will do a lot worse.

'For how long?'

'Always.'

The Scientist nods. 'Are they getting better, staying the same, or getting worse?'

'Worse.'

Her father holds his hands out to the side. 'There's the proof. He's had over two decades longer than any of the others. He should be grateful.'

'And you want to fit this to Maggie?' Terra asks. 'You want to kill her too?'

He shakes his head. 'Of course not. The answer only came to me a few days ago. What do all the subjects have in common?'

'You tortured them.'

He ignores her reply. 'They're all male. I haven't tried the control implant on any females.'

'So you're going to test it on her?' Terra asks.

'It will work. Not only is she female, but she is the prototype's mother. I'm convinced that is key. He survived and so will she.' He turns away from Terra and finally looks down at Gryffin. 'Your mother will be so proud of your sacrifice.'

Gryffin tests his restraints again. The monitors hooked to his implants beep loudly as his heart rate increases. The Scientist is immediately by his side. 'I need your implants in perfect working order. Control your heart rate or I will have no choice but to harm

Terra, and neither of us wants that.'

Gryffin concentrates and links with the control implant. His levels immediately return to normal. The Scientist nods and moves back to his screens. 'It will all be over soon, I promise.'

The Scientist looks up at the ceiling as the lights flicker twice before shutting down, plunging the room in to darkness.

∞

Garvan moves away from the lighting controls and pushes the body of a technician off the seat. The man slumps to the ground and lands on top of one of his colleagues. Garvan sits on the blood stained chair and reaches down to a pocket on the leg of his combats. He pulls out the charge and reaches under the table. The small metal box locks into place on the power supply for the shielding. As soon as the device locks on, the timer begins its countdown. Garvan leaps to his feet and races from the room.

He just rounds the corner when the shockwave hits, throwing him against the wall with bone rattling force. He falls to his knees and squeezes his eyes shut. His lungs struggle to pull in air and the newly acquired broken rib isn't helping. It seems like hours later when his screaming lungs finally get what they need again. He forces his eyes open and finds himself surrounded by black smoke. In spite of his situation he can't help but smile. That'll put a serious dent in any Foundation plans. He pushes to his feet and looks around to get his bearings. Fingers crossed, the fleet will be making its move on the facility. Technically, his part in the plan is over. He should move back to the shuttle and wait for backup.

Garvan faces the corridor that will lead him back the way he came, then turns to the one opposite. That one will take him to the centre of the facility. It's where Gryffin and Terra will be. He scratches his jaw as he considers his options. Staying in the corridor is out of the question. Security will be on the way. He looks back down the corridor. Gryffin will probably kill him, but he can't leave without them. It's just not in his nature. Besides, he owes Bray. The brothers may not be close, but they're still blood.

Decision made, he dusts himself off and moves towards the centre of the base.

∞

The fleet of Nomad, Hunters, Foundation, and Rogue ships comes to a stop just outside of weapons range of the Foundation ships on the surface. There's no visible sign of any defences. There will be protection, but it's well hidden. The Foundation clearly doesn't want to attract attention to their shiny new colony.

'Sir! The shields have just dropped.'

Roman breathes a sigh of relief and opens a link to the other ships. 'Garvan's done it. Everyone know what they're doing?'

One by one, the confirmations come through. 'Move in!' He lowers into his leather command chair and watches the fleet on the screen beside his seat. Each of the ships approaches the colony from different angles. 'Any resistance yet?'

'Not yet, sir,' a helmsman reports.

Roman is uneasy. The colony will be within range in less than a minute. The Foundation should have made an appearance by now. 'Anything from Gryffin?'

'No, sir.'

'Ready the guns.' As he finishes speaking the Foundation appear in front of the fleet. His breath catches in his throat when he sees clearly what they're facing. For every one of their ships, the Foundation has at least two fighters. He opens a link to Chayse. 'Status.'

'We're in position. I'll give you a shout once we're done here,' Chayse signs off and Roman stares out the window at the planet. 'I'll see you soon old friend,' he mutters under his breath. 'Time we had a heart-to-heart.'

∞

Chayse closes the link to *Infinity* and settles back in his new leather chair. He composes himself as he checks the comms to the Hunter ships with him, then gives the order. 'Attack!'

His fleet moves towards the Port. As soon as they get in range, Foundation fighters appear out of nowhere. He spent month patrolling the area and only saw a handful. The Foundation must have hidden them in the surrounding area just in case. 'How many?'

'Sixteen, sir. They were hidden in the debris field.'

Not a problem. It's been too long since *Nemesis* had a proper fight. She needs to stretch her legs. 'Let's thin them out.'

The large battleship moves closer to the swarm of angry fighters like she doesn't have a care in the world. One on one, the smaller ships pose no threat. In a group, it's a very different story. Her main guns target the smaller, more manoeuvrable fighters. One explodes in a burst of light, taking its not so lucky wingman with it.

'Two down, sir. The prison moon has taken down another one.'

Chayse smiles. Not a bad start. He links with the other ships. 'Keep them from attacking as a group.'

'Captain!' the tactical officer shouts. 'They've locked on to us!'

'Evasive moves! Now! Don't let them take the shot.'

Her powerful engines roar as they respond to the command. *Nemesis* tilts sharply to the side to evade the lock. 'Sir! We've got a lock.'

'Fire!'

Nemesis vibrates as her guns fire on the nearest Foundation ship. The missile hits and reduces the fighter to debris. Chayse dismisses the kill and targets the next one. There'll be time enough to celebrate when they're surrounded by nothing but Foundation debris.

'Sir, they've locked on!'

'Lose them!'

'It's too late they've fired!'

Nemesis jolts as the missile hits. The shock wave throws the helmsman and comms officer from their seats. 'Return fire!'

'Direct hit, sir.'

'Target the defences on the Port. We need to take it or we're all screwed.'

Nemesis veers around and comes at the Port from the back. The screen in front of him displays the data from his scan. The Hunters on the moon have taken care of another three fighters. Only four more Foundation left.

'We've lost the main engine. Auxiliary down to eighty-percent power. They're locking on again.'

Chayse curses. 'Get us out of their line of fine! Now!' *Nemesis* lurches to the side then rises to fly over the top of the Port. Chayse examines the information continuously being updated by the ships scans. The Port is a lot better armed than they thought. *Nemesis* jerks to the side again and alarms screech to life as she takes another hit.

'Sir, their powering up to fire again.'

Chayse leans back in his seat as *Nemesis* speeds away from the fight. He closes his eyes and curses himself. He's a failure. Chayse opens his eyes and one of the tattoos on his arm catches his attention. The small purple griffin glares up at him from next to his wristband. Gryffin wouldn't run from a fight. He'd keep fighting until he was dead.

Chayse suddenly leaps to his feet and goes over to the helm. 'Turn back to the Port and let them hit us.'

Gryffin's night vision kicks in as soon as the lights drop. Killing the lights was Garvan's idea. He wanted some way of letting Gryffin and Terra know he got to the control centre. He silently watches as the Scientist fumbles in the dim emergency lighting. He trips over his stool and yelps in pain. Like him, Forty-Three seems unaffected. The cyborg silently watches the other man struggle in the gloom.

'What's going on?'

Forty-Three shakes his head. 'I don't know.'

'Well find out!' Callum makes his way over to the pod and breathes a sigh of relief. 'It's just the lighting. Power is still getting to the pod.'

Forty-Three works on one of the consoles and nods in agreement. 'There's no response from the control room.'

'Well get down there and fix the lighting. How can I operate when I can't see?'

A large rumble works through the lab, throwing the two men off their feet. Gryffin smiles. Garvan's come through. At least Terra will be out of here soon.

The Scientist drags himself to his feet and wipes his hand on his forehead. He stares at the blood tainting his fingertips and frowns. It takes several seconds for him to finally snap out of his daze. He looks over at Gryffin and his face hardens. 'What did you do?'

When Gryffin doesn't reply the Scientist lifts a blade from the floor where it was thrown during the explosion. He thrusts it into Gryffin's leg, just below the metal. Gryffin doesn't give him the satisfaction of screaming as the pain sears through his already tender limb. Gryffin can hear Terra screaming at the Scientist to stop, but he ignores her and impales Gryffin's other leg with a second blade. This time Gryffin can't hold back a grunt of pain.

The Scientist sneers at him and turns away to search nosily through drawers to Gryffin's right. He finally reappears and switches on a torch, blinding Gryffin's sensitive eyes. He points it at Forty-Three. 'Get her out of here. I don't want them anywhere near each other until this is rectified.'

'No!' Gryffin hears the word escape his mouth before he can stop it.

The Scientist twists the knife in Gryffin's left leg. 'How many times over the years have I said this to you? You don't have a say. You have no rights. You belong to me.' He points his light at the console behind him. 'You're just like this console. Far more valuable, but my possession nonetheless.' He leans closer and Gryffin grimaces as rancid breath hits him. 'You will never touch her again. She is my daughter and you are a machine. The idea is ridiculous.' He snorts. 'I can't say I'm surprised Jensen let it carry on as long as it has. He always had a soft spot for Terra.' He steps back as Forty-Three pulls Terra up to the table. 'Say goodbye.'

Gryffin fights to get out, but the Scientist points to his own neck. 'Ah ah ah, remember the collar. Behave yourself.'

Gryffin forces his limbs to lie still, but the anger burns deep inside him. Terra grunts in pain as Forty-Three shoves her up the stairs to the walkway. Her eyes never leave his as she is dragged to her feet when she loses her footing. They reach the upper level and Terra trips again. When Forty-Three stops to pull her up, she slams her shoulder into his stomach. He grunts and doubles over. She brings her hands down against the back of his neck, driving him to his knees. Terra makes a move for his weapon, but he gets there first. He pulls her upright and jams the gun to her temple.

'Stop fighting, Terra.'

She looks down at her father and sneers, 'Not going to happen.' She nods at Gryffin. 'He's going to kill you and I'm going to do nothing to stop him.'

The Scientist shakes his head sadly. 'Get her out of here.'

Gryffin twists his head as much as he can to watch as Terra is dragged from the room.

∞

'Anything yet?'

The reports all confirm Bray's worst fears. Nothing from the surface. The cloaks lowered, then nothing. No communications. He grips the railing and pushes back against the metal. He should be down there with Gryffin. He's worried about Terra even though everyone keeps telling him Gryffin would die before he lets anything happen to her. Not incredibly encouraging considering the Scientist probably has him and is more than likely cutting him open.

Sayber looks in his direction. 'Gryffin will get her out. You know what he's like. Damn fool won't quit — no matter what.' Sayber curses as *Perses* is hit. 'Quinn, stop letting them fire on us!'

Quinn redirects *Perses* and the large ship veers to the side and returns fire. The two Foundation fighters skim along *Perses'* hull, peppering the large vessel with fire as they pass. The helmsman puts the ship in a dive, leaving the fighters facing *Styx*. The smaller Nomad ship takes out both fighters before they can react to its presence. 'Cheers, Vance. Guess we make a good team.'

'For now.'

Sayber laughs and cuts the link before he turns back to Bray. 'You're putting a dampener on a perfectly good fight. Get out of here before you ruin the fun for everyone.'

'What? I'm not leaving.'

Sayber turns him around and points him towards the door. 'Yes you are. Go to the surface. You're no use to me if your mind is down there and not on the command deck.'

Sayber's right. His mind isn't in the game right now.

Sayber pushes him towards the door. 'Would you just get out of here. I've got stuff to do.' Bray smirks and nods. Sayber calls to him as he gets to the door. 'Just don't come complaining to me if you get blown up, Commander.'

'Deal. Thanks.'

Sayber shakes his head. 'I'm sending you out into a battle in little more than a tin can. Nothing to thank me for.' Sayber dismisses him by shouting orders at the command crew. Bray races from the deck. He calls down to the cargo bay, ordering a transport be ready for him. He's thinking with his heart right now, but there's not a lot he can do about it. Even with everything that's happened, he still loves Terra, and, as much as he wants to deny it, Gryffin is his brother. It'll take a miracle to have anything resembling a normal relationship with him, but they're blood. He owes it to his mother to at least try to get him back in one piece.

His boots pound on the metal gantry as he runs through the lower deck. He bursts through the door and gestures at a Hunter working in the control booth. 'Open the cargo doors.'

Bray climbs up the ramp, shuts the door behind him and locks the harness around his body. He starts the ignition process and contacts the command deck. 'Heading out now, sir. Try not to blow me up.'

Sayber chuckles. 'Not promising anything. Anyway, you've got yourself an escort.'

Bray powers up the engines. 'Escort?'

'I sent word out that you're heading down. The Rogue ship will cover you.' Bray hears Sayber shout as the ship is rocked by another direct hit. 'Bray, if you're going, go now.'

Bray shuts down the comms with the command deck and turns the ship around. He clears the bay and smiles as he sees his escort waiting for him. Rua's ship, *Lir*, moves closer and her voice comes over his comms. 'Death wish, Hunter?'

'I guess you could say that. Thanks for the back up.'

'I owe you a rematch. It must be a reputation killer to lose hand-to-hand combat with a woman.'

Bray grimaces and rubs his still sore ribs. The Rogue captain proved to be a competent fighter and had him on his back on the mat within a few seconds. Even though it was embarrassing, he enjoyed training with her. 'Let me just get down there first.'

She laughs and closes the channel. *Lir* spins around and fires on a Foundation fighter that gets too close to Bray. *Lir* may be smaller than *Perses*, but the fierce looking ship is as lethal as her captain. By the look of the damage to her hull, the ship's seen more than her fair share of combat. The metal on her hull is mismatched, dented, and buckled.

The transport clears *Perses'* transport bay and bursts into the fire fight. It ducks around the side of *Perses* and towards the surface. An enormous Foundation ship appears from behind a neighbouring moon and moves towards the surface. 'What is that?'

'Whatever it is, it's Foundation,' Sayber replies. 'Imagine how much that beast would have cost. Colonies are struggling and they stuff that monster in our face.'

'That's the Foundation Council's ship, *Alpha*,' Roman says.

Bray snorts. 'Please tell me the pompous idiots didn't call that ship *Alpha*.'

'That's the Council for you,' Roman says. 'They're full of self-importance. She usually never leaves Earth's orbit. The Council must be here. That's unsettling. If the Council are here, it means they're involved. I'd hoped it was just a corrupt group of admirals we were clearing up after. Not the Council as a whole.'

Bray doesn't really care who he's fighting — Council or admirals. They're all Foundation so they're all targets as far as he's concerned. 'You know her capabilities?'

'Not much. She's a carrier, not a battleship. She wasn't built for combat. That may have all changed since we left. Don't underestimate her.'

'Got it.' The ship makes *Infinity* look like a large shuttle. *Alpha* is impressive. Unfortunately, she's also in their way. 'We should try to take her.'

'Not right now, Bray. She's the biggest, most technologically advanced ship in the group. There isn't a hope of taking her without massive losses.'

Bray doesn't reply. Roman knows best when it comes to the Foundation, but Bray likes a challenge. *Alpha* will be taken at some point — he'll make sure of it.

He moves the transport away from the safety of *Perses* and, ignoring the battle going on around him, directs it towards the surface. Rua sticks close to him. *Lir* twists and dodges quicker and more aggressively than any ship he's seen before. Alarms screech to life. He curses as the system confirms a Foundation fighter has a direct lock on him. He opens the link to *Lir*, but the ship is already reacting. Her bow ploughs straight through the middle of the fighter. The large pointed barb protruding from the front of *Lir*, easily punctures the fighter. The barb retracts, pushing the fighter off the ship, and then extends again.

Bray whistles. 'Hey, thanks. Remind me ever to get in the way of that.'

'My own invention,' Rua says. 'Pick up the pace, Hunter.'

Bray increases power to the engines and speeds towards the surface. Luck is on his side. The larger vessels are more focused on each other than a tiny shuttle. Rua's ship continues to run interference with any ships that gets too close. Within a few minutes, he reaches the planet.

Bray opens a channel. 'Thanks for the escort.'

'No problem,' Rua responds. 'Good luck.'

Bray speeds away from his escort and accelerates towards the surface. Bringing up a map of the colony, he guides the ship towards the large building about a mile outside the main settlement

∞

Terra stands on the balcony and looks out over the new colony. It's like a scaled down version of the Foundation capital on Earth. The roads and paths are dug in perfect lines, but have yet to be paved. The white, boxed housing units look identical to every other one on the colony. Some have two or three linked to make larger units. They must be for important colonists.

She turns away and looks back into the stark room. Everything is white — white walls, white floor, white furniture. She wanders back into the room and drops down on the first chair she sees. The wall panel opposite her is still sitting on the ground. She couldn't find anything to help. The room is isolated. There's no way to check what's going on in the rest of the building.

Terra gets to her feet again and wraps her arms around her chest as she paces. The gut wrenching worry is getting worse by the second. What was she thinking bringing Gryffin here? She should have stood up to his suggestion. Should have fought him. All she had to do was leave him in the cell and come alone. She could still have smuggled Garvan in. Everything could have worked out the same without having to give him back to her father.

Her stomach threatens to empty again so she takes deep breaths to steady herself. He's not her father — not anymore. The man she knew and loved did die years ago. Whoever the man in the lab is, it's not him. She wants nothing to do with him or his twisted plans. She briskly rubs her arms, trying to get some warmth back into them. Seeing Maggie in the lab has truly shocked her. The only small glimmer of consolation is that she's not aware of anything that's happening. Terra got a good look at the display on the pod. The woman is brain dead. The pod is just keeping her body alive and nothing more. She may not know a lot about the implants and how they work, but she seriously doubts anything can be done to bring Maggie back.

A large engine roars outside the window, bringing her out of her disturbed thoughts. She hurries to the balcony and looks outside. A large Foundation ship uncloaks beyond the settlement. She squints as a large flood light reflects off the highly polished hull. As she watches, men are pushed and shoved down the loading ramp by half a dozen cyborgs. Their red glowing eyes visible even from this distance. The restrained men are led into one of the larger houses at the end of the street. Her stomach churns as the truth hits her. They're the latest test subjects for her father.

Her attention moves back to the ship. Something is familiar about it. The transport beside it moves out of the way and she sees the name stamped on the hull. *Alpha*. She frowns. It doesn't make sense? *Alpha* is the Council's ship. If she's here that means someone from the Council is here. She knew the Foundation was involved, but never thought the actual Council had a hand in it.

They're in a lot of trouble if the corruption goes straight to the top.

Infinity comes in to land at the end of the line of houses. Roman leads the teams off the ship and they hurry away as Infinity rises from the ground and re-joins the battle above them. The teams take shelter behind two of the houses until the ship lifts off. Roman takes his ten-man team around to the other side of the settlement. They hurry around the side of the town towards the control building. Their night vision goggles pick up the outline of the path weaving through the colony. The rest of the surface is in darkness, the glow of weak emergency lighting can be seen above the door and in some of the windows.

He contacts Garvan on his comms. 'Are you back at the transport?'

'Afraid not,' Garvan replies. 'I couldn't leave them.'

Roman can't help but smile. 'Where are you?'

'On the bottom level, Basement Two. From what I can see, it's the main lab. Terra's not here though.'

'I got her signal.'

Roman frowns. 'Bray? What are you doing here?'

'I'm a control freak. Had to be here myself. You get Gryffin, my mother, and the Scientist, I'll get her.'

Roman pauses. He didn't want Bray anywhere near the place in case they couldn't get Maggie. 'Very well. Garvan, I'm on my way. Stay put until I get there.'

He checks the map on his unit and points in the direction they need to go. They clear the ground and reach the main building. He leaves some of the men on guard and the rest approach the building. The guard at the door looks in their direction, his glowing red eye searching the undergrowth. Roman nods and the team to his right moves in. As soon as the cyborg turns in their direction, Roman shoots him in the side of the head. They hurry to the door. Two of his team drag the body around the corner while another deals with the door. The officer attaches the detonation device and they hurry around the corner. The small explosion takes care of the control pad and the doors silently open.

Roman's night-vision goggles bathe the entrance lobby in an eerie green glow. He takes out his unit and checks for a signal from Terra's Foundation tracker implant. The signal flashes on the screen, three floors above them. He nods to one of the teams. 'Go help Commander Bray and Commander Rush. Level Three. If you meet any cyborgs, shoot to kill. Team Two, to the first basement level. Clear it out.' No one argues with his orders and moves to their targets leaving him standing alone in the lobby. It's no secret he has his own target to go after. He's not going to leave this building until he's had a chat with his old friend.

Roman walks through the lobby. Shrink wrapped leather chairs sit along one wall facing a large marble table. A shrink wrapped drink dispenser fills the alcove behind the chairs. A large artist impression of the finished facility covers the wall facing the chairs. It looks sterile and impersonal. A little bit of Foundation Earth in the savage Outer Sector. Roman shakes his head and turns away. It looks like the

Council invested a vast amount of credits in this project.

He walks past a wall with four elevators, through an office space and out into the service corridor. He dismisses the signal from his team's transmitters and searches for Garvan's signal. Roman quickly memorises the route and stuffs the unit into his pocket. He silently moves through the darkness to the service stairs and cracks the door open. He waits and listens, but the only sound he hears is from his own racing heart. Roman takes a cautious step out of the doorway and scans the stairwell above and below him. Still nothing, so he descends into the dark.

∞

Terra releases the breath she was holding when warm hazel eyes meets hers. 'Bray!'

He races over to her, hugs her tightly then pulls back to examine her. 'You okay?'

She nods and then remembers the collar. 'Well apart from this.' She pulls down the neck of her shirt and Bray curses.

'Please tell me that's not like the one Gryffin had?'

'One of the cyborgs, Forty-Three, has the remote.'

Bray runs a hand through his hair and turns away. 'Great.' He activates the mic behind his ear. 'This is Bray. I have Terra. We're on our way out.'

She shakes her head. 'No way, Bray. Not without Gryffin.'

'Yes, we're leaving. Roman and Garvan will get him out. He'll be fine.'

She pulls out of his grip. 'I can't leave. We need to get the remote for the collar.'

He takes her arms in his hands and bends down to look in her eyes. 'I'll get the remote. I promise. But you need to get out of here.'

'And what if it is set to blow if I leave the building?'

He sighs and looks up at the ceiling. 'Fine. But you stick to me.'

She nods and holds out her hand. 'I'll need a gun.'

∞

Nemesis' auxiliary engines slowly turn her to face the Port again. The Nomad at the helm is still not fully confident with this great plan and Chayse can't blame him. There's not a lot else they can do. *Nemesis* is in serious trouble. With no main engines, she doesn't have the power or the manoeuvrability to dodge the hits coming her way. Shields are down to twenty percent and he's out of options. The hits are coming too fast, giving them no time to lock on and target their own defence.

Chayse readies himself as they near the Port.

'They've locked on again, sir.'

'Remain on current course.' Chayse sits back and braces for the impact. Three seconds later, *Nemesis* shudders. 'Now!' Chayse shouts. The engines and stabilisers shut down. *Nemesis* drifts towards the Port, appearing to anyone watching, that she's dead in the water. Chayse curses to himself as they approach the Port and drift closer to her guns. The defences are automated. Fingers crossed they'll scan *Nemesis*, see she's not a threat, and stop firing. It's a long shot, but he's quickly learning that being captain means taking chances and hoping that everything pays off. This is one of those times.'

'We're within range.'

Chayse stands up and walks to the railing at the edge of the deck. 'Any weapons lock on us?'

'Nothing.'

'Not yet. We're only going to get one shot. How many of the guns are within range?'

'All but four.'

'Reroute everything to our guns and auxiliary engines.' Chayse looks at the scan data in front of him. Three left. That should be enough. 'Fire!' Chayse commands.

Nemesis' guns swing into position, each one targeting one of the defences on the outer shell of the Port. As one, they attack, driving their missiles into the surface of the portal. His comms screeches to life as reports come in from the prison. The Foundation have suddenly realised what's happening and turned any available fighters to the Port, but it's too late. Fifteen seconds after she fired her first round, the fight is over. The Hunters protecting the moons intercept the Foundation fighters, taking out all of them before they can come anywhere near the heavily wounded *Nemesis*.

'Release the beacons. I want this area locked down,' Chayse orders. The large defence beacons launch from *Nemesis* and take up orbit around the Port. 'Activate.'

'Confirmed,' the helmsman reports.

'I want a full damage report ASAP.' Chayse sits back in his chair, takes a deep, calming breath and smiles.

∞

Roman finally reaches the dark underbelly of the facility. While the upper levels smelled of fresh paint and new flooring, this level is a far cry from that. The one word that springs to mind is death. He's in the right place.

He grips his gun tightly and moves further along the poorly lit corridor. He cautiously approaches the metal door at the end and comes face to face with a large gun. He freezes, then smiles. 'I surrender.'

Garvan lowers his gun. 'Don't sneak up on me like that, Roman.'

'Didn't think you'd be the jumpy sort.'

Garvan shudders. 'It's this place. Gives me the creeps. Everything okay up top?'

'We're holding our own. I've sent a team to Bray and Terra. He nods to the door. 'Is Callum in there?'

Garvan nods. 'Gryffin too. Only one small problem, the place is full of cyborgs.'

Roman curses. 'How many are we talking?'

'Dozens.' He points to the door and Roman creeps forward to take a look. The cyborgs Garvan mentioned appear to be on stand-by. A single torch beam cuts through the dark. The light jumps frantically along the walls and ceiling of the cavern.

'Have you seen them move?'

Garvan shakes his head. 'Not yet.'

Roman checks his gun. 'I'm going to get Gryffin out.'

Garvan nods. 'I'm with you.'

'You don't have—'

'I know,' Garvan interrupts. 'You distract your mate. I'll see to Gryffin.'

Roman doesn't argue. Any help is a good thing. Roman pulls open the old metal door open, grateful for its well-oiled hinges. He takes the lead, leaving Garvan to follow. Roman carefully steps out onto the walkway and descends into the cavern. Someone mutters in the room below the walkway. The voice of his former friend cuts through any uncertainty he might have previously felt. He clears the bottom few steps and enters the small room.

'About time,' Callum shouts. 'What happened to the lights?'

'So, you really are alive.'

Callum spins and stares at him. 'Jensen?' His face slowly breaks into a smile and he bows. 'You look older, dear friend.'

The light from the banks of monitors helps to show him everything he needs. He looks over Callum's shoulder and holds back a growl when he sees Gryffin. His son is strapped to a table. His chest is rising and falling rapidly as he looks at Roman. A large blade is sticking out of each leg and blood glistens on the table. Blood drips from the tool in Callum's hand. He moves closer and clenches his teeth when he sees a piece of Gryffin's ocular implant hanging off the side of his face. He forces his eyes away from the mutilation. 'Do you really want me to tell you how you look?

Callum nods and walks closer to him. Roman moves to the right of the room and Callum mirrors his movements, bringing him around so his back is facing Gryffin. 'We have both adapted to our new roles. I hear your career has come to a spectacular ending. Traitor, siding with the enemy, stealing a ship, conspiring against the Foundation — the list goes on and on. I'm sure your folks are proud.'

'I chose the right side. They'll understand.'

'Shame you can never talk to them and explain your side. They'll die thinking their perfect son betrayed them and everything they believe in. How can you sleep at night?'

'I can ask you the same thing. I went to your funeral. I mourned the loss of my best friend. Terra said goodbye to her father. What possessed you to throw your life away... for this?' He looks around the dank room. 'You're hiding in the shadows, experimenting on living people, for what? Money? Power? What could the Foundation possibly be giving you that could entice you into this life.'

'You wouldn't understand,' he sneers.

'Maggie.'

Callum rushes to Roman and shoves him back against the units. 'Don't you dare say her name!'

'Where is she, Callum?'

A slight flicker of his eyes tells Roman more than Callum wanted him to know. He easily pushes his friend away and walks around the far side of the equipment into the small alcove at the side of the room. His feet lock to the floor when he sees her in the stasis pod. She looks the exact same as she did when he last saw her. The love he always carries for her surges to the surface and fires the rage burning inside him. 'You sick bastard,' Roman begins as he launches at Callum. He grabs the smaller man by the front of his coat and pushes back over the bank of consoles. They crash to the ground with Roman still holding on to Callum. 'What have you done to her?'

Callum tries to push Roman away, but years spent hiding in labs has weakened him. 'I'm trying to save her.'

'She's dead. You can't save her.'

'If I can take the implant from the prototype, I can fit it to her and bring her back.'

Roman stares in horror at Callum. The man he spent most of his childhood with, grew up with, is gone. The twisted remains in front of him may look similar, but there's nothing to compare to his friend. 'Let her go, Callum. She wouldn't have wanted this.'

'You still think you know what's best for her, even after all this time!'

Roman frowns and pushes back a little. 'What are you talking about?'

'You and your obsession with Maggie. You told me you only dated for a few months. You promised that nothing happened between you.'

Roman is well and truly confused. 'And?

'You forgot to mention him!'

Roman shakes his head, not understanding what Callum is saying.

Callum rolls his eyes. 'Your son, Gryffin. Daegan!' he spits in response.

Roman's stomach lurches. He assumed no one in the Foundation knew about his relationship to Gryffin. He'd made sure to erase the results of the DNA test and the only existing records are on the system on Ultar. Nothing the Foundation has access to.

Callum laughs loudly. 'If you could see your face right now. Yes, Jensen, your big secret is out.'

'How long—'

'Remember when we were invited to the beach for the weekend with Maggie and Dean?'

'Yes.'

'Her two boys came too. The eldest, Daegan, was about nine and the younger one was about four or five. As soon as I saw the older boy I knew.'

Roman swallows deeply. 'Knew what?'

'That you were his father. I knew the second I saw him that you had lied to me. You swore nothing happened yet here was the proof stating otherwise. You must have been laughing behind my back for years. Poor naive Callum. He'll never figure out the truth.'

'I didn't—'

'But I did figure it out!' Callum shouts. 'It's your fault she only saw me as a friend. It's your fault she never wanted to date me.'

'She didn't want to ruin your friendship. It was too important to her, you know that.'

'I didn't want friendship,' he spits in reply. 'I wanted her. After I saw your son, I knew my old life was over. Admiral Balfe had approached me months before about using my engineering skills in a new project. I initially declined, but after that weekend on the beach I decided things had to change. So, I decided to put you back in your place. I had been working behind the scenes developing cybernetics. My work had attracted his attention, so I met with him. As soon as he described the project I knew I wanted to be part of it, needed to be part of it.'

'You're telling me that you knew what was going to happen? You knew what they would do to the children? You really are a monster.'

'Perhaps, but what I have accomplished is more than I ever imagined. And I caused you pain while doing it.'

He's struggling to keep up with what Callum is telling him. 'How?'

Callum frowns. 'By using your son, of course.'

Roman lets go of his friend and takes a step back. His heartbeat crashes loudly in his ears. 'Callum, what did you do?'

'Your precious son was handpicked by me. You lied to me, deceived me for years, so I took your son from you.'

Gryffin connects fully with the control implant, takes a deep breath and pulls his metal arm back as hard as he can. Nothing happens. He closes his eyes and resists the urge to curse out loud. Footsteps hurry towards him and he tenses, not having a clue what to expect. He frowns as Garvan's face appears above him. 'Ready to get out of here, Captain?'

'You were meant to go back to the transport.'

Garvan nods. 'You know, you're right. I'll go back there now.' He disappears from view.

'Wait!' Gryffin hisses.

Garvan reappears and smiles. 'Thought not. Now, how do I unlock these?'

'Under the table. There's a separate power unit for the restraints.'

Garvan nods then ducks under the table. Several seconds later, the locks click open. Garvan pops back up and looks towards the room where Roman and Callum are still arguing. 'What about your eyepiece?'

Gryffin ignores him and pushes onto his elbows. He glares at the two blades sticking out of his legs. He sits up, takes one in each hand, and clenches his jaw. Gryffin grinds his teeth together as the searing pain explodes from each leg as he withdraws the blades.

Garvan grabs a roll of bandage from an upturned drawer on the floor then stands beside Gryffin's legs. 'Bend your legs.'

Gryffin pulls his legs up and Garvan hurriedly wraps each leg to stop the bleeding. 'Where's Terra?' Gryffin asks.

Garvan quickly secures the dressing. 'On an upper level. Bray has her.'

'He get the collar off?'

Garvan shakes his head. 'Still looking for the cyborg.'

'Help them.'

Garvan crosses his arms as he looks down at him. 'How exactly are you going to go anywhere with those legs?'

Gryffin swings off the table. 'I'll be fine. She's the one in trouble at the moment. The only way to disarm it is with the code or the remote. It could blow if she steps outside the building.'

'Okay. I'll meet up with Bray. What about you? Can you see okay?'

'The other eye still works.' He looks up the stairs that leads to Terra. He wants to go after her, but he can't walk away from this. The need to kill her father is too hard to ignore. He makes a fist and winces as the power travels down his arm. 'I have something to do first.'

∞

Roman's stomach lurches as Callum says the words. 'You deliberately took my son?'

Callum's face instantly brightens at his reaction. 'That's right. How does it feel knowing that your actions only served to seal your son's place here? It's funny — I pointed him out to the Foundation as a target, but never expected him to be so useful. I merely used him to test the implants before they were fitted to the actual viable subjects. No anaesthetic, no aftercare, nothing to help him in any way, yet he survived and thrived. I did everything I could to make him suffer and all he did was get back up and take more. I put that down to Maggie's blood in him — not yours.'

Roman stares in horror at the stranger in front of him. 'I didn't know he was my son until last year.'

Callum laughs nervously and shakes his head. 'Nice try, friend.'

Roman looks him straight in the eye. 'Maggie kept it to herself.' Even though the words taste foul as he says them, he continues. 'All that effort to hurt me was wasted. As far as I was concerned, a friend's son had disappeared. I was upset for her, but it meant nothing more than that.'

Callum's face turns dark. 'Lies!'

Roman shakes his head. 'Do you honestly think I'd just sit back and do nothing if I knew my son was missing? You know full well I'd have ripped the Sector apart looking for him. I wouldn't have stopped until I found him and the people responsible for taking him. I just never imagined it would be you.'

Callum looks away and shakes his head. 'Why didn't she tell me the truth?' he mutters under his breath. He ignores the gun pointed at him and hurries over to Maggie. 'Why didn't you tell me while there was still time?'

Roman roughly shoves Callum back. 'Time for what?' Callum continues to ignore him. 'Time for what!' Still getting no response, Roman pushes his gun tightly to Callum's forehead. 'What did you do?'

'She found out the truth.'

'Callum!'

'She found out I was still alive. Bumped into me at a market on one of the border worlds.' He laughs. 'What are the odds? She was with Dean, her husband. They were looking for your son. She was suspicious straight away. Dean tried to call for security so I had to stop him. Maggie went crazy when I killed him. I didn't mean to squeeze her neck as hard as I did. I didn't mean to hurt her. You have to believe me.'

Any response Roman was trying to formulate disappears as Gryffin suddenly appears out of the shadows

∞

Gryffin steps up to the Scientist and shoves his metal fist against the side of his head. 'Time's up, Roman.' The electricity travels down his arm, stopping at Gryffin's wrist.

'I just need a few more minutes.'

'He's told you all he's going to. He targeted me, killed the woman, and lost his damn mind. Nothing else to explain.'

'He can tell me why.'

Gryffin swipes his fist against the Scientist's head. The man grunts and drops to his knees. Blood oozes from between his fingers as he presses his hand to his head. 'We're out of time.'

Gryffin walks over to the pod and looks down at... his mother. Part of him still expects some jolt of recognition, but it's just like every other time he's seen her. There's nothing there. 'Get her out of here.'

Roman looks at his former friend. The self-assuredness that was plastered over Callum's face has all but vanished. In the space of a few seconds, Gryffin has reduced him to a pathetic mess huddling on the floor. 'What about him?'

Gryffin glances down at him. 'I'll take care of him.'

Roman looks like he wants to argue, but he doesn't. He unhooks the cables from the pod and wheels Maggie towards the door.

'Don't leave me with him, Jensen!'

Gryffin puts his boot on the Scientist's chest, forcing him to the ground. Roman looks down at the Scientist and shakes his head. 'Goodbye, Callum.' Roman looks away and wheels Maggie from the room.

As soon as the pod turns the corner, Callum screams, 'Bring her back!'

Gryffin kicks him in the side. The Scientist screams again as a few ribs break. Gryffin grabs a handful of clothes and lifts the scrawny man off the floor. The Scientist puts up a fight, but Gryffin doesn't pay him any attention. One of the cyborgs lining the room decides to step in. Gryffin slams the cyborg back against the wall and his lifeless body slumps to the ground. The little display convinces the rest to keep out of his way. The cyborgs may have something built in to stop them from hurting their creator. That doesn't mean any of them will put their life at risk to help him. You don't earn loyalty by torturing people.

They watch in silence as Gryffin slams the Scientist onto the operating table. The man's feeble struggles are no match for him and his raging anger. He fastens him to the table and takes a step back. Gryffin spent most of his life terrified of the Scientist. He's the first person he really remembers and it isn't the best memory. The pleasure this man took from his pain, the look of joy plastered to his face as he tried new implants on his test subjects — that's the bit that he will never get his head around. The procedures were bad enough without him actually enjoying it.

Gryffin looks around the theatre. Tables of instruments line the walls. Each one is covered in blood — some of them still fresh. He's experienced the pain most of the instruments cause, but there's two in particular that he hates more than the others. He starts the drill and his stomach rolls as the sound brings back sickening memories. He turns off the drill and picks up the bone saw. The rusted blade looks old enough to be the one that removed his hand. The drill and the saw were the first things used on him. The first steps towards becoming the 'new and improved' model. The brand was put on his shoulder while he was unconscious so he had no memory of that. The saw and drill are another matter.

He turns to face his tormentor and places the saw on the man's chest. A large wet stain darkens the front of the Scientist's trousers.

'Please. What are you doing? I made you! You can't hurt me!'

Gryffin places the drill beside the man's head and turns it on. He swallows deeply as the sound echoes in the cavern. 'I overrode that programming. I'm going to need the code to her collar.'

The Scientist's eyes dart in his head as he begins to accept the reality he's faced with. 'Don't do this. Terra! She'll hate you if you kill me!'

Gryffin leans over. 'I think she'll hate you more. Code.'

'I don't have it! Really!'

Gryffin squeezes the Scientist's scrawny arm in his metal hand until it breaks. He screams in pain as Gryffin keep pressure on the broken limb. 'Where's Forty-Three? How can I track him?'

Tears run down the Scientist's face as he battles with the pain. 'I don't know. He should have come back by now. You love, Terra, right?'

Gryffin gets right in the Scientist's face. He wants to make sure his face is the last one the man sees. 'This isn't about her. This is about you and me.'

'Please don't!'

'I begged you to stop, but you still drilled into my head. You still cut off my hand.' Gryffin stands back and holds his arms out to the side. 'You turned me into this while I begged you to stop. You preferred it that way.'

'I can undo my work!'

Gryffin snorts. 'No, you can't. I'm dying — you and I both know that.'

'I can help give you more time! I'll do whatever you want!'

Gryffin places the saw against the Scientist's restrained wrist and moves it through the soft flesh. 'Beg me to stop.'

As one, the other cyborg occupants of the room smile as the Scientist screams.

∞

Gryffin slowly inches along the corridor. The Scientist's blood stains his hands. He can't fully believe that part of his life is over. That man will never hurt anyone else, but that knowledge gives him little comfort. He still managed to affect too many lives. About a dozen or so of those lives are destroying all the computers and equipment in the lab.

After he killed the Scientist, the group of cyborgs stood to attention in front of him. Apart from being creepy as hell, it was recognition he didn't want. There's enough for him to work through without adding commanding those men to his list. To get their attention away from him, he ordered them to destroy everything then wait at the rendezvous point. He feels responsible for what happened to them. If he didn't survive all those years ago, they would still be in prison instead of walking around with chunks of metal on them.

Reports from the various teams on the surface buzz in the earpiece Garvan gave him. Gryffin smiles. The Port is theirs. It nearly cost them *Nemesis* but Chayse succeeded. Not that he doubted the young man would. Chayse is nearly as stubborn as he is.

'Gryffin.' Roman's voice sounds loudly in his ear. 'Where are you?'

'South access corridor, Section...' he looks up at the digits stamped into the metal above his head. He'd recognise those two numbers anywhere. 'Section 35.'

'Bray and Garvan are heading your way. Target should be approaching from Section 42. I'll send back up. Don't do anything stupid.'

Gryffin closes the channel. Their versions of stupid are miles apart. He continues down the corridor that extends a long way ahead of him. It's the longest corridor he's ever seen. He ignores each of the locked doors along its length. There's no time to check every room. The sound of hurried footsteps echoes down the empty corridor. He ducks behind a large electrical supply unit, biting back a curse as his legs protest about the position. He releases a little more of his control to the implant. If his legs give up, he's screwed.

Gradually, the silence in the corridor is disturbed by voices. He struggles to keep control when he sees Forty-Three with a man wearing the Foundation uniform. He fights against himself to stay where he is. His mechanical side wants to rip the two men to pieces, but he barely manages to keep it under control.

The small group disappears into the adjoining corridor. Gryffin uses the electrical supply unit to pull himself to his feet. He breaks cover and clears the distance as quietly as he can. He presses tightly against the wall and peers around the corner. They're just up ahead. Large steel doors seal the corridor, blocking them from entering the cargo bay. Sparks jumps from Gryffin's damaged robotic eye as he tries to zoom in on the keypad as Forty-Three enters a code. Before the doors open fully, Gryffin steps out and charges his arm. Forty-Three hears him before the other man. He spins around and pulls his weapon out. 'Hello, brother.'

Gryffin looks away from his brother to the other man. A wide sash crosses his body over his Foundation uniform. His top lip lifts off his teeth in something resembling a smile. 'Well, I presume you're the prototype.'

'Who the hell are you?'

'You may call me One. I am head of the Foundation Council.' He takes a step closer and Gryffin's skin crawls at the way the man is examining him. 'You are impressive.' He turns to speak to Forty-Three. 'His legs?'

'Minor damage. He wasn't behaving, sir.'

One nods. 'I see. You have a habit of not following direction, Thirty-Five. It is not a good quality.'

Gryffin wants to shoot the pompous Council member but his hand won't move. He concentrates but it's like something is blocking the order from his brain to his hand.

One takes another step and his creepy smile gets bigger. 'Having a bit of trouble?'

'What have you done?'

'You're programmed not to harm your creator.'

'I just killed him.'

One shakes his head. 'No, you see my fellow Council members and I are the actual brains behind... well, you. Balfe, Avoca, The Scientist, Rayde, they were all working for us. Indirectly of course. We can't have our names muddied by being directly involved in a project that would harm children. That would be damaging to our careers.'

Gryffin concentrates hard, but his hand ignores him.

'Stop fighting. You will only harm yourself.' He steps right up to Gryffin and looks up at him. 'We can't have anything happen to you just yet. We're not quite finished with you.' He pats Gryffin on the face and turns back to Forty-Three. 'Remote, please.'

Forty-Three passes the remote to him and One holds it up to Gryffin. 'Is this what you want?'

'Don't.'

One frowns. 'Are you telling me what to do? It doesn't work that way. I tell you and your brother here what to do. Forty-Three, would you please shoot him.'

Gryffin can't do anything except stand on the spot as Forty-Three lifts his gun and shoots Gryffin in the leg. He smiles as Gryffin roars in pain and crumples to the floor. 'You forget, I helped build you. I know your weaknesses, brother.'

Gryffin tries to get more power from the implant, but it's at its full capacity. He tries to put weight on his leg, but the damn thing won't support him.

One crouches down in front of him and smiles again. 'See you soon, okay?' He holds up the remote and mouths 'Boom' as he pushes the button to detonate.

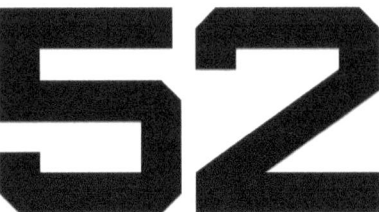

Bray covers Terra as a loud explosion ruptures out of the corridor up ahead. 'What was that?' she asks.

Bray shakes his head and activates his radio. 'Nothing. Whatever it was, it's screwing with the comms.' He takes her hand. 'Stay close.'

They approach the corner and Bray pushes her behind his back as someone steps out of the shadows. Bray recognises the build of the man. 'Garvan, that you?'

He steps out of the shadows. 'Well, hello. Any idea what that was?'

Bray shakes his head. Something doesn't feel right. He's got a sinking feeling in his stomach. They reach the corner and Bray runs his hand over a black burn mark on the wall. He spins around the corner with his gun raised and freezes. Gryffin is lying on the ground. Electricity is pulsing over his prone body. 'Shit.'

Terra and Garvan join him and Terra curses when she sees Gryffin. Garvan holds her back before she touches him. 'Gryffin!'

He slowly opens his eye and looks at her. 'You're okay?'

'Of course I am. What was that?'

The electricity abruptly dissipates. 'They detonated the collar. I thought you were dead. I released some power.'

Bray examines the collar. 'It's powered down. What happened?'

Gryffin rolls onto his back and screams in pain. Bray looks down at his brother's leg and grimaces. A strip of bloody metal is sticking out of his torn leathers. He is about to pull the metal out of his leg when Gryffin shouts at him to stop.

'That's a part of my leg. Must have snapped off when Forty-Three shot me. He's working with the Council.' Gryffin pauses and squeezes his eyes shut for several seconds.

Terra brushes sweaty hair from his face. 'Hey, it's okay.'

'It's not okay!' Gryffin opens his eye and looks at Bray. 'Forty-Three knows everything the Scientist does. If he's working for the Foundation they can keep producing cyborgs!' he shouts and beats his fist against the floor. 'I have to kill him.'

'You're not going anywhere except back to *Ares*.' Bray activates his comms and pulls off his jacket. '*Ares*, this is Bray. I need immediate evac. Gryffin's leg is... broken.'

'Five minutes,' Desyl replies.

'I'm not going anywhere until he's dead,' Gryffin says through clenched teeth.

'No choice, I'm afraid. I need to strap up your leg.'

'Will it work?' Terra asks.

Bray shakes his head. 'Only one way to find out.' His hand hovers over Gryffin's leg. 'Ready?'

Gryffin nods. Bray takes a deep breath then pushes the metal back against his leg so it lies flush. Gryffin roars in pain as Bray secures the metal against his leg. Once the makeshift bandage is tied, they lean him back against the wall. Gryffin holds out his hand. 'I need your gun.'

Bray shakes his head. 'Stop being ridiculous. Your leg is broken — seriously broken, your eye is a mess, and I don't even want to know what's under the two bandages on your legs. I'll get the cyborg while you go back to *Ares*.'

Gryffin shakes his head, but Bray forces his point when he gently prods Gryffin's leg with his finger. He smiles when Gryffin grinds out a curse. 'Do I need to do that again or will you stand down and let me get him?'

'This has to end.'

Bray nods. 'Trust me to do this. I'll make him suffer — you have my word.'

Instead of answering, Gryffin nods once.

Bray stands up and checks his gun. 'I'll come with you,' Garvan says. 'I still need to pay you back for saving my skin.'

Bray looks down at Terra. 'You good to stay with Gryffin?'

'Of course.'

Gryffin meets Bray's eyes. 'Sure you want to do this?'

Bray smirks and nudges Garvan. 'We've got this. Besides, it's not the first time a Hunter has to clean up after a Nomad.'

∞

Bray skids to a halt and melts against the wall. He gestures to Garvan and the man creeps closer. He points out the door towards *Alpha*. 'That's him.'

Garvan nods. 'Now what?'

Bray doesn't respond immediately. Forty-Three is marching towards the cargo hold of the enormous Foundation ship. Three cyborgs are loading boxes into the back. Bray recognises some of the units as the ones the Scientist had when he worked on the freighter. Seems Gryffin is right. They're taking the technology back to Earth. 'Well, how about we just walk out there and shoot until we're the only ones standing?'

Garvan shrugs. 'Simple, yet effective. After you?'

Bray nods and walks purposefully from the doorway. He takes down two of the cyborgs and Garvan takes care of the last one. Bray climbs up the loading ramp and puts a round in each of the units from the lab. Garvan fires over his shoulder and a cyborg falls off the railing above them. Their attacker lands with a loud crack as bones shatter on a stack of metal boxes. Bray weaves through the cargo, closely followed by Garvan. Bray holds up a hand. Footsteps move to his left, then stop. Bray readies his weapon and waits.

The ship smells new. No taint of fuel in the air, no smell of stale sweat from the crew. Unless of course Foundation crew don't sweat. Bray wouldn't put it past the Foundation to have a rule banning sweat. He steadies his breathing and listens for anything that will tell him where Forty-Three is hiding. 'Screw it,' he mutters. 'Forty-Three,' he shouts, his voice echoing across the vast cargo hold. 'I know you're hiding in here somewhere. You afraid of two little humans?'

Forty-Three replies with a deafening roar from his own weapon to their left. Bray and Garvan turn in unison as Forty-Three approaches from behind a transport.

'Step into the open,' Bray says. 'I've wasted enough ammunition on you. Do us both a favour and let me kill you quickly.'

Garvan takes a shot, but Forty-Three ducks for cover. Bray decides to take a leaf from the cyborgs book and drops behind a large metal crate with Garvan.

'Surrender!' Forty-Three commands.

Bray glances at Garvan. 'Fancy that?'

Garvan shakes his head. 'Not especially. How many you got left?'

'Three. You?'

'I'm out.'

Forty-Three sends three rounds towards them. Sparks fly off the metal box as the bullets hit a little too close for comfort. Bray leaps up and fires just before the cyborg retreats behind his shield. The man screams as Bray's last round penetrates his hand, removing all his fingers. Forty-Three drops the weapon and clutches his ruined hand to his chest.

Garvan and Bray step out and approach the man. Bray stops in front of him and smiles.

'What are you smiling about? You've got no rounds left.'

Bray shakes his head. 'You don't know anything about Hunters do you?' He steps right up to Forty-Three. 'We prefer to get up close and personal when we kill.' He cocks his arm back and swings at the man, catching him in the centre of his ocular implant. He is about to take a second hit when the ship shudders.

'What the blazes is that?' Garvan asks.

Bray groans. 'We're taking off.'

∞

Roman leaves Maggie in the capable hands of the medical staff and races up to the command deck. He relieves the officer in command and takes his place. Only four fighters remain and Rua is having fun taking care of them alone. Three Nomad and two Hunter vessels fell during the battle, but the Foundation suffered a much more catastrophic loss. The area around *Infinity* is scattered with the debris of dozens of fighters. He's disgusted at what the Foundation forced them to do.

'Sir, *Alpha* is leaving the surface.'

Roman turns to the view-screen and watches as the large cruiser lifts off the ground. 'Target her. I want all Foundation presence removed.'

Infinity turns her guns towards the large ship and Roman is about to give the order to fire when *Ares* contacts them. He opens the channel. 'What is it?'

'Bray and Garvan are on the ship!' Terra reports. 'They went after Forty-Three. Bray and Garvan went after him to kill him. I've just tracked Garvan's transponder to *Alpha*.'

'Okay, change of plan. Bring her down in one piece. Where's Gryffin?'

'Desyl is getting him to the command deck. We'll use *Ares*' tethers to secure *Alpha.*'

'Won't work,' Roman says. 'She's too big.'

'*Perses* will go too,' Sayber interjects.

Roman nods and looks out the front of *Infinity*. 'Very well. Go get them.' He closes the link to *Perses* before he talks to Terra again. 'Can you talk?'

'He's okay, sir,' Terra replies, reading his mind before he has a chance to ask the question. 'His leg is badly damaged. Milla may have to come up with a miracle repair.'

'That bad?'

'Yes, sir.' She takes a deep breath. 'I don't see what she can do for him.'

'Okay, just get Bray back first, then we'll worry about Gryffin's leg. I'll warn Milla.' He signs off and watch as *Ares* and *Perses* break away from the rest of the fleet.

∞

Gryffin drops heavily into his chair and straightens his leg. He ignores Desyl as his second in command cuts his leathers open to get a better look at the damage to his metal leg. Desyl's curse doesn't fill him with confidence. 'Just patch it up for now.'

Desyl shakes his head. 'It's way beyond being patched up, sir. The metal and the flesh have separated.'

'Just wrap a bandage around it.'

Whatever protests Desyl is about to make disappear under Gryffin's cold eyes. 'Yes, sir.'

Gryffin leans over the screen and hooks up to the system. He opens a channel to all the ships. 'This is Gryffin. We need to stop *Alpha*. Bray is on board so don't blow the damn thing up.' He shuts down the channel and concentrates on the screen. The air is filled with Nomad, Rogue and Foundation fighters, but through the chaos, *Alpha* is hard to miss. The large ship moves through the other fighters and turns towards the Port. 'Sayber, you got it?'

'We're on her tail. Just try to keep up.'

Gryffin doesn't bother responding. *Ares* matches *Perses'* speed through the debris as they both close in on the larger vessel. Gryffin grits his teeth as Desyl tightly wraps a bandage around his leg to keep it together. He can barely think straight through the pain.

Ares easily weaves through the smaller fighters gaining ground on *Alpha*. Desyl continues to poke and prod his leg. 'Just leave it.' His leg is gone. Nothing Desyl can do to help it.

As soon as *Ares* gets closer to the transport, the craft picks up speed. The larger vessel is faster than it should be. Desyl echoes his thoughts. 'Ship must be modified.'

The Foundation ship enters an asteroid field. The Nomad at the helm curses and slows the ship as he guides her into the field.

Gryffin beats his fist against the arm of his chair. 'Push her harder!'

'There's too many obstacles in the way. I can't manoeuvre her around the debris at top speed.'

He may not be able to, but Gryffin can. 'Get me to the engine room.'

Gryffin is grateful when Desyl doesn't argue. Desyl and Terra support his weight as he hops down the stairs. He clenches his jaw against the roaring fire that's consuming his leg. He'd remove his leg right now if he could.

They stumble as they enter engineering and Gryffin screams in pain as his knee hits the ground. Desyl wheels a chair over and they lift him into it. Terra pushes him to the directed console and Desyl rips the side of the computer drive off. He connects a cable from it to Gryffin's ocular implant.

'Sure about this, sir?'

Gryffin ignores the question and merges with *Ares*. Once linked with the ship, he takes control of the helm before opening a channel with the command deck. 'I've got the helm. Keep her speed at its limit.'

Gryffin blocks out all the other sounds around him and

concentrates on the signal from the Foundation ship speeding away with his brother. He just hopes *Ares* survives what he's going to ask of her. The engines roar as he forces as much power as he can into them.

'Sir, take it easy. That's too much power for you! Break the link, sir!'

'No. Load all the tethers.'

Desyl curses, but does as ordered. 'Sir, Sayber wants to know what you're doing.'

'Just tell him to watch our back,' Terra says.

The ship vibrates around them as he pushes her engines. A searing pain builds in his ocular implant, but he ignores it. He doesn't care if his whole damn implant melts. Bray and Garvan are only on that ship because of him. He never leaves anyone behind and he's sure as hell not going to leave them. He guides *Ares* through the asteroid field, skimming by rocks as she speeds past. Alarms scream in the background so he shuts them off.

He feels blood drip out of his nose, but he ignores that too. They're gaining on the Foundation ship. His relief is short-lived as a large circular structure slowly uncloaks in front of the giant transport. Panic rises in his chest and tightens his stomach. It's another Port. He's vaguely aware of the sudden increase in comms chatter. Questions fly around the group, but he shuts it all out. It's a bit late to discuss how they missed this Port. The point is, they did and Bray is about to fly right through it.

The distance shortens, but he doesn't let up. If it kills him, he'll stop that ship from entering the Port. He resists the urge to open fire on the vessel. He can't risk accidentally injuring them. The starboard engine overloads and grinds to a halt. His crew reroutes power to the other engines. Gryffin hopes they'll be able to withstand the surge.

Time slows down for Gryffin as they gain ground on the larger vessel. He just needs to close the gap by another few meters so he can launch the tethers. Just as they are about to reach the maximum distance, *Ares* veers off course. It takes him a second to realise he changed their course. Gryffin concentrates and tries to turn them around, but the helm is locked. What the hell is going on? The crew seem to be as confused as he is. The ship shudders violently as her engines struggle to bring her to a halt before she gets too far away.

Perses launches her tethers, but the larger ship is too powerful for the Hunter vessel. He hears Sayber cursing him over the comms as he's left with no choice but to disengage before *Perses* gets dragged into the Port.

Desyl attempts to take back control, but the system refuses to allow him access. Gryffin tries everything he can think of from within the system. His programming has locked down the system.

Alpha disappears through the Port and the barrier closes behind it. Gryffin hears a scream tear from his throat, but can't stop or control it. Pain surges along his ocular implant and through his head. He's vaguely aware of the bitter tang of blood in his mouth. Voices ring in his ears and random blurry shapes appear in front of him before his vision shuts down, plunging the world into darkness. Someone disconnects him from *Ares* and lowers him to the ground.

White-hot pain travels along his chest implant and meets with the pain in his head to create an unbearable agony. His breath freezes in his lungs as they shut down. He gasps for air, but can't find any relief.

Bray's gone and it's his fault.

∞

Bray groans. Every inch of his body aches. Someone shakes him and calls his name, but he can't get his body to cooperate. The shaking continues and his hand finally moves to swat the person aside.

'Open your eyes, Bray.'

He finally convinces his eyes to do as they're told. A very blurry image swims in his vision. He blinks a few times and Garvan comes into focus. Blood trickles down his face from a large gash and there's a very impressive black ring decorating his left eye. 'What happened to you?' Bray croaks.

Garvan grins. 'Should take a look at yourself first, Commander. You okay?

Bray frowns and assesses his body. He wriggles his toes and fingers. 'Everything's still attached.' He tries to sit up, groaning as his body protests. 'But it's damn sore. What happened?'

Garvan points behind him and Bray props himself up on an elbow to look. The twisted body of Forty-Three is draped over a wooden crate. He's either very limber or his neck and limbs are broken. 'He's dead?'

Garvan reaches out and touches the side of Bray's head. Bray yelps and pulls back. 'He got you full force on your implant. Knocked you out cold. I sorted him out for you.'

'Is the metal still attached?'

Garvan nods. 'Don't know if it's good or bad, but it's still there.' He gets to his feet and helps Bray up. Garvan holds him steady as the room tilts violently for a few seconds. Bray closes his eyes and concentrates on breathing through the dizziness and queasiness. He's tempted to go over and put a bullet in Forty-Three as payback. 'We still on *Alpha*?'

Garvan nods and dabs the blood from his face with his sleeve. 'Bigger problems than that.'

Bray frowns and walks to the small porthole Garvan is looking out of. It takes him a few seconds to realise the Foundation fighters are gone along with the Nomad and Hunters. Garvan taps on the glass to the left and Bray groans out loud when he sees a large planet in the distance.

'Now,' Garvan says as he stares at their destination, 'it's been a few years, but that looks a lot like Earth.'

Bray rests his elbow on the wall and holds his head in his hand. Two ex-convicts on a Foundation ship heading straight for

Foundation Earth. 'We're in a hell of a lot of trouble.'

EPILOGUE

One week later

Gryffin looks up as Roman knocks on the door to his new room. 'You don't have to knock, it's a damn cell.'

Roman lowers onto the bench in the centre of the room and clasps his hands together. 'Force of habit. How are you?'

Gryffin pulls himself into sitting position. The metal framework clamped tightly around his thigh, catches on the blanket as he drags his leg up the bed. He hates the feel of it but it's all that's holding his leg together at the moment. He massages his leg, easing the pain that's been a constant since he woke up. After a lot of scans while he was unconscious, Milla and Chayse came to the conclusion that they can't undo what the Scientist did to his leg. Even if they could remove the metal, the damage to his limb is too severe. They're looking at alternatives, same with his eye, but he's not holding his breath on either count. 'I'm fine.'

Roman smiles and shakes his head. 'You're as stubborn as your mother.' His smile suddenly disappears as he points towards his nose. Gryffin reaches up and wipes the blood away before it runs down his face.

'Do you want me to get Milla or Chayse?'

Gryffin shakes his head. 'It'll stop in a minute.' It's just another souvenir of his stunt on *Ares*. On top of his damaged leg, linking to the ship had overloaded every one of his implants. He suffered from a blood clot in his brain, a damaged lung, and a heart attack. Both his human and mechanical side shut down. It was touch-and-go for a while and Chayse still doesn't know what long term damage there is. His condition is deteriorating and, as of yet, no one can figure how to stop it.

It's been six days since Bray and Garvan disappeared back to Foundation space. It took Chayse and Milla until this morning to figure out why he subconsciously changed *Ares'* course. Someone, presumably the Scientist, had embedded something in his programming to stop him from entering the Port. Each of the Foundation gateways emits a signal unique to the Foundation. It acted like a repellent to him and his damn programming. Without being aware, it kicked in when he got within a certain range. The Scientist clearly didn't want his prize invention in Foundation space. Not only is his leg a problem, so is his programming. Milla and Chayse are worried there could be more changes they haven't found, and so is he. Once again he's a threat. Until his programming can be picked apart, he has to stay in the cell.

Roman clearly forces a smile on his face. 'We've linked Garvan's transponder signal to *Perses*. Sayber has everything he needs to track the signals on the other side. He'll find Bray. I'm sure of it.'

Gryffin grunts, but doesn't respond. He should be going after Bray, not the Hunters. He doesn't know where this protective streak has come from, but deep down, he feels the need to keep Bray safe. Roman and Bray both came through for him. It's like there's this strange connection between them. He can't explain it, but it's there.

Roman takes a deep breath. 'I know you want to go yourself,' Roman says, echoing his thoughts, 'but Sayber will find him. Avoca knows the area like the back of his hand. He'll help bring them all back. Oh, and Rua is taking her ship, *Lir*, too.'

'The Rogue?'

Roman nods and smiles. 'It appears Bray made quite an impression on her. Baila and Dare tried to talk her out of it, but she insisted.'

'No harm in having back up. I should be going.'

Roman rests his arms on the back of the bench and crosses his legs at the ankle. 'You don't have a lot of choice, Gryffin. There's something going on with your implants.'

As if to prove Roman's point, the image from his artificial eye flickers before it shuts down. It's been struggling since he woke up yesterday morning. Hooking up to *Ares* and controlling her for so long is still causing havoc with his components.

Roman gets up and walks closer to the bars. He crouches down so he's eye level with Gryffin. 'Maggie's funeral took place this morning. She's been laid to rest in the village graveyard. I can take you to see the grave it you'd like.'

'No. If you let me out once, exceptions will keep being made. Terra's having a hard enough time without confusing things. I have to stay here until my programming is examined. No exceptions.'

Roman looks at the floor and nods. 'I know. I've let you down — both you and your mother. You may not believe what I'm saying, and I know the whole father and son relationship is not top of your to-do list.' Roman drapes his arms over his knees and faces Gryffin. 'Understand one thing. Callum and the Foundation betrayed me in an indescribable way. I want revenge. Simple as that.'

Gryffin sucks in a breath as a sharp dagger of pain spears through his artificial eye.

Roman's eyebrows draw together. 'Your eye again?'

Gryffin nods. 'I'm tempted to cut the damn thing out myself.' He presses the heel of his hand against the implant on his face. 'Callum is dead.'

Roman nods. 'Callum is dead, but his work is still hurting people.

Hurting my son. Until his work is stopped and hopefully reversed, I will not rest. I can't allow the Foundation do this to anyone else. I won't allow it. That's all I can do for you, and with you, if you'll work with me.'

He nods, but doesn't share Roman's enthusiasm. If Terra's father knew how to fix the terminal malfunctions, he would have made the adjustments.

'I brought lunch.'

Roman smiles at Terra and gets to his feet. 'I'll leave you two alone.' He winks at Terra then leaves the room, shutting the door behind him.

Gryffin doesn't have the heart to tell her that the thought of food turns his stomach. Instead he forces a smile and braces himself against the bars as he gets to his unsteady feet. The fiery pain sears through his broken leg as he hobbles over to the bars. He drops heavily into the chair beside the door and stretches his leg out in front of him.

'So,' she mumbles around a mouthful of fruit, 'did Roman tell you about Rua?'

He rests the tray on his knee, but doesn't attempt to eat anything. 'She's a good fighter. She'll keep things interesting for Sayber.'

'Sayber is going to Earth. I really don't think he needs things any more exciting for him.' She stabs another piece of fruit with her fork. 'What about you? Is there anything I can get you? Do you need more ship reports?'

He attempts a reassuring smile, but it's not something he's ever practised. 'I'm good.'

She smiles. 'You know, for a mercenary, you're a really bad liar.' She puts her tray on the ground beside her and holds out her hand for his. 'Hand it over. You look like you're about to be sick.'

He does what he's told then rests his head against the cell wall.

Terra kneels at the far side of the bars and chews thoughtfully on her bottom lip.

'What?'

'Can I ask you something?'

Gryffin stills for a moment. He has a horrible feeling he knows exactly what she's going to ask him. Ever since he woke up, he's been waiting for her to question him about the Scientist, ask him what he did to her father. So far, everyone has avoided talking about it. 'Are you sure you want to ask?'

She pulls back from him and looks in his eye. 'I need to know what happened.'

'Terra, I'm not going to tell you what I did to him.'

'And I don't need to know.' She frowns and looks down at the ground. 'You killed him — that's all I need to know about it. I wanted to ask about the people he said you killed in the lab. What happened?'

'No, Terra.'

'You can't just say that.'

'Well, I did. I done with your father and his damn experiments. I don't want you to know about that place. Do you understand?'

'It's not going to change anything between us. I love you Gryffin. Nothing can change that.'

'What if I don't want to take that risk.'

She smiles in spite of the conversation. 'Trust me. I'm not going anywhere.'

He scratches the irritated skin under the leg brace as he collects his thoughts. Gryffin looks back down at his hands. 'I was number thirty-five out of the initial batch of people. I don't know who the others were or where they came from — everything in the first few weeks is a blur. After we were branded, we were dumped in cages and only taken out when he wanted to experiment.' He pauses and his throat tightens at the memories. 'He had started fitting implants to us. We all had to watch as he worked. Even with your eyes closed, you could still hear the screaming. You couldn't escape. The Scientist left to get some supplies one day. About half the group had already died. Something went wrong with the locks on my cage and I managed to crawl out.'

Terra reaches out and places her hand on his cheek. 'What happened?'

'I tried to get them all out but I couldn't open the locks.' He pauses again. He's never talked about his time with the Scientist. Breaking the cycle with Terra wasn't in his plans. He considers ending the conversation, but Aleena's words echo in his head. He has to let her in at some stage. Maybe this is the first step.

He meets her green eyes and decides to go against his instincts. 'I couldn't leave them. It was better to be dead than have one more day there.'

Terra wipes a tear from her face, but nods for him to continue.

'He got back just as I killed the last. I was thrown onto the table and tied down. He said I had balls for doing what I did.' He gestures to his groin. 'That was my punishment. Balls for balls. The Foundation arrived and distracted him half way through.' He snorts. 'Never thought I'd be glad to see the Foundation.'

Terra tilts his face up and cups his cheek. 'Thank you for telling me.'

Gryffin frowns at her reaction. 'You're not leaving?'

She smiles and shakes her head. 'You saved them. You did what you did to spare them from any more pain. I just wish I could have stopped him before—'

'He's dead. It's done.' Terra plays with his hair through the gaps in the bars. 'How do you do that?' he asks.

'What?'

'Make things seem better.'

Her hand pauses briefly before it works through his hair again. 'I'm not doing a great job.'

He lifts his head and frowns at the tears running down her face. 'Why'd you say that?'

She angrily wipes some tears away. 'You're in a cage. I swore this would never happen to you again. I swore to myself that I'd never let it happen. Yet here you are.'

'I'm on Ultar — it's not the same.'

'A cage is a cage, Gryffin.'

He shuffles around in the chair and reaches through the bars to turn her face towards his. 'Hey, this was my decision. No one forced me in here. As soon as we figure out what's going on up here,' he says, tapping the side of his head, 'I can get out.'

'And what if nothing can be found? Do you stay in here forever?'

He shrugs. 'I don't have the answers right now. I'm fine. Really.'

She laughs and shakes her head. 'When are you going to learn that I know you, Gryffin? I know you're far from fine. I know you're having frequent nose bleeds. I can feel the tremors running through your body. Your artificial eye has shut down and you constantly feel sick. It's happening, isn't it? What my father said would happen. Your implants are failing, aren't they?'

Yes, but he's not going to say that to her. He's seen how upset she is at him being in the cell. The truth won't help her. Terra gives up waiting for an answer he can't or won't give. She pulls the chair close and sits down next to him, her head resting against his through the cell bars.

Gryffin closes his eye and tries to ignore the pain from his abused and damaged body. It may be in his very near future, but he's not ready to die. Not anymore. For the first time in as long as he can remember, he actually does care about his future. He always accepted that he wouldn't survive to be an old man and didn't have a problem with it. But the longer he spends with Terra, the bigger that issue becomes for him. He didn't realise how much of an issue until faced with his own mortality. He's tired of surviving from day-to-day, tired of not looking beyond the end of the day. He's far from ready to settle down with a farm on Ultar, but he started to hope that Terra would stay with him on *Ares*. A few days ago, he would have been adamant she should keep away from him, but he doesn't want that anymore. She makes him feel like a man instead of a machine, and it's a feeling he could get used to.

He takes a deep breath and inhales her fresh scent. He'd be quite happy to live in the cell if it meant he had years to spend with her. Instead he's facing a few short weeks, if he's lucky. He may never know if Bray is found and that really pisses him off. The Foundation has taken his life — they shouldn't take his brother's life too. He wants to bring down the Foundation, fighting side-by-side with Bray. It's what they both deserve.

Gryffin focuses on the rhythmic movements of Terra's fingers through his hair. He'll fight whatever is happening to him. Whatever it takes, whatever he has to do, somehow, he will stand in front of the Foundation Council with his brother.

And then they would find out exactly how dangerous their creation can be.

∞

The two cloaked battleships slow down as they enter the sector. Rua holds her breath as *Lir* follows *Perses* past the fleet of Foundation fighters guarding the Port. The ships are completely unaware of their presence as they concentrate on their task. They're not expecting anyone to come from the other direction. Even if they were looking, they wouldn't see anything to make them suspicious. Rua never thought she'd be thanking the Nomad for anything, but their cloaks are effective.

Perses and *Lir* clear the other vessels. She releases her breath and gets to her feet. Like the rest of her crew, her ancestors hail from Earth, but the Council decided they couldn't offer anything of value to the system and shipped them through the Port.

Retracing their steps had never been on her radar.

'Sayber wants to talk.'

She nods at the comms officer and he opens the channel. 'Like the view, Rogue?'

She bites back her harsh reply. Fighting with their one and only ally in this Sector would be a bad start. 'Not particularly. Ready to go hunting, Hunter?'

He laughs and Rua can't help when a small, brief smile crosses her face at the sound. 'Oh, we're more than ready. Let's find Bray and bring him home.'

If you enjoyed *Nemesis*, please leave a review and tell somebody about the book. Reviews and shares are always welcome.

Thanks for your support!

K.A. Finn

EXCERPT FROM PERSES (BOOK 3)

'Never thought I'd have to wear one of these,' Garvan grumbles to himself.

Bray glances over at him, barely managing to hold back a laugh at the sight of the large man struggling to force his thick arms into the tight sleeves of the Foundation uniform. 'It suits you.'

Garvan glares at him before focusing on his task again. 'You just couldn't have found someone the same size as me, could you?'

Bray finishes pulling on his own Foundation issue jacket. 'Slim pickings.'

Garvan grunts. 'Slim is right.'

Bray fastens his borrowed jacket, all too aware they could have company any minute. As soon as they realised their excursion was going to end in an unplanned holiday on Earth, they set to work erasing any evidence of their presence. The large vessel was quickly gaining ground on Earth leaving little time for the task. They barely had enough time to drag the body of Forty-Three to one of the smaller storage rooms off the main cargo bay before the ship landed. After some desperate searching, Garvan finally found the perfect hiding place. The access tunnels that ran behind the wall panels of the ship would keep the body out of sight until they were far enough away.

'How do I look?' Garvan holds his arms out to the side and spins around. In spite of the seriousness of their predicament, Bray can't help but laugh. How the large ex-prisoner had managed to convince the sleeves of the Foundation jacket to accommodate his arms he'll never know.

'Ridiculous. It'll have to do though.' He takes the cap from the body at his feet and pulls it over his hair to hide his implant. 'Give me a hand with these two.'

Garvan frowns at Bray. 'That supposed to be funny?'

Bray glances at the two severed right hands on the box beside him. He grins and shrugs. 'Bad choice of words. C'mon.'

Garvan takes hold of the feet of the first hand donor while Bray grabs the man under his arms. After a bit of manoeuvring, he joins Forty-Three in the cramped space. Garvan steps back and smiles.

'Don't they look cosy.'

Bray thumps him in the arm and gestures to the third body. 'Even cosier once he joins them.' Bray helps Garvan unceremoniously stuff the man on top of his colleague and Forty-Three. Not quite the Foundation-styled send off the men probably deserved. It's just their bad luck they were in the wrong place at the wrong time. Killing the men didn't sit well with Bray but they had no choice. All doors in and out of the base have palm scan locks fitted.

As soon as Bray and Garvan left Earth as criminals, their identification had been marked. Their palm prints, retinal scans, and any other means of identification was permanently flagged. If they were caught, they'd be back in prison before they knew what was happening—if they were lucky. Escaped convicts infiltrating Earth without permission is bad enough. Add killing Forty-Three and the other men to that, and it probably earned them a place at the top of the most wanted list.

Garvan makes sure the panel is secured back on the wall while Bray packs his own clothes into the bag at his feet. Garvan passes him the guns they borrowed from the men. Bray hides their Outer Sector weapons in the bag under their clothes then pushes the Foundation issued weapon into the holster on his hip. He stands up and takes a deep breath.

'Ready for this?'

Garvan rubs his hands together. 'Can't wait.' He looks around the small storage room. 'Still wish we had time to cause some mayhem here. Seems a shame to miss such a great opportunity.'

'I hear you. Our best chance of getting off the ship in one piece is as soon as she lands. We need to jump ship along with the rest of the crew. There's less chance of us standing out in a large group.'

Garvan nods but is far from happy. 'I just wanted to have a little fun before we leave, is that so wrong?'

'We'll come back and destroy something later. Will that make you happy?'

'I'll hold you to that.' Garvan grins and nods. 'Fair enough. Lead the way.'

They step out of the relative safety of the storage room and enter the vast cargo hold on *Alpha*. Her enormous loading ramp is lowered, showing an enormous hangar housing the ship. Dozens of drones march up and down the ramp, carrying boxes of supplies in and out of the ship. A gleaming transport is being loaded with some of the heavier crates taken from the new colony. Bray's eyes narrow as he tries to make out the details on the boxes. One of them holds the Scientist's personal computer along with all the data from every procedure he carried out.

Like damaging the ship, the cargo from the new colony will have to wait. It tears at Bray to walk away and leave it here, but again, they have no choice. They're just two men and they need to get as far from here as possible while they figure out what to do. Bray glares at the crates being loaded onto the shuttle. Whatever happens, he will locate and destroy the data from the Scientist's system. There's no way he's leaving Earth if the Foundation have the knowledge and ability to make more cyborgs, to destroy more lives for their own personal gain. The experiments have to stop. No one else should have to suffer like himself and Gryffin have.

Garvan nudges him in the side discretely. 'One foot in front of the other, Commander. You're looking a tad suspicious.'

Bray nods and clutches the strap of the bag in his hand. Full of illegal weapons, Outer Sector clothes, and two severed hands, he can't afford to let it go for even a second. He straightens his shoulders and strides through the cargo hold towards the ramp. It appears luck is on their side. The cargo bay is so busy with transports entering and leaving in quick succession they manage to slip out unnoticed. Using a transport as cover, they keep pace beside it as it exits the ship and travels along the length of the far wall.

Bray tries to focus on where he's going but his eyes continue to wander around the space they are in. In stark contrast to Ultar's crude stone hangar, the Foundation base is made of highly polished, immaculate metal. Powerful lights embedded in the towering ceiling bathe every inch of the space in a harsh white light. Lines and lines of fighters and cargo vessels take up the entire right side of the hangar and occupy the numerous levels like a giant beehive. Human and drone technicians mill around the ships seeing to repairs and maintenance.

'Ultar doesn't stand a chance against this,' Bray mutters to Garvan. 'We have to find a way to warn Gryffin and the others.'

'Agreed. How about I ask someone if I can make a call?'

'I'm being serious,' Bray hisses.

'So am I, Commander. Right now, it's our own lives I'm worried about. Stop thinking with your heart. Our first priority is to get out of here. We're no good to anyone as corpses.'

Bray bites the inside of his cheek to stop any reply. Garvan is right and that irritates him.

'So, Commander, any idea where the exit is?'

Bray nods towards the far end of the hangar and the glowing red emergency light. 'Must be down there.' They slip out from behind the automated transport and crouch behind the cargo containers lining the wall. Ducking and diving behind the crates, they near their target. Bray stops all of a sudden and grabs Garvan's arm. 'Wait.'

'Are you serious?' Garvan hisses.

Bray crouches down to examine a crate. He taps his fingers against the side of the box. 'This came from the new colony.'

'That's nice.'

'I'm serious, Garvan.'

'So am I,' he replies, harshly. 'We've talked about this.'

Bray gets to his feet and leans closer to Garvan. 'The cargo is why we were on *Alpha* in the first place. Everything about the cyborg program is on that computer.'

'Yeah, I know. You agreed we had to leave it for the moment. Look around you. We're seriously outnumbered, Commander. I know the Foundation having that information is a bad thing, but if we're going to have any chance of getting out of here, we have to leave it. It's going to be hard enough getting the two of us out without lugging a flipping big crate along for the ride.'

'But—'

'But nothing. Have you forgotten the small matter of a dead cyborg and two personnel hidden in the wall on the ship? Once they're found, they'll know someone hitched a ride. I want to be long gone before they come looking for us. Move!'

Bray opens his mouth to argue, but changes his mind when he sees a group of technicians moving in their direction. 'You're right. Time to go.'

He picks up the bag and aims for the door again. Every step of the way, Bray fully expects someone to shout for them to stop. It seems the buzz created in the bay by the return of *Alpha* is keeping everyone busy. Bray crouches down in front of the door to rummage through the bag while Garvan keeps watch. Bray takes the two hands out and passes one to Garvan. The large man makes a face as he splays the fingers out. 'This brings back memories.'

Bray glances over his shoulder at him. 'You've handled a severed hand before?'

Garvan smiles. 'Long story, Commander. Perhaps when we have more time.'

Bray raises his eyebrows and turns back to the door. He passes one of the two stolen key cards to Garvan. 'You want to go first?'

They hold their breath as Garvan presses the hand against the scanner at the side of the door, and slips the card into the reader. The light above the door turns green and the metal slides silently into the wall. Garvan steps through and the door secures behind him. Bray repeats the procedure with the other man's hand and joins Garvan on the far side.

Bray stares in wonder around him. Instead of the maintenance tunnels he expected, they're in an enormous glass lobby area. The room must be at least ten stories high and made entirely of seamless glass. Their scuffed boots squeak on the highly polished white floor as they cross the vast space.

Garvan attempts to pull the sleeves of his coat down so the cuffs are in the same vicinity as his wrists. 'I feel like we're leaving a trail of grime after us.'

Bray nods. 'I know what you mean. We don't exactly blend in.' He looks around and grimaces when he sees two security personnel and two drones standing at the door to the outer courtyard.

Garvan turns his back to the guards and Bray follows suit. 'Drones randomly scan faces. Don't think they'll like what they discover with us.'

'We have to get out of the open.' Bray gestures to three doors at the back of the lobby and smiles. The door on the left has 'MAINTENANCE PERSONNEL ONLY' stamped on a red plaque attached to the door. 'Best option for us.'

Garvan follows Bray to the door, and after using their acquired hands again, they disappear into the corridor. Garvan stoops to talk quietly to Bray. 'No way we're going to be able to mosey out the front door. Could be a bit risky using the prints out in the open like that. Nothing screams we're trouble quicker than taking a severed hand out of your bag.'

Bray readjusts his cap to make sure his implant is concealed.

'There are drones everywhere. We need to get out of here and regroup. Somewhere away from so many Foundation security measures.' They continue along the maintenance corridor, checking each of the doors they pass for more guards or drones, but they're alone. They reach the last door and Bray pulls the "borrowed" hand out of his pocket and holds it up to the panel. He looks at Garvan and raises an eyebrow. Garvan rests his hand on his gun and nods. Bray places the palm against the panel. The light flashes and Garvan steps outside.

'All clear.'

Bray joins him, blinking as the bright sunlight hits him. Once the spots clear from his vision, Bray finds himself in a large maintenance yard lined with rubbish compacters and recycling units.

Garvan spins and grabs Bray by the arm. They duck down behind the nearest compacter and slump to the ground. Garvan points to the far wall. Bray risks a quick look and sees what caught Garvan's attention. 'Security units, Commander. No doubt motion detectors and facial recognition. Best keep out of the open.'

Bray closes his eyes and takes off the cap. He runs a hand through his sweat-soaked hair and rests his head back against the wall.

What a bloody disaster. Garvan is only in this mess because of him. He should have gone after Forty-Three alone. If he'd acted immediately, Forty-Three would be dead on the landing deck of the colony and Garvan would be in the Outer Sector. Now they're both stuck here and the Foundation still have access to all the data. He presses the heel of his hand against the implant on his face. As if things aren't bad enough, the metal hurts like crazy. The blow from Forty-Three probably did some damage to the useless component.

'You okay?'

He opens his eyes and grimaces at the look of concern on Garvan's face. 'Yeah. We can't stay here. You know anyone in the area?'

Garvan shakes his head. 'Last I heard, my family relocated to the colony on Mars after my arrest.' He smiles but there's little warmth in it. 'Doubt they'd be too welcoming anyway. In their eyes I'm a criminal.' He rubs the back of his neck as he looks away from Bray. 'Don't get me wrong—I'd give anything to see them. Hell, I'd give my life to see them, but not like this. I want to clear my name before I go anywhere near them.' He shrugs and looks back at Bray. 'You?'

Bray makes a face. He's got family on Earth and that's part of the problem. His uncle, Morgan, was incredibly close to his younger sister, Maggie, and took it especially hard when she died. It didn't help when Bray took a slightly grey path in life. Morgan's wife Shayla had spent most of her time separating the two of them or stepping in when Bray and his cousin Erin got in trouble for doing something they shouldn't have. The last time he saw Morgan, the man had made it clear Bray was a disappointment, and he never wanted to see him again. 'Yeah, like you, I'm not sure how welcomed I'll be.'

Garvan holds up his hands, mimicking scales. 'Uncomfortable family reunion verses being killed by the Foundation.'

Bray looks down and sighs.

Garvan drops his hands and frowns. 'Seriously? What the blazes did you do?'

'Everything I wasn't supposed to... and more. I guess we don't have much choice though.'

Garvan clasps his hands together. 'Fantastic. Uncomfortable family reunion it is. They near here?'

Bray shakes his head. 'That would be too easy. They live a couple of hours from here. We'll need transport of some kind. Stealing a shuttle is out. The Foundation will have plenty of time to track us down. We'll be picked up before we leave the city limits.' Bray leans back against the unit and chews his bottom lip. Something on the side of the compacter catches his attention. 'I think I have an idea. You're not going to like it though.'

PERSES

NOMAD SERIES BOOK 3

AVAILABLE IN EBOOK, PAPERBACK AND AUDIOBOOK

On a mission to stop the Foundation from creating an army of cyborgs, wanted felon Brayden Sawyer is trapped far from his ship and crew in the last place he wants to be...Earth.

With the Foundation hot on his heels, Bray must ask his family for refuge - a family who always preferred his brother Gryffin over him and kicked him out of their lives a decade ago.

When his family rejects him a second time, Bray wonders if saving Gryffin - and completing his mission - is worth it. All his life, he's been second best to his brother, a brother he never really knew. But turning his back on Gryffin is out of the question and he won't let the Foundation do to others what they've already done to him and Gryffin.

Breaking into Foundation headquarters, Bray comes face to face with the horrible truth about his brother's cyborg enhancements as well as his own modifications. And that's not all...the Foundation is set to destroy a planet of innocent people, using Gryffin as their number one weapon.

With time running out, Bray must finish what he started. Together with Garvan and his family, Bray must escape Earth with the necessary technology to save Gryffin and stop the Foundation's evil plans. But can one man stand against the all-powerful and tyrannical Foundation? If Bray can save Gryffin, he may just have a fighting chance.

CHAOS

NOMAD SERIES BOOK 4

AVAILABLE IN EBOOK, PAPERBACK AND AUDIOBOOK

Twenty-five years ago, two futures were changed.

Before becoming a Nomad and a Hunter, brothers Daegan and Brayden Sawyer were like everybody else on Foundation Earth. Then Daegan leaves for a school trip, a decision that would lead them to travel very different paths.

With his older sibling declared dead, Brayden's grief causes him to spiral out of control. After being banished by his family, he becomes even more self-destructive. When he's arrested and given a death sentence on the infamous Tyrat Prison, he realizes how far he's fallen.

However, Daegan is alive, though he may wish otherwise after discovering he's the latest recruit for the cyborg project. Years later, he finds salvation on the battleship, *Ares*. With their help, he becomes Gryffin and carves a formidable reputation for himself.

Chaos follows them as they fight their own demons and strive to find who they were always meant to be.

MANIA

NOMAD SERIES BOOK 5

AVAILABLE IN EBOOK, PAPERBACK AND AUDIOBOOK
(JAN 2021)

PRE-ORDER AVAILABLE

Twenty-five years ago, two futures were changed.

Gryffin uses his unwanted cybernetics to make the Nomad a group you fear. They travel the Outer Sector, taking what they want until they encounter an enemy. He's forced to do something he never thought possible – protect the very people he was intent on harming. Soon, those who were once friends can no longer be trusted and Gryffin's authority as Captain of *Ares* is questioned.

Brayden is in hell, accepting he'll die on the moon keeping him prisoner, his years there leaving scars, both hidden and visible. Resigned to his fate, he's given a chance at salvation, but there's a catch. Destroy the cyborg project once and for all by hunting down the sole survivor.

What happens when these brothers prepare to go face to face for the first time in nearly two decades? Will their bond be stronger than those they've forged while apart or could the truth destroy them both?

Mania follows them as they fight their own demons and strive to find who they were always meant to be.